Also by Kathryn Freeman

The New Guy

Up Close and Personal

Strictly Come Dating

MR RIGHT ACROSS THE STREET

KATHRYN FREEMAN

One More Chapter
a division of HarperCollins*Publishers*
1 London Bridge Street
London SE1 9GF
www.harpercollins.co.uk
HarperCollins*Publishers*
1st Floor, Watermarque Building, Ringsend Road
Dublin 4, Ireland

This paperback edition 2021
First published in Great Britain in ebook format
by HarperCollins*Publishers* 2021

A catalogue record of this book is available from the British Library

ISBN: 978-0-00-846226-0

Chapter One

Mia pressed the phone to her ear and tried to focus on what her mum was saying, but it was hard to when her eyes kept sliding to the flat directly opposite hers. Not the one just to the left, oh no. That was heart-sink territory. The sure way to make her feel like a total failure as a human being. Who on earth looks that put-together at nine o'clock in the morning? Earlier, even, though Mia couldn't say for certain how early because Immaculate Woman was always there, at her desk, by the time Mia staggered out of bed. Didn't the woman know that tracksuit bottoms, baggy jumpers and dressing gowns were all perfectly acceptable dress codes in your own damn home?

'Are you sure you're okay, pet? Your dad and me, we worry. One minute you're living round the corner. Next you've upped sticks all the way to flipping Manchester where you're living all by yourself, away from your friends and family. It's not right.'

Mia sighed. *Here we go again.* 'I'm thirty, not thirteen, Mum. And it's not like it's the first time I've been away from you guys. I managed to survive three years at uni.' In truth, Bath hadn't been that far away, and though 'survived' was accurate, boy had she missed her family. Oh and when she'd got her degree and a job, she'd moved to a house in the next street along from her parents.

'I know you can survive,' her mum countered. 'But I want my little gumdrop to be happy.'

Mia groaned. Seriously, how many thirty-year-olds get called a little gumdrop? And yet … her eyes begin to prick. She'd always been her mum and dad's gumdrop, just as Elle, her elder sister, had always been their little peanut. Because that's what they'd been nicknamed in the womb. God, she missed her family.

'Mia?'

Mia drew in a shaky breath. Nope, now wasn't the time to show weakness. At the first hint of it, her parents would jump into their car and bomb up the ruddy motorway. 'I am happy, Mum.' Or at least she would be, once she'd made a few friends up here. So far the only person she'd spoken to was Stan, her neighbour. Sixty-seven, divorced, overweight and lonely, he wasn't exactly who she imagined hitting the nightlife with.

'Have you met anyone else yet, aside from your neighbour?'

As Mia debated how to reply, she glanced at the time on her computer and saw it was ten o'clock. Immediately her eyes skimmed over to the flat opposite. Bingo.

The highlight of her day.

'Are you still there?'

Guiltily Mia tried to recall her mum's question. 'Of course I've met people.' Did it count if you hadn't actually spoken to them? All you'd done was ogle them from across the courtyard while they'd lifted weights? Or, in the case of Immaculate Woman, glowered at them every morning. 'But I've only been here two weeks and friendships take time, so please quit worrying. I'm perfectly content. I've got plenty of work to do and my new place is great.' With a dynamite view between ten and eleven in the morning.

Dear God, Hot Guy Opposite, as she'd nicknamed him, had started his routine with bicep curls. Even from across the courtyard, she could see the pump of his arms. The hard muscles of his naked chest…

'That's something, I suppose.' Her mum's voice jolted Mia out of her lusty thoughts. And the way she paused to clear her throat, sent alarm bells ringing. 'I saw Debbie yesterday, who'd spoken to Anne.' In other words, the gossip grapevine. 'Pete's been asking around for your new mobile number.'

Mia froze at the mention of the reason she'd had to leave the comfort of life in Somerset. Maybe it had been too comfortable, maybe moving to Manchester would turn out to be an inspired idea, but fact was, she'd not been drawn here by the idea of a better life in singleton city (apparently it had the highest concentration of single people in the UK, so at least she wouldn't feel too out of place). She'd come here to escape Pete. The boyfriend who'd seemed so nice.

Until he'd proven he wasn't. 'It's okay, Mum, he won't get my number. The only people who have it are family and my best buddies, Heather and Gill.'

'Good. Because if I find that despicable man sending my gumdrop any more nasty messages, I'll hunt him down and ... and...' Mia's lips began to twitch as she waited with interest. 'I'll knock his block off.'

Mia burst out laughing. 'Way to go, Mum. With you in my corner, I have nothing to fear.' And really she wasn't afraid of Pete; he hadn't hurt her physically. But in the year she'd dated him, his messages had gone from sweet, to possessive, to downright mean when she'd told him she no longer wanted to see him. Yet another boyfriend who'd turned out to be vastly different from advertised. Clearly, her judgement when it came to men totally sucked. Either that, or there were only two decent men left in this world; her dad, and Dave, her brother-in-law.

God, what a depressing thought.

The guy in the flat across from her, the one flashing his muscles, caught her attention again. If her theory was right, he was probably an axe murderer, and all this weight training was to help him wield the deadly weapon with greater precision.

'Mia, are you still there?'

Shit. 'Sorry, yes I'm here.' Just a tiny bit distracted.

'Well whatever it is you're looking at, you need to stop and listen to your mum. I know friendships take time, but I don't want to think of you up there with only your pensioner neighbour to talk to. It would be okay if you worked in an office, but all you do all day is sit in front of a computer.'

'I don't only sit here. Sometimes I work.'

'Very funny. Now promise me and your dad that you'll drag yourself away from that screen and go … wherever you youngsters go these days to meet people. A café, bar, gym.'

'Gym? Do you not know your daughter *at all*?' Mia had never fancied the idea of sweating next to gym bunnies in tight lycra. She preferred exercise with a purpose. As a kid she'd tried out loads of sports before finally finding one where her individuality – or as her school mates had called it, her weirdness – was respected, not mocked. 'I've found a local judo class, Mum.' She omitted the part about it not starting up again until September. 'As for meeting people, we youngsters do everything online now. No need to brave the outside. I can view prospective dates from the luxury of my own four walls.'

'Not that Grinding app I hope. Debbie said she overheard her niece talking about it and it was like dial-for-sex, no, wait, swipe-for-sex.'

Mia burst out laughing. 'God, Mum, have you any idea what you're talking about? But okay, message received,' she added quickly before her mum could take the conversation down any further dodgy alleys. 'Now I need to get on and do some sitting at my computer. Love to Dad and I'll phone next week.'

As she ended the call, Mia gave the view opposite a final ogle before dragging her eyes back to her computer screen.

Luke rattled the bar back onto the rack and heaved a sigh of relief. Shit, this was getting harder, not easier. Was it possible that at thirty-four, he was getting *old?* A shudder ran through him. No way. He was just having an off day. Probably his body was exhausted following the workout it had been given last night by Tanya; long legs, flaming red hair and apparently boundless energy.

After giving Pickles a pat on the head and her daily carrot – the name wasn't his idea, nor was the rabbit, but he was stuck with both – he dived into the shower. At exactly 11.29 a.m. – Fridays were one of the days they opened for lunch – he slammed his front door behind him and bounded down the stairs.

'Morning boss.' Sandy, waiting outside the bar for him to open up, glanced at her watch. 'A whole three seconds early today. Wow, you spoil me.'

'I cut out the shave.' He waggled his eyebrows. 'Tanya reckons the rugged look suits me.'

'Tanya?' Sandy raised her right brow. 'What happened to Sophie?'

Luke flipped on the lights and started lifting the chairs off the tables and onto the floor. 'Nothing *happened* to Sophie. We saw each other for a bit, now we're not.'

As Sandy mumbled something along the lines of not being able to keep up, Luke took a moment to survey his domain. Ten years since he'd moved into his flat and started work at the bar beneath it – and yes, the one-minute commute to work had been part of the appeal, though the decision on where to live hadn't solely been his to make. Those first few years had been tough, money had been tighter than a duck's arse, and he'd lived on tips, his wages gobbled up by a mortgage and … other expenses. But he'd worked his butt off, learnt the trade thanks to Bill, and over the years, actually begun to enjoy working there. Then Bill had decided to sell up – said he was looking to reduce his hours and stress – and Luke figured the opportunity was too good to miss. As of a month ago, the place – cleverly or lazily named The Bar Beneath, depending on your point of view – was his. No longer the employee, but the employer.

Who the chuffing heck would have thought it?

Had he always wanted his own bar? No bloody way.

Could he imagine himself doing something else now? His eyes skimmed across the dark wood furniture, the black and white tiled floor, the polished mahogany bar with the lines of optics behind it, back lit in green, put in last week as a homage to his part-Irish ancestry. It was home to him now, just as much as his flat. And for a guy who liked people, liked shooting the breeze, it wasn't a bad career to stumble into.

'Hey Mateo, you're looking hot. Great haircut.'

Luke glanced round as Sandy greeted the youngest member of their staff. Mateo was twenty-five, and though he had the swarthy looks of a Spanish matador, he had the accent of a Mancunian. A combination that was proving to be a hit with the female punters.

Mateo flashed her his grin. 'Thanks, babe.'

Luke stared at Sandy and cleared his throat. 'I assume I wasn't told I was looking hot because you didn't want to be accused of sucking up to the boss.'

Sandy threw back her head and laughed. 'Whatever helps you sleep at night.'

It was banter, and as Sandy had been a friend a lot longer than an employee – all the way back to school days, in fact, when she'd started dating his mate Jim – he was well used to it. Still, together with the more-arduous-than-usual weight session this morning, it added up to him feeling *old* again.

Not that long ago he'd been the sexy young bartender the girls had come to flirt with.

Now he was the bar owner, with a responsibility towards the people he employed. Hell, he was finally growing up, as his brother liked to mock. His phone buzzed with a text and when he glanced down at it, he grinned.

> Hey hot stuff. Had a great time last night. Let me know when you're up for a repeat. Tanya xx

Fine, he was growing up. But he still had some appeal with the ladies.

'Are you going to help us, or are you going to leer at your phone all day, as usual?' Sandy stared at him, hand on her hip.

Guiltily he stuffed his mobile back in his pocket. Old habits were hard to break but Sandy was right, he was the boss now, he had to set an example. 'I take exception to *all day, as usual* and the word *leer,*' he replied mildly, pulling down the rest of the chairs. 'Especially leer. I mean, that's what dirty old men do. I was smiling. Aside from that, you have a point and I apologise.'

'That wasn't a smile. It was an I've-just-had-an-invite-for-sex smirk.'

Luke stared back at Sandy. 'You could tell that, just from my expression?'

'Duh, you're acting like I haven't known you for twenty years. When you look at your phone, which you do far more than anyone else I know, by the way, you leer when you get a booty call, and give out a pained sigh when the booty call gets too keen.'

Her observations were a bit too close to home to be comfortable. What did it say about how many times Sandy had seen him pull those faces that she'd learnt to recognise them? 'Haven't you got lunch menus to be putting out?' he muttered, not liking the way he felt right now.

Sandy must have seen something in his expression – clearly she really *could* read what he was thinking – because her face softened. 'I wasn't having a go, you know. It's up to you how you live your life.' She paused, wrapping the end of her ponytail round her fingers in a gesture he knew of old. It meant she was gearing up to saying something she knew he wouldn't like.

'Come on, spit it out.' He gave her a half smile. 'You once told me I was an irresponsible prick. It's not worse than that, is it?'

'No.' She caught his eye and he didn't miss the fondness

in her expression. Or the edge of sympathy. 'I just … I can't help hoping one day you'll find what Jim and I have.'

Luke tensed. There had been a time when he'd believed he *had* had that. God, he'd been dumb. 'You mean a life where the highlight of your week is eating take-out curry in front of *Britain's Got Talent*?'

Sandy narrowed her eyes at him. 'Yes, okay, I can go with that. It is a highlight, because the person you're sitting on the sofa with is the same person you woke with your arms around that morning. The person who kissed you goodbye until your knees went weak, then sent you a silly text in the afternoon to make you laugh. That evening they listened to your gripes about work, hugged you when you felt low. Then made love to you to remind you what was really important in life.'

Because he didn't want to hear what she was saying – it wasn't the first time he'd had the lecture – Luke silenced her by placing his hand over her mouth. 'Quit rabbiting. No amount of fluff can hide the fact that in your scenario, *Britain's Got Talent* is on the television, so no thanks. Now get your arse into gear. I've got a business to run here.'

She huffed and walked towards the cabinet where they kept the menus. 'What if I'd said *Match of the Day* was on?'

'Same answer.' Fact was, the picture of domestic bliss she'd painted suited her, suited his brother and yeah, suited a lot of people. Didn't mean it suited him.

Chapter Two

Mia glanced again at the clock on her computer. How sad did it make her that she was still sat in front of her computer at nine o'clock on a Saturday night?

Her mum would go ballistic.

Stuff it though, it wasn't like she was working. Monday to Friday she designed websites, but at the weekend, she created. Well, she had been, up until the last half an hour, when the words to the rom com she was trying to write – maybe she should add a *still* in there, because a year on and she was only a third of the way through – anyway, the words had dried up and the time spent gazing out of the window had increased exponentially. There wasn't even anything to look at. Immaculate Woman wasn't at her desk. Hot Guy Opposite was probably out somewhere showing his diligently acquired muscles to some lucky woman. Or man.

With a resigned sigh, Mia rose to her feet. Her mum was

right, not that she'd ever tell her. Sitting here all day, *and* all night, would lead to a pretty lonely existence. Sure, she didn't lack friends, she'd talked to both Heather and Gill only a few hours ago, but it was all on the phone. When was the last time she'd spoken to someone face-to-face, other than Stan? Even that conversation had been three days ago, and had revolved around the best local supermarket. According to Stan, the Co-op was the closest, but it was more expensive than Lidl, though neither were as well stocked as Sainsbury's when it came to ready meals for one.

Yep, she'd officially reached rock bottom.

Walking to the bathroom, she gave her face a cursory glance in the mirror, mainly to check there was no evidence of the tomato sauce she'd shoved all over her sausage and mash dinner. Don't mock. At least she'd cooked it herself. Satisfied she was clean, if not looking her best – the green dye she'd streaked her hair with had seemed like a good idea at the time, but now looked like someone had emptied grass cuttings over her – she grabbed her trusty black handbag and walked out of the flat.

A few minutes later, she stood, staring, at the bar beneath the flats. It was early June and many people sat outside. The area had a continental feel, with strings of lights wrapped around pots of bay trees and flickering tea lights on tables. A brightly lit sign depicting the name, The Bar Beneath, cast a green light across the space.

Inside was similar; green plants, tea lights, dark wood furniture.

It looked warm, inviting. Yet the laughter, the constant buzz of chatter, the sheer numbers of people … it was intimidating as hell to walk into alone.

The alternative was crappy TV or another chat with Stan. Maybe this time about the residents' association.

Suck it up.

Squaring her shoulders, she walked up to the bar, slipping onto the only free stool. When she looked up to catch the bartender's eye, she nearly fell off the ruddy thing.

It was Hot Guy Opposite, far taller than she'd thought, muscles threatening to burst out of his black fitted shirt. Chestnut brown hair, sparkling green eyes.

'Hey there, welcome to The Bar Beneath.' Her stomach cartwheeled as he flashed her a smile. White even teeth and dimples. Honest to God, dimples. That wasn't a smile, it was an invitation to have sex. 'Luke Doyle at your service. What can I get you?'

Mia swallowed to get the saliva working in her mouth. 'A bottle of whatever beer you recommend.'

'Beer?' For a split second, his smile faltered, before returning in full force. 'Are you sure I can't tempt you into a cocktail?' Reaching behind him, he grabbed a cocktail shaker and flipped it up in the air, catching it neatly. 'An Alabama slammer? Black velvet? Campari and soda?' Another grin. 'I can go through the whole alphabet.'

There was something about the high-watt smile, the easy bartender chat, that helped Mia relax. Hot Guy Opposite was a fantasy she'd created and yes, Luke looked like the man she'd been ogling across the courtyard, but he was just a guy. And she'd been handling them, one way or another, all her life. 'Thanks, but I'll stick with the beer.'

'Your loss.' He bent to slide a bottle from the chill cabinet, unscrewed the cap and placed it in front of her. 'Slice of lemon? Snappy little green umbrella?' He picked up one and whirled it round with his fingers.

'Thanks, but no.' She cocked her head at him. 'Out of interest, if I'd wanted a cocktail beginning with *z*?'

'I'd have mixed you a Zombie. Light rum, dark rum, grenadine, a mix of different juices.' He winked. 'Honestly, it's a right pain to make so I'd probably have told you to pick something else.'

'What about beginning with *x*?'

He laughed. 'Then you'd have had our Xellent martini.'

'Okay, I'll take the bait. What's so excellent about it?'

Another wink. 'The name.'

She rolled her eyes, and he disappeared off to serve someone else. Mia tried not to feel too self-conscious, but it was hard when she knew people were giving her sideways glances. The girl sitting by herself with odd green streaks in her hair. Belatedly she glanced down at what she was wearing. Crap. She'd not even changed out of her slobbing-at-home outfit; leggings and an oversize shirt.

'Regretting the beer yet?' Luke was back, giving her another of those big, Tom Cruise-like smiles.

'Nope.' He gave the cocktail shaker he was holding a final shake, and poured a vivid green mixture into a cocktail glass. 'And now I've seen that, definitely no. Is it radioactive?'

He laughed. 'Well it can scramble your brain, but only if you have too many of them.' He leant across the bar. 'Between you and me, it's a screwdriver, with a dash of blue curacao.'

'What is it to the customer you're serving it to?'

'It's the house special.' He nodded towards the brightly lit green sign on the wall behind the bar, and then to the one in the window. 'Green is our colour, but then you knew that.'

'I did?'

His eyes skimmed over her. 'Your highlights were for our benefit, yes?'

His attention was caught by someone at the end of the bar and he murmured an 'excuse me' before heading off. And yes, her eyes did stray to his bum. It was … damn, it was perfect. No wonder the clientele were mainly female. The sexy, flirty bartender was a total cliché, but it also worked. Even if she didn't talk to anyone else all evening, already this was better than sitting on her own in her flat.

Luke served the next customer quickly, keen to get back to the newcomer. There was something about her that appealed. She wasn't his type – he tended to go for tall, slender women who dressed up to go out, and who flirted back – but she intrigued him. Turning up to a bar by herself, dressed in clothes she might have gone to bed in, not a trace of make-up, she was … unusual. Different from the women he saw in the bar most nights.

And he'd enjoyed sparring with her.

Indicating to Mateo, currently picking up empties from the tables, that he wanted him to take over at the bar, Luke headed back to the girl with the green stripes in her hair.

'Ready for something radioactive yet?'

Her gaze jumped to his and she smiled. 'I like my brain unscrambled, thank you.'

Freckles. How had he not noticed them earlier? A cute dusting of them across her nose. Bending to pick up a beer from the fridge, he twisted off the cap. 'Mind if I join you?'

'Aren't you supposed to be working?'

He grinned. 'The boss is very understanding.'

She angled her head, scrutinising him, and he wondered what was going on behind those big blue eyes. He was used to being appraised by women, but usually it was accompanied by a flirty smile and a glint in their eye. Not this sober appraisal. 'Let me guess,' she said finally. 'You're the understanding boss.'

He laughed. 'Why do I get the feeling nothing gets past you?'

A cloud seemed to cross her face. 'That would be great, if it was true.' Her eyes fell to the beer bottle and she wiped at a drop of water before glancing back up at him. 'So how long have you worked here?'

'Too long, probably.' He worked the dates out in his head and experienced a small jolt. Where had the time gone? 'Worked behind a bar since I left school, and behind this bar for nearly ten years. Took it over from Bill a month ago, though you'll still see him here when he covers my days off.' He flashed a grin. 'Older guy, bit of a belly. Hopefully you'll notice the difference. Assuming you come back, of course.' When she didn't reply, he added, 'I promise not to force a cocktail on you if you do.'

She laughed and he liked the sound of it; warm, natural. Some of the women he'd met laughed to get attention. This one seemed to laugh for her own joy, just as she seemed to dress how she wanted to, not to please others.

'I suspect I'll be back.' She shrugged. 'I'm new around here, so it's been good to talk to an actual person for a change. I've been relying on Facetime and Skype for the last three weeks.'

'Ah, I thought I hadn't seen you before.' He made sure to catch her eye. 'You're kind of hard not to notice.'

She didn't blush, or give him a coy smile. 'It's the green hair.'

He shook his head, gaze not leaving hers. 'It's more than that.'

Her eyes widened. 'You're really going to call me out on my tracky bottoms?'

'What?' He could honestly say he'd forgotten what she was wearing.

She gestured down her body. 'Come on, nobody else in here is wearing their slob-in-front-of-the-TV clothes.'

He glanced around him and nodded towards the group who were sitting at the back. 'How do you know they don't watch TV wearing a tight dress and five-inch stilettoes?'

'Because they couldn't *breathe*?'

'You make a good point.' Leaning against the counter behind him, Luke took a mouthful of beer. This didn't feel like work, not now. 'So ... wait, I don't know your name.'

'Mia.'

He smiled. 'Nice. Pretty, easy to spell, but not ordinary. So, Mia, what brings you to this metropolis, beside the lure of a great bar?'

'Ah.' She avoided his eyes and took a slow drink of her beer. 'I fancied a change of scenery.'

He could bullshit with the best of them, and frequently had done. Mia's evasive reply wouldn't fool anyone. Just because he knew there was a story behind her move though, didn't mean he had a right to prize it out of her. Even if he was surprisingly interested. 'A change from where?' he asked, figuring it was less contentious than the question he wanted to ask: *why?*

'Somerset. Famous for cider, Cheddar cheese, Glastonbury and the country's smallest city.' Her face relaxed as she spoke, seeming to back up his theory that her move was more about getting away from something or someone, than moving to Manchester.

'They're quite compelling reasons to stay. Then again, we have got *Coronation Street*, Oasis, Vimto and the best football club in the world.'

She grinned, pointing her bottle at him. 'Now that's what sold me.'

'You're a fan of the reds?'

Laughter spluttered out of her, her eyes crinkling with

mirth. 'You're sadly deluded if you think the reds are the best club in the world, when they haven't won a Premier League title in ten years. Arguably right now the blues are the best.' He wanted to butt in, tell her Man U had won other trophies since then, but even diehard United fans like him had to admit, as of now, that she was right. 'What is indisputable,' she continued, her face as animated as he'd seen it all evening, 'is that Oasis are a brilliant rock band.'

It was his turn to be amused. 'Thank God you went for that. If you'd said you were a fan of Corrie, I'd have to assume you were drunk on one bottle of beer.' From the corner of his eye he saw Mateo waving at him. Yep, he was drowning under a sea of punters wanting another drink. 'Sorry, looks like duty calls.' He gave her his best, slow smile. 'What do you say we carry on this chat another time, when I'm not working?'

Surprise flashed in her eyes, and she gave him another of her quiet appraisals. 'Maybe.'

Before he could push any more, she'd slipped off the bar stool. For a moment he thought that was that, but as he watched her head towards the ladies, he relaxed. Hopefully he'd get his date before the end of the evening.

Chapter Three

As Mia washed her hands with green liquid soap, the green walls of the ladies reflected back at her in the mirror. He'd not been kidding about it being their colour. She stared at her face; flushed cheeks, bright eyes. Yep, for the first time in months, over a year's worth of months, certainly since she'd begun to realise Pete wasn't as advertised, she looked excited. That's what a little light flirting with a dishy guy could do.

The door pushed open and two women almost fell inside, giggling away.

'Ooops, sorry.' The dark-haired one glanced over at her. 'Hi.'

Mia smiled back. 'Hi. I'm Mia.' Her mum would be proud of her, she thought wryly. That's two people she'd spoken to tonight.

'Donna,' she pointed to herself, 'and the wasted one

with me, is Chloe,' she added, nodding to the blonde standing next to her.

'Four cocktails doesn't make me wasted,' Chloe complained. 'Just makes me horny.'

Donna groaned. 'Oh God, don't get her started. One more and she'll be hitting on Luke again.'

Mia wasn't sure why her heart jumped at the sound of his name. 'The bartender?'

Chloe raised her perfect eyebrows. 'You know him?'

'He served me, that's all.' *He hit on you. For a few minutes he made you feel special.*

'Did he flirt with you?' Chloe asked, then shook her head. 'Don't know why I bothered asking, he must have. He flirts with everyone.'

'He was friendly, yes.' *He basically asked you on a date.* Maybe he hadn't though. Maybe he'd suggested meeting up because he'd taken pity on the new girl.

'That's Luke for you. Friendly and flirty.' Chloe sighed. 'And sooooo dreamy. He's got this sexy as fuck smile. And a body a girl just wants to get her hands on.' Leaning against the wall, she closed her eyes. 'Tanya says he's great in the sack, too. Like he really knows what to do with his hands, his mouth and his—'

'We got the message.' Donna opened the door to one of the loos. 'Go and pee some of those cocktails out.'

Chloe staggered into the cubicle and the door bounced shut behind her.

'Excuse her.' Donna smiled. 'She's a nightmare when she's drunk.'

'Hey, I heard that. I'm not drunk.' There was a loud curse from the cubicle and a roll of loo paper rolled under the door, landing at Mia's feet.

Donna frowned and bent to push it back under before turning to face Mia. 'I don't think I've noticed you here before. Are you local?'

Mia pulled down a paper towel and dried her hands. 'I am now. I moved here from Somerset a few weeks ago. I live in one of the flats.'

'Ah. Not far to stagger home then eh? Result.' She gave the closed cubicle door a wry look. 'Maybe Chloe should buy one.'

The toilet flushed and Chloe lurched out, cursing again. 'Bollocks. I've caught me bleeding nail in the frigging door. I think it's broken.'

Mia's eyes widened as Chloe waved the offending nail at Donna. She had talons on the end of her fingers. Honest to God, *talons*.

'Don't panic.' Donna gave the nail a quick glance. 'It's not that bad. We can fix it with glue and a teabag. But first, I've got to pee.'

A tea bag? Mia's mind boggled.

'Cool.' Disaster seemingly averted, Chloe turned to wash her hands. 'We're staying for one more, yeah?' She called over her shoulder.

'Maybe.' Donna pushed open the cubicle door. 'As long as you're still on your feet when I come back out.'

Chloe shrugged at Mia in the mirror. 'She used to be a right laugh. But then she,' Chloe raised her fingers and mimed quotation marks, 'fell in love. Now she's a party pooper.'

'Up yours, Chlo'.'

Donna's voice echoed from behind the door and Chloe giggled. 'Don't take notice of her, I'm not wasted. Just got my happy on.'

Mia watched as Chloe proceeded to take out her lipstick and draw a wonky line around her lips. 'Err, you've kind of missed a bit.'

Chloe frowned, and rubbed her lips together, spreading some of the vivid pink lipstick even further from her lips. 'Better?'

Mia winced and pulled out another paper towel. 'Can I?'

'Go for it. Make me look so gorgeous Luke's gonna want to shag me.'

Ignoring the twist in her gut, Mia carefully rubbed off the smudges. 'There you go.'

'Fab, thanks sweetheart.'

Donna emerged from the loo and after washing her hands, she turned to Mia. 'Are you here with anyone?'

'Nope, just me.'

'Then you have to come and join us.' She nodded towards Chloe. 'We're not all as bad as this one.'

'I'd love that, thanks.'

Wait till she told her mum, Mia thought a few minutes later as she was introduced to Michele and Tanya. She now knew the names of five more people. And so what if one of them had slept – or was it present tense? – with the guy who, for a few moments, had made her feel a little bit special?

'Who's for another drink?' Michele looked like a model. She had shiny auburn hair, like they did in shampoo adverts, and though Mia wasn't an expert on nails, unlike everyone else's Michele's perfectly varnished red nails actually looked like they could be real.

'I'm gagging for one.' Chloe winked. 'But I'll get them in. It'll give me another shot with Luke.'

Tanya – tall, endless legs and long red hair she must have ironed flat, because no way did anyone have hair that straight – sighed. 'Leave it, Chlo'. I know you're just trying to wind me up.'

'Maybe I am.' She shrugged. 'Or maybe I figure as you guys aren't actually dating, I've got as much right to chat him up as you have.'

Mia watched as she sashayed off to the bar. When Luke turned to flash Chloe the same wide, sexy smile he'd given her, the tiny kernel of excitement she'd felt earlier, shrivelled.

She shrugged the disappointment off. The bar owner was clearly a major player. One of those men who flirted with anything in a skirt, and possibly slept with them all, too. She didn't need a man like that in her life. What she did need, was friends. And maybe she didn't have much in common with these girls with their high heels, fake tans and long, painted nails, maybe she'd found it easier talking to the guy behind the bar, but at least their company was real.

Luke kept the smile on his face as he served Chloe. It wasn't that he didn't like her, he did. Recently though, she seemed to have got it into her head that she fancied him. Wrong. Sure, he had a pretty solid ego, he knew to many women his smile and his muscles were attractive, but that wasn't what Chloe saw in him. She only saw a chance to prove she wasn't cut up over being dumped by her ex.

How did he know all this? He was a bartender, people talked to him, especially once they'd had a drink.

'So, when do you get out of here?' Chloe fluttered her long false eyelashes at him as he poured the house cocktail into the waiting glasses.

'When the last customer has left, the rubbish cleared, glasses washed, bar wiped down and the floors mopped.' He smiled. 'Nobody said owning a bar was easy.'

Though her face fell a little, she gave him a valiant smile. 'I can wait. Help you out, you know, if you like.'

Oh Christ. He ran a hand down his face, wondering if there was an easy way to do this that he hadn't discovered yet. 'That's a great offer, Chloe, but you've got better things to do than hang out here.'

Her eyes dropped to the credit card she clutched. 'What if I haven't?'

He took the card from her, placing it on the bar before wrapping his hand around hers. 'Chloe, don't do this.' Her gaze snapped to his and she tried to pull her hand away, but he held on. 'You're better than me, better than this.' He indicated between them. 'Clive was too dumb to realise what he had, but other guys won't be. Give them a chance to realise you're single again, and they'll come running.' He smiled. 'You'll be able to take your pick.'

'Yeah, right.' She sighed. 'That's just your way of turning me down.'

'No. It's my way of telling you that if we started anything, you'd regret it.' He looked her straight in the eye. 'I want you to keep coming to my bar, Chloe. I enjoy chatting with you, serving you. I don't want that to stop because we got into something you regret and were too embarrassed, or too angry to come back.'

'You sleep with Tanya.'

'Sometimes, yes. But she's different to you. She's happy keeping things casual. You're not that kind of girl, Chloe.'

She stuck out her bottom lip. 'I could be.'

He dropped a kiss on her knuckles before letting her hand go. 'No, don't go changing. You stick out for what you really want. There are plenty of guys looking for a gorgeous woman to settle down with. Plenty who'd bend over backwards for a chance with you.' He winked. 'You never know, maybe you'll meet him here. And if you do, you'll thank your lucky stars you didn't chuck away your principles and tumble into bed with the bartender.'

'Chuffing Nora, Luke. You sure know how to turn a girl down.' After a long exhale, she gave him a sly look from under her lashes. 'Can't promise I won't stop flirting with you.' Then she leant across the bar and flung her arms around his neck. 'But ta for the ego massage.'

As he peeled Chloe off him, Luke caught sight of Mia, waiting behind her. A dart of satisfaction shot through him; she was still here. He smiled over. 'I'll be with you in a sec.'

To his disappointment, she shook her head. 'I'm just here to give Chloe a hand carrying the drinks back.'

Chloe started to giggle. 'Bummer, I nearly forgot yours, Mia.' She turned to him. 'And a—'

'Bottle of beer. Got it.' He bent to retrieve one from the fridge, looking again at Mia. 'Sure I can't tempt you to the radioactive cocktail?'

She smiled, shaking her head, but though it was friendly, he sensed a wall that hadn't been there before. 'I don't want my hair going any greener.'

Chloe's mouth fell open. 'You're kidding, right. I mean this stuff,' she looked down at the tray of vivid green cocktails, 'it isn't going to turn me green, is it?'

'Only if you have too many.'

'What?' Then she burst into laughter. 'Oh right, you mean because I'll be sick. No flaming way. I'm not chucking them up, not after all the money I've spent on them.'

Picking the card off the bar, Luke quickly took payment for the drinks. As Chloe reached for the tray, he put his hand on hers. 'I'll take them over.'

She gave him a wide, flirty smile. 'Such a gentleman.' Then tottered back to join the others.

Mia set off behind her, but Luke touched her shoulder, only realising then how *short* she was. 'Hey, wait a sec.' Slipping round the bar, he fetched the tray of drinks. 'Good to see you still here.'

'I met up with Chloe and Donna in the ladies. They persuaded me to stay.'

He gave her a crooked smile. 'So it wasn't the lure of continuing our conversation?'

'Which conversation was that? The one about Somerset versus Manchester, cocktails—'

'The one where I suggested meeting up outside this place,' he interrupted, wondering if he'd got this totally wrong. He'd been certain there'd been a spark between them earlier. Sure, she was different from the women he usually chatted up at the bar, but that was part of the interest. He didn't meet many women who had the confidence to come into a bar alone, and without the need to squeeze into a tight dress or put on make-up for the occasion.

Nor did he meet many people who outsmarted him in the banter.

'Oh, that conversation.'

He was interrupted by Helen, one of his regulars, who gave him a smacker of a kiss on his cheek. 'Luke, I've not seen you all evening.' She darted a look at Mia. 'Seems others have claimed your attention. I'm going to be upset if you don't drop by our table when you've finished here. Lizzie, I know, will want to say hi. She was telling us how much she missed your pretty face.'

'You're busy.' Mia's eyes followed Helen as she walked back to her table.

'Yeah, sorry, Saturday nights are usually mad. It's quieter during the week. Easy to talk.' When she didn't reply to his opening, he gave it one last shot. 'So, can I have your phone number? Maybe meet for coffee one day?'

'Umm.'

'I've lived here most of my life. I could be a pretty useful guide while you settle in.' He grinned. 'Cheapest coffee, best take-out, prettiest place to eat outside, most scenic running route if you're into that.' Crap, he sounded desperate.

Her eyes flicked over to where Chloe and … damn, Tanya was there. Was that what had put Mia off? She thought he was dating Tanya? 'Look, I don't know what you've heard, but—'

'They're waiting for the drinks.' She gave him a small smile. 'Thanks for the offer. I know where to come if I decide to take you up on it.'

'Okay.'

She took the tray from him and nodded to where Helen was watching them. 'Thanks, I've got it from here. You'd best go over there before she gets upset.'

He was left feeling confused, a little put out and, yeah, he had to admit, a lot disappointed.

Chapter Four

Sunday was quiet. Mia went running – surprise, surprise, she was capable of finding her own routes, quiet and short being the key criteria. Who needed scenic when it took all her effort to put one foot in front of the other? After that, she tried out Lidl, thanks to Stan's recommendation. She'd keep the excitement of ready meals for one at Sainsbury's until she'd been here at least a month.

If she thought, just occasionally, about the guy from the bar, it was because it had been a long while since she'd enjoyed chatting to a member of the opposite sex quite so much. Not because she regretted not giving him her phone number.

Pete had taught her a valuable lesson. No longer was she giving her number out easily. And considering her track record of dating men who appeared decent, but turned out to be total jerks, no way was she about to date a man who seemed like a bit of a jerk at the outset. Sure,

Luke was gorgeous, charming and easy to talk to, but God, the bar seemed littered with women who'd either slept with him (Helen had to be an ex), were sleeping with him (Tanya, for one), or wanted to sleep with him (Chloe, plus all the girls who had sat at the bar and fluttered their eyes at him).

Monday, Mia woke to the usual routine. Drag herself out of bed, eat breakfast (Frosties) while checking on Immaculate Woman (dressed today in navy, her hair coiled in a bun). Take mug of coffee to desk. Turn on computer while glowering at Immaculate Woman. Work.

At 10 a.m. she stopped everything to ogle Mr Hot Guy Opposite … damn, she guessed she'd have to say ogle *Luke*. The idea felt uncomfortable because even though he was undeniably still hot, now she knew who he was.

Opposite her, Luke picked up the bar of weights and jerked it above his head. As his muscles bulged, Mia felt her pulse quicken, her blood heat, and she huffed out a resigned sigh. Fine, when it came to ogle worthiness, apparently she could overlook his womanising ways.

She sat and stared as he bent to put the bar back on the rack. When he straightened, his head angled in her direction and … shit no, please say he hadn't caught her looking. Mia pushed her chair back, away from the window, and the connection, if there had been one, was lost. Breathing a sigh of relief, she pulled her desk towards her and watched the rest of the show from the shadows.

When it was over, she worked solidly until her stomach complained, then ate a sandwich at her desk while trying to avoid crumbs falling onto her keyboard. Later in the afternoon she took a call from her sister.

'Yes Elle, you can tell Mum I'm still alive.' Absently she glanced down and winced. Balls, she'd forgotten to shower and change. Wearing a dressing gown and pyjamas at three in the afternoon was not cool.

'Please tell me you got out at the weekend. And going to the supermarket doesn't count,' Elle added, ruining Mia's witty reply.

'Actually, you'd be proud of me. I went to the local bar on Saturday and had conversations with actual people.'

There was a pause. 'Sorry, can you repeat that? I thought I heard you'd gone to a bar.'

'Very funny.'

'So, who are these actual people you spoke to? Any dishy men?'

It was Mia's turn to pause. 'Sort of.'

Elle gasped. 'OMG Mia, come on, spill.'

Damn, why was she chronically incapable of keeping her big mouth shut when it came to her sister? 'Chill Elle, there's nothing to spill. I went to a bar, met a few local girls and had a nice evening.' Nice, pleasant. Funny how it had felt a lot less bland than that.

'But where did the dishy men come in?'

'Man,' she corrected. 'There was a dishy man.' For the first time since this morning, when she'd nearly got caught ogling, Mia allowed her gaze to drift over to the flat opposite her. And her jaw dropped open. 'Whoa, what on earth?'

'Err, Elle calling Mia. What's happening up there?'

Mia shook her head, but when she stared back at Luke's flat again, the sheet of paper was still there in the window.

One simple word:

Hi

It couldn't be meant for her. Could it?

'Mia? Do I need to call 999?'

'What? No.' Heart racing, she stared at the message. It probably wasn't for her. Luke was clearly well known round here. He could be saying hi to anyone. And God, since when did she attract men like him? Flashy, good-looking men? *He asked for your number.* Her palms felt sweaty, her heart loud in her ears. So what if it was for her? *He's a player.*

She paused to take a breath.

'Mia, will you tell me what the pissing hell is going on before I get really fucking angry, really sodding worried or both.'

Ouch. Elle didn't often swear, but when she did, it wasn't pretty. 'Sorry sis.' She drew in another breath, organised her thoughts. 'The dishy man I mentioned was the bar owner. He chatted to me, like bartenders do, and he sort of flirted a bit and I was sort of interested for a bit. Then I found out he was sleeping with or had slept with half the women in the bar – slight exaggeration, but you see where I'm coming from. So I said no to his offer to meet up.'

'Holy shit, give me a minute to work that through, it's a

lot to digest.' Mia imagined Elle shifting on the sofa, rubbing her hands across the hugely swollen belly that was keeping Mia's nephew safe until he decided to pop out.

'While you're digesting that, the reason I went radio silent on you was because I've just noticed a sign in his window saying "Hi".'

'Err, you know where he *lives*?'

Ah. 'Yes, kind of, because it's the flat directly opposite mine.'

'You've been *spying* on him?'

'No, of course not, that would be all sorts of wrong.' Guiltily she remembered spending one sad evening looking at binoculars online. She hadn't bought a pair though, that was the important part. 'But if he decides to work out slap bang in front of the window, people are going to see and, well, watch.'

'By people, you mean you.'

She guessed, given he lived directly opposite, she probably was the only one with such a clear view. 'Okay, yes, me.'

Elle's voice went quiet. 'How big are his muscles? Are we talking just starting out, or Dwayne Johnson?'

'Why are you whispering? Is Dave around?' Dave was Elle's saint of a husband.

'What, no? I don't want The Wriggler to hear me asking about a man who isn't his dad.'

Mia snorted with laughter. 'I thought he was Turnip?'

'God, you're so out of date. That was week seventeen. After that we went through Pepper, Mango and

Cauliflower. By the time we got to Cabbage, Dave said he'd had enough and nicknamed him The Wriggler.'

'For which I'm sure my nephew will be eternally grateful.'

'All of which is a distraction from my original question about the size of the muscles on the dishy bar owner who lives opposite you.'

Mia bit into her lip as she thought. 'I guess, if we're going with your food analogy, we're talking melons for his biceps.'

'Melons? Wow, honeydew, or watermelon, or—?'

'Stop! God, Elle, maternity leave is clearly making you even more bonkers than usual.'

Her sister sighed. 'Okay, yes, good point. I shall stop thinking of my sister's hot neighbour. But I will ask if you're going to reply to the sign.'

'It's probably not for me.' Men like Luke, cocky and good-looking, didn't go for geek girls, she reminded herself. She attracted the shier, solid guys, who then turned out to be flakier than a Danish pastry.

'You've just said your flat is dead opposite his,' Elle protested. 'And presumably this is the first time he's put up a sign since you moved in, or you'd have noticed. Quite a coincidence that, you meeting him, him wanting to take you out, and now a message popping up in the window that looks directly into yours.'

Crap, maybe he *had* seen her.

'Sounds like he's trying to attract your attention.' Elle's voice took on that sort of excited hush again. 'Just think of it, Mia. Running your hands over all those straining muscles.'

Mia burst into laughter. 'Err, hello pregnancy libido. I think it's time you made yourself a chamomile tea and went to lie down. And I did some more work.'

'So you *haven't* thought about sex with the hot guy opposite?'

Nope, she wasn't getting suckered into answering that one. 'Bye Elle, talk to you later in the week.'

Mia put down her phone and stared back at the sign.

Then she shook her head and pulled down her blind.

The kick of disappointment he'd felt on Saturday night when Mia had turned down his offer to meet for a coffee had rolled through Luke again on Sunday when, despite his constant checking, she'd not walked through the door of the bar. He'd had to acknowledge it was possible his chance of seeing her again had all but disappeared.

But then this morning, when he'd been lifting weights and looking out of the window, which he did because lifting on his own at home was boring as shit, he'd spotted a flash of green hair opposite him.

No mistaking that hair, that face. The fact she'd still, as far as he could see, got her dressing gown on.

So he'd shifted even closer so she could see him, and he could see her. And yes, he'd flexed, pumped his muscles harder than usual. Some girls dug a guy who worked out, others preferred lean. As he had no hope of being the latter, he had to make the most of what he had, and hope Mia liked it.

Had she watched? He wasn't sure. After that initial glance at her, she'd disappeared into the shadows.

Still, not being the sort to give up, before he'd left for work he'd scribbled a quick *Hi* on a sheet of paper.

Then he'd stuck it to the window with Blu Tack and gone off to the bar feeling mildly hopeful.

Falsely hopeful, it turned out, as there'd been no reply in Mia's window when he'd come back last night.

Worse, she'd pulled down the blind.

He supposed that could be construed as a big f-off sign in itself.

Of course, there was a chance the blinds were down because it was too sunny. Also a chance she hadn't replied as she didn't realise the message was intended for her, though he couldn't believe a smart woman like Mia wouldn't have connected the dots.

'What do you reckon, Pickles?' He bent to give the creature a scratch behind her long floppy ears. 'If she pulls the blind up at ten, that has to mean she's interested, yes?'

Pickles twitched her nose and stared back at him. A brown and white lop-eared dwarf, she had the run of the flat and was the only girl he'd ever lived with. Maybe that was how his life was destined to be. And hell, it wasn't a bad life. Pickles was easy, undemanding company and helped with the occasional loneliness he felt coming back to an empty flat. Even if it did mean he had to clean out her poo tray. For adult conversation, he had the punters at the bar, and for those times he wanted to unwind in the arms of a willing woman, well, he had numbers on his phone he could call; women who were happy to see him, no strings asked for or given.

It wasn't how he'd pictured his life evolving when he'd been cramming for his exams, university only a few months' hard study away.

'No point looking back though, is there girl?' Pickles angled her head, whiskers bobbing up and down as she chewed on the treat he'd given her. 'Life's what we make it, and I'm not about to complain. Not when I've got the day off.'

Rising to his feet, he ducked into the bedroom, shrugged on his shorts and headed for the spare room where he'd set up his weights.

His note was still stuck on the window. With a sigh he tugged it off, his shoulder dropping, just a little, when he saw the blinds opposite were still down. Before he could think twice about it, he picked up the pad of paper and scrawled a new one:

Hi Mia

Not eloquent, not clever. But at least now there was no doubt who the greeting was directed towards.

Yet as he sweated through his work out, the blinds to her room remained down.

Feeling out of sorts, he headed for the shower where he

gave himself a strict talking to. He had a damn bar to run now. Complications, and women definitely came in that category, were not what he needed right now.

He'd been at his makeshift desk in the spare room – a plank of MDF laid across two dumb-bell racks – for ten minutes, poring over invoices and orders, when his phone rang. Seeing Sandy's ID, he picked up.

'Hey, what's up?'

'Me and Mateo have been waiting here for ten minutes, that's what's up.'

'So, why are you telling me? Isn't Bill there?'

'Why would Bill be here? He's down for Wednesday. Today's Tuesday.'

Luke glanced at the rota he'd stuck on the wall – Blu Tack was mighty handy – saw she was right, and swore. 'On my way. Don't kill me when I get there.'

There was a long suffering sigh. 'I guess I can promise that, though there might be some serious dismembering.'

Unconsciously, he placed a protective hand over his groin. Then he grabbed his keys, wallet, jacket and legged it out of the flat.

Notes to a woman he barely knew. What the shit was he playing at? He couldn't even cope with the stuff he already had going on in his life. He didn't need adding to it.

Chapter Five

By Thursday afternoon, Mia was proud of herself. For three days she'd not opened her blinds.

She didn't miss the sight of Immaculate Woman. She didn't miss ... okay, there was no other positive she could think of. She missed the daylight, the sight of something other than a blank brown canvas (if she was going to keep doing this, she'd have to invest in some non-cow pat coloured blinds). And damn yes, she missed the ten o'clock Luke show. She hadn't realised how much it had motivated her to be at her desk.

She'd updated Heather and Gill on the situation yesterday. Heather had told her she admired her discipline, even though she'd have messaged back because, 'duh, hot guy'.

Gill had told her she was bonkers. 'Fine, don't reply, but shutting the blinds, are you crazy? How many times in your life are you going to get a free show like that?'

Her sister thought she was being a coward. This morning, after Mia had admitted yes, the blinds were still shut, Elle had messaged her:

> What are you going to do, keep the ruddy things closed forever?

She had a point, Mia supposed.

And Luke must surely have got the hint by now. Or, quite probably, he hadn't even noticed she'd had her blinds down because *he didn't care*.

God, she was being crazy. This had to stop. With a ruthless snap of her wrist, she flicked the blind up.

A moment later, her heart cartwheeled in her chest.

There was no denying now that the original message had been intended for her. The way he'd added her name after the *Hi*, kind of gave it away.

Doesn't mean you have to reply.

Mia forced her eyes back on her monitor and her focus back on work.

She managed to keep it up for ten whole minutes before her gaze bounced back to Luke's window and that damn piece of paper with its cheesy smile next to her name.

With a huff of impatience, she phoned Elle.

'So I opened the blinds, only to find he's put my name next to the *Hi*. What am I supposed to do now, smarty pants?'

Elle whooped. 'Yay, you have no idea how much I

needed this. Your love life is about the only thing stopping me from going stir crazy.'

'I don't have a love life. I have a … a dumb note stuck in a window with my name on it.'

'Aw, come on, don't be mean. He's wooing you. It's romantic.'

Mia stared again at Luke's window. If she hadn't bumped into Chloe and the girls last Saturday, hadn't heard them talk about Luke's casual approach to sex, hadn't seen him with his arms around Chloe, and a moment later seen another woman act all proprietorial in front of her. If she didn't know he was having sex with Tanya… If none of that had happened, maybe she would think this was romantic.

And maybe she would send him a message back.

'Is it romantic, or is he just acting true to type?'

'So cynical, baby sis. You barely know the guy, you can't possibly have him down as a type already.'

It was true. She usually she only found out a guy was a tosser once she'd started dating him. With Luke though, she had a feeling she'd had a lucky escape. 'He asked for my number when I know for a fact he's sleeping with at least one of the women I met last week. I rest my case.'

'Umm, that is a bit yucky.' Elle sighed. 'What are you going to do about the message?'

'Ignore it.'

'Okay. Boring, but okay, I can see why Pete the Prick could have put you off men for a while.'

'It isn't just Pete the Prick, though he was by far the

worst. It's also Danny the Dick, Andy the Arsehole, Chris the—'

'Yep, I can see where you're coming from. The thing is though, Mia.' A pause. 'The thing is.' Another pause, this time with a huff.

'Jeeze, get to what the bloody thing is. Please. Unlike you, I do actually have some work to do.'

'I am working, I'm incubating your nephew.' Elle blew out a breath. 'So anyway, the thing is, if you just ignore the message ... where the hell am I going to get my entertainment from?'

Mia spluttered with laughter. 'God, you're so cranky at this stage of your pregnancy. I'd forgotten.'

'I'm sitting here feeling like a beached whale, my ankles are like tree trunks, my back aches, my husband thinks it's hilarious I look so huge and keeps taking photos of me naked. You'll be bloody cranky when you're thirty-odd weeks pregnant.'

Elle said it so emphatically, as if there was absolutely no doubt that Mia would, one day, not only be pregnant, but also have a husband who wanted to take naked photos of her. Yet as she said goodbye to Elle, Mia realised she couldn't picture any of that. All she could see was her inhabiting the same four walls she was living in now. Immaculate Woman would probably have left to live in some four-bed house in a leafy lane, Luke to live with some rich woman who wanted him for his body. And she'd still be here. All alone.

Mia rummaged in her drawer for a marker pen, then

picked up a sheet of paper from the printer. For a few moments her hand hovered over it. Then she exhaled heavily and pushed the paper away.

Lonely was fine. It didn't bring angst, didn't screw with your mind or play havoc with your emotions.

An image of Elle and Dave on their wedding day came to mind. Their joy as they'd exchanged vows. Then later, the joy on her parents' faces as they'd danced together as if *they* were the newlyweds.

Sadly, lonely didn't bring happiness, either.

Saturday night and during a welcome lull – he supposed now the bar was his, he should leave out the welcome part as busy meant profit – Luke stepped into the back office and pulled out his phone. Still nothing back from Grace.

Fingers flying across the keys, he messaged again.

> Having too much fun, avoiding me, can't be arsed? Any other excuse for lack of reply to my text from yesterday? X

He supposed he should give her a break, but he wasn't used to not seeing her. He especially didn't like not hearing from her.

A tap on the door, and Mateo stuck his head round.

'Thought you might like to know, she's back.'

Instinctively Luke knew, but because he didn't want to look *that* keen, he raised an eyebrow. 'Who's back?'

Mateo grinned. 'You're not kidding me, boss. I've watched you look out for her every night this week.'

He could carry on the charade, but then he'd look like more of a loser than the guy who looked up every time someone came into the bar, hoping they had green hair. 'I check out everyone who walks through the door. It's important to know who the punters are.'

'Yeah, especially those with green hair, freckles and a spark in their big blue eyes.'

Luke gave Mateo a double take. 'Sounds like you're the one who's been looking out for her.' Yeah and that idea didn't sit well with him.

'I'm a single guy.' Mateo winked. 'And some women prefer their men on the younger side. More stamina.'

Thankfully Luke's phone beeped at that moment, preventing him having to reply.

TOO MUCH FUN! Will phone soon. Promise. G x

His mouth curved, imagining Grace's face. Fine, he could live with the lack of communication, as long as she was happy.

Maybe now he could find himself a little taste of happy.

It wasn't hard to spot Mia. She was the only woman standing at the bar with green stripes in her hair, no make-up and wearing a T-shirt that declared: [2b || !2b]. What on earth?

'Hi.' Not his finest opening line, but like the messages

he'd left in his window, the ones she'd ignored, his wit seemed to have deserted him around her.

Her gaze shot over to him and she gave him a careful smile. 'Hi yourself.'

'Can I get you a drink?' Duh. He gave himself a mental slap. Why else would she be at the bar?

'Thanks, but Mateo's serving me.'

Fucking Mateo. Ignoring the flare of irrational jealousy, he nodded to her chest, trying not to look at the curve of her breasts – holy shit, beneath the loose clothes she'd worn last time, she'd been hiding the body of a porn star. Stop staring, stop staring.

Drumming up all his willpower, Luke forced himself to read the wording on her shirt, rather than imagine what was under the shirt. Beneath the line of utter gobbledegook, [2b | | !2b], was written: *that is the expression*. 'Interesting T-shirt.'

She glanced down, as if she'd forgotten what she was wearing, which was highly likely to be the case. 'Oh, right. Computer nerd humour. To be or not to be?'

'Ah, right.' He laughed softly. 'I barely know how to use one, never mind how to make them work. Is that what you do then?'

'Yep.' She smiled at Mateo as he settled her bottle of lager on the bar top. 'Thanks, and three of the house cocktails.'

Luke glanced over to the back of the bar, where Tanya, Chloe and Donna were sitting. Chloe gave him a wave, Donna a smile. And Tanya winked and blew him a kiss.

'Seems I'm sitting with your fan club,' Mia remarked dryly.

'Hardly.' He wanted to add that they were just regulars, but he suspected she knew Tanya was a bit more than that. They weren't dating though, so it didn't make him a douche to have asked Mia out. Did it?

Mateo returned with a cocktail shaker which he proceeded to shake with a flourish before pouring the vivid green contents into three waiting glasses. 'One day we'll persuade her to try the cocktail, hey boss.' He smirked at Luke before grinning back at Mia. 'But be sure to ask me to make it for you. I've got a, let's call it a *more delicate* touch.'

While Luke gritted his teeth at the clear innuendo, Mia laughed. 'I'll remember that.'

'I think the lady at the end of the bar is in need of your *more delicate* touch.' Luke glowered at Mateo, who gave him a jaunty smile before strutting off to serve the waiting customer.

There was a beat of silence while Luke struggled to regain his balance. This was totally unlike him. He was the master of bar banter, so why was he struggling with Mia? *Because she turned you down.* 'It's good to see you back here.' He held her gaze. 'I'm glad we didn't scare you away.'

She shrugged. 'I don't scare easily.'

'No?' Luke felt the elephant in the room start to shuffle its feet. 'Seems I might have scared you with my message in the window.'

Her eyes widened in surprise. 'Scared me, no. But I wasn't sure how to reply.'

'A *Hi* back would have been nice.' He smiled. 'The drawing takes an artistic touch, and with you being into computers, you'll probably struggle to compete with me.'

Her laughter eased some of the tension he'd felt. At least he hadn't totally screwed things up with her.

Still, she didn't reply to his comment. Instead she glanced down at the tray of drinks on the bar. 'I think I'd better get these to their owners.'

As he started to walk round the bar, she put a hand on his arm, stopping him. A light touch, yet his skin tingled. 'You've got people to serve. I can manage.'

It felt like another brush-off, though her smile was warm as she picked up the tray.

'Okay, enjoy your evening. I hope to see you here again soon. Oh and Mia,' he added, just before she set off. 'Keep a look out at my window. I might message you again.' He smiled. 'Three times a charm?'

She rolled her eyes, but didn't say anything further. As he watched her walk away he wondered what she thought of his messages, of *him*. He'd caught her watching him lift, so there was something, maybe. Equally though, she'd turned down his offer to meet up, ignored his notes, and kept her blinds closed nearly all week, so yeah, it was likely she'd only been staring out of the window. Normally he'd take the hint – no point chasing after someone who didn't want to be chased, when plenty did – yet nothing about his reaction to Mia so far felt normal.

Chapter Six

Monday morning and Mia had just settled down at her desk when her doorbell sounded. With a groan of impatience she pushed back her chair and went to answer it.

Stan stood there, greasy hair, straggling beard and a body shape that screamed type 2 diabetes; large belly hanging over his trousers, the buttons of his shirt under serious strain.

'You know about this modern technology.'

She tried to hide her smile. Her neighbour clearly wasn't a fan of the long preamble. Or even the short pleasantry, apparently. 'Good morning, Stan.'

He humphed. 'Yes, yes, but this is an emergency. My TV doesn't work.'

'Your TV?'

'That's what I said.'

'I work with computers, Stan. Not televisions.'

'You use a screen, don't you?'

'Well, yes, just like I use a car. It doesn't mean I know what happens under the bonnet.'

Ignoring her, he walked to his front door – three strides away – pushed it open and waved for her to go inside.

Bloody great. Checking she had the key to her flat, she followed him in. The two places were side by side, mirror images of each other in terms of layout, but entering Stan's was like going into an eighties time warp. Everything was beige, except for the plants which seemed to have taken over the flat, like Triffids. Two giant speakers were set at either end of the living room, and next to one of them was a literal tower of CDs. She imagined somewhere there were stacks of VHS videos lurking on orange coloured pine shelves.

Snatching up the remote control, he pointed it at the TV. 'See here, flaming thing is frozen. I can't turn it off, can't change channel. I'm stuck with that bloody Piers Morgan.' He glowered at her. 'I can't stand the guy.'

'Okay, I see your issue. He is a bit Marmite.' When Stan looked at her blankly, she added, 'You either love him or hate him?'

'At least with Marmite you can put a ruddy lid on it.'

'Good point.' She held out her hand for the remote. 'Can I take a look?'

'I'm a pensioner, not a geriatric,' he grumbled when she opened the battery case. 'I know how to change the batteries.'

There was only one other thing this computer nerd

could think of. Mia walked to the wall behind the TV and turned it off at the plug. 'At least that's got rid of Piers for you.'

Stan didn't look too impressed. 'I could've done that. Bet he's still there when you turn it back on.'

'Ah, then you'd be betting against the magic power of the reboot.'

The screen flickered to life, and Mia pressed the remote control. As she changed it over to BBC1, cutting Piers off mid rant, a smile spread across Stan's face. 'You're a bloody genius.'

She could point out she'd only turned it off and on again. Or she could take the praise. Mia figured the latter was the most neighbourly, so she smiled. 'You know where to find me if Piers gives you any other problems.'

'This calls for a brew.' He waved his hand towards the beige sofa, complete with stains Mia really didn't want to think about. Or sit on. 'Sit yourself down lass, I'll put the kettle on.'

'That's kind, but I am meant to be working.' *And in fifteen minutes, I may want to stare out of my window into the flat opposite.*

His smile slipped. 'Oh, right, not to worry. Another time.'

Don't look at his sad eyes. Damn it. 'But I've got time for a quick drink.'

His face lit up again, and if she looked past the awful beard and the terrible hair she could see he actually had a good, kind face. One that didn't deserve to be as lonely as he seemed to be.

While he pottered around in the kitchen, Mia looked out of the window, wondering how different his view was than hers. And maybe also wondering how much he could see into Luke's flat. Not a lot, it appeared, as the blinds in the opposite room were down. Luke's bedroom? Swallowing, she shifted her gaze along, and her breath caught when she noticed a new sheet of paper taped to Luke's second window. Because of the angle, she couldn't read what it said, but it hadn't been there last time she'd looked.

'Checking out the guy opposite, I see.'

Mia gave a guilty start and knew she was blushing. Accepting the mug he offered, she gave a shrug she knew didn't convince either of them. 'Just looking at your view.'

'The lass in the flat before you used to invite her mates round at 10 a.m.'

She nearly choked on the tea. 'Seriously?' Then realised she was giving herself away. 'Umm, what for, exactly?'

Stan chuckled. 'If you weren't blushing so hard, I might believe you've never watched him take his shirt off, or whatever you girls seem to enjoy.'

Clearing her throat, she took another sip. Strong and stewed, exactly how she didn't like it. 'I'm guessing from this angle you can't see what the fascination is.'

Stan's eyebrows shot up. 'Don't tell me he's one of those Chipmunks.'

Mia burst out laughing. 'Sorry?'

'You know, men who prance about in their underwear.'

'Ah, Chippendales.' She had to work hard to get her laughter under control. 'Sadly no, he only works out with his weights. So I hear,' she added, totally unbelievably. Then, because she couldn't stop staring at the window she knew contained another sign for her, she asked, 'Do you know him?'

'Sure.' Stan slurped noisily at his tea.

The guy who'd taken an hour to tell her where the nearest supermarket was, chose *now* to use one-word replies? 'That's all you're going to give me?'

He slid her a sly smile. 'What more do you want?'

'What do you think of him?'

Another chuckle. 'Doesn't seem to matter what I think. You're clearly smitten.'

'I'm not.' *Then why are you asking about him?* 'I'm not smitten,' she clarified, 'just interested. Not in him,' she added quickly, then realised she was kidding nobody. 'Okay, maybe a bit in him. He seems to have a large female following.'

'Aye, there's no shortage of young women hanging around the bar, that's for certain.'

'And?'

Stan shrugged. 'You're better off asking some of them. I can tell you he's worked in the bar and lived opposite for as long as I've been here. Friendly bloke. Never had any trouble from him, as far as I know.' He paused. 'Rumour has it he's been through all the single women in this block, mind.'

Mia sighed. 'Yeah, that's what I thought.'

Silence descended and Mia realised the feeling sitting heavy in her gut was disappointment. She'd hoped Stan would tell her she'd got it wrong, that the hot bar owner with the twinkly eyes and the ready smile, wasn't a player.

Stan looked down at his watch. 'It's ten o'clock.'

She smiled. 'So? Are you kicking me out?'

He grinned, showing he had nearly all his teeth. 'I can take off my shirt instead, if you like.' As her eyes rounded in horror, he cackled. 'Or we could sit down and finish our brew.'

Relieved, she pushed away thoughts of the work she had to do. 'Let's do that. And you can tell me about the women hanging round your place.'

For a second his shoulders slumped. 'Nothing to tell on that score.' But then a slow smile spread across his face. 'Though like your barman, I've had my moments, over the years.'

It took Luke ten minutes to realise there was something missing with his usual workout routine.

A pair of big blue eyes watching him.

Did it make him vain that he preferred it when he knew Mia was watching? Probably. What he couldn't work out was why. Sure, he admired her self-assurance, enjoyed the way she could give as good as she got in a conversation, liked, okay really liked the way her nose wrinkled when she laughed, the blue of her eyes, the freckles. And yes, even the green hair. All of it said she was her own person.

That said, he thought about her way too much than was comfortable.

Beside him on the window ledge, his phone pinged.

Hey, I'm in Manchester next week. Fancy catching up? Vicky xx

Automatically he reached to reply:

Sure, Wednesday works.

But his thumb hovered over the send button. Did he *want* to see Vicky? She was fun, a sales rep he enjoyed hooking up with when she was in town.

So why wasn't he feeling it this time? Why was he hesitating?

Hastily he deleted his words and messaged instead:

Bar worker to bar owner = big change, little time off. Will have to give it a miss this time. L

He dumped the phone back on the ledge and snatched at the dumb-bell. At this rate he was going to turn into a bloody monk.

While he worked the dumb-bell, he glared at the sign he'd put up this morning for Mia. It was a picture he'd printed off the internet of scattered coffee beans in the shape of an owl, with two mugs of coffee for the eyes. Beneath it he'd scrawled:

Morning.

He'd hoped it would nudge her into putting up a message back. Either the owl wasn't cute enough, or he wasn't.

Frustrated with himself, he focused back on his weights. He was trying way too hard on Mia, and not hard enough on the stuff that was important. Like his business.

The week dragged.

On Thursday Sandy caught him looking at his phone and gave him a knowing smirk.

'Let me guess, Tanya?'

He shoved the phone away. 'No.' The message had been from Vicky, double checking he didn't want to meet up as she was leaving on Friday.

'Tanya been given the boot, has she?'

'You tell me, you seem to think you know my love life as well as I do.'

Sandy's eyebrows flew up. 'Oooh, a bit tetchy today are we?'

Luke forced himself to take a breath. Sandy was right. They'd had this banter over the women in his life for years, so why was he making such a big deal of it now? 'Not tetchy at all. Just focusing all my energy on the bar for now.'

That shut her up. 'Really?'

He nodded, aware he was telling the truth. Owning a

bar was very different to working in one and he was coming to realise he had less time now for distractions like Vicky, or Tanya. *Or Mia.*

He'd already ruined one career opportunity by losing focus, being irresponsible. He couldn't afford to ruin another. His finances and his self-esteem needed him to make a success of the bar.

Still, when he got home, he couldn't resist grabbing a sheet of printer paper, writing on it and sticking it in his window.

GNITE

And when he spoke to his brother the following evening after work – Phil was a night owl, like him, so always up for a midnight chat – it seemed he couldn't stop talking about Mia.

'You've done *what*?'

'Put a couple of signs up. Our flats are directly opposite each other, so from the room she works in, she can look into my spare room. I just … well, said *Hi*.' Now he was saying it out loud, it sounded stupid. 'She's not messaged me back.'

'I'm not surprised. Leaving a message in your window, God Luke, it's … hell, it's frigging weird, even for you. She probably thinks you're some sort of stalker.'

Shit. He flushed hot and cold. He hadn't considered she might be upset by the signs. 'Seriously? You think it's creepy?' He jumped up from the couch and strode down the hall to the spare room. There he stared at the potentially offensive signs. 'I only said *Hi*, or *Morning*. Tonight I wrote *Goodnight*.'

'Goodnight like you're watching her go to bed?'

'No, damn it, of course not. I can't see into her bedroom.' His stomach lurched. Christ, did she really think that he was some sort of pervy peeping Tom? 'I can only see when she's right against the window, like when she's sitting at her desk. That's the only time I've seen her in her flat,' he added, to reassure himself as much as Phil. Hadn't he caught *her* staring at him? Then again, maybe she'd been doing it in a *What the hell are you doing looking at me?* sort of way.

'Hey, I believe you.' Phil, the bastard, sounded amused. 'Maybe she's ignoring you because she doesn't like you, not that she finds you creepy.'

'Yeah right, not helping.' Feeling shaky, he knelt down and tore off the sign. That was it, no more acting like a sap.

'What is it about this Mia that's got you making such a dork of yourself?'

Luke slumped to the floor, scrunching up the sheet of paper. 'I don't know. Maybe it's not her, it's me. Could be an early mid-life crisis, stress over the bar.' *You felt a connection, one you've not felt for a long time.* 'Anyway, whatever it was, I'm over it. No more signs, no more distractions. The Bar Beneath has all my attention from now on.'

'Glad to hear that, because I've been going through the books.'

Phil, older by three years, was the responsible, sensible

one. The son who got married, became an accountant, produced two grandchildren their parents doted on. Luke knew, by the way his brother hesitated, that what he was about to say was going to be bad news. 'And?' he prompted. 'Whatever you've got to say can't be worse than Mia thinking I'm creepy.'

'That depends. How wedded are you to keeping your flat? To retaining your staff?'

'What?'

'It seems some of the money we thought was in the business, isn't. The last guy who did the books looks to have been skimming money off the place and now, well, there's a bloody big hole in the accounts.'

Luke's stomach lurched. 'Hit me with it.'

'Either you remortgage your place, lay someone off, or somehow manage to persuade a lot more customers through your doors, especially during the week.'

'Fuck.' Nausea rose inside him and Luke hung his head, his whole body starting to shake. 'Do you think Bill knew?'

'No way. I suspect he didn't take notice of the books, trusted the accountant to do everything.' Phil hesitated. 'Might have been an idea to have got me to look through all this before you bought the place.'

'You think?' Christ, what a mess. He'd worked in the bar, hell, worked for Bill for ten years, so he'd taken the whole thing on trust. *Because you're an idiot.*

After ending the call to his brother, Luke stared out of the window and over to Mia's. To think, ten minutes ago all he'd had to worry about was trying to get her to message him back.

Now he wasn't sure how much longer he'd be able to live in his flat. And his dreams of owning something, being someone, seemed as far away as ever.

Chapter Seven

Mia discovered that instead of making her own coffee in the morning, she could buy it from the café downstairs. Of course it meant she had to get dressed, but that was a good discipline and the coffee was worth the effort.

As a bonus, the lady who ran the café was a real hoot.

Naomi, part Caribbean, part Mancunian, part *who the Lord knows?* – her words – greeted Mia with her signature beaming grin. 'It's my favourite green elf.'

'How many five-foot-two elves do you know?'

Naomi winked. 'Not as many as I'd like to. Come for your latte?'

'Yes please.' She looked around at the empty tables. 'You're quiet this morning. What have you done with everyone?'

Naomi chuckled. 'Have you looked at the time, lady?

You're running early. It's only five past nine. You're my first customer.'

Mia stared at the clock on the wall. Wow. Clearly worry, in this case about whether she was being rude, or just plain dumb to ignore Luke's messages in the window, upset her body clock. If she carried on like this she might actually be at her desk before Immaculate Woman.

'You all right love?

Mia shook herself. 'Sorry, yes. Just stuff on my mind.'

Naomi gave her a knowing smile. 'Boy stuff.' When Mia opened her mouth to object, she flapped a hand at her. 'Don't you go pretending otherwise. I know the look on a woman's face when she's thinking about a man.' She placed a lid over the takeout cup and handed it to Mia. 'If you tell me the problem, I might be able to help, on account of this.' She tugged at a strand of silver hair. 'The grey represents years of experience on the subject. And the wrinkles. Lord, I swear, men are not good for the complexion.'

Naomi had told Mia, on their first meeting, she was sixty-two, yet she looked at least ten years younger. Accepting the coffee, Mia decided she needed a dose of that wisdom. 'Okay, if you'd met a guy who was really … well, hot, but also funny, you know? And easy to talk to. If you'd met him and liked him, but then found out he was a total player so you turned down his offer to meet up.' She paused to take in a breath. 'If he then put some messages in his window that he knew you'd be able to see, what would you do?'

Naomi's dark brows shot upwards. 'Heavens to Betsy, this sounds like the plot of a book. What did the notes say?'

'Nothing really, just greetings. Hi, goodnight.'

The older woman sighed. 'Damn girl, that's sweet.'

Mia's shoulders slumped. 'It is, isn't it?' She sighed, twisting the coffee round in her hands. 'I haven't replied. Is that mean?'

'You said you liked him?'

Mia thought back to that first conversation in the bar, how effortless it had been to banter back and forth with him. 'Yes.' But Tanya, Chloe, Helen. 'I don't want to date him though. I've trusted too easily in the past and been badly let down. The next man I date has to be a good one. This guy, with his sweet talk and easy smile, is more good-time-only.'

Naomi's deep brown eyes were full of sympathy. 'Sounds like you'd better steer well clear then, love. Ignore the notes and wait for the right one to come along.'

'That's what I thought.' So why did she feel so disappointed?

'How's that neighbour of yours?'

'Stan's good. How did you know we were neighbours?'

'Ah, nothing gets past old Naomi. Of course, it may have helped that he told me he had a new neighbour with green hair.' She chuckled. 'He wasn't quite sure what to make of you at first. A bit of a traditionalist, our Stan, though he's a sweetheart beneath the bluster. And the bone dry humour.'

Mia eyed Naomi speculatively. 'Is he a regular here?'

'He comes from time to time.' She nodded towards the highly calorific cakes and buns. 'Can't resist a custard donut. Tell him I've got some in especially for him.'

Mia had a feeling Stan was more than just a customer to Naomi. 'I will.' She took a sip of the coffee, savouring the flavour. 'Well, I guess I'd better get some work done. Thanks for the coffee.' She smiled. 'And for the advice.'

'Anytime time, love. I'm here for both.' She chuckled. 'And I only charge for the coffee.'

Laughing, Mia opened the door. And almost careered into the next customer.

Tall, built like a brick wall.

Smelling like shower gel, citrus and man.

'Hey.'

Her heart bounced. She'd know the voice anywhere. Deep, low and smooth with a soft Manchester accent. 'Hi.' Feeling awkward, she glanced down at her take-out cup. 'Just getting my caffeine fix.'

'Me too.' He smiled, dimples flashing either side of his mouth. But then a guard came down over his face. 'Err, do you have a minute?'

'Yes, sure. I should be working though, so…'

'It won't take long.' He glanced back to the bar, but then seemed to change his mind about asking her over. Instead he took a step back and shoved his hands into his pockets. It was a restless, awkward gesture for a man Mia had only seen as relaxed and confident. 'I just wanted to apologise.'

Mia frowned. 'For?'

His eyes met hers. She'd seen them glint with humour,

blaze with confidence. Now they seemed unsure. 'The notes to you in my window. I thought I was being … hell, I don't know, cute I guess.' He gave her an embarrassed look. 'That sounds cocky, but what I'm trying to say is I didn't mean any harm by them. Quite the opposite.' His huge shoulders lifted and fell as he sighed. 'It was pointed out to me last night that rather than being charming, I was in fact coming across as a total creeper.' A shudder ran through him. 'Christ, the thought that I might have upset you—'

'You didn't.'

He stilled, those brilliant green eyes searching hers. 'No?'

'Definitely not.'

He exhaled a long, deep breath. 'Okay. Good.'

Quiet descended and Mia struggled with how to fill it. She felt awful knowing her lack of response had made him think she'd been offended by his messages. Before she could say anything though, he was speaking again.

'I'd better let you get back to work.' He glanced into the coffee shop and gave Naomi a wave.

'I don't usually see you up and about so early.' *Not before 10 a.m.* Mia cringed, wondering how much she'd given away. Here he was, apologising for acting like a creeper with his notes, when she was the one who couldn't stop staring into his spare room every morning.

But he looked like he had other things on his mind than her voyeurism. 'Yeah, the bar's giving me a headache at the moment.' He laughed softly. 'And before you ask, it has nothing to do with the radioactive house cocktail.'

Relieved they were back to bantering, she smiled. 'Ah, so you admit it's radioactive then?'

He shook his head, eyes amused. 'I'll admit to it looking green and packing a punch.' There was another beat of silence and Luke shifted on his feet. 'So, I'll see you around?'

'No escaping me. I live here, remember?'

His gaze trapped hers, and he gave her a small, wry smile. 'Hard to forget.'

As she walked back to her flat, Mia did so with a little more lightness to her step. She didn't know why, but it felt important that she and Luke were still on friendly terms.

Ten minutes after bumping into Mia, Luke was sat in his spare room with his brother, both of them huddled round Phil's laptop, though only one of them currently staring at it. Luke's eyes kept straying to Mia's window.

'Something important going on over there?' Phil gave him the raised eyebrow. 'More important than looking at the big fat hole in your accounts?'

Of course it wasn't, but as he took a sip of his now lukewarm coffee, Luke couldn't help but wonder if Mia had finished hers. *She's out of bounds.*

Or was she?

'You were wrong, you know.' He nodded towards the window he'd been … yes, okay, gawping at. 'Mia wasn't upset by the messages I put up.'

Phil heaved out a sigh and sat back on the chair. 'I thought you said you were going to focus on the bar from now on?' He scratched at his chin. 'I guess I shouldn't be surprised at the quick U-turn. You've always been distracted by the opposite sex.'

Luke flinched at the unsubtle dig. Yet even as the barb sunk home, he plastered a smile on his face because that's what he'd learnt to do. Smile so his family couldn't see how much their criticism stung. 'Even you have to admit women are more interesting than accounts.'

Phil frowned. 'Even me?'

'You're the king of the spreadsheet, big brother.' Luke swigged back the last of the coffee. 'At one point I thought you'd rather go to bed with one than an actual woman. Then you met Janet and I figured maybe you'd persuaded her to recite numbers to you as foreplay.'

'That would be funny, if I didn't feel a bit weirded out that you've spent time thinking about my sex life.'

Luke grinned. 'Not that much time. I'd rather focus on my own.'

Phil gave him a shrewd look. 'And how's that going?'

Usually he'd give him a flippant reply, but for some reason the words wouldn't roll off his tongue. 'I don't know.'

'What about, who was the last one, Tabitha?'

'Tanya.' Luke raked a hand through his hair. 'Yeah, I see her now and again.'

'And the sales rep?'

'Vicky's not been around lately.' He didn't like lying to

his brother but if he admitted he'd turned down her invite to meet up, Phil might read something into it he didn't want him to.

'And here you are, mooning over the girl living opposite.' Phil shook his head. 'You do know decent women aren't impressed by guys who sleep around?'

Irritation pricked. 'I'm a single guy. The women I've been with know the score. Hell, they feel the same way, they don't want to be tied down either. Nobody's getting hurt here. We're just having fun.'

Phil gave him a long, steady look. 'And yet you don't look like a man who's enjoying himself right now.'

Damn Phil and his ability to read him so well. 'Of course I'm not. You've just told me the business I bought has been leaking money like a sieve.' Anxious to get the conversation back on track, he pointed to the computer screen. 'Come on, show me what the damage is, so I can work out how many kidneys I need to sell.'

'Put it this way, if you had three it would help,' Phil countered dryly, which did little to stem Luke's growing feeling of being utterly out of his depth.

An hour later, while Phil packed up his computer, Luke put the kettle on. What he needed was a double brandy, followed by a whisky chaser, but a large cup of hot caffeine would have to do instead.

And from the look of things, he'd have to settle for making it himself, ditto all his meals. His days of grabbing take-outs, even in the form of a coffee from Naomi's, were over. He had to plough all the money he could into the bar.

And find a way of increasing the takings by half as much again.

His stomach churned. Shit, why the hell had he ever thought he could run a flaming business?

'Whatever you're thinking, stop.' Phil clasped his arm and squeezed it tight. 'You'll find a way, Luke. You know the business inside out. This is just a temporary blip.'

'An hour ago you called it a big fat hole in the accounts.'

Phil gave him a sympathetic look. 'That was before I saw you looking so shell shocked.' He turned towards the window. 'So what are you going to do about the girl who lives opposite? Try another message?'

Luke shovelled a large spoonful of coffee into the mug. 'I think I've got enough on my plate at the moment.'

'Probably a wise decision.'

'*Probably?* This coming from the guy who told me I'm too easily distracted by the opposite sex?'

Phil smiled. '*Probably*, because while it's the right decision for your business, I'm not sure it's the right decision for you.' He shifted his glasses further onto his nose and gave Luke a quiet study. 'I've not seen you quite so keen on a woman for a long time.' Before Luke could correct him – he wasn't keen on Mia, just intrigued by her – Phil marched towards the door. 'I'll see myself out. Give us a call if you need anything.'

'Yes, and Phil?' Luke waited for his brother to turn round. 'Thanks for going through everything with me, for finding the issue. For having my back.'

Phil nodded. 'Always.'

It was true. His brother had been there for him when his parents hadn't. Was still there for him. As for their parents, Luke could almost see them shaking their heads in disapproval at this latest fuck up.

He felt a brush against his feet. 'Hey gorgeous.' Putting down the mug he'd been holding, Luke bent to pick up his furry friend. 'Come to tell me you have my back too, huh?' Stroking her ears, he walked them both back to his desk in the spare room and settled her on his lap. 'Right, no weights today, we've got work to do. We need a plan for how to increase business at the bar, or it's no more carrots for you, and no more roof over our heads for both of us.'

Straightening his shoulders, he opened a blank Word document.

That's when Pickles nudged his arm with her nose.

'Hey, I can't stroke and type at the same time.' When she looked up at him with her big brown eyes, he huffed out a laugh and resumed stroking her ears. 'Okay, message received. One-handed typing it is.'

Briefly he glanced over at Mia's window.

Then he forced his attention away from where he wasn't sure it was welcomed. And back to the computer, where it was needed.

Chapter Eight

It was the two-month anniversary of her move to Manchester.

Mia glanced down at the mug of tea in her hand. Sad or sensible that she was spending the Saturday by herself in her flat?

It hadn't been the plan. At one point her sister had been due to join her for, as Elle had put it, 'my last taste of freedom for a while'. But Dave had apparently put his foot down and told his wife she wasn't hightailing it up the motorway by herself at thirty-eight weeks pregnant. He was happy to come with her, but that would mean bringing their daughter Caitlin too. And just like that, Elle's idea of them shopping till they dropped around the Trafford Centre had fizzled out.

This morning, Mia had been ready to drive down, even though she was aware celebrating being in Manchester for two months by *not* being in Manchester, wasn't exactly confirmation of the brilliance of her decision to move.

Anyway that idea had been squashed, when Elle had calmly announced that she thought her contractions had begun.

'And no, I don't want you driving down today. Let me push The Wriggler out first. Come and visit when I'm back from hospital and looking serene with my newest cherub nestling quietly in my arms.' She'd finished the call with the classic comment, 'I don't want you stewing in your flat by yourself. Go to that bar with your new chums tonight. See the dishy owner you're pretending not to like.'

Mia really wasn't sure she could stomach an evening of Chloe fawning over Luke, or Tanya relating yet another tale of when she and Luke couldn't keep their hands off each other. All while she was worrying about her sister.

Of course the girls could have chosen to drink somewhere else, and Mia would be left drinking at the bar, worrying alone.

Then again. Maybe she could persuade Stan out? And yes, it came to something when she was considering asking her pensioner neighbour out for a drink, but wasn't it better than the alternatives?

Pushing the mug onto the kitchen work-top, she snatched her keys and headed next door to ring Stan's bell.

He opened it cautiously, the safety chain in place. 'Oh, it's you.'

'Yep. Your friendly neighbour.' When he didn't move the chain, she started to laugh. 'Err, you do know I'm friendly, yes? You can safely release the chain and I promise not to push you aside and storm inside.'

'Sarky woman.' He huffed as he released it, then stood in the doorway with his arms crossed. 'What do you want?'

'I'm here to invite you over to the bar for a drink.'

His shaggy grey eyebrows shot up. 'You're asking me out?'

'In a manner of speaking, yes.' His eyes widened to the extent she worried they might pop out. 'We're talking you and me, in the bar, having a drink instead of sitting on our arses all by ourselves in our respective flats. We're not talking candlelit dinner and coming back to bonk.'

He chuckled so loudly his chest rattled. 'Damn shame, that, though might be for the best. It's been so long since I bonked, not sure I can remember how to do it.'

Mia tried not to laugh, but in the end the situation was too ridiculous not to. 'Crap, Stan. That's no good. Maybe if you come with me to the bar we can find you someone.'

'Offering to be my wingman, are you?' He gave her a sly look. 'Or maybe I'm your wingman, and you're there to catch the Chipmunk's eye, huh?'

Again, Mia found herself laughing. 'That's wrong on so many levels, but what the heck. If it gets us both out of our flats for a few hours, let's do it.'

He looked down at his clothes. 'Do I need to change?'

His shirt had a smear of what she assumed was brown sauce, and his jeans had a hole in the knee that was more old age than design. Still, she wasn't looking so great herself, though at least her T-shirt was clean, and her jeans were from this decade. 'Not on my account. Just grab your wallet and keys.'

'Wallet? You invited me.'

'That I did.' Was she really this desperate for company? Apparently.

When she directed him towards the stairs, Stan gave her a baleful look. 'Why aren't we using the lift?'

'Because the exercise will do us both good.'

He huffed and puffed his way down, muttering words like *evil woman* and *I didn't sign up for this torture*. When they finally got to the bottom he halted, crossing his arms across his chest. 'What's this really about?'

And just like that, her confidence crumpled. 'Sorry, you don't have to come with me. I just…' She sighed. 'I should be with my sister this weekend, but right now she's in hospital, giving birth, and if I stay in all I'll do is worry and sit by the phone. The last couple of times I went to the bar I met a few girls and they might be there, but they mainly talk about guys and tonight I'm really not in the mood.'

He waggled his eyebrows. 'You'd rather talk bus passes, the good old days and hip replacements?'

'If that's what it takes to get you to come with me.' A lump of sadness caught in her throat. 'You're in the unlucky position of being the closest I've come to a friend up here, Stan. And right now, I need one to take me out of my head for a while.' *Luke would have done that for you.* She pushed the unhelpful thought away.

His craggy features softened and he held his arm out for

her to take. 'Then let's go and get that drink, love.' He winked. 'And don't forget, you're paying.'

'I won't.' Slipping her arm through his, they walked towards the bar. 'Maybe once I've got a few drinks down you, you'll tell me how well you know Naomi.'

He came to an abrupt halt. 'She owns the café.'

'I'm aware.' Tugging on his arm, she encouraged him to keep walking. 'She asked after you today. Said she had some custard donuts in for you.'

'She did?'

Mia tried not to laugh at Stan's hopeful look. 'She did, so you'd better get down there tomorrow.'

'Aye, I might just do that.'

Her own love life was in the doldrums, but Mia took comfort from the fact she might have helped nudge two other people together.

Luke tried not to stare at Mia too often, and mostly he succeeded. Old Stan was an unusual choice of companion for an attractive young woman on a Saturday night, but then again little about Mia was expected or conventional.

So far he'd only managed a quick smile in her direction. Mateo had been the one to serve her and it had been a rushed job – yes, Luke had been watching – because, hallelujah, the bar was heaving.

Still, it didn't stop him clocking when Mia's glass was

empty. Nor did it stop him making sure he caught her eye as she weaved her way back to the bar.

'Hey.' He nodded to where Stan was sitting at the back. 'He's not pulled the dodgy hip excuse to get you to buy him a drink has he?'

She smiled, but the spark he'd come to associate with her big blue eyes, was lacking. 'I invited him, so I buy the drinks.'

'Then he's lucked out twice tonight.'

Her gaze dropped away from his and down to the two empty glasses she'd brought back. 'I'm not sure about that. My company's a bit crap, to be honest. Hence the need for a refill.' She pushed the pint glass forward. 'He's on the house bitter. And I'm on merlot.'

'No problem.' He took a clean glass and slid it under the bitter pump. 'Everything okay?'

Her gaze bounced back up to his. 'Yes. Why?'

He shrugged. 'You seem a bit flat.' Sliding the full glass onto the bar, he shot her a grin. 'And crap is not a word that could ever describe your company.'

'Thanks.' It looked like she was about to say more, but then Chloe – bloody Chloe – muscled in next to her. 'Mia, I didn't realise you were here tonight. How's it going, love? You want to come and join us? We're over in the usual corner.'

'Thanks, but I'm with Stan.' Mia waved over to where Stan was sitting and Luke had to bite the inside of his cheek to stop from laughing as he watched Chloe's mouth gape open.

'The old geezer?'

Mia nodded, her face perfectly straight. 'He's good company. Tonight I've learnt all about how hard it is to live off the state pension.'

'You're having me on, right?' Mia simply smiled, and Chloe laughed. 'God, you probably have talked about that. Me, I prefer my men built and a hell of a lot younger.' With that she winked at Luke. 'Speaking of, how's my favourite bartender?'

She wasn't the woman he wanted to be flirting with, but Luke pasted on a smile. 'Mateo's gone to wash some glasses. He'll be back in a minute.'

Chloe laughed. 'Dead funny. You know I mean you.'

'I'm good, thanks. Busy, but not going to complain.' He glanced to where Donna and Tanya were sitting. 'If you want to go back to the others, I'll come and grab your orders when I've finished here.'

'Ooh, personal service. Tanya will be chuffed. Apparently you've been a naughty boy and not replied to her last two texts. She thinks you're avoiding her.' She waggled her fingers at Mia. 'Ta-ra for now love.'

As she tottered away on her spikey heels, Luke smiled at Mia. 'I'll bet a fiver she's gone to tell them you're dating Stan.'

'I'm not taking that bet. It's too obvious.'

Earlier her eyes had lacked their usual spark. Now the smile she directed at him looked strained. 'What is it?' he asked quietly. 'What's wrong?'

She shook her head. 'Nothing.' Then handed over her card.

Together with the closed-off expression, it was a clear signal their conversation had come to an end.

Feeling unsettled, he watched her walk back to Stan. Did she simply not like him but was too polite to say? Did she like him, but was pissed because Chloe had made it sound like he and Tanya were an item? And shit, that was something he needed to tackle. Or was Mia simply indifferent to him? He was the bartender she didn't mind bantering with, but in between her appearances at the bar, he dropped off her radar?

And why, when his business was crumbling round his ears, was he obsessing about any it?

Shoving thoughts of Mia to one side, he went to serve Chloe and the rest of the gang. 'Ladies, what can I get you?'

As they shouted over their orders, Tanya wrapped her hand around his arm. 'Can we talk?'

'Sure. Will it wait till things quieten down?' A busy bar was not conducive to the sort of conversation they needed to have. One that she deserved, rather than his cowardly text avoidance.

An hour later, he caught Tanya's eye and nodded towards the small office to the side of the bar.

When she slipped in, he closed the door behind her. 'I'm sorry I didn't respond to your texts.'

She nodded, moving to perch on his desk. As usual she was carefully made up, her hair poker straight, her red dress hugging curves he'd enjoyed unwrapping on and off over the last six months. 'Too busy for sex?'

Her directness was one of the things he enjoyed about Tanya, but on this occasion he struggled with how to answer. His head might be stuck on Mia, yet it wasn't like they were ever going to happen. 'In a way, yes. The bar is proving to be a headache and for now it needs my full focus.'

'Okay.' Disappointment came and went in her eyes, but she smiled brightly at him. 'I'm going to miss you shagging me senseless, but I guess I understand.' Slipping off the desk, she put a hand on either side of his face. 'Before I go, let me remind you what we have together.' With that she tugged him towards her for a long, slow kiss.

Usually he'd be up for it, he was a huge fan of kissing, but tonight his head wasn't in it. Carefully he drew back, dropping a final kiss on the top of her head. 'I won't forget,' he whispered, before going to open the door.

Head high, shoulders back, she walked out ahead before turning and pausing to rub at a spot on his mouth with her thumb. 'Red lipstick isn't a good look on you.' Giving the side of his face a gentle pat, she smiled. 'When you've rid yourself of the headache, you've got my number.'

He wasn't sure he'd be able to solve the headache that easily, nor if he did, that he'd ever use her number again. Still, he smiled back. 'You'll have found someone better by then. Maybe fallen in love.'

She threw back her head and laughed. 'Love is bullshit, we both know that.'

Yeah, they did. 'Well, don't be a stranger, the bar needs the sales.' He gave her a look loaded with affection. 'And I need to see a friendly face now and again.'

She went to join the others and his eyes drifted back over to where Mia was sitting. At that moment she looked up and as their gazes collided, he felt that pull again. It wasn't lust, not like he'd felt with Tanya and others before her. This was something more, deeper, a pull he felt in his core, as well as his groin. He wanted to ask her again what was wrong, because it was obvious something was, but she clearly didn't want to tell him, so he had to respect her privacy.

Giving her a brief smile, he headed back to the bar. Moments later, he saw her and Stan head out.

Chapter Nine

Going to the bar with Stan had helped in a way. While she'd been stewing over Tanya, wondering about her texts to Luke, about the kiss they'd obviously shared in his office, she'd not been worrying about Elle.

Now she was back in her flat, and still she hadn't had an update from Dave or her mum. Sure, it must be hard being the mum-to-be, pushing eight pounds of squirming baby out, and the dad-to-be, watching the pushing, but it was also bloody hard being the aunt-to-be. Even if it was second time round for all of them. Especially hard, because Elle had not had an easy time with her first, Caitlin, who ended up needing forceps to prize her out. *Instruments of torture that have no place near a woman's delicate parts,* Elle had moaned afterwards. When Mia had gone online to find out what the forceps actually looked like, she'd almost lost her breakfast.

For the umpteenth time she stared at her phone, willing it to ring. Until it did, she wouldn't be able to sleep.

Sighing, she returned her gaze to her computer screen, though it was more in hope than anything else. It turned out worry wasn't conducive to writing romantic comedy.

That's when she caught sight of movement in the window opposite. Holding her breath, she watched as Luke stuck up a sign.

JTOU.

Just thinking of you. Her heart bumped, but he wasn't finished. A moment later there was another one next to it.

Hope UR OK.

Tears pricked at her eyes. This man she barely knew had known something was wrong, and had cared enough to show his concern.

She'd pushed him away because she had no place in her life for a player, yet she had a huge gaping hole in her life for a friend. What if he was offering that?

Before she could overthink it, Mia grabbed a black marker pen, scrawled three letters on a sheet of printer paper and stuck it in the window:

Thx

As she sat back on her chair, her phone finally burst into life. Mia snatched at it.

'He's out.' Elle's voice sounded both euphoric and full of emotion.

'Oh God.' Mia bit at her lip to try and stop the tears. 'Are you okay? Is he okay?'

'I'm knackered, but fine. He's … oh Mia, he's not a turnip, or a cabbage. He's frigging perfect. Two eyes, a nose, fingers and toes. Everything. Here, Dave wants a word. He'll tell you.'

There was a sound of rustling, and then her brother-in-law's voice came on. 'Hi Mia, your sister is a bloody marvel. A bit of gas and air, a lot of shouting, and then your nephew popped out. He's got one hell of a set of lungs on him, just like she has, and he's handsome like his dad. He's looking forward to meeting you.'

It was all too much. Mia had tears streaming down her cheeks. Waves of longing, of acute loneliness, washed through her. She'd drive down tomorrow and take Monday off, catch up the work in the evenings. Eight weeks was too long not to see her family. And twelve hours too long not to see her brand-new nephew.

Just as she'd dried her face, her mum came on the phone which precipitated another round of over-emotional, happy tears.

As she finally got ready for bed, Mia looked across at Luke's window again. Taking up the marker pen, she scrawled:

New nephew!

Then crashed out with a smile on her face.

The next morning, the first thing she did was check her phone. No missed calls, no new messages. Everything must be okay.

The second thing she did was look across at Luke's flat. There she did find a new message.

Congrats Aunt Mia

A grin slid across her face. Maybe it was daft, but his messages made her feel less alone. Like she had someone looking out for her.

He might, if you give him a chance.

The thought stuck with her on the long journey down to Somerset. The moment she knocked on her sister's house though, all she could think was how amazing it was to hug someone. And how incredibly cute her new nephew was.

'OMG, he's like a doll.'

Dave, who'd answered the door, looked at her in horror, his protective genes already kicking in. Caitlin, three but wise beyond her years, giggled. 'Jakey is a doll.'

'Jacob is a baby,' Dave corrected, reaching to stroke his son's cheek. 'And until your aunt realises that she doesn't get to cuddle him, because you have to be very careful with babies.'

'My doll lost its head,' Caitlin told Mia proudly. 'I pulled it.'

Mia winced and mouthed *sorry* to Dave, who shook his head and muttered something about her always being a trouble-maker. 'Your parents are on their way and Elle's in the bedroom, trying to find some clothes to cover her saggy bits. Her words. I'm sure she won't mind you going up.'

Mia dashed up the stairs and threw her arms around her sister.

'God, I've missed you, missed this,' Mia said as they sat side by side on Elle's bed. They talked birth and babies, including how a minor tear was far easier to handle than an episiotomy – not that Mia would ever have to worry about it, the way her love life was progressing.

'We won't leave it so long next time.' Elle bumped shoulders with her. 'Mum's going to be here any minute, and you know I need an update on the hot bar owner. Any more messages?'

Her sister's expression went all soft and gooey when Mia told her about the ones from last night. 'He was thinking of you? That's so sweet.' She took hold of Mia's hand and squeezed it. 'You know, just because he isn't boyfriend material, doesn't mean he wouldn't make a good friend.'

'I know. And I messaged him back so, well, we'll see.'

'I'm so going to get a vicarious thrill from this.' Elle beamed at her. 'And it would make a great plot for your next book. Just think, ogling across a courtyard, secret messages in windows, friends to lovers.'

'Whoa, I haven't written the first one yet. And you just agreed he wasn't boyfriend material.'

'Hey, I'm enjoying a moment here, don't ruin it.' Her sister clasped her hands against her chest in a totally over-the-top romantic gesture. 'Who said I'm talking about the bar owner, anyway? Stan's the man who's already had a date with you.'

She tried to say it with a straight face, but soon the pair of them dissolved into fits of laughter. It was only as they finally managed to gather themselves that Mia acknowledged how much she'd missed exactly this. Laughing so much it hurt, with someone she felt comfortable enough to really let go with.

Sunday was proving to be a bleh sort of day for Luke. The bar wasn't as busy as it should be, the rain putting off the crowd who usually gathered on a late summer afternoon to while away a few hours before meandering home for dinner.

In the past quiet days had been easy days. Now Luke spent them worrying.

'For God's sake *smile*.' Clearly worried he'd forgotten how to do it, Sandy gave him a big cheesy demonstration. 'Your current look isn't good for business.'

'Err, remind me who the boss is?'

She rolled her eyes. 'The boss is the one who seems to have lost his mojo.'

'Hey, I've not lost anything.' Except money, though technically that had vanished before he'd taken over.

Sandy studied his face, and whatever she saw made her frown. 'Something's up, what is it? Grace okay?'

'Yes, she's fine. She's in Italy now, or she was last time she called.' Their conversations had been too infrequent, but it wasn't her fault he needed more, it was his. He missed her. He might spend most of his life surrounded by people, but there were very few he could really talk to.

'Okay, so if it's not Grace, what?'

He owed Sandy and Mateo a conversation, he realised. After all, if he failed to turn things round, they would be affected, too.

'Grab Mateo and meet me in the office.' Walking over to the door, he flung the sign to *Closed*. Then waved at the few customers still left. 'If you fancy another drink, help yourselves. We're in the office if you need us.'

Closing the bar and giving away free drinks probably wasn't on the *how to make your bar profitable in five easy steps* list. Then again, he'd yet to find the damn list.

He didn't sugar coat the issue, though he did try to remain upbeat. 'This is just between us. Phil knows, because he's the one who discovered it, but we tell nobody else, is that clear?' When they both inclined their heads, he added, 'I'm not planning on losing the place, or any of the staff. Instead I'm working on ideas to increase business. Themed evenings, maybe flyers to the residents, giving them a discount.' He eyed them both. 'If you've got stuff to add, don't hold back. The only stupid idea is the one you keep to yourself.'

Mateo flexed his biceps. 'How about topless bar staff?'

Sandy raised an eyebrow. 'I presume that's just for the men?'

'Okay, let me rephrase,' Luke interjected. 'The only stupid idea is the one you keep to yourself, or anything that turns the place into a strip club.'

'Gotcha.' Sandy gave him a considered look. 'Have we got a Facebook page? A website?'

Luke groaned, rubbing his hands over his face. 'How bad would I sound if I admit I don't actually know?'

'Hey, give yourself a break, man.' Mateo gave him a cheeky grin. 'All that modern stuff's hard to keep track of when you're old.' Ignoring the glare Luke directed at him, Mateo slipped his phone out of his pocket and tapped on the screen. 'The Bar Beneath is listed on Google but doesn't have a website or a Facebook page. Bill was hardly social media savvy. He probably didn't bother with it all.'

'Okay, I'll ignore the age dig and put it on the list.' Luke shot himself an email reminder, not because he was old, but because it was the smart thing to do. Like having the accounts of a business checked properly before buying it. And knowing basic things about it like its online presence.

'You know who could help you with the website.' Mateo had a small smile on his face. 'She comes to the bar now and again.'

'Who?' As Mateo's smile turned into a smirk, Luke had a feeling he already knew.

'The lady you've got a thing for.'

'What lady?' Sandy glanced between the pair of them. 'And why don't I know about this?'

'You don't know, because it's a secret.' If anything, Mateo's smirk had got even … smirkier.

'Nobody knows,' Luke interrupted, 'because there is no *thing*.' Before Mateo could drop him in it any further, Luke added, 'Right, we'd better get back out there and look after the few customers we do have.'

Mateo jumped to his feet and dashed out, sneaky coward, but Sandy put a hand to Luke's chest and stopped him. 'Three things.'

'Three?' He stared at the clock on the wall. 'God, I might never get out of here.'

Sandy punched him on the arm. 'First, the stuff I said about the social media. If you do anything about it, I want in.'

He'd already decided to ask Sandy to do it, so that was an easy win. Still, wouldn't harm to make her sweat a bit, considering all the grief she gave him. 'I'll consider it. Next.'

She huffed, but clearly decided to save her fight for another day. 'This hole in the accounts. Does Bill know about it? I really like the guy, but if he's diddled you—'

'Chill.' Because she looked so fiercely protective, Luke brought a hand to her face, cupping it gently. 'I appreciate the loyalty, but Bill's been like a dad to me. No way was he aware of this.'

Sandy stared back at him, then exhaled long and slow. 'Crap, you're not going to tell him either, are you?'

Luke dropped his hands and turned away. How could he? Sure, Bill could give him the contacts of the previous people who'd done the books, and maybe then Luke could find out who'd screwed the business, maybe recover some of the money, but at what cost? Bill would be mortified.

Worse, he'd probably want to pay him back, and Luke knew for damn sure finding that sort of money wouldn't figure in Bill's retirement plans.

'Luke?'

He swivelled back to face her. 'This is my issue, Sandy, and I'm going to fix it. All Bill needs to know is we're trying to increase turnover.'

There was a pause while she studied his face. Then she sighed. 'Fine.' Surprising him, she kissed him on the cheek.

'What was that for?'

'Being one of the good guys. Most people in your situation would have gone to the previous owner, all guns blazing.'

'No, most would have done their homework properly before buying the place.' But he'd learn from it. 'You said three things?'

'Who's the girl Mateo mentioned? The one you've got a thing for. And before you deny it, remember I'm your oldest friend. We *talk* about this stuff. At least we used to.'

Because she looked not just put out, but upset, he wrapped an arm around her and hugged her close. 'I'll tell you when and if there's anything to tell. I promise.'

'Okay.' She threw him a look as they reached the door. 'I think I might have a chat with Mateo and swop one of my shifts to the evening. Just, you know, to see what goes on.'

He laughed, aware Sandy would wheedle it out of him sooner or later. But until she did, he would enjoy this spark, these shoots of something. Because yesterday, Mia had messaged him back. Not only that, she'd shared her good news with him. He could even have been one of the first she'd told. Call him soft, but that meant something.

Later that evening, after the bar had closed, he paced his flat, wondering whether to leave Mia another message. He wanted the connection, but given her initial reticence he didn't want to seem too pushy. It was likely she'd only replied yesterday because she'd been on emotional overload, swinging between worry about what he guessed was her sister giving birth, then joy knowing she was an aunt.

She'd had all day today to message him again, but she hadn't.

He'd not seen any lights on in her flat since he'd been back though, so maybe she wasn't there. Maybe she was visiting her new nephew.

Sod it, he'd never been one to back down. Taking the pen he'd left by the window, he considered what to write. He wanted to ask to meet up, but he suspected that might scare her off again, so he settled for something he figured a new aunt couldn't ignore.

Cute rating 1–10?

Chapter Ten

Mia drove back to Manchester on Monday evening following a lunch catch-up with Gill and Heather. The conversation had gone something like: yes the guy opposite was still sending her messages, yes she'd replied, no she wasn't interested in dating him. After her last answer, they'd both cracked up laughing.

'We always pegged you as the smart one,' Gill had observed, wiping tears of laughter from her eyes. 'But you've lost some brain cells if you think you're going to remain immune to a hot guy sending you love notes in his window.'

She'd tried to argue they were hardly love notes, but it had been no use. The pair of them were clearly writing their own script.

Lunch had been followed by dinner and another inquisition, this time from her parents. Yes she was fine, yes she was meeting people and no, there was nothing to add since they'd asked the same questions two days ago. In the boot of her car, along with her overnight bag, she now had three Tupperware boxes of shepherd's pie, three of corned beef hash (her mum was big on mashed potato), a tin of rock-hard cookies and a large Victoria biscuit that clearly hadn't understood it needed to actually rise before it could be called a sponge cake.

'Couldn't drag your mother out of the kitchen yesterday morning,' her dad had grumbled as he'd helped her load up.

'The mash concoctions are probably edible, but since when has Mum believed she can bake?'

He'd given Mia a long-suffering smile. 'Since you decided to up sticks to Manchester. She's worried you aren't eating properly.'

At which point her mum had joined them. 'Of course I'm worried. It's all black pudding and Eccles cakes up there. Our gumdrop needs some proper food inside her.'

There had been no point arguing that by that yardstick, Somerset was all cider and Cheddar cheese. Or that some of what was in the boot could not be given the label 'proper food'. Not when her mum was on a roll.

Especially not when her dad had whispered, 'Be grateful. You should see the batches we had to throw away.'

Mia felt a squeeze on heart as she recalled the look on his face, the doting expression beneath the dry humour. He loved her mum because she was a little loopy, a little odd, not in spite of it.

Would anyone ever feel like that about her?

By the time she arrived back at her flat, she was tired, stiff and missing her family already. *You're lonely.* The words circled her head, dragging her mood down further.

Unwilling to give in to the dark cloud, she picked up her hold-all and carried it into her bedroom. As she emptied the contents onto the bed, she noticed a flash of white in Luke's window.

Had he put up another sign?

Heart beating that little bit faster, she abandoned the bag and dashed into the spare room so she could read it properly.

Cute rating 1–10?

She let out a huff of laughter and picked up a pen and paper.

Nephew or ?

To her surprise, there was immediate movement in the window opposite. Glancing at her watch, she realised it was just after eleven o'clock. He must be back from the bar.

Suddenly her heart began to speed up. Had her reply sounded flirty? She didn't want to send mixed messages.

Nephew

Phew, okay. That she could deal with. Picking up the pen again, she wrote:

11

She was about to turn away, when she saw the flash of paper again, followed by the outline of Luke as he stuck another message up:

Mateo?

Her stomach began to flutter.

8

She held her breath. He wouldn't, would he? Because if he did, she wasn't sure how she could answer him…

Stan?

Laughter burst out of her.

Easy 7.

He wasn't finished, and as Mia waited for his next sign, the flutter returned. She was enjoying this, she realised. As long as…

Final answer?

Smiling, she messaged back.

Final answer.

Part of her wanted him to ask the obvious, but a bigger part was scared he would. This tenuous friendship they'd begun felt too important to ruin with flirty comments.

See U + or - 7 soon?

Her answering smile was as much relief as it was amusement. Hastily she scrawled:

Yes

Quick as a flash he put up another message:

Sweet dreams

She wrote back:

U 2.

And when she crawled into bed, she realised she didn't feel lonely anymore.

On Wednesday, Mia decided to have a change from her usual lunch – cheese and/or ham sandwich – and see what Naomi had to offer.

The café was busy and Mia had to wait in a queue to be served. 'Well hello.' Naomi gave her a broad grin. 'Here for another coffee?'

'I've come to see what you have to offer on the take-out lunch front.' She pointed to the bacon, cranberry and brie panini. 'That's exactly what I need.'

Naomi scooped it up and slotted it into the toasting machine before leaning across the counter. 'How's the hot guy?' she whispered. 'The one leaving you messages?'

Mia could feel a blush scald her cheeks. 'Ah.'

'Oh Lordy, this sounds good. Come on, confess all.'

'There's nothing to confess.' Mia glanced over her shoulder, relieved to see nobody was queuing. 'We've been messaging a bit.'

Naomi whooped. 'Wow, girl. And here's me thinking you didn't want to encourage him. What made you change your mind?'

'I'm not … we're not…' Mia sucked in a breath. 'It's not like that. The messages are just friendly.'

Naomi turned to slide the panini out of the toaster and into a cardboard container. When she handed it over, her eyes were brimming with mischief. 'But you still think he's hot.'

Mia glanced down at the box, then up at Naomi. 'This panini is hot, doesn't mean I want to date it.'

As Naomi rang up the cost on the till, she chuckled. 'But you do want to gobble it up.'

Mia raised her eyes to the ceiling. 'I want to gobble it up

because it's got bacon in it.' A diversion was needed. 'Did Stan come in for his custard donut?'

'He did that.' Naomi shook her head. 'I know what you're doing, but I'm afraid it won't work. Nothing's going to happen between me and Stan. He's far too shy, and despite appearances, I'm too much of a traditionalist to want to do all the running.' She winked at Mia. 'But you've got a guy sending you messages by window. If that's not romantic, I don't know what is. I can't wait to hear the next instalment.'

Mia walked out laughing, her eyes automatically glancing towards the bar. As if there was some invisible thread between them, Luke, who was rearranging tables outside, chose that moment to look up. A slow, wide smile slid across his face, and her pulse kicked up a gear.

He's a player, she reminded herself. *You don't need the angst.*

Still, his smile was so infectious, she couldn't help but smile back. Or walk towards him.

'Hey.' He straightened, eyes seeming to take an inventory of her face. 'How's eleven out of ten?'

'Jacob's…' She rolled her eyes. 'Okay, I'm a besotted aunt. He's incredible. All tiny and perfect.'

'You went to see him?'

'Of course, what sort of aunt would I be if I deprived him of a cuddle?'

'A terrible one.' Luke's dimples winked on either side of his mouth as he grinned back at her. 'I hope he realises how lucky he is.'

Warmth surged through her, leaving Mia feeling unbalanced. She didn't want him flirting with her, and yet … God, she was flattered.

As she was trying to work out how to reply, a dark-haired woman burst out of the restaurant, dashed over to Luke and threw her arms around his neck.

'Whoa.' Luke put his hands on her hips, presumably to steady them.

'You didn't need to do that,' the woman said, though it was clear whatever Luke had done, she was fully in favour of it. Then she seemed to become aware of Mia, and as she untangled herself from Luke, she gave Mia a wide-eyed look. 'Crap, sorry. I didn't realise I was interrupting.'

'You're not.' Holding up the panini, Mia forced a smile. 'You're saving me from having a cold panini.' With a quick nod to Luke, she headed back to the stairs, trying to ignore the heavy feeling in her gut. She didn't even know what she was disappointed about. That she and Luke had been interrupted? That here was yet another woman treating him with obvious familiarity?

'Bugger, that was her, wasn't it?'

Luke looked to where Mia was retreating faster than the profit column in his accounts. He figured there wasn't much point denying it. Not if his face had registered even half of the curdling frustration he felt. 'Yep.'

Sandy placed a hand on his upper arm and squeezed.

'Fuck. I'm a moron.' When he didn't say anything, she nudged him. 'It's okay, you can agree with me.'

'You're a moron.' He sighed. 'But let's hope you're less of a moron than me, now you're head of our communications.'

She gave him a sly glance. 'Does it mean I can ditch the waitressing?'

'Nope. It means you get the fabulous opportunity to sort out our online presence *and* be a waitress.'

'Hence the pay rise.' It was her turn to sigh. 'I came out here to thank you for it, because it was a ridiculous but very generous thing to do, considering how tough things are at the moment.' Her eyes filled with apology. 'Didn't realise I'd end up scaring off your crush. Some thank-you gesture, huh?'

He gave her a wry smile. 'She was already wary, so no biggy. As for the pay rise, if you get more people through the door, you'll more than earn it.'

'And if I don't?'

'Hopefully your next employer will have the decency to match the inflated salary.'

Her shoulders sagged. 'Crap. That assumes he or she will want to employ a mouthy know-it-all.'

Luke laughed. 'Exactly, so don't screw this up, for both our sakes.'

'Gee, thanks boss, no pressure.' She looked towards the direction Mia had taken. 'This crush, does she have a name?'

'Mia. And she's not a crush. She's…' Hell if he knew

what she was. Only that he felt drawn to her, somehow. 'She's someone I'd like a chance to get to know.'

Sandy frowned, looking up at him. 'You realise that isn't what you usually say about women, don't you? I get *Sandy, she's hot*, or *she's game for some fun*, or even—'

'I've got it.' He felt a kick of embarrassment at the stuff he'd probably said. He enjoyed women, yet somewhere along the line he'd chosen to forget where the real joy came from. Instead he'd clung to the surface, the looks, the fun, because it was safer than getting to know the person. Safer than being dragged into deep water and then being spat out, like a riptide.

'Do you have a phone number for her?'

Sandy's voice pulled him back into the present. Taking a moment to make sure the old, unwanted memories were locked away, he shook his head. 'No, why?'

'Because I want to tell her about your big fat non-crush.' Alarmed, he opened his mouth to argue and Sandy raised her eyes heavenwards. 'God, I'm joking. Mateo said something about her maybe being able to help with the website?'

'Ah, yes, okay.' As the panic settled, he managed a laugh. 'I never know with you. Sometimes you're scary. I don't know how Jim manages to keep his sanity.'

'He loves me.'

The words were simple yet it was the certainty behind them that had him envying, not for the first time, what his best friends had. What he'd once wanted, until he'd taken a different path.

'So, how do I contact her then, this Mia?' Once again, he was yanked out of the past. 'Do I need to hang outside Naomi's and hope she buys another panini?'

It was an excuse to pop another message in the window, yet the thought of using what he saw as a personal, an *intimate* method of communication, for a work-related reason felt wrong. 'Leave it with me.'

He wrestled with the thought all day, and when he got back to his flat the first thing he did was walk into the spare room/gym/study/messaging-Mia room and look over at her window.

There was no message. He hadn't expected one, and it felt absurd that he should be disappointed, yet he was.

Pickles scampered into the room and he bent to pick her up. 'Sorry love, I forgot to say hello to you first. Pretty unforgivable, huh?'

She pushed her nose under his hand, and he got the unsubtle message and began to stroke her.

'What do you think I should do, huh? Wait until I bump into her again, or message her?'

He could loiter outside Naomi's on the off chance she went there most mornings for coffee or lunch, but what if she didn't?

Yet if he put a note in the window, what could he say? He glanced down at Pickles. 'What do you reckon she'd say to something along the lines of… *Can we meet up and chat about you maybe building me a website but really I just want to talk, you and me, about anything you want. I'd love to see if this connection I feel is real or me going through some approaching mid-life too fast, crisis.'*

Pickles twitched her nose.

'Really? Too long for a window message, huh? Maybe it's just as well.' If Mia was wary now, that would bring her blinds down permanently.

Still, maybe he could work with the first part. She'd turned down his offer to meet up before, but hadn't they established a rapport now?

One you could be about to blow.

Indecision wormed through him, and he hated it. This dithering twat wasn't him. Sod it. He placed Pickles back on the floor and snatched up a pen. This was no longer about him wanting to chat to her away from the bar, away from interruptions. This was about the bar, and the people who relied on him.

Carefully he sketched out a coffee cup and the words:

Naomi's

11 a.m.?

Did it sound too abrupt? Grabbing a second sheet, he added:

On Me

'There.' He glanced down at Pickles, who was sniffing at his shoe. 'Let's see what tomorrow brings, eh?'

His mobile started to ring, and he glanced at the screen. 'Big brother keeping an eye on me,' he muttered as Pickles scampered away, no doubt in search of something more interesting to sniff. And then possibly chew. Internet cables were her preferred choice.

'No need to worry about me,' he said in lieu of a greeting. 'I'm a big boy now. I can sort out my own mess.'

Phil cleared his throat. 'I'm calling to ask if you want to come over for dinner on your next day off. Janet says it's been too long since we saw you. And the girls keep asking after you.'

'Ah.' Feeling like a batsman who'd been clean bowled, Luke slumped to the floor. 'Way to make your brother sound like a prick.'

'Serves him right for being such a sensitive arsehole.'

Luke winced. 'Sorry. I got a bit defensive there.'

'Yes.' A pause, and when Phil came back on, his tone was more sympathetic. 'But you have your reasons for it.'

Phil had always managed to keep on the right side of their parents, but Luke knew if push came to shove, his brother would stand firmly in his camp.

'Am I allowed to ask how things are going?' Phil asked into the silence.

'Plans are in place; social media, website, local promo. Sandy's sure she can create a buzz.'

'And are you sure?'

'Of course.' He crossed his fingers like a ten-year-old being caught in a lie by his mum.

'Great. And how about the girl opposite? Are plans in place there, too?'

Luke glanced at the signs he'd put up. And felt like crossing his damn fingers again, only this time for luck. 'Ask me again this time tomorrow.'

Chapter Eleven

Mia glanced at the clock on her computer. 10.45 a.m. She had time to change her mind.

Or did she?

She'd noticed his message in the window when she'd sat at her desk, bleary eyed, at nine this morning. It had done more to kick start her system than coffee ever could. The trouble was, all that adrenalin, instead of being used to enhance her productivity, had been spent working out what to reply. After thirty minutes of furious thinking, she'd come up with:

Okay.

To say no would have been rude, she'd reasoned, and … and … bugger, no point in lying to herself. She wanted to meet him.

At ten o'clock she'd watched him tape a in his window.

And yes, she had glanced at him as he'd worked out, but only because that was where her eyes fell when she stopped to think. Working on a mind-numbing website for a courier company, a girl needed all the inspiration she could get.

Then the show had ended, presumably so he could go and shower for their meeting.

She looked back up at the time. 10.58 a.m.

Her heart bounced, and she pushed her chair back. Okay, no big deal. She was going to meet a friend for coffee.

Her mum would be pleased, her sister frigging delighted when she told her who the friend was.

Grabbing her purse – she didn't need him to buy her coffee – she dashed out of the flat.

Halfway down the stairs, she realised she'd not checked if she had toothpaste/marmalade round her mouth. Or thought to change.

But this was her, and she couldn't see the point of pretending to be any different. She'd tried once, as a teenager at school, but it had been too exhausting. Instead she'd learnt to smile as they'd called her names – geek, nerd, weirdo – and to use humour to deflect the sting.

She'd also, eventually, learnt to be happy with who she was.

Pushing on the door to the café, she noticed Luke was already there, his back to her as he stood chatting to Naomi at the counter. Somehow he looked even bigger today, his wide shoulders encased in a white T-shirt, long legs in jeans that fitted nice and snug over a very neat bum.

As a view, it was enough to send her girl hormones buzzing. And that was before he turned and smiled.

Her stomach dipped, and heat flashed through her. It was hardly surprising this guy had women flocking. And if a good time was all a girl wanted, she'd like to bet he'd deliver.

'Morning, Mia.' His eyes, all warm and green and twinkling, skimmed over her face before settling on hers.

'Morning.' She was glad her voice sounded steady, though the saliva had vanished from her mouth, which was frigging ridiculous. He was crazy good-looking, and charming, and he'd sent her sweet messages from his window, but she didn't need a flirt in her life.

'What can I get you?' He nodded towards the seating area. 'I'll bring it over if you want to find a seat.'

'Is this force of habit, feeling the need to serve me even when you're not at work? Because I can order and buy my own drink.'

His smile slipped, just a little. 'I invited you, remember?' And then it was back again, in full force. 'Next time you can pay.'

She wasn't going to argue about next time, not in front of Naomi. 'I'll take a latte, thanks. And as you're buying, a pastry too.'

He laughed. 'Fine, any preference?'

'You choose.'

'Are you sure? You didn't trust my judgement when it came to cocktails.'

'Ah, but I trust Naomi. She won't sell anything as awful as your radioactive green sludge.'

Naomi chuckled, but the look she levelled at her was full of questions. Mia had a feeling she was in for a grilling the next time she came to the café.

'Sludge?' Luke put a hand to his chest. 'You wound me. For that, I'm going to pick something boringly healthy.' He scanned the selection and grinned. 'I've got it. A granola bar. The one without chocolate.'

'I asked for a pastry. Getting me anything different would be rude.'

He returned her verbal lob with a sly grin. 'I don't mind being rude.'

More customers entered the shop and Mia left him to it, finding a spare table in the corner. As she sat down, she realised she was smiling. Luke was everything she needed to steer clear of, but he was also fun. And it turns out when you're feeling lonely, fun is in really short supply.

Maybe that explained why she was here. Her brain knew she needed to keep Luke at arm's length, but her soul desperately needed to laugh.

Luke walked over a minute later carrying two mugs in one hand, and a plate laden with pastries in the other.

When she goggled at them, he smiled. 'I didn't want to risk you not meeting me again, so I asked Naomi for a few of each.' He reached behind him into his back pocket and produced a handful of serviettes and a paper bag. 'You can take those you can't eat now back with you.' A flash of those dimples. 'Think of me as you drop pastry flakes all over your keyboard.'

Her gaze bounced to his. 'How do you know I eat over my keyboard?'

'Ah.' He grabbed at one of the pastries. 'I could say you mentioned you worked with computers, and I assume like most people, you snack when you get bored. But actually, when I lift weights I can see you at your desk.' He gave her a wide grin. 'It pushes me to work out harder.'

Crap. Could he tell she ogled him? 'You can really see me?'

'Well, the shadow of you.' He considered her while he munched on a mouthful of pastry. 'First thing I noticed was the flash of green hair, that's when I realised it was you living opposite. But you must have shifted your desk back because after that I couldn't see you as clearly, only your outline.'

Relief surged through her. 'It was getting too hot right next to the radiator.'

'Too hot, that explains it.'

His lips twitched and as amusement flickered in his eyes she squirmed on her seat. *He doesn't know you've been watching, not for sure. He's only guessing.* 'So, anyway, as enjoyable as this is, sitting in front of a plate of pastries, why did you want to meet?'

He took a swig of his coffee before placing it back on the table and meeting her eyes. 'You know why. I asked you out the first night you came to the bar, but you turned me down.'

Her heart began to race. *This is what happens when you play with fire.* 'I said I knew where to find you, if I needed a guide.'

'True.' He leant forward, searching her face. 'But we both know that meant thanks, but no thanks.'

There wasn't much point lying about it, not when he was being so upfront. 'It did.'

'Am I allowed to know why?' He glanced down at himself, then back at her. 'Are you into skinnier guys? Men who know their way around a computer rather than a bar? Or maybe it was the ropey sense of humour that put you off?'

'I like you and your ropey humour just fine.' She made sure to look him straight in the eye. 'But I don't want to have sex with you.'

It wasn't the first time he'd been turned down, but it was the first time it had been done quite so … Luke wanted to say brutally, because that's how it felt, yet she'd also said she liked him. And she was smiling, which definitely took the edge off her words.

'Okay.' He jammed a hand through his hair and tried to find his balance. 'I wasn't just talking about sex. I thought I could show you around, take in a meal, maybe the cinema.' He felt his pulse quicken as he gazed into her big blue eyes. 'But yes, I'd hoped sex was part of that package.'

She paused, brushing at flakes of pastry that had fallen

onto her T-shirt. This one he noticed said *I write code so I know stuff*. 'The first part, I'd like,' she said finally. 'It's the last part I'm not up for. And I know that's not something you usually hear, what with you looking like you do.'

He seized on the comment like a starving man being offered a plate of chips. 'You think I'm attractive?'

Her mouth curved. 'I'm not blind.'

'But you still don't want to have sex with me.'

'I don't want to join that list, no.'

'List?'

'Come on, at the bar I'm surrounded by women you've slept with.'

He was starting to regret this whole conversation. 'Not true.'

She quirked a brow. 'Helen, I bet she's an ex.'

'Exactly, an *ex*. It was a long time ago.' How had he gone from flirting with her about watching him lift weights – and yeah, she'd definitely watched – to dissecting his love life?

'But you admit you've slept with her. And, who was the other woman she mentioned, Linda?'

'Lizzie, and that was brief. She's happily married with two kids now.'

'Chloe?'

'No.'

'She seems keen.'

He wasn't enjoying this, not one little bit. 'She is. Doesn't mean I've slept with her.'

'Sandy?'

'Christ, no, absolutely not.' He was getting both

flustered and frustrated now. Part of him wanted to say forget it, he'd received the message and wouldn't trouble her again. But damn it, when was the last time a woman had challenged him? Even if right now he wasn't enjoying it. 'I've known Sandy since school. We used to go round in a four, her and Jim and me and … hell, it doesn't matter.' He exhaled an exasperated breath. 'Sandy's been married to Jim almost forever. I've never dated her. God, just the thought of it.' A shudder ran through him. 'It would be like dating my sister.'

Mia's eyes flickered with amusement. 'Fine, it seems I can cross her off the list.'

'This frigging list is beginning to piss me off.'

Her teeth settled over her bottom lip as she clearly tried not to laugh. 'I can see that.'

'But you're enjoying this too much to stop, huh?'

A smile crept across her face, and if she wasn't needling him so much, he'd have enjoyed watching it light up her features. 'Afraid so. What about Tanya?'

Crap, he'd known they were heading in that direction. 'Yes, okay. We've…' he trailed off, unsure how to describe it without it sounding coarse.

'Hooked up? Tangled in the bedsheets? Fucked?'

He flinched at the last one. 'We've enjoyed each other from time to time.'

To his surprise she reached across the table and patted his hand. 'That was rude. Sorry.' As she drew her hand away, she sighed. 'This sounds like I'm judging you, and I'm not, honestly.' She gave him a wry smile. 'I mean, you're single, good-looking, quite funny and you own a bar. It's not hard to see why you're so popular.'

'Quite funny?'

She giggled, and it was the first time he'd heard the sound. He wished it didn't affect him, didn't make the breath catch in his throat. 'I don't want you getting big headed.'

'All these obvious charms, and yet you're immune to them?'

'I didn't say that. It's just that moving here, being away from my family and friends ... it's been tougher than I thought. Having sex with a hot guy isn't high on my priority list.' Her gaze drifted away from his and out of the window. 'I've spent the last few years bouncing from bad relationship to bad relationship. I want time on my own, time to be content being single.' When her eyes found his again, they were wide and vulnerable. 'What I really need right now, is a friend.'

A friend. His mind circled the idea. 'Is that a friend with benefits or—'

'God, you're terrible. A friend.'

She was smiling again, and there was no way his face could resist smiling back. Aside from Sandy, he'd not been friends with a woman since ... the memory brought a wave of sadness. Yeah, it had been a long time.

Maybe this was for the best. The bar was going to drain his energy and his focus for the foreseeable future. Sure, sex would be great – hell, it was a fanfuckingtastic stress buster – but it was clearly not on the table with Mia. The chance to see her now and again though, have a laugh with her, be challenged by her, sounded like something he wanted more of.

He held out his hand for her to shake. 'Friends.' When her fingers clasped around his, he ignored the tingle of awareness that shot up his arm. No sex. 'This friendship thing, it includes looking out for each other, yes?'

'Yes.' She withdrew her hand and eyed him warily. 'God, you're not going to ask me to fix your IT issues now are you? Because I get that all the time.'

'Not as such.' He tried his most charming smile. 'I was thinking more along the lines of I'll show you round your new environs, the best places to eat, the ones to avoid, the parks, the shops that are off the beaten track, the museums, sports venues—'

'Yes, yes, I get the idea. And in this marvellous new partnership you're describing, what have you got me signed up to do in return?'

He almost couldn't look at her, his smile decidedly sheepish. 'Help me with a website for the bar?'

Her brows flew to her green-tinted hairline. 'Seriously? You're a half-assed travel guide, showing me stuff I could basically find on my own anyway. And in return, I spend my free time making you a website, which means I won't actually be able to do any of the stuff you've just mentioned?'

Ouch, when she said it like that, he felt like a git. Before he could tell her to forget it though, her eyes had narrowed on his.

'Is this why you asked to meet me? Why you put all those messages in the window? To get a free website?'

'Whoa. No, of course not.' The sting of her words ricocheted through him but it was hard to be offended when her eyes were telling him she was hurt. 'I asked for your number the first time we met, remember? I wanted to get to know you well before I was told you made websites. And I never said I expected it done for free.' He rubbed a hand down his face, aware if he didn't pass this test, the tentative friendship was over before it had started. 'Truth is, you fascinated me from day one. I thought we had a connection, but you didn't seem keen to explore it, so I told myself that was that. But then I saw you in the window opposite and I figured maybe I could persuade you to change your mind, so I started the messages.' He tried to gauge what she was thinking, and failed. 'The website is a separate thing, and you don't have to help. Mateo mentioned you developed them for a living, so we thought we could tap into your brain for some ideas of where to start.'

'We?'

'I've put Sandy in charge of sorting things out. Social media, websites.' He shot her a wry smile. 'Thanks to Bill, who used to own the place, I know the best local brewery, how to mix a cocktail, and where to get cheap but decent-looking cutlery. Anything outside that, I'm lost.'

'You said you'd only just taken over the bar from him?'

'Yeah, a few months.' He shrugged, like it was no big deal. 'Still learning the ropes.'

She sighed heavily. 'Damn, I'm sorry.' His stomach plummeted and she must have read his expression because she held up a hand and started to laugh. 'No, no, I'm sorry I was a bitch before, about the website. I jumped to an assumption, which wasn't cool.' She bit into her lip. 'I guess I'm trying to work out why you, with all those charms we mentioned, want to get to know *me*? Don't get me wrong, I'm bloody awesome, but not to someone like you.'

'What do you mean, like me?'

'Come on, I've seen some of the women you've … for the sake of politeness, let's call it dated. None of them look anything like me.'

He couldn't disagree. What Mia didn't know was that he'd deliberately gone for the obvious, the carefully made-up women in tight dresses who flirted, because what they wanted had matched what he'd been looking for. Easy, uncomplicated, undemanding.

Then he'd met Mia. And now he was questioning what he really wanted. 'Tastes change. They mature.' Smiling into her eyes, he added, 'Now I'm into bloody awesome. So Mia … what's your surname?'

'Abbott.'

He rolled it round his head. 'Nice. Okay then, bloody awesome Mia Abbott.' He flashed a grin. 'What about this website?'

Laughing, she scrunched up her serviette and threw it at him. 'I'll talk to you about a website once you've taken me somewhere in Manchester I wouldn't have gone to by myself.'

'Deal.' He winced. 'Though my hours do suck, so it can't always be at the weekend.'

'That's okay, my hours are my own.'

Relieved, he grinned. 'Do I get your phone number now?'

Her gaze darted behind him and when it returned her eyes had lost some of their amusement. 'For reasons I don't want to go into, the only people who have my number are my two best friends and my family. I'd rather keep it that way.'

He didn't like the flicker of unease he saw but he wasn't about to upset things, so he nodded. 'I don't suppose there's any point in me giving you mine?'

She shook her head, smiling sadly. 'Thanks, but I won't phone it, because if I did—'

'I'd have your number,' he finished for her. 'Okay, no problem. Keep an eye on my window then.'

'Oh, I will.'

'And I guess if we're doing this, we need to invest in some flip-chart paper. A4 doesn't give much scope.'

'That sounds like cheating, but okay, I'll consider whether the investment is worth the reward.'

He detected the beginnings of a smirk, and though she quickly schooled her face into a bland smile, it didn't hide the mischief in her eyes.

Chapter Twelve

Mia wasn't sure when to expect Luke's first message, or even if there would be one. He'd seemed keen yesterday, but there was every chance he'd mulled it over and decided he didn't need to be friends with someone who wouldn't even give him her mobile number. Oh, she'd been tempted, so, so tempted. But Pete had seemed like a good guy, then turned out not to be. In a different way, so had Danny et al. before him, so she couldn't rely on her judgement when it came to sussing out the opposite sex.

All of which she was trying to explain to her mum the next morning, while also trying not to fixate on the window opposite.

'That Pete was a vile, nasty man.' Her mum was on a roll again. 'I told you he wasn't good enough for you right from the start, didn't I?'

She hadn't, though she had said he was a bit quiet and

she didn't know what to say to him, which was quite something coming from the world's most chatty woman.

'Well just in case Luke turns out to be another Pete, I don't want to give away my number yet. We're leaving messages on our windows instead.'

'Like semaphore?'

Mia had an image of her and Luke flailing flags around wildly in the window and started to laugh. 'We're not waving our arms about, Mum. We're putting notes in the window.'

'But how can that work? Putting what you want to say on a scrap of paper?'

Yep, it would never work for her mum, that's for sure. 'We'll have to be creative. At least this way, if he turns out to be a nutter, I only have to close my blinds to shut him up. Not buy another new phone.'

'I suppose.' She didn't sound sure. 'But if this man with his muscles and his messages *is* a nutter, he can work out where you live.'

Note to self, never mention the words 'nutter' and 'man' in the same sentence when talking to Mum. 'The way the flats were built, he'd have to get the floor plans to know exactly which was mine. Besides, he's lived here for years Mum, he owns the bar. He's not going to turn into a psychopath overnight.' It's just that he might, just might, turn into another Pete. 'And anyway, how do you know he has muscles?'

'Not from my gumdrop, that's for sure. I had to hear from your sister that you had a man putting a show on for you at ten every morning from his window.'

Oh God, she was going to murder Elle. 'He works out at ten every morning,' Mia corrected. 'It's not for me. I just happen to see him sometimes.' *Most times.*

There was a long pause, before her mum whispered, 'How big are these muscles, exactly?'

Mia burst into laughter. 'You're as bad as Elle. I'm not getting into another conversation about this. He's agreed to show me Manchester. As my friend. The size of his muscles, his smile or any other part of his anatomy is irrelevant.'

Her mum cackled with laughter. 'Your sister didn't say it was *that* kind of show.'

'God, it's not. He lifts weights.' She started to feel all hot, just thinking about ... *no, stop it.* They'd agreed to be friends, and female friends did not think about the size of their male friend's penis.

That's when she saw him. Well, to be exact, she saw his arm in the window, though for a heartbeat, with the conversation she'd just been having going through her head, she'd done a double-take.

'You've gone all quiet on me, gumdrop. He's not flashing you, is he?'

It was all too much, the bizarre conversation, the glimpse of, albeit innocent, flesh. Mia started to giggle. 'Relax, he's putting up a sign.' On larger paper, she noted with a smile to herself.

1st non-date Sat

CU 10 a.m. @ bar?

And there was another drawing, what looked to be a donut and a snowflake.

'Come on, don't leave your poor mum hanging. What does it say?'

'I don't know. Looks like we're going out on Saturday to … eat a frozen donut? Or maybe eat a donut in the cold?'

'Eat a donut?' her mum scoffed. 'See, I told you this one-page nonsense wasn't going to work. Either that or you were right about him being a nutcase.'

On an impulse, Mia typed *donut ice Manchester* into her computer. And started to laugh. 'There's a place called the Chill Factore opposite the Trafford Centre, Mum. It's an indoor snow park where you can go down a slope in rubber donut rings. I guess we're going there.'

'Oh.' Mia smiled to herself as she imagined the look on her mum's face. 'Well make sure you wear a helmet. And you'll need a big warm coat, and gloves and—'

'I'm thirty, Mum. I don't need to be told to put my coat on before I go out.'

There was a pause on the other end, and when her mum spoke again, her tone was softer. 'You sound happier, gumdrop.'

'I am.'

'Is that because of this Luke?'

Mia stared out of the window, watching as Luke began his routine. 'I've been here over two months now. I'm starting to get know people.' The girls at the bar, Stan,

Naomi … and yes, Luke. She was already looking forward to Saturday.

More than any of that though, she was getting used to being by herself. No family round the corner to pop in to. No old friends to hang out with. No boyfriend to rely on. At first the idea of it had seemed enormous, but now it felt more manageable. In time, she might even come to enjoy her independence.

After she ended the call with her mum, Mia scrawled out her reply – yes, she'd also ordered some sheets of paper – and stuck it in the window.

It's a non-date

As she sat back in her chair, she thought back to the conversation she'd had with Luke yesterday, and the way she'd flown off the handle at his mention of the website. It had been a sore point, because Danny the Dick had asked her to make one for his fledgling photography business. Before dumping her a week after she'd finished it.

It was unfair to assume Luke was anything like Danny though, so at the risk of being a shmuck again, she was going to make the bar a website. And she'd do it for free. Not because she was attracted to Luke – God, definitely not that. Not even because he was going to show her Manchester. No, she'd do it because when he'd admitted to feeling lost beyond the basics of running a bar, she'd felt an answering tug deep in her chest. For all the confident display, this was a man who clearly felt out of his depth. It was a feeling she knew, one she'd experienced the moment she'd moved up here. Yet Luke, with his friendly overtures, had helped her feel more settled. It was only fair she help him, in turn.

Involuntarily, her gaze zeroed in on his window. Watching him work out felt wrong, now they'd agreed to be friends.

Deliberately she forced her gaze away and onto her computer.

Luke had dithered about their first date … shit, non-date. He had to remember that.

A meal out had seemed safe, but lame. In his experience, women liked the process of getting dressed up to eat, often more than the actual eating. As Mia hadn't got dressed up to go to the bar, he wasn't sure she'd be a huge fan of the trendy Manchester restaurant scene. Plus his first night off wasn't till Tuesday. Too long to wait.

Saturday he didn't need to be in work till three, giving him a morning and lunch. He'd considered, and discarded, a walk (lame again) and a trip to a museum (if he used 'lame' again, had he officially regressed to being a teenager?).

The tour of Old Trafford had been a possibility, but she'd seemed more impressed by City and there was no way he could force himself to sit through a tour of the Etihad.

He'd rather have his eyelids tattooed.

That was when he'd messaged Grace for ideas.

Take her on a donut. If she's as cool as you say, she'll totes be up for it. G x

As he waited for Mia by the bar on Saturday morning, he hoped to God Grace was right. All he could think was what woman in her right mind would want to spend a summer morning in a giant fridge, careering down an ice slope in a rubber ring?

And suddenly there she was, and his heart jumped, just a little, at the sight of her; hair tied back in a ponytail, flashes of green amongst the blonde, skinny jeans, bright yellow T-shirt.

All those curves, in a deliciously short package.

'Hi.' She lifted the plastic bag she was carrying. 'Before we go, are we really eating frozen donuts, or are we going to the Chill Factore? Because I don't need my waterproof trousers and coat if it's the first. Unless it's a very big donut.'

He laughed and, unable to resist, bent to kiss her on the cheek. A light touch, a friendly gesture because that's what they were. Friends. Had her cheeks pinked? He wasn't sure. 'What would you rather do?'

She gave him a quizzical look. 'You can really take me to a frozen-donut shop?'

'For you, anything.'

She rolled her eyes. 'And now you're working out where

you can buy donuts and how much room you've got in your freezer.'

God, she cracked him up. 'Such little faith.' Taking her bag, he nodded towards the car park. 'Luckily I've got something more exciting planned. Come on, or we'll miss our slot.'

'Exciting by whose definition? I might love frozen donuts.'

He screwed up his face. 'That sounds really hard on the teeth.'

'No harder than if I fall off this rubber ring you're planning on sending me hurtling down a slope on.'

He stilled for a moment, scrutinising her. 'We don't have to go, not if you're not up for it.'

'What, and miss the chance of whooping your arse?'

'Oh no.' He picked up pace again, leading them towards his car. 'Heavier people go down faster.' He glanced sideways at her. 'You're a tiny thing compared to me.'

'I may be lighter, but I'm also more aerodynamic.' She waved a hand towards his shoulders. 'Those big things aren't going to help you.'

Why on earth had he worried?, he thought as they reached his car. This woman was exactly who he'd first thought she was: funny, brave. Her own person. She wasn't going to be intimidated by a bit of ice.

'Nice wheels.'

He bent to open the car door for her. 'Not going to tell me it matches my stereotype? You know, the playboy barman, or whatever it is you've got me down as?'

She slid neatly into the passenger seat, her five-foot-and-a-bit frame fitting in far more easily than his six-foot-two one did. 'I'm a computer geek. You're not going to get me stereotyping anyone. I hate it.'

A tiny part of the jigsaw that made up Mia Abbott slotted into place. 'I bet you do.' He also bet that's why she rebelled with her green hair and her non-conformist attitude.

'She's a TVR, yes?' she asked as he squeezed into the driver's seat and turned on the engine, smiling when he heard the rumble.

'Correct on both accounts.'

'Both?'

'The fact she's a she, and a TVR. A twenty-year old Chimaera, to be exact.'

Mia laughed, brushing a hand along the walnut dashboard. 'She had to be a girl, she's so pretty.'

'I hope you're still saying that when she breaks down on the way back.'

'But you can fix her, yes?'

'Why do you say that?'

'Because only a stupid guy would buy a British sports car and not be able to do basic repairs.' She glanced sideways at him. 'And you may be a playboy barman, but you're not stupid.'

How long since anyone had shown that sort of belief in him? 'Not sure I deserve your confidence but thanks.' He was aware of her eyes on him. 'What?'

'One day I'm going to ask why a guy who's so full of

himself when it comes to the opposite sex, puts himself down when things get more personal. But not today.'

He wasn't sure how he felt about her soft threat. 'Why not today?'

'Because today is about me getting on that donut and leaving you for dust … err, snow.'

'Yeah? Bring it on, Leprechaun.'

She groaned. 'First Naomi with the elf, now you. I'm dyeing it red tomorrow.'

He laughed, enjoying himself. 'Good. Red Riding Hood is cute.'

They kept the banter going while he parked, and while they changed and had their helmets fitted. In fact all the way until they stood at the top of the long icy slope.

'It looks scarier up here.'

Her voice had lost some of its boldness. Because he didn't want her thinking about it too much, he walked to the lane next to hers and plonked himself down in his rubber ring. 'It'll look even scarier when you're staring at the back of my head.' He raised his hands aloft in a mock celebration. 'Victory is mine.'

He'd never seen anyone move so fast. One minute she was standing, the next she was whizzing down ahead of him.

By the time he'd reached the bottom, she was back on her feet, cheeks flushed, eyes dancing. 'What was that about victory?'

'That wasn't a victory, it was blatant cheating.' He cursed as he struggled to get out of the ring he'd somehow wedged himself in, which only made her expression more gleeful.

'Need any help there? I know I said your big shoulders wouldn't help, but I didn't realise your backside was going to let you down too. Here.' She held out her hand and tugged.

They were still on snow and it was slippery as shit, so though he made it out of the ring, he unbalanced, which caused him to knock into her and they both went down, limbs tangled, helmets colliding.

He found himself sprawled over her, staring straight into a pair of shocked blue eyes. Chest resting against the most amazing pair of breasts he could ever remember pressing against. Clearing his throat, he croaked out, 'Are you okay?'

She nodded. 'Feel I've been sat on by an elephant.'

That's when he realised she was taking all his weight. 'Crap, sorry.' He rolled off her, sitting up, then started to laugh. 'FYI, you were pretty comfy.'

She snorted. 'Just what every woman wants to hear.'

'Hey, it was a compliment. No angular, bony bits. Just a lush, bountiful softness and – oof!' He received a harsh prod to his stomach.

'Confucius says, when in a hole, stop digging.'

Laughing, he stood and held out his hand to help her up but she shook her head. 'Seriously? You think it went that well the last time?'

'You won't hear any complaints from me.' He watched

while she struggled to her feet, dusting the snow off her legs. 'So, want to go down again?'

She smirked back up at him. 'As long as you don't mind getting beaten by a girl.'

He shrugged. 'You've called me a playboy bar guy with a huge backside who weighs as much as an elephant. I figure I've reached my threshold for insults.' Reaching out his gloved hand, he brushed a flake of snow off her nose. 'Wow, you've got some serious freckles going on there.'

Her eyes narrowed. 'Call me cute and I'll push you down the slope without the ring to cushion that big bum of yours.'

'Not cute.' He bit into the inside of his cheek to stop himself from laughing. 'Oh no, you're not cute at all, Leprechaun girl.'

But damn it, she was. As Luke followed her back up the stairs to the top of the slope, he wondered how he was going to manage this friends lark, when all he kept thinking about was how much he wanted to kiss her at every conceivable opportunity.

Chapter Thirteen

Mia hung back as Sandy served a customer with what looked to be a large glass of rosé. What did it say about her screwed-up feelings that she was seeing her through clear eyes now she knew Luke and Sandy were only friends?

Just like she and Luke were only friends.

It didn't matter that there were times her pulse sped up when he looked at her, or butterflies buzzed in her belly when he touched her. It only mattered that she was smart enough to ignore it.

Sandy did a double-take when she saw her. 'Hi, it's Mia, isn't it? I almost didn't recognise you.' She waved at Mia's new highlights. 'The blue suits you. It matches your eyes.'

'Thanks, I fancied a change.' And red had been rejected; she didn't mind elf and leprechaun but she drew the line at being a little girl. Red Riding Hood, yuk. 'Have you got a minute?'

Sandy scanned the outdoor area. There were a handful of customers, clearly enjoying the combination of sun, alcohol and the knowledge that most poor sods were spending their Monday afternoon working away in an office. 'All quiet here. Just have to watch the boss doesn't catch me skiving. How can I help?'

'It's more whether I can help you.'

'Oh?' Sandy's dark brows came together. 'Is this about the website? Because I was told you couldn't do it.'

'Couldn't, or wouldn't?' Mia asked wryly, feeling a twinge of discomfort. Saturday had been … well, the best day she could remember having in months, maybe years. And the orchestrator of it deserved that she kept an open mind and didn't compare him to her past disasters.

'He said you were too busy to help.' Sandy scrunched up her face. 'Oh no, don't tell me you guys had a row. Sometimes he forgets to put on his filter and says stuff without thinking. If you were upset by any of it, I can assure you he didn't mean it.' She huffed out a breath. 'He likes you, Mia.'

'And I like him. As a friend,' she added quickly when she saw Sandy start to smile. 'Which is why I wanted to tell you that I'm happy to help in any way I can.'

'Really? Like you'd be willing to recommend some good website companies for me, tell me what I should be looking out for, or—'

'I'll work with you to build one.'

Sandy's face lit up. 'Oh wow, that's fantastic. I'm so chuffed he's trusting me to sort this out, but I know Jack shit about computers, or websites. My other half might disagree, he reckons I spend far too much money buying stuff online, but sneaking a few online purchases from Next and developing a website for a bar are like chalk and flaming gorgonzola.'

Mia laughed, immediately seeing why Luke and Sandy were friends. Both were funny, and both had a natural way of talking that made you feel as if you'd known them for years. 'The fact that you use websites yourself is going to be very useful, so tell Jim you need to do more,' she raised her hands to mime quotation marks, 'research.'

Sandy smiled. 'I'll try. And don't think I haven't noticed that you know my hubby's name, by the way. My Poirot powers of deduction tell me you guys must have talked about me.'

'Guilty.' Mia didn't see there was any reason to lie. 'I might have accused you of sleeping with him, for which I sincerely apologise.'

Sandy let out a huge bellow of a laugh. 'I can just imagine how well that went down. He probably went hot and cold all over.'

'It was an interesting conversation.'

Sandy started to say something before stopping and shaking her head. Then she cursed. 'Bollocks, if we're going to be working together you're going to find I'm not one to hold back if I've something to say, so I'm just going to come out with it. Don't judge Luke too harshly by the company he keeps. Plenty of girls who come to the bar do so in the hope of leaving with him, and when it's served up on a plate like that, waved in front of your face, it's damn easy to accept. Especially when you've got no reason to say no.'

Mia found Sandy's gaze hard to hold. 'We're not, that is, Luke and I aren't…' She expelled a sharp breath. 'We're friends, Sandy. That's all. He's going to show me Manchester, I'm helping with the website.' Sandy didn't say anything, just nodded, her eyes studying Mia's face for so long, she started to feel uncomfortable. 'So, anyway, have a think about what you want the website to do, and we'll take it from there.'

'Great, thanks.' Sandy dug into her apron and retrieved a pad. 'Can I take your number so we can sort out a time to meet?'

Mia hesitated. 'Tell Luke when you're ready. He knows how to contact me.'

'Okay.' She looked slightly puzzled as she pushed the notepad away. 'See you soon then.'

Mia smiled and started walking away, but then she remembered this morning's note in the window. 'Oh, and do me a favour and tell your boss Wednesday is fine, though I'm not convinced about the singing. And the forecast isn't for rain.'

Sandy's eyes widened and she started to laugh. 'Oh God, what has he got you guys doing?'

Mia pictured the message again in her head.

A few musical notes coming out of a person's mouth. A rain cloud. And the words:

Weds @ bar 6pm.

'You know what, I really don't know.' She shrugged, feeling a smile slide across her face. 'But it's kind of fun that way.'

As he waited for Mia outside the bar, Luke could feel several pairs of interested eyes inside, watching him. There was Sandy, who'd finished her shift, yet for some reason wasn't in a rush to go home.

And Mateo, who'd clearly been unconvinced by Luke's 'we're only friends' spiel. Possibly because when he'd suggested he might ask Mia out, Luke had lost his cool.

'She might only want to be friends with you, boss,' he'd boasted. 'With me, she might want to do the horizontal tango.'

Luke had been battered by an alarming wave of jealousy. 'You do any sort of dancing with her, ballroom, dirty or otherwise,' he'd retorted through a clenched jaw, 'and I'll…' Thankfully he'd stopped short of actually threatening his employee. Instead he'd ended with a lame, 'I'll be bloody annoyed.'

The moment he caught sight of Mia though, the still-simmering anger died, replaced by what he was sure was an embarrassingly daft grin.

'My favourite Smurf.'

She raised her eyes heavenwards. 'Thanks.'

God, she looked so damn cute he felt the urge to lift her

up and hug the daylights out of her. Then kiss her until she was breathless.

But eyes were watching, and though she might be up for the first, he knew Mia definitely wouldn't thank him for the second, so he bent to kiss her cheek and hoped Mateo was watching. Just because Mia had insisted on 'friends' didn't mean he wasn't as protective as hell around her. Wet behind the ears barmen could sling their hook.

'Lack of rain hasn't put you off then?' he asked as they walked towards the bus stop. It was an easy bus ride to Quay Street and this way he left his options open for after. Plus he refused to pay rip-off NCP car park prices for the privilege of putting the TVR on a few square foot of tarmac for a couple of hours.

She gave him the look he was really starting to enjoy. The one that said she knew he was winding her up and could handle anything he threw at her. 'You didn't cancel, so it clearly isn't a problem.'

'What about the singing? Are you up for some karaoke?'

For a brief second alarm flittered across her face, but then she smirked. 'As long as you go first.' Laughing, he reached for her hand as they crossed the road, the gesture totally unconscious. She slid him a look. 'I can cross by myself. I don't need my hand held.'

He winked. 'Where's the fun in that?' As soon as they'd reached the other side though, she slipped her hand away, leaving him oddly disappointed.

The bus was busy, standing room only, and as she grasped a handrail he manoeuvred himself so he she could lean against him. A gesture he'd have made for any girl he'd taken out, yet with Mia he'd done it instinctively.

'You know I was wrong about the Smurf,' he remarked a few stops later when the crowding had eased and they were the only ones left standing. 'You're more of a Smurfette.'

She craned her neck to look up at him. 'I hope that isn't a heightist joke.'

He bit into his cheek to stop from laughing. 'Smurfette was the female. You're not small at all. I mean you make it all the way up to my shoulder, so that's definitely taller than the average Smurf.'

She elbowed him in the ribs and he couldn't stop himself. He started to laugh.

'There's nothing worse than being average,' she muttered, which only made him laugh harder. At which point she gave up and started to laugh with him. He could see the rest of the bus watching them, but he didn't care. He was enjoying being with this girl with blue-tinted hair, sparky humour and a take-me-as-you-find-me attitude.

Enjoying himself so much, he almost missed their stop.

'Shit, we need to get off.'

Just as the doors were closing, he wedged himself between them and they clambered out. 'At last we've found a use for your hulking shoulders.'

He grinned as he headed towards Quay Street. 'You think I've got broad shoulders, huh? Like the heroes in all those romance novels?'

'Not in mine.'

It was the sly look she gave him that made him pull up

short. 'Wait, are you talking about the book you're reading, or…?' he trailed off when she raised an eyebrow at him. 'Damn it, I don't know if you're having me on or not.'

'Can you really see me writing a romance novel?'

He couldn't. Not that he had any clue what a romance writer looked like, but surely it wasn't blue hair with attitude? 'That Barbara Cartland woman. She wrote romance and I remember seeing pictures in the newspapers when she died. She wore pink and had this daft long-haired mutt with her.'

'So you're saying all romance writers have to wear pink and have a small dog?'

'Well no, obviously not, but…' He huffed. 'Put me out of my misery. Have you written a book?' Now he'd asked her outright, she looked less cocksure. In fact as she turned away from him, he'd go so far as to say she'd gone shy. 'Wow, you have, haven't you? You're a frigging author. That's awesome, Mia.'

'No, I'm not.' She shrugged, finally turning back to him. 'I'm trying to write a book, but I've got a long way to go.'

'Long as in, what? You've only just started? Halfway through?'

'I've written fifty thousand words.'

His jaw dropped open. 'To a guy who finds writing a shopping list taxing, that's one hell of a lot of words. Are you sure you need to write any more?'

The edge of tension he'd seen in her face disappeared and she snorted with laughter. 'If I want to write a proper book, you know, one with a start, a middle and an end, one someone might want to publish, then yeah. I need to write about the same again.'

'That's your goal?' They started walking again and this time when he reached to grab her hand to cross the road, she didn't tug it away when they'd reached the other side.

'It is. I don't know why, but something in me has always wanted to write books.'

'You mean instead of developing websites?' He banged a hand against his forehead. 'Shit, I forgot to say thanks for agreeing to do ours. Obviously I'll pay you—'

'No.' She glanced up at him, a small smile on her lips. 'Friends don't charge. I get a free Manchester guide, you get a free website. We're quits.' Clearly seeing he was about to argue, she waved a hand at him. 'In answer to your question, yes, maybe, one day, if I'm good enough, I'd love to write books instead of building websites. For now though, I want to write for fun and see how it goes.'

For the first time since he'd met her, he was aware of the gulf between them, not in class or wealth, but in education. Intelligence. 'I can't imagine writing being fun,' he admitted. 'Same as I can't imagine working on a computer, doing all that whizz-bang techno stuff you do.'

He was aware of her eyes on him, as if she was trying to see inside his brain. 'Because you're a humble bartender, huh?'

He tried to laugh it off. 'Nah, I'm not humble. I'm an ace bartender. It's not just about mixing the cocktails, you know. It's about multi-tasking, keeping your cool when it's busy, keeping busy when it's not. Being what the customer needs you to be, a shrink, a friend.' He winked at her. 'A flirt.'

'You've certainly got that last one nailed.' But then she did something that caused his heart to flip. She squeezed his hand and added softly, 'Don't put yourself down. You can't imagine writing a book or writing code. I could never run a bar. I'd get flustered at the first sign of a queue, I'm not sufficiently organised or forward thinking to sort out stock and not good enough with people to make them want to come back every week.'

A lump rose into this throat and he couldn't shake the gruffness out of his voice when he spoke. 'Thanks. And for the free website. It means a lot.' He swallowed a few times before attempting to speak again. 'So this book, what's it about?' The question had been intended as a distraction but a thought occurred to him and he halted, tugging her round to face him. 'Holy shit, it's kinky, isn't it? Please tell me it's full of smut, leather and furry handcuffs.'

'Furry handcuffs are the best smut you can manage?'

'Hell no. I can go as smutty, as dirty as you want to go.' And God help him, with Mia he wanted to go everywhere and anywhere she did. 'Obviously I draw the line at sheep, or any animal frankly, unless it's in the background, watching. On second thoughts, that might be a bit intimidating, being stared at by a cow when you're going at it in a field, but it takes a lot to put me off my stride, so—'

'For the love of all that is holy, stop!' She put her hand up, laughter bubbling out of her. 'Can we please change the subject? Maybe tell me where we'll find this rain you promised?'

As if he'd choreographed it – and for all her sweet words about his organisational skills, he certainly wasn't that good – a few steps later they arrived at their destination. Tugging at her hand, he nodded at the advertising screen outside the Everyman cinema. 'There's your rain.'

Chapter Fourteen

As Mia stared at the advertising screen, it slowly begun to sink in. 'We're going to the cinema.'

Luke pulled a face. 'Please, don't insult me. I'm not taking you to any old cinema. This is the best boutique cinema in Manchester.'

'And we've come here to watch *Singing in the Rain*.' She tried to think back to what she knew about the film, other than it was a musical and really, really old. 'Is it even in colour?'

'Of course.' He hesitated, then frowned back at the advert. 'Well, I assume it is.' His smile was typical cocky Luke, but his eyes said he wasn't as confident as he looked about his choice of date. *Non-date.* God, how easy to slip into thinking this was a real date. Holding her hand, using his big body to cushion her against the jolts on the bus. Even the way he'd greeted her, as if he'd wanted to kiss her but then realised he shouldn't.

The easy self-assurance was part of his charm. Yet how could a woman trust that charm when his track record showed how quickly he became bored, moving from conquest to conquest? Leaving a trail of women wondering what they'd done wrong. She'd spent too much of her life wondering why, had too many rugs yanked from under her feet. Now she wanted to focus on *finding* her feet

'If you don't fancy the film we can try somewhere else.' His quietly spoken words jolted her out of her head. 'Or we can just have a drink here because it is a really cool place and you might want to come back if there's something more, I don't know – funny, gory, sci-fi.' He gave her a sheepish grin. 'Honestly, I only picked this film because it made a funny message. I really wanted to watch *Star Wars* but I figured if I put a Death Star symbol up you might run a mile.'

Mia burst out laughing. 'And here's me thinking you were some sort of film buff.' She stared back at the screen advert. '*Star Wars* is my favourite, so I'd have totally gone with you for that, but you know what, I've never seen *Singing in the Rain*. Just snippets of Gene Kelly twirling his umbrella.' She linked arms with him. 'Let's do it.'

And wow, by the time she'd settled into the plush red velvet sofa – yes, the place didn't have grubby seats but real, honest-to-God, two-seater velvet sofas – she didn't actually care what film they were about to see. It was stunning. A real luxurious old-world vibe, taking people back to the days when going to the cinema was a rare treat, not something they did when they were bored on a rainy day.

'You're kidding.' She gaped as a waiter placed two fancy-looking cocktails and a selection of nibbles – cashews, almonds and of course popcorn – onto the wooden table fixed to the arm of the sofa. 'I don't get Coke in a plastic cup with a straw?'

'You know I've been dying to get a cocktail down you.'

Cautiously she eyed up the vivid turquoise and blue creation. 'What is it with you and nuclear cocktails?'

'It's not on the menu. I had to ask them to make it specially for you.' He leant in to her, looking ridiculously pleased with himself. 'It's an Electric Smurf.'

Her gaze flew to his and she could see he was struggling not to laugh. 'Very funny.'

'I know.'

Merriment danced in his eyes, making them twinkle, and the breath caught in Mia's throat. This man was stunning. Beyond good-looking, with his beautiful green eyes, his dimpled smile.

In front of them the screen came to life. Mia was grateful for the diversion and the chance to regain her balance. Luke was her friend, this wasn't a date. Even though they were sitting side by side on a velvet sofa, his thigh occasionally touching hers.

Around them the lights went down, the atmosphere becoming even more intimate.

She cleared her throat and took a sip of the cocktail. Not bad. 'What's in this deadly concoction?'

Angling his head, he whispered in her ear, his breath warm against her neck. 'Blue curacao, Malibu, pineapple juice, some lemonade. It should have pineapple rum too, but they didn't have it.' She could feel his smile against her skin and a shiver went through her. 'I didn't think you'd notice.'

'Any more rum and I'll sleep through the film.'

He shifted closer, so now it wasn't just the occasional brush of his body against hers. The contact was there, warm, solid and … God, she was tingling. And then, just as she was trying not to make a big deal of it, he raised his right arm and slid it across the back of the sofa behind her. 'If you feel yourself nodding off, lean on me. I'm a pretty good pillow.'

She had no sarky response, her brain too full of him; the citrus tang of his aftershave, the heat of his big body. It wasn't how she imagined friends should feel. Wasn't how she wanted it to feel.

For God's sake chill, Mia. It's not a big deal. You'll get used to him.

She took another sip of the cocktail, and then another, feeling the alcohol start to relax her. 'It's really called an Electric Smurf?' she whispered.

'Of course. Thank God you didn't go for the red highlights. The Red Riding Hood cocktail is a nightmare. Strawberry liqueur and champagne. It would have blown the budget.' He fake shuddered. 'We'd have had nothing left for popcorn.'

Laughing softly, she grabbed the container of popcorn

and shoved it at him. 'Here, get your fill now. I don't want to hear you munching when the film starts.'

'Spoilsport, that's all part of the cinema experience.' Once again he shuffled closer to her so he could whisper in her ear. 'As is making out on the back row.'

Her stomach flip-flopped and she turned round to check there was still a row of seating behind them. 'We're not on the back row.'

His grin turned wicked. 'Yeah but nobody is sitting behind us, so technically you could argue we're at the back.'

Now her heart was pumping, knocking against her ribs. 'Technically you could argue friends don't make out.'

There was beat of silence, followed by his quiet laughter. 'Neatly put in my place.'

Finally, thankfully, the film began to start and it wasn't long before Mia lost herself in the musical. She couldn't believe how many songs she recognised. Nor when she looked back on it later, would she believe how quickly she became used to sitting close to Luke. Once she'd turned off her paranoia, the act of leaning into him became as natural, and as pleasurable, as relaxing against the pillow he'd said he'd make. Except pillows weren't as solid, or as warm. They didn't move gently up and down as they breathed. And her body didn't feel so achingly aware of them.

As the credits rolled, Luke stood to stretch his legs, hoping the tightness around his groin area wasn't as obvious to anyone else, as it was to him.

He'd loved every moment of feeling her soft body pressed against his.

But she wanted to be friends, so where he'd spent most of the film itching to draw his hand away from the back of the sofa and onto her shoulder, down her arm, over her breasts … yeah, when he'd thought of doing that, he'd had to reel himself back. He could truthfully say it was the first time he'd been to a cinema with a woman and not spent a lot of the time with his tongue in her mouth and his hands on her body.

Bizarrely though, he'd enjoyed himself more tonight than he could remember doing in ages. Maybe he was one of those guys who got a buzz from being denied.

Or maybe Mia was the most fascinating, funny, straightforward woman he'd ever met.

Reaching out his hand, he tugged her to her feet. 'Has an old movie and two cocktails done you in for the night, or…?' He paused, trying, and failing, to judge her mood.

'Or?'

'Or, has it put you in the mood for more cocktails?' He flashed her a hopeful smile. 'I can probably even rustle up a place that does beer.'

'It wouldn't be called The Bar Beneath by any chance?'

He tapped her lightly on the end of her cute nose. 'Funny, but no. I was thinking somewhere you hadn't been.

Another one to cross off on your top one hundred places to visit in Manchester list.'

'Top *one hundred*?'

He shrugged. 'Of course. You didn't think I was going to fob you off with ten, did you?'

'You must really want help with this website,' she muttered as they made their way out of the theatre.

He turned to her. 'You think that's all this is about?'

'What else?'

I can't stop thinking about you. She'd run a mile if he phrased it like that. Yet when they exited into the balmy Manchester evening, he found he couldn't simply make a joke of it, so he placed his hands on her shoulders and turned her to face him. 'I enjoy being with you.'

He watched her throat move as she swallowed. 'You do?'

He nodded, wondering what was going on behind those huge blue eyes. The longer he stared into them, the longer he took to reply, and the more charged the air around them became, until it felt as if electric sparks were pinging between his hands and her skin. She must have felt it too, because a shutter fell across her face and Luke silently cursed himself. *Keep it light, you muppet.* 'I do,' he repeated, his voice sounding gravelly. 'I can truly say this is the most fun I've ever had with a Smurf.'

It was exactly what she needed, because the tension left her face and she laughed. 'Then you obviously haven't met the right Smurfs.'

'Clearly, but in the absence of any of your more

entertaining blue cousins, I'm going to have to make do with you. So what is it to be – home, or cocktails?'

She pursed her lips, and he tried like hell not to look at them too closely. Not to think about how they might feel beneath his, or trailing across his skin…

'I'd hate to let down my Smurf family.'

He shoved his carnal thoughts aside and mentally high fived at her choice. 'Of course you would, so cocktails it is, yes?'

She narrowed her eyes. 'Maybe we should make that cocktail, singular, because I do have to work tomorrow.'

'Okay then, I know just the place.'

Linking arms with her, he began to walk towards a Latin bar he knew. He told himself he'd chosen it because it wasn't far, though in truth there were several other bars also in short walking distance. But they didn't have the option of a dance floor.

He'd always been a hopeful kind of guy.

Considering it was a Wednesday night the place was pretty busy – busier, he'd like to bet, than his own. There was no wait at the bar though, and he ordered for both of them.

She didn't look too impressed. 'A Manchester bee cocktail?'

'Sure, when in Manchester.'

'What does it have in it that I have to worry about?'

'Recipes vary but in this one I think there's honey, lemon juice and a garnish of orange peel. Oh and gin and champagne.'

She groaned, but didn't protest. 'Why the bee?'

'It's the symbol of Manchester. Represents how much it was a hive of activity in the Industrial Revolution. Basically, Mancunians are all worker bees. We buzz around, doing lots of stuff for little reward.'

'You're a boss now,' she argued as they sat down. 'You're like the queen bee, getting your staff to buzz around for you.'

'Yeah, maybe. Though there's not enough buzzing.' He wondered if Bill and Mateo were managing even a flap of their wings tonight. It hadn't mattered before; the place had earned enough to keep them all happy. But now he had a huge financial hole to fill.

'Everything okay?'

Mia's concerned voice brought his shitty train of thoughts to a welcome stop. 'Sorry, started to think about work.' He raised his glass. 'Here's to our second non-date. And the next ninety-eight to come.' She laughed, shaking her head at him, and once again he was struck by how natural she was, how unaffected. 'So Mia Abbott, you dissected my dating history, I reckon it's only fair I get to ask about yours. Who was the last guy you dated?' He paused, remembering the conversation they'd had at the coffee shop. 'And did he have anything to do with your reluctance to give me your number?'

She stared down at her cocktail. 'There isn't enough alcohol in here for that conversation.'

Luke felt a vicious flare of anger and he had to take a

deep breath before he could trust his voice. 'Did he hurt you?'

'No.' She glanced over at him and his thoughts must have been mirrored on his face because she immediately placed a hand over his and squeezed. 'Thank you, but no, he didn't, at least not physically. You can call off the dogs.'

Some of the tension left his body. 'Will you tell me what happened?'

She sighed, then took another sip of the cocktail before speaking again. 'I've got a shitty track record when it comes to choosing men. The last one, Pete, started off sweet, then became possessive. When I finished things he kept phoning and bombarding me with messages, begging me to reconsider. I blocked him, but he just got another phone and started again. In the end I had to get a new number.' She caught his eye, her expression apologetic. 'Only my parents, sister and two closest friends know the new number. I didn't want to risk anyone else giving it to him.'

'And you don't want to risk it happening again,' he finished for her.

'No.' She exhaled in frustration. 'It sounds awful, I know. I mean, I'm basically accusing you of being a psycho and I'd be pissed if someone did the same to me.'

'Hey, I'm not angry. At least not with you,' he qualified, his stomach churning at the thought of Pete and how much emotional hurt he'd caused her. 'I need to earn your trust before I earn your number, I respect that.' He grinned. 'Anyway, where's the fun in communication that uses an unlimited number of words?' She smiled and he gauged she looked relaxed enough to be asked another personal question. 'You said you had a shitty track record. How come you keep choosing the duffers?'

'Good question.' She shrugged. 'I think maybe it goes back to school. I was always the geek – you know, the weird one who enjoyed maths and raced to be first to computer lessons so she could grab the best terminal.'

He laughed. 'Nope, don't remember coming across a geek before. Probably because I was the one who bunked off maths and was still snogging Lusty Linda round the back of the bike sheds when the computer class was due to start.' They shared a smile and he couldn't explain how good it felt to make her laugh, to banter with her like this. 'But what does being a geek have to do with choosing duff men? I thought it would make you *better* at picking, like maybe you'd have an algorithm for it. If he sits at the back of class, reject. If he holds the door open for you, go to next question.'

Laughter burst out of her. 'Why didn't I think of that? Oh, I know, because I wasn't *that* weird, Mr Snog Alot. Just weird enough that the cool guys didn't fancy me, so I was left with a skewed sample of misfits and the odd shy, decent guy. Somehow the ones I chose turned out to be not so decent, after all.'

'Would I fit into the cool group?'

She blinked. 'I'm totally walking into a trap here but yes, okay, as you treated me to a pretty stellar night out, I'll humour you. You'd be in the cool group.'

He put down his cocktail and pulled her to her feet. 'Come with me.'

'What? Where?'

'Don't panic, just to the dance floor.' When she froze, he smiled. 'I know we're only friends, but just let me do this? Please?'

He sensed her reluctance as they climbed down the stairs and onto the small dance floor. The live band was playing jazz, and the mood was just right for what he wanted.

Pulling her into his arms, he held her loosely and began to move them slowly to the gentle beat of the music. 'This is me, proving to you how wrong you are.'

Her hand curled round his bicep as she stared up at him. 'I'm rarely wrong.'

He chuckled, risking holding her just that tiny bit closer. 'I'm sure, but this is one of those rare exceptions.' Bending, he whispered into her ear, 'It isn't just the misfits and shy guys who fancy you, Mia. Cool guys do, too.'

Chapter Fifteen

One of the advantages of Facetiming her sister rather than calling her was that Mia could easily read Elle's thoughts, rather than relying on working them out from the nuances of her voice. In this case, she knew, without doubt, she'd managed to shock the pants off her.

'He said *what*?'

'I just told you.'

'I know, but I think I must have misheard you, because you said you and this Luke were only friends. And now you're telling me he said he fancied you.'

'I know.' One of the disadvantages of Facetiming with her sister, was that the thought reading went both ways.

'God, you're happy about it, aren't you? Happy that Mr Muscles Opposite has the hots for you.'

'No, no, it isn't like that. He doesn't.' Except she'd been on the end of his flirtatious smile, heard him admit he'd wanted to date her, have sex with her. And on Wednesday, when he'd held her in those strong arms, she'd been shocked at how right it had felt to rest her head against his brick wall of a chest. And how much she'd melted when he'd told her cool guys fancied her, too. 'Okay, he does like me.' *I like him too, and I'm afraid if I'm not careful, it won't stop at like.* 'That's not what this is about though. He'll soon find another woman to focus his energy on, and the last thing I need in my life is another failed relationship. We *are* just friends.' The smile she'd tried to suppress burst across Mia's face. 'But God, Elle, he's doing amazing things to my ego. I have always had a hang-up about guys not fancying me, and I think that's sometimes led me to—'

'Settle for anyone who showed an interest,' Elle finished for her.

'Wow, that's harsh.'

'Sorry, maybe it is, but I've never thought any of your boyfriends were good enough for you.'

'That's 'cos you're my big sis.'

'Maybe, but I'm also a woman. I can't wait for you to introduce me to a guy who I'd think, *wow, if I wasn't married, I'd totally go for him.*'

Mia cleared her throat. 'Err, except you wouldn't, obviously, because he'd be my *boyfriend.*'

Elle burst into laughter. 'Ooops. Blame the hormones.'

'Which hormones are these? Because I've seen my nephew so I know you're not pregnant anymore.'

'Trust me, my hormones are all over the place. Some of them are plummeting, others are raging. I'm going to be an emotional basket case for a while to come yet. Not that little

Jacob isn't absolutely worth it.' Mia grinned as she watched Elle's eyes automatically glance to the sleeping bundle of cuteness in the bassinette next to her. 'Anyway, I've been talking to Dave and Mum and we're all planning to come up and see you in a few weeks, so be warned.'

'That's crazy, I'll just come down again.'

'Oh no, you're not escaping that easily. We want to see you on your home turf. Check out your environs, the bar you mention, your neighbours, like Stan next door.' She winked. 'And the hot one opposite you.' Her eyes lit up. 'Please tell me he works out at the weekends, too.'

Mia felt her face going hot. Ogling Luke now they'd agreed to be friends still felt wrong. And if she thought of her sister … and God, maybe her mum standing in her window staring at him… 'He doesn't do weights at the weekend,' she lied, making a mental note to keep the blinds down if they were around in the morning. 'Even if he did, you're married, with two young children. You can't be seen spying on my neighbour.'

'When did you turn into such a spoilsport?' In the background, Mia heard the sound of gurgling and a moment later, Elle held Jacob up to the camera. 'Your nephew's woken up to say hello.'

Mia cooed at him. 'Hello handsome.'

'I guess I should say goodbye and feed this monster.' Elle's expression was utterly besotted. 'Just before I go, have you had any more messages from your *friend* since you last saw him?'

'Only one this morning, asking if I'll be at the bar

tonight.' It was still in his window and she smiled as she looked at it.

2night

Me = bar

If U = bar

Me = happy

'Are you going?'

It was hard not to, after a message like that. And Mia knew if she was going to grasp this being single and independent lark by the scruff of the neck, she needed to venture out on Saturday nights. 'I think so, yes.'

When she walked into the bar several hours later, there was a satisfying hum to the place. The sound of conversation, of laughter. Immediately she spotted Luke serving, his face animated as he laughed with the … striking brunette. Mia bit into her lip and reminded herself it was his job. He charmed, he flirted. Just because the woman looking doe eyes at him right now was leggy and slender, her dress emphasising her sleek body, didn't mean Luke was interested.

He flirted like that with you the first time you met him.

The memory was still vivid; how flattered she'd been, how much she'd enjoyed it. But she'd taken the sensible option, the best option for her, and decided not to take him up on his offer of a fling.

So it doesn't matter who he flirts with.

'Hey, Mia, over here.' Chloe waved her arms around from the group's usual table. Mia spotted Tanya, Donna and Michele with her. Presumably Donna's other half, who she'd learnt was a nurse, was working nights again.

Mia smiled and walked over, feeling a little burst of pride. She'd been here, what, ten weeks, and she could walk into a bar by herself and see familiar faces. They weren't friends, not like Heather and Gill back at home ... oops, back in Somerset, but they'd been kind enough to take her under their wing.

Unconsciously her eyes strayed back to Luke. He caught her gaze and directed a full-watt smile at her that she was sure had most of the female customers wondering what she had that they didn't.

Aside from blue hair.

'Who's ready for another drink?' she asked as she joined them.

Tanya shook her head, slinky straight hair cascading over her shoulders. 'I'm getting this round.' She winked at Mia. 'You can do the next one.'

Inevitably the conversation veered to what they'd been up to and it was only when she mentioned she'd been to the cinema with Luke, that Mia realised quite how it sounded. 'Oh no, it's not like that,' she added hastily when she saw their jaws drop. 'He's promised to show me Manchester, that's all.'

'Who's showing you Manchester?' Tanya asked as she arrived back with the drinks.

'Luke. As a friend,' she clarified quickly, wondering quite how sharp Tanya's long nails were. And if she was about to find out.

'Oh?'

Tanya's cool response made everything inside Mia tighten. 'Yes. Somehow I've been conned into making him a website. Frankly, him showing me the occasional Manchester hot spot in return is the least he can do.'

It was the right thing to say. Tanya rolled her eyes. 'That sounds like Luke alright, using his charm to wangle something from you. I suspect he wants something from me, too, as he's asked to meet me for coffee tomorrow.' She took a large swig of her cocktail. 'But here's hoping it'll be less about work and more about pleasure, if you know what I mean.'

Everyone laughed and the moment passed, but the happiness Mia had felt earlier had been dented. She didn't want to resent Tanya, to feel this sting of jealousy knowing the other woman, the one Luke *enjoyed seeing from time to time*, was, in fact, seeing him tomorrow.

She wanted to laugh it off, to take the piss out of Luke for living up to his playboy reputation when she next saw him, as friends would surely do. She just wasn't sure she was that good an actor.

And damn it yes, she had just admitted her friends-only claim was an act.

It was frustrating, seeing Mia and not being able to talk to her. Yet Luke couldn't complain, not when the reason was a busy bar and ringing tills.

He winked when he caught her looking in his direction, and felt a twinge of worry at the weakness of her answering smile.

Whatever Tanya et al. were saying, she wasn't happy about it.

'Can't take your eyes off, her I see.' Mateo smirked over at him.

'Just being friendly to our website designer.'

Mateo laughed. 'I'm sure that's all she is to you, boss. Like I'm sure Man United are just a football team.'

Luke opened his mouth to argue that Man United were far more than a team, they were a religion, a family. A love affair. Then snapped it shut when he realised Mateo's devious trap. 'Exactly.' He slid the guy a superior smile. 'Sometimes things are just what people say they are.'

At that moment he spotted Mia walking to the bar, and immediately blew his own theory by almost falling over his feet in a dash to get to her first.

'Hey there.' Behind him he could hear Mateo chuckling loudly, but he ignored the bugger and kept his eyes on Mia.

'Hi.' She gave him a suspiciously bright smile. 'You're busy tonight.'

'Are we?' He flashed her a flirty grin. 'I hadn't noticed. All I see is you.'

She groaned, shaking her head. 'Does that line really work?'

He waggled his eyebrows. 'I don't know, you tell me.'

'I can't, because we're friends, remember? Friends don't try corny pick-up lines on each other.'

'Corny? You wound me.' Automatically, because he knew what the group usually ordered, he began lining up the cocktail glasses. 'And anyway, why can't friends try out chat-up lines on each other? Aren't they there to help?'

'I don't think you need any help in that department.'

It was the slight edge to her voice, rather than the words themselves, that caused him to pause. 'Why do I get the feeling that isn't a compliment?' Her eyes avoided his and once again he wondered what the group had been discussing. 'Mia?'

She seemed to shake herself. 'Because you're feeling weirdly sensitive?'

Was he? 'Maybe.' He twirled the cocktail shaker – Tom Cruise eat your heart out – and poured it into the glasses. 'So, what have you ladies been discussing?' he asked casually.

She arched a brow. 'You think we've got nothing better to talk about than you?'

Crap. Clearly his casual needed some work. Still, if he was going to be accused of being a closet narcissist, he might as well own it. 'Why wouldn't you want to talk about me?' He grinned to show he was joking. 'I am fascinating.'

'You're something,' she muttered. When her gaze found

his again, it was guarded. 'They asked what I'd been up to, and I told them about our trip to the cinema.'

'Okay.'

'Is it?'

'Of course.' He frowned, not quite understanding. 'What's the issue? It's not a secret that we've been out a couple of times.'

'As friends,' she added, and yes, he hadn't missed that that was the second time she'd emphasised the friends part. 'So you haven't deliberately kept our non-dates from Tanya?'

'What? No, of course not.' He waited until she looked back at him. 'I told you before, Tanya and me, we're just—'

'People who have sex with each other from time to time,' she cut in quietly. 'It's clear that's what you think, but is it what she thinks?' Before he could answer, she held up her hand. 'You know what? Forget I said anything. It's really none of my business. I just thought, as your friend, you should know Tanya wasn't happy when she heard I'd been out with you. Obviously I made it clear you were only showing me Manchester as payback for me doing your website.'

'Obviously,' he returned wryly, disappointment settling in his gut. He'd hoped Wednesday night, when she'd melted in his arms, would prove to be a turning point and she'd realise how dumb her friends-only rule was. Hell, the chemistry pinging between them was so palpable even Mateo had picked up on it.

She might be aware of it, but she doesn't want it.

He sighed. There was that.

'So, thanks for the drinks.'

As he took her card and rang up the drinks, he reminded himself 'friends' was better for him, too. Women were complicated; they didn't always think the way he did. They were like a puzzle, and just when he thought he'd found the answer, he'd be blindsided by something he'd not expected. The bar was providing enough complications, he didn't need more.

Besides, Mia wasn't a girl a guy had a fling with, and he was a guy who only did flings.

Seeing Mia again as a mate, though? Someone who'd take him out of his head for a while, with the added bonus that he enjoyed her? That he could look forward to. All he had to do was stop thinking about how unconsciously sexy she was.

Or how much he wanted to peel off her simple black shirt and jeans so he could get his hands on the curves he knew lay beneath.

Curves he bloody well had to stop thinking about. Shaking himself, he handed her card back. 'I'll see you soon, yes? For non-date number three?'

She nodded, her fingers touching his as she reached for it. Immediately he felt a fizz across his skin. Her gaze jumped to his and he knew she'd felt it too, those blue eyes blazing with heat, and with confusion. But then she quickly ducked her head and spent the next minute meticulously placing the card back in her purse.

When she finally looked back at him, her feelings were

back under control. 'I'll keep an eye on your window for my next adventure.' Her lips twitched. 'That is unless you've run out of Manchester hot spots.'

He laughed, relieved. 'There's ninety-eight more of them. You're in this for the long haul, Mia. Better get used to the idea.'

Maybe by then she'd get so used to it, to *him*, she'd drop her guard and let him in, he thought as she walked away.

And while he was on the elusive maybes, maybe by then he'd have turned the bar round, and no longer be waking up in a cold sweat, wondering if he really was capable of any of this. The bar or the woman.

The following day, Luke met Tanya at a café near her flat. Usually when he took her out he went to her place first to pick her up, but he didn't want to give the wrong impression.

Today there'd be no hasty sex in the hallway. No forgetting the date entirely and spending it in her bedroom instead.

'Well, this is a first.' Tanya gave him a breezy smile as she slid onto the chair opposite him. 'I don't usually get the joy of your company in the morning.'

He signalled for another cup of coffee, allowing her words to sink in. Sure, he hadn't met her for coffee before, but surely… 'I've never stayed over?'

Slowly she shook her head. 'I asked a few times, but you

said something about having to get back to feed a rabbit.' She gave him a wry smile. 'I assumed it was an excuse.'

'It wasn't.' Yet it clearly had been, because it wasn't like Pickles would have starved if she'd missed a morning feed, though she might have sniffed out a wire or two to gnaw through instead. 'I do have a rabbit.'

'Wow.'

'Long story.' And that was one thing he'd never done with any of the women he'd dated. Delved into the long stories. It wasn't what they wanted from him. He was the bartender they enjoyed flirting with, the guy with the muscles they wanted to hook up with. And it suited him just fine.

Well it had, until Mia had come into his life. Now he wanted to talk, to do things that didn't involve getting horizontal on a bed. Scratch that, things that didn't *only* involve getting her on a bed.

The waitress settled the mug in front of Tanya and he stared guiltily back at the woman who should be his focus this morning.

'I'm sorry I never stayed over,' he told her quietly. 'You deserved more from me.'

She shook her head. 'I didn't expect any different. I know what we're about.'

It was true, yet he couldn't help but feel a prick of unease. Of guilt. He hadn't always been this man, the one who had sex with a woman but didn't stay over. Sometimes didn't even take her out on a date, first.

'Maybe I should have put that in the past tense.' She

smiled sadly at him. 'You've got that look on your face. Like you're about to tell me something you don't think I want to hear.'

He winced. 'Shit, I'm never playing poker with you.' Taking a swig of his coffee, he looked her in the eye. 'I've loved our times together, but I don't think we should keep seeing each other. Not now.'

She nodded, her expression giving nothing away. 'Because?'

Yeah, great question. He was still a free agent. Mia didn't want to date him, so why was he about to give up sex whenever he wanted it? *Because it no longer feels right, not since you met Mia.* He swallowed, choosing his words carefully. 'It isn't fair to keep this going, not now my head is mixed up with the idea of another woman.'

Her eyes snapped to his. 'Is it Vicky?'

He shook his head. 'No.' Shame coiled through him. Both had known about the other, but where before he thought that made it okay, now he could see it only meant he'd short-changed all of them.

'Chloe?'

The conversation was starting to remind him of the one he'd had with Mia in the coffee shop, and he didn't like how it made him feel. 'Nothing happened with Chloe, and nothing's happened with this person, either.' He huffed out a breath. 'It probably never will, but it still doesn't feel right to continue seeing you.'

'I see.' She took a long, slow sip of her coffee, and when

she finally looked at him again, her smile was tinged with sadness. 'Well, it was good while it lasted, right?'

God, he hated doing this, hurting someone, yet it was clear that Tanya had been more invested in their time together than he'd thought. Reaching across the table, he took hold of her hand. 'It *was* good, but you deserve better. And now you're not seeing me, you'll find it.'

She nodded. 'Maybe. And what about you? Will you find it, too?'

That was a great question. 'I don't know.' He gave her a wry smile. 'I only know I've reached a crossroads and rather than keep going down the same path, I'm wondering about taking a different one.'

Chapter Sixteen

When Mia made it to her desk on Monday morning, coffee mug in hand, still wearing her PJs, she found activity going on in the flats opposite. Immaculate Woman was feverishly typing away on her computer, fully dressed, though this time her long brown hair was loose. In Luke's window, there was not one, but two messages.

Sandy says

coffee @ Naomi's

2day 11 a.m.

Nerd stuff

She suspected the last line was Luke's own.

The second message was definitely from him, another

two lines accompanied by a drawing of what looked like a paint palette.

Non-date no 3

Weds p.m.?

Good Lord, what on earth was he planning this time? Picking up a sheet of paper she wrote:

Sandy – yes

After sticking it on the glass she wondered how to reply to his invite to … paint? It couldn't be an art gallery could it? Not that she had anything against them, but he really didn't seem the type. As she deliberated she saw the shadow of him in the window. It looked like he was writing and sure enough, a few seconds later, he'd removed the message from Sandy and stuck another in its place.

No 3 is not to view

my etchings

Honest.

Laughter burst out of her and before she realised what she was doing, she'd scrawled:

Shame

Of course the moment she'd stuck the sheet up, she regretted it. They didn't do flirting – wait, no, she didn't do it, because she couldn't flirt with a guy at the same time as saying she didn't want to date him. It gave out mixed messages.

He must have shifted closer to the window, because now he wasn't a shadow. Now she could clearly see him as he posted his reply. And then looked straight into her window.

For U

I will learn 2

etch

Prickles raced across her skin as her gaze connected with his. Oh God, what was she doing, playing with fire like this? It was dangerous and yet … her heart began to race, her stomach to swoop. When had she last felt such excitement?

Mia drew in a deep breath, made herself remember why Luke was so wrong for her. Not just that he was a charmer, a man who couldn't help but flirt with every woman he saw. Or a player who seemingly couldn't help but sleep with most of them. He was also the cool guy, the dishy, ripped man all the women wanted. History had taught her cool guys didn't go for nerds. *Yet the coolest guy you've ever met has said he fancies you.*

Once again she felt the dip of her stomach.

Picking up the pen she carefully wrote:

Weds 3 p.m.

No etchings needed

Releasing the breath she hadn't realised she'd been holding, she stepped back, away from the window. And caught his final message just as she sat down at her desk.

Shame

Sandy was a breath of fresh air. Like Naomi – who had given her a fair amount of stick since she'd found out Luke was the *hot guy* leaving her messages – Sandy was funny and totally grounded. Unlike Chloe and the girls, who Mia enjoyed but didn't feel a kinship with, she suspected if she'd met Sandy at school, she'd still be best mates with her now.

'You really don't mind helping with this?' Sandy glanced down at the sketches she'd made, outlining how she wanted the website to look. 'My artistic talent is almost as good as my tech skills, which basically means a lot of this rests on you. Seems a teeny bit unfair considering you're not actually being paid for it.'

Mia laughed. 'Don't worry, I'm getting my pound of flesh out of Luke. Apparently I have another ninety-seven non-dates to look forward to.'

She gave Mia a sly smile. 'Non-dates, huh?'

'Yep, non-dates.' Mia willed herself not to blush. 'You know we're just friends,' she added, which was probably a mistake because Sandy started to giggle. 'We are.'

'Oh, I know you're both saying that, but I've never seen Luke like this over a woman.' Leaning across the table, she whispered, 'The other day, Mateo joked that he might ask you out, and Luke threw his toys out of the pram.'

A warm, satisfying pleasure pulsed through her, and Mia had to work hard to stop from smiling. Knowing someone in her 'new life' cared enough to worry about her, was a pretty bloody special feeling. 'He was being protective.' Mia eyed Sandy, and decided there was no reason not to be open. 'He knows my previous track record of relationships, and how I'm focusing on being single right now. He was just trying to warn Mateo.'

'You think?' Sandy pursed her lips, her fingers fiddling with the teaspoon on her saucer. 'When did you discuss your ex-boyfriends with him?'

'Why?'

'Because Luke threw his toys at Mateo last week, when he was waiting to take you out on your second date. Sorry non-date. So your theory of him being protective would only work if you'd told him about your exes *before* then.'

Mia felt the flush creep up her neck and knew she didn't need to give Sandy a reply. Especially when Sandy burst into delighted laughter.

'You're the picture of a Union Jack right now, Mia. What with your streaked blonde and blue hair and your red face.'

'Thanks.'

Sandy reached across the table and patted her hand. 'You know I'm only ribbing you because that's what I do, right? Ask Luke. It's my way. The only people I don't take the mick out of are those I don't like.'

The words, the warm smile … it was impossible to be upset with Sandy. 'I think I can see why you and Luke are such good friends. You both, in your own ways, know how to charm.'

Sandy grinned. 'We've got stuff in common, sure, and we've certainly got a lot of history. I can't remember a time when I didn't know Luke Doyle. Still, it's not the reason he's my best friend, after Jim obviously.'

'Obviously,' Mia added dryly, aware Sandy was merely laying the bait but far too curious not to take it. 'I'll bite, what *is* the reason?'

Sandy's face sobered. 'You see him as this player, which is fair enough on current evidence, but it isn't the man I know. Not deep down. The Luke Doyle I grew up with had the biggest heart of anyone I've ever met.' Her eyes searched Mia's. 'He still has, but over the years he's tried so hard to protect it, he's forgotten how to use it.'

So she wasn't the only one with a bad relationship history. Luke had told her he was thirty-four, she guessed it shouldn't come as a surprise that he'd had a serious relationship at some point. Yet from what she'd seen, what she'd heard – *rumour has it he's been through all the single women in this block* – it was clear he wasn't ready for another one. *That makes two of us,* she reminded herself. 'He seems to be trying with Tanya.'

Sandy's eyes crinkled with amusement. 'Why do you say that?'

Yes, Mia, why did you? 'Just that I know she was seeing him last Sunday.' God, that hole she was digging herself was in danger of swallowing her.

'I guess you haven't seen her since, so you don't know that he arranged to see her so he could end things.' As Mia tried to digest that bombshell of a statement, Sandy added, 'Not that they were ever together, not in the true sense of the word. But he's stopped their arrangement.'

'Oh.' Yep, that was about as eloquent as she could manage right now.

It didn't stop Sandy laughing delightedly. 'Oh indeed. But it's fine, I'll go along with the friends-only story you guys keep telling yourselves. Just know that I will smile smugly when you both come to your senses.'

Chapter Seventeen

Luke pulled into the car park and nodded towards the impressive stainless steel and glass Lowry building. 'Welcome to non-date number three. Known as not quite Salford's Guggenheim.'

Mia scrambled out of the TVR – elegant was one word he couldn't use to describe her. He climbed out more sedately and when she turned to him, she looked decidedly suspicious. 'I didn't put you down as an art fan.'

'Lots you don't know about me, Mia.'

'Clearly.' Her gaze swept away from the Lowry and across the quays. 'Yet why do I have a sneaky feeling you brought me here not for the galleries, but so you can ogle Old Trafford?'

Laughter shot out of him. 'Christ, you're way too smart for me.' But he grabbed her hand and tugged her in the direction of the Lowry. 'Still, as we're here, you should cross this one off your list.'

They didn't spend long studying the paintings, neither of them knowing much about art.

'I think my etchings would have been better,' he murmured to her at one particularly weird canvas of swirls and splodges.

She stifled a giggle, and his chest puffed out a little. Making her laugh was becoming one of his favourite pastimes. 'Maybe, but then I would have had to go to your flat to see them.' She gave him a sly smile. 'As you've pointed out, I'm too smart to fall for that.'

Yeah, he couldn't deny she had his number.

They moved on to the next gallery; the permanent exhibition of Lowry paintings.

'He used to live in Salford,' he told Mia as she came to a stop in front of one of Lowry's famous industrial landscapes. 'I kind of have a soft spot for his matchstick people.'

They stood next to each other, studying the picture, and Luke was acutely aware of everything about her. How she smelt – floral with a hint of spice – the warmth of her body. The soft look of her hair, which his hands itched to touch.

'I love how he didn't care about the usual rules and conventions.' Mia lifted her shoulders. 'He did his own thing.'

Luke slid her a look. 'Is that a rebellious streak you've got there?'

'I'm not a rebel.' Her eyes remained fixed on the painting. 'But I hate to be pigeon-holed. People making assumptions based on how I look or what I do for a living.'

'Is that the reason for the coloured streaks in your hair? You want to keep people guessing?'

Another shrug. 'I decided way back when I was in school that I wasn't going to invest time and energy in trying to be something I wasn't. I mean, I enjoyed maths, so why say I didn't? Sure, I got the mick taken out of me, but that was easier to cope with than having to pretend all the time.'

'What you see is what you get, huh?'

Her lips curved in a smile that added sparkle to her eyes. 'Exactly right.'

Unable to resist, he nudged his arm against her shoulder. 'I like what I see, Mia Abbott.'

A faint flush crossed her cheeks. 'Yeah?'

'Most definitely.' An odd lump settled in his throat. Shit, he had a feeling he more than liked this woman. As if she sensed his churning emotions, her eyes widened and the air around them filled with a taut silence. 'You're without doubt the best Smurf I've toured Manchester with.'

Her answering laugh was so loud people turned to look at them, but Luke didn't care. The tension was broken, and his chest felt free again.

'Come on, let's get out of here before we're kicked out. We can grab a quick coffee on the quay.' He took her hand – he loved the feel of his fingers wrapped around hers – and led her out towards one of the cafés that lined the canal. As it was a rare sunny day in Manchester, they opted for the outdoor seating and ordered two lattes.

'How did you get on with Sandy the other day?' he asked as the waitress placed their drinks in front of them.

'Good. She told me how she wants the website to look and gave me all the social media links to incorporate.' Her lips quirked in a half-smile. 'Apparently I have to like the new Facebook page.'

He smiled sheepishly at her. 'Sorry, she can be pushy at times.'

'Maybe, but she's also really nice.'

'Sometimes she's nice.' Luke took a sip of the coffee. 'Sometimes she's a giant pain in my backside.'

Mia laughed softly. 'Only because she cares about you.' Across the table, she caught his eye. 'She told me you ended things with Tanya.'

Her statement caught him by surprise. 'Yes.' Was she making conversation or was she interested? 'It didn't seem right to keep seeing her when I've got my eye on someone else.'

'Oh?' Her gaze avoided his. 'Is it Michele? Her hair is amazing, so sleek it's like a flaming shampoo advert. And did you know her nails are natural?' Mia glanced down at her short, unvarnished nails. 'Sometimes I wish I could grow mine. Just a bit, so they don't look like I chew them. Which I kind of do now and again, so I guess it's my fault.'

Luke struggled not to laugh. 'You think that's what guys look for in a woman? Nice hair and nails?'

'On current evidence, it seems to be what *you* look for.'

'It isn't.' He hesitated, unsure whether to say the words that hovered over his tongue. Surely there was no point hiding what was so blinking obvious? 'You know who I was referring to, Mia.' Immediately a blush swept over her face and this time, when she darted him a glance, she looked uncomfortable. Maybe some things *were* better left unsaid. 'But it's okay,' he added quietly. 'I'm enjoying life with this really cool, funny girl just as it is.' When her eyes lifted to his, he smiled. 'Turns out non-dating is more fun than I thought.'

A slow smile started across her face, and when it reached her eyes, the blueness was as vivid as he'd ever seen it. 'You mean that?'

He nodded. It was the truth, though if she wanted more, he'd give her it in a heartbeat. 'Especially when my non-date decides galleries are okay, but what she really wants to do this afternoon is go on a tour of Old Trafford.'

Mia threw back her head and laughed, the sound so infectious he ended up laughing, too. God, she was gorgeous, so natural, so pretty, even though she'd probably hate him for calling her that.

The phone he'd left on the table buzzed, and he glanced at the screen.

I'm around next week. Hope we can get together. Vicky x

Damn, there was still one more loose end to tie up.

When he looked back over at Mia, she quickly averted her eyes, pretending an interest in a couple who were trying, unsuccessfully, to encourage their toddler into a pushchair.

Had she seen?

After settling the bill, he took her hand again and led her towards the footbridge that crossed the canal. The one that would bring them out at the Theatre of Dreams.

'We'll have to up the pace if we're going to make it in time for the five o'clock tour.'

Her head snapped round to his. 'You booked it already?'

Say yes, he'd be presumptuous. Say no, he'd be a liar. He gave Mia his most winning smile. 'Maybe?'

She rolled her eyes, yet the smile that had been so full, so easy a few minutes ago looked strained now, and Luke's heart sank. Of course she'd seen the bloody text. He supposed there was a chance she was annoyed because she was jealous, yet more likely she was annoyed because she felt he was being less than truthful with her.

What was certain was that Vicky's text had considerably dented his chances of persuading Mia he wasn't the player she had him down as.

And likely blown any chance of shifting their relationship to more-than-friends at some point in the future.

Chapter Eighteen

Mia looked over at Stan. He wore what she was starting to realise was his stubborn expression; narrowed eyes, jutting chin. It was Saturday night and she'd spent the last ten minutes trying to persuade him to come to the bar with her again.

'Give me one good reason why you want to turn down the offer of a free beer with a charming companion and instead spend the night on your own, nursing a Horlicks?'

He humphed. 'I'm not that bloody old yet.'

'You must be, or you'd join me in the bar.'

He waved his hand at her. 'It's too noisy for me, that place.'

'Thought you said you weren't old. That's a really old person's excuse.' She received a baleful glare.

'Why do you need a wingman anyway? Thought you and the Chipmunk were friends.'

'We are.' It's just the Chipmunk – God, Luke would die

of laughter if he knew they were calling him that – the man had also told her he'd ended things with his regular hook-up because he wanted to … what? Hook up with her instead? Date her for real? Yet how could it be the latter if he was also still seeing some woman called Vicky?

And wow, seeing that text had really hurt. Yet it shouldn't have done, because she wasn't supposed to want anything more from him.

Her heart also shouldn't have leapt at the message he'd posted earlier.

If U go to bar

2night

Me = v happy

She was a basket case. So keen to see him, yet so terrified about how little effort it would take for him to persuade her into doing something she really shouldn't. A flirty suggestion, that smoulder in his eye, a flash of his wicked smile. Any combination and she could find herself waiting for him after the bar had closed.

Hence she'd taken to pushing poor Stan out of his flat, against his will.

The man took one look at her face and sighed. 'I'll get my wallet.'

Guilt pricked. 'You don't have to, you really don't.' But

because she needed him to, she added, 'If you do come, I'm paying.'

'No bloody way.' Stan loped off to fetch his wallet and key from the sideboard. 'Can't have you buying me drinks twice in a row. People round here will talk.' He pointed for her to lead the way. 'Besides, don't want that man of yours becoming jealous. Reckon he might just have the edge over me if it came to fisticuffs. Him being a bit younger.'

'Maybe a tiny bit bigger, too? And slightly fitter?' Feeling a rush of affection for her sometimes curmudgeonly, yet also utterly loveable, neighbour, Mia wrapped an arm around his ample waist. 'Luke's not my man, Stan, he's my friend. Don't fret though, if it comes to a fight, I'll be in your corner.'

He huffed. 'Lot of good a damp sponge will do me.' But his arm slipped around her, too, and when he squeezed her waist, emotion balled in her throat. She missed her dad something fierce, but in Stan she was starting to realise she had a substitute.

The place was exactly how Stan had said it would be; humming with noise. Something he took great glee in telling her. 'How's anyone supposed to have a conversation in here?' His gaze swung towards all the women lined up at the bar, bodies encased in tight dresses, hair perfectly styled, all fighting to get Luke's attention. 'Suppose most aren't here for a chat, mind.'

'No.' Glancing down at her leggings and converse trainers, she pushed down the unhelpful stirrings of jealousy. What had Luke told her? *I like what I see.* 'Let's find a seat somewhere quieter.'

But just as she was about to turn, Luke glanced up. The bloom of pleasure that crossed his face when he saw her, the beaming smile he aimed her way, sent her heart cartwheeling.

It also sent Stan into a fit of unlikely laughter. 'That bloke isn't friends with you,' he rasped. 'He wants to get in your knickers.'

'Keep your voice down.' As Luke continued to smile in their direction, Mia hoped to God he couldn't lip read.

'Just saying it as I see it.'

Giving Luke a little wave – the gesture felt ridiculously coy, yet somehow she couldn't stop grinning – Mia set off towards the tables outside, where the noise was at a more reasonable level for a sixty-seven-year-old.

'If we're just saying things how we see them,' she said as Stan levered himself into a seat, 'what about you and Naomi? In your own eloquent words, do you want to get into *her* knickers?'

Stan spluttered, then started to cough so loud he began to wheeze. 'Good God, girl. Where on earth did that come from?'

'Observation.' She leant on the table, eyes on Stan to watch his reaction. 'You're both dancing around each other like a pair of shy peacocks. No wait, I should say a shy peacock and a shy peahen. I don't know what the collective noun is.'

'Peafowl.' As soon as he'd said it, Stan stilled, his

expression almost comically shocked. 'Wait, you're saying she's interested?'

Mia rolled her eyes. 'Of course she is, dummy. Why else does she get me to tell you the custard donuts are in?'

'Because she needs to sell them?'

Mia started to laugh. 'Okay, that's true, but the reason she buys them in the first place, you dozy fool, is because she wants you to go into the shop. She wants to *see* you.' Standing back up, Mia smiled at him. 'Now while you think on that, I'll get the first round in.'

Her pulse began to race as she turned to walk into the bar, yet just as she was about to step inside, Luke's large frame blocked her way.

'Hey.'

The sexy low tone made her heart leap in her chest. 'Oh, hi. I was just heading in to get some drinks.'

His smile was lazy, dimples winking at her. 'I've come to find out what you want.'

'Wow, personal service, huh? Is that all part of Sandy's drive to get more customers through the door?'

He laughed softly. 'No Mia, it's part of my drive to take care of my favourite customer.'

'Favourite.' Her belly fluttered. 'Stan will be pleased.'

Amused green eyes bored into hers. 'Stan's a good bloke, a good customer, but you know he's not my favourite.' Luke leant forward, the touch of his lips a gentle brush against her ear. 'For the avoidance of doubt: you, Mia Abbott, are my favourite customer.'

Butterflies were no longer fluttering in her belly, they

were having a dance, and doing it so vigorously they must have taken all her breath because she found she could hardly talk. 'I…' She swallowed a few times, trying to find her balance. 'I'm honoured. Does that qualify me for anything? Like a discount, or…' she trailed off at the dart of heat in his eyes.

'Or?' His gaze dipped to her mouth, and her lips tingled in anticipation.

He's not going to kiss you here.

But God, it looked like he *wanted* to. 'I don't know.'

His finger trailed down her cheek and he smiled right into her eyes. 'It qualifies you for a drink after the bar has closed.'

'A lock-in?'

'If you like. A private lock-in.' Another smile, his eyes darkening. 'Just you and me.'

'Oh.' She could barely get the word out, so dry was her mouth, so loud the heartbeat pounding in her ears. *This was why you brought reinforcements.* 'What about Stan?'

Luke raised his right eyebrow. 'Do you want him to stay?'

Okay, he'd very firmly knocked the ball back into her court. Now was the time to stop the flirty stuff – there was no doubt that was what they were doing – and say yes, she'd invited Stan so of course he should stay.

'Mia?'

'I guess it might be too late for him.'

A slow smile spread across Luke's face and once again

his eyes drifted to her lips, before finally meeting hers again. 'Then I'll see you later.'

Luke was struggling, his mind not on the job, but on what was waiting for him when the job was over. When he'd got rid of the staff and the customers. All except for Mia.

Who had nearly invited her sixty-odd-year-old neighbour to the lock-in. *She's not as keen to be locked in with you, as you are with her.*

'Boss, pull your head out of your arse.' Mateo's voice drifted over to him. 'I said I needed three margaritas. Not three mojitos.'

'Bollocks.' Luke stared down at the drinks he'd just poured. 'Who were they for?'

Mateo nodded towards the three girls sitting to the left of the bar. 'You can try your charm on them.' He gave Luke a sly grin. 'Or maybe you're not allowed, now you're dating Mia?'

'Who's Mia?' Bill, who'd actually come for a drink with his wife and a few friends, was nursing a beer at the bar, claiming he needed a breather from the incessant chat about holidays.

'Mia is a customer who's kindly helping make our website. And I'm not dating her.' Though the statement was accurate, it rested on him like an ill-fitting suit. They went out together and held hands. He'd almost kissed her right here, in the bar, a couple of hours ago. It felt like dating.

'You're doing something with her.' Mateo's dark brows lifted and he smirked. 'Enough to totally put you off your game.'

Bill chuckled. 'That's fighting talk, lad.' He slid Luke a glance. 'But I reckon your new boss is too wise to rise to that bait.'

'Too wise? Or too scared of failure?'

Mateo was needling him, but Bill was right. He was a businessman now. Too mature, too sensible to let the younger man get under his skin. 'You think I'm off my game?'

Mateo grinned. 'So far off it, I no longer think we can say you have a game.'

Luke snatched at the tray holding the glasses. 'Watch and learn, upstart. Watch and bloody learn.'

It seemed he'd lied about the mature and sensible part. This was what he did though, what he was good at; charming the punters, harmless flirting. Without it, he didn't know what he could offer the bar. He couldn't do the numbers like Phil, or the social media tech like Sandy. He didn't have Mateo's youth or swarthy good looks. Nor Bill's second-hand car buyer's skill at negotiating with wholesalers.

He only had his smile, and his gift of the gab.

'Ladies.' With a flourish, he set the mojitos on the table. 'Have you tried one of these? White rum and soda with a dash of lime juice, a sprinkle of sugar and a hint of mint. It's basically summer in a glass.'

'Sounds amazing.' One of them reached for a glass, but her friend stopped her.

'Wait, we ordered margaritas.'

'No problem, I can take these away and make some for you.' He paused, giving them all a wide smile. 'Or you can try it and tell me what you think.'

They all took a sip, and he knew from their expressions he'd won them over. 'Still want the margaritas?'

'No way.' One of them eyed him over the top of her glass. 'You seem to have sussed what we like. How about you keep the surprises coming?'

He bowed and when he turned back to the bar, he bumped straight into Mia.

'Whoa, sorry.' He put his hands on her arms to steady her, steady them both. The feel of her skin beneath his palm sent a bolt of arousal through him, which only intensified when he stared down into her surprised blue eyes. 'Scratch that,' he corrected, lowering his voice. 'Bumping into you feels too good to apologise for it.'

She shook her head, but her eyes smiled. 'That's such a line.'

'Oh, he's good at those.' Bill shifted on his stool to give Mia a quiet appraisal. 'You must be the famous Mia.'

'Famous?'

Luke's heart shot into his mouth. He knew how wary she still was of his reputation as some sort of Mancunian Don Juan. The way she'd backed away from him after seeing Vicky's text still weighed heavily on him, their tour of Old Trafford lacking the ease, the teasing banter of earlier in the day. He didn't need Bill poking the wound, making things worse. Luke was well aware he was cocking up enough on his own.

'Aye love, I hear you're the one making a website for the bar.'

Okay. Luke's heart settled again. 'I am.' She studied Bill and smiled. 'You must be the famous Bill. One-time bar owner, now semi-retired.'

Bill gave her the same goofy, smitten smile he'd seen other men give Mia when she showed them attention. 'That's me. Pleased to meet the lady that has our Luke muddling up his cocktails.'

Mia gave Luke a puzzled look and he sighed. 'I got my margaritas and mojitos mixed up. But I sorted it,' he added firmly, with a silent one-fingered gesture towards Mateo. 'In fact the ladies now want me to choose a cocktail for their next round.'

Bill started to laugh. 'I see the Doyle blarney is still alive and kicking.' He turned to Mia. 'Watch him, love, or before you know it he'll be talking you into stuff you had no intention of ever doing.'

'Will he now?' Luke tried to keep his expression neutral as Mia gave him a long, contemplative look. 'Thanks for the warning, but I'm pretty strong willed.'

Yeah, he could attest to that.

Yet when she slipped onto a spare stool to the right of Bill, he realised she'd clearly said goodbye to Stan, and was now waiting at the bar. For him.

Maybe he hadn't lost all his powers of persuasion.

Chapter Nineteen

Luke closed the door behind Mateo, who was the last to leave, and the bar instantly became quiet. Just her and the man she was becoming increasingly aware of.

Mia had always known Luke was good looking yet tonight, as she'd watched him charm his way through the evening, her appreciation of his looks had become even more acute. It wasn't just his face. He had a body that featured in most women's fantasies, or it would if they'd been lucky enough to see it. She had, but only the top half through her window, from a distance.

Tanya had seen it all, and Vicky, whoever she was. A lot of women had seen him naked.

'Hey, are you okay?' Luke slipped his hands into his pockets, his expression concerned. 'You don't look too happy to be locked in with me.'

Crap, she needed to stop thinking about him with other women. Or him naked. 'Sorry, I was remembering what Bill said earlier, about you charming people into doing things.' She glanced around her at the empty bar. 'This is my first lock-in.'

'Then we'd better make it a good one.' He strode round the bar and picked up a silver cocktail shaker, his movements easy; a man totally in tune with his body. 'So, the big question is, do you trust me?'

'Well I'm locked in here with you, so I guess I must.'

He grinned, a flash of straight white teeth, and her heart gave a little dance. 'Enough for me to make you a cocktail?'

'Of course. I enjoyed the Electric Smurf and the Manchester Bee.'

'Ah, but they weren't made by me.' He flicked the cocktail shaker upside down and caught it casually, eyes appraising her. 'Any special requests?'

'You managed to convince those women to let you choose one. I'm sure you can convince me to do the same.'

Another smile, though this one was more cautious. 'You know that's just the job, don't you? That I only see them as customers.'

'Sure.' She glanced down, flicking a non-existent fluff ball from her leggings. 'I was one once.'

'You were never just a customer, Mia.' At his quietly spoken words, her eyes jumped to his. 'Right from the outset, you intrigued me. I felt, I don't know, some sort of magnetic pull towards you. I mean, you shot me down, but I still wanted to see you. Can't say that's ever happened before.' He gave her a wry smile. 'Must be that blue-green hair. I reckon you're some sort of witch.'

'Ha, first I'm a Leprechaun, then a Smurf, now I'm a witch. Make up your mind.'

He turned towards the line of spirits hanging behind the bar and squirted a measure of vodka into the shaker. 'I'll let you know if I find a broom and a pointy hat.'

'Fair enough. So what are you making me?'

'*Star Wars* is still your favourite film?'

She gave him a quizzical look. 'Err, I'm not sure that answered my question, but yes.'

'Okay, let me just check in the kitchen.' She watched as he disappeared into the room behind, his bum looking just exactly right in his black jeans.

Friends don't ogle each other's bums.

She groaned, aware she was failing so badly at this friends-only rule she'd instigated, it seemed futile to carry on with it.

A few seconds later he emerged, a wide grin on his face as he shook the cocktail shaker. 'Okay, so it's not exactly as per the recipe, but behold…' He poured the mixture into two waiting glasses. 'The Giggling Yoda.'

'The, what? Seriously?' God, he cracked her up with his daft cocktails. Laughing, she took a sip. 'Are you making all these drinks up?'

He gave her a mock affronted look. 'Of course not. They're all genuine cocktails.' He took a swig of his own and grimaced. 'Though I'm not sure the apples work as well as the pear would have.'

'I'm sure Yoda won't mind. Being a Jedi Master and all

that, he's probably got more important things to worry about.'

They shared a smile, and Mia found she couldn't drag her eyes from his. The longer they stared at each other, the more her skin began to prickle, her belly swooped and heat pooled between her legs.

Luke cleared his throat and carefully placed his glass onto the counter. 'I've got to be honest, this doesn't feel like friends, Mia. It feels more. Much more.'

'I know.' She avoided his eyes, the atmosphere feeling suddenly charged and heavy, like before a thunderstorm. 'But I like having you as my friend.' She caught at the condensation on the glass with her finger. 'I'm scared if we change that, we'll muck our friendship up.'

'Why would we?'

'The nerd and the cool kid, really?'

'It seems to be working so far.'

She shrugged, trying to feel casual when inside everything felt tight. 'I told you, my track record with men is terrible.'

'They were the wrong men.'

She snorted. 'They definitely were, but they didn't start out that way.' Taking a swallow of her drink, she raised her eyes to his. 'In the beginning, they seemed like the right men.' It made Luke even more of a non-starter, because he wasn't even right for her now. At least not on paper. When she was with him, though? When he held her hand, made her laugh, danced with her … then he felt perfect.

He exhaled sharply, jamming a hand through his hair. 'I

can't lie to you, Mia. It's hard to be just your friend when every time I see you, I want to kiss you.'

God, she didn't think her heart could take much more of this, it was beating so fast. 'I know that, too.'

'You do?'

The look he gave her was full of longing, yet it was the doubt mixed in with it that made her chest squeeze. As if he had no clue of the effect he had on her. The idea was so crazy, it made her smile. 'You seriously think I don't want to kiss you?'

A slow smile spread across his face. 'Well, I was wondering if I'd lost my touch.'

The reminder that he was used to women wanting to kiss him was a welcome blast of cold air to the heat raging inside her. 'No need to fear, your reputation as a sex god is safe.'

As if she'd slapped him, he took a step back, a flash of hurt in his expression. 'I guess I deserved that.'

'No, you didn't.' God, she was a bitch. Who was she to judge him? A hugely attractive guy, working in an environment that brought him into contact with lots of women out for a good time ... what single guy wouldn't take up what was on offer? Yet she couldn't pretend to like it, either. 'I'm sorry. It was meant as a joke, but I guess it came out a bit snarky.'

For a few beats he said nothing, just went to pick up his drink again, the cocktail glass looking so delicate in his large hands, attached to his big, strapping body. Finally his green gaze pressed hers. 'I've not slept with another woman since I met you.'

His quietly worded admission stunned her. 'Why? We're only friends.'

'So you keep saying.' With a sigh he nodded over to one of the green leather sofas. 'Why don't we sit somewhere more comfortable? I've had enough of standing behind this bar tonight.'

Luke needed to sit. His legs ached from standing all evening, his balls ached from wanting to lift Mia onto the bar and kiss the life out of her, and his chest … well, he wasn't sure why that ached. Maybe it had something to do with knowing that Mia wasn't ever going to be more than a friend.

Mia slipped off her Converses and sat cross-legged on the sofa. He eased in next to her, giving his balls a little more teasing. *Here she is, all natural and warm and smelling like spring, but you can't touch her.*

'The other day, when we were at the Lowry.' She spoke softly, eyes downcast. 'I saw the text from Vicky.'

'I know you did.' Her gaze jumped to his and he gave her a half smile. 'The mood between us changed. You were less relaxed. I figured either you'd seen Vicky's message, or you were cheesed off that I'd booked the tour of Old Trafford.'

Her lips twitched. 'Then you decided it couldn't

possibly be the latter, because who in their right mind wouldn't want to see the Theatre of Dreams?'

'Exactly.' He shifted so he was facing her. 'Vicky is a sales rep I used to see from time to time when she was in the area.' Reaching into his pocket, he dug out his phone and scrolled through his messages. 'She wanted to meet up a few days after I'd left that first message in the window to you, but I declined. As soon as I got back home after the Old Trafford visit, I messaged her to tell her I wouldn't be seeing her again. Here, take a look.'

Mia stared at the phone, then shook her head. 'I don't need to see your private messages.'

'Okay, I'll read it out to you. *Hi Vicky, wanted to let you know I've met someone. She's unlike anyone else I know and I'm rapidly becoming besotted, hence this is goodbye.*'

Mia took a big gulp of her drink, then coughed, the vodka clearly hitting her throat. 'That's, well, a bit cold? Just goodbye?'

He tried not to let it bother him that she'd focused on that, and not the first part. 'We had a relationship based purely on sex, Mia. She wouldn't expect … wouldn't want anything else.'

Her big blue eyes searched his and he wondered what she was thinking. That he *was* cold? Ruthless even? That wasn't him though. Maybe it was how he'd become, but detached sure as hell wasn't how he felt now, sitting next to her in the deserted bar, the lights above the bar casting a soft glow across the place.

After a few more beats of silence, her lips curved upwards. 'Besotted, huh?'

God, he loved looking at her mouth. Loved looking at *her*. 'I'd say that was a fairly accurate description.'

She knocked back the rest of her cocktail. 'I think I may need another drink.'

It wasn't the reaction he'd hoped for, but he climbed to his feet. 'Sure, any requests?'

'Nope, you choose.' She waggled her eyebrows at him. 'Though I don't know how you can follow a Manchester Bee, an Electric Smurf and a Giggling Yoda.'

'Such little faith.' Though as he crossed to the bar, he wasn't sure either. He surveyed the optics, thinking about the woman on the sofa, and immediately reached for the blue curacao.

Now for the less obvious. Mia was razor sharp, yet she was warm. Genuine. Vodka, he thought. Rum was too sweet, brandy too sophisticated. Gin could work, it was dry, like Mia's humour, but it was flowery where Mia was more earthy. He added a squirt of lemon juice for the sharpness of her mind, and some soda for the fizz of her personality. Finally, once he'd mixed and poured two glasses, he added some cocktail stirrers which were supposed to look like fireworks, coloured foil cascading from the top of the sticks.

Her eyes widened as he brought them over. 'Don't tell me. It's called Fireworks over the Blue Danube.'

'Clever, but wrong.' He touched her glass with his. 'Here's to the Blue Mia.'

'There's a cocktail called Mia?'

He grinned, enjoying her excitement. 'There is now.'

Her eyes widened. 'You named a cocktail after me?'

'I developed *and* named a cocktail after you.' He took a swig. Not half bad. 'Go on, give it a try.' She took a cautious sip, looking at him over the top of the glass. 'What do you think? How do you taste?' And yes, he was aware of the innuendo.

Clearly so was she, because she shook her head. 'I'm not going to answer that. Just tell me what's in it.'

He listed the ingredients and why he'd chosen them, and was rewarded with a shy smile.

'And the crazy firework stirrers?'

'They dazzle. Just like you do.'

She pealed with laughter. 'Oh no, no way.' Her gaze dropped down. 'Look at me, I'm sat here in leggings. I'm not dazzling anyone.'

Irritation burned through him, not with her, but with whoever had made her unable to see what, to him, was so bloody obvious. 'I *am* looking at you, Mia. The glint of laughter that's nearly always in your eyes, deepening their glorious Smurf blue.' He received a roll of her eyes, but her gaze remained fixed on his and he knew he had her attention. 'The translucence of your skin. The softness of your natural pink lips, the ready smile. The way you're not afraid to say what you think, no bullshit, no guile. The way you challenge me, make me laugh, proper belly laugh, more than I can remember doing in a long time.' Unable to resist, he brought a hand to her face, smoothing his thumb across her perfect skin. 'You dazzle *me*.'

Her throat moved as she swallowed, that blue gaze riveted on his, a world of questions behind it. Not, he thought, for him, but for herself. Did she really want to do what he was so clearly asking – hell, he was almost begging. Was it right for her? Could she ever trust him?

'You're pretty damn dazzling yourself right now.' Her hand covered his, eyes continuing to search his. 'Are we really going to do this?'

His heart leapt, sensing her opening up to the possibility, but he didn't want it to happen like this, him persuading her. He wanted her to be as desperate for it as he was. 'We're not going to do anything until you decide it's what *you* want.'

She nodded, bringing his hand down and clasping it in hers. 'What if I want to kiss you? Just, you know, to see if we're any good together.'

'You really think there's a chance we *won't* be?'

A smile played around her mouth. 'Honestly, no. I can't see you being anything other than a dynamite kisser.' She licked at her lips, causing a bolt of lust to zap through him. 'Still, we should try, because if it's rubbish, we can forget it happened and carry on being friends.'

His gaze wouldn't shift from her mouth. He wanted to kiss her more than he wanted to breathe. 'And if it's not rubbish?'

Another lick of her lips. 'Then we can maybe do it again.'

He laughed softly. 'Can we remove the maybe in that

sentence? If we're going to do this right, we need a proper incentive.'

'Of course we do.' Amusement flickered across her face, but then her breathing changed from smooth to choppy, and her eyes darkened, the blue turning to more of an indigo. 'Damn it, kiss me, Luke. The anticipation is killing me.'

He needed no further instruction. 'Sit on my lap,' he told her. She eyed him dubiously and he laughed. 'Come on, I'm not going to bite, at least not our first time.'

'You say that like there'll be a second time.'

'I *know* there'll be a second time.' He pointed to himself. 'Dynamite kisser, remember?'

'God, I should never have said that.'

She scrambled over and straddled him, her buttocks settling on his thighs, brushing against his groin, which immediately perked up. 'Jesus, you feel good.' He ran his hands down her back, resting them on her hips when what he really wanted to do was nudge her core even closer to the part of him that ached and throbbed.

She must have felt him because he saw her swallow, her cheeks flush. And when she spoke, her voice had turned husky. 'You promised me a kiss.'

Instead of wasting any more precious moments talking, he angled his head and captured her mouth with his.

Instantly a zing of pleasure shot through him. Softer even than he'd imagined, her lips felt perfect against his and for a few moments he contented himself with simply exploring them, nibbling, licking, teasing. Soon the desire for more, for deeper, tore at him and he nudged her mouth with his tongue, letting out a groan when her lips parted. Had kissing ever felt this good? Over the years he'd done less and less of it, preferring to get to the main event, but now he realised what he'd been missing out on.

Or maybe it was Mia who made his body hum, his nerve endings fizzle, just from the feel of her lips, the dart of her tongue. The heat of her.

It was almost too good, because his hips started to shift restlessly, pushing up against her, needing more contact. More of her. Breath heaving, he had to drag his mouth away before he started something she might regret.

She looks as blindsided as you. That was his first thought as he took in her flushed cheeks, her bright eyes. The choppy puffs of breath.

'So?' he asked, smiling. 'Worth doing again some time?'

She nodded, but as she eased off his lap and back onto the sofa, her quiet sigh made his stomach dip. She might be blindsided, but he had an awful feeling she was also conflicted.

'I get the sense you'd have preferred it to have been rubbish.'

Her eyes met his and she gave him a dry smile. 'It would have been easier.'

She had a point. Friends was cleaner, simpler, less messy than a relationship. Yet, even though his attraction to Mia was inconvenient, he didn't care. What he was starting to feel for her was worth the risk, worth the mess. Then again, that's because what he was gaining, for however long it lasted, was Mia, in all her gorgeous, natural, unconsciously sexy glory.

What was she gaining? A guy she didn't trust, who owned a bar that was probably going bust. No wonder she was backing away.

Chapter Twenty

Days after her lock-in with Luke, and Mia couldn't stop thinking about the kiss. Whenever she closed her eyes, whenever her brain had nothing to focus on, it came slamming back to her.

Dynamite was exactly the right word for the way he kissed. It had been explosive.

'Are you listening to me, or are you ogling that guy opposite again?'

Elle's voice shattered Mia's daydream. The one where Luke hadn't pulled away. And she hadn't dashed back to her flat feeling both turned on and terrified. 'Sorry. I'm listening. The phone signal must have dipped.'

'I'll pretend to buy that dodgy excuse,' Elle countered dryly. 'I said we're thinking of coming up to see you next weekend. Does that work?'

'Does next weekend mean this weekend, or the following one? I never know.'

'Next weekend always means next weekend. If I'd meant this weekend, I'd have flipping *said* this weekend, wouldn't I?' Elle let out a long sigh. 'And I thought it was my post-pregnancy brain that was scrambled.'

'Okay, okay, next weekend. Great.'

'And if I'd meant this weekend?'

'I might have a thing on Saturday.' Mia screwed up her face, waiting for the onslaught of questions. Being evasive with Elle never worked, but she couldn't help it. Since the kiss, planning to see Luke no longer sounded innocent.

'A thing? You mean a date?'

'No.' It certainly wasn't that, because they wouldn't be alone. It was just that what he'd invited her to seemed more coupley – was that a word? – than a non-date.

Elle huffed. 'God, come on Mia. I've got a saggy middle, leaking breasts, bags under my eyes from getting up seventy thousand times a night – only a slight exaggeration. All I do all day is feed, burp and wipe up poo. Throw me a bone. I need to live through you now.'

'The feeding, burping and poo – is that you or the kids?'

'Ha bloody ha. Gossip, Mia. That's what I need.' Her voice lowered. 'Please tell me you're shagging the man with the muscles.'

Mia groaned. 'Of course I'm not. Friends don't shag.' They don't kiss like they did the other day, either. 'Luke invited his brother and a few friends out for lunch on Saturday.'

There was a pause down the line before Elle's voice

came back. 'You're going to lunch with Luke's brother. And Luke's friends.'

Mia swallowed, knowing very well what her sister was thinking. 'Yes.'

'So you're doing the girlfriend thing, meeting his family and friends.'

'No, absolutely not.' But God, that was exactly what she'd thought when Luke had asked her after their kiss on Saturday night. Just before she'd fled to her flat. 'He's introducing me to some more locals. I thought you and Mum would be happy with that.'

'Oh we are.' Mia knew from her voice that Elle was grinning. 'We'll be even happier when you reciprocate and introduce Luke to your family next weekend.'

Mia raised her eyes to the ceiling. How had she walked into that one so easily? 'Come on Elle, I'm only meeting his brother.'

'As your sister, I'm only asking for the same courtesy. Plus Mum and Dad, obviously, or they'll whine something rotten.'

It was easier to agree, or at least to pretend to agree. 'I'll see what I can do.' Which had to be nothing, because introducing him to her parents wasn't just dipping into girlfriend/boyfriend status. It was diving straight into it.

Saturday came around way too fast. All of a sudden, Mia was scrabbling in her wardrobe trying to find something to wear.

And God, this woman yanking clothes out and throwing them onto her bed Was Not Her. Since when did she care what people thought of her? If people didn't like what they saw, it didn't matter because they weren't her sort of people. Yet here she was, dithering about putting on a dress, yep, a flaming dress. She couldn't blame it on the venue either. Not after she'd messaged him last night:

Dress Code?

He'd messaged back:

You do code

I do cocktails

Okay, it had been witty, but it hadn't helped. Neither had his second message, added a few seconds later:

Casual

Do I get to see

your legs?

Her usual self would have ignored his comment, but this

giddy one had shaved her legs in the shower. And was now looking at her two summer dresses.

It was hot, she reasoned. A dress would be more comfortable than jeans or leggings. Taking a quick photo of them both, she sent it to Gill and Heather in their group chat.

Going to meet Luke's brother and his friends. Which one? M x

Immediately Heather pinged back a message:

Still just friends?!?!?!??!?! Yellow, but you need to phone us. We need details H x

A second letter Gill sent one:

It's a yellow from me 2. But OMG, fill us in ASAP G x

With a wry smile to herself, Mia slipped the yellow one on.

And tried not to blush when Luke's eyes widened with delight as she walked up to him in the car park.

'Good God, Mia.' Resting against the TVR, legs crossed casually at his ankles, his gaze ran up and down her body. 'You don't just have legs. You have bloody gorgeous legs.'

She glanced down, feeling oddly shy. 'I don't know what to say to that.'

'How about, *Luke, I promise to always wear a dress for my dates with you from now on*?'

The appreciative way he looked at her, the flirty tone, the heat she could see banked in his eyes. It all left her flustered. 'Non-dates.'

A flicker of disappointment crossed his face but he didn't comment. Instead he held the door open for her.

She'd been so focused on trying not to look at him, so he wouldn't see how nervous she felt, it was only now she noticed what he was wearing. A white T-shirt that moulded to his impressive chest and cargo shorts that revealed he worked out every bit as hard on his lower body, as he did on his upper.

They were man's legs. Dusted with dark hair, bunching with muscles.

'You have legs too, I see,' she commented as she climbed into the low-slung TVR. Not easy with a flipping dress on.

He slid her a smile. 'Not as sexy as yours.'

Not from where I'm sitting. She swallowed the words, reminding herself of the dangers of giving out mixed messages. *So why did you ask him to kiss you?*

God, she really was making a mess of this. It was a wonder he still wanted to talk to her. 'I don't believe you can judge your own legs.' Before he asked her to judge his, she added, 'So, where are we heading and who's going to be there?'

His glance told her he knew she'd deliberately changed the subject. 'We're meeting the gang at Altrincham market. It was given an overhaul a few years ago – it's now one of the trendy places to head outside the city. It's got artisan food traders selling local produce, plus lots of craft stalls.' He shrugged his broad shoulders. 'I figured you might enjoy it.'

Her pulse sped up a gear. 'Hang on, we're heading there for *me*?'

He pulled up to a traffic light and looked over at her. 'Is there something wrong?'

'No, it's just, well I thought you'd planned to see your friends anyway, and I was just tagging along.'

His green eyes were steady on hers. 'I wanted you to meet my friends. This way you can also cross another item off your list.'

Panic bubbled but she tried to squash it. It wasn't like she was his girlfriend. If his friends didn't like her, it didn't matter.

Except he'd specifically arranged today so they could meet her. And she really, really wanted them to like her, because she really, really liked Luke.

As if he could see her mind racing, he touched her cheek. 'Don't overthink this. I thought you might like to meet some more locals, that's all.' He gave her a small smile just as the lights turned green. 'People who don't live in the same block of flats, or frequent the same bar.'

The panic receded. She was getting ahead of herself. They'd kissed, he wanted more, but only *sex* more. Not *relationship* more. And like it or not, she was a relationship kind of girl. 'These people, are they as crazy as you are?'

His laughter filled the car, erasing the knots of tension.

'My brother's wife, Janet, is sane. Phil is bordering on sane. Jim, Sandy's husband, is a saint, which of course he has to be, to put up with her. As for Gary and Tony, they're both single so they'll probably try and flirt with you.'

'Are they as good at it as you?'

His expression was enigmatic as he glanced briefly in her direction. 'I'll leave you to judge.'

Luke rested his arm along the back of Mia's chair, the gesture both protective and proprietorial. As he'd suspected, Gary and Tony were all over her, partly because she was uniquely attractive and razor-sharp funny. Partly because they were the biggest flirts out. And yes, it hadn't escaped his notice that she'd said he was good at flirting, which he knew wasn't a compliment. The thing is, he wasn't a natural flirt, as any of the friends around the table could testify. His skill, if he could call it that, was being able to talk to people, put them at their ease, and when it came to his customers, to make them feel important. Flirting was different. It was compliments, cheeky innuendo, smiling into the other person's eyes, all done because you fancied the pants off them. It was why he'd flirted with Mia when she'd first walked into the bar, but it didn't mean he did it with every woman he served.

And he sure as hell hadn't done any flirting with anyone else since he'd met Mia.

'Luke took you to Old Trafford?' Tony burst out

laughing. 'Christ, he's seriously losing his touch.' His so-called friend spoke to Mia as if Luke wasn't within earshot, sitting just the other side of her. 'If you want a proper tour of the Mancunian highlights love, just say the word. I even work civilised hours.'

'What Tony's not telling you is he's a Blues fan,' Luke interrupted. 'First place he'll take you is the Etihad.'

Tony scoffed. 'I've more class than that.' He winked at Mia. 'We'll head for a Maccy D's first.'

'Aye, and the guy's so tight he'll probably make you pay,' added Phil, earning a big brownie point from Luke.

'It's clear Mia needs a man with more class than you lot.' Gary flashed her a cheesy grin. 'I won't take you to footie stadiums, I'll wine and dine you. Dinner and jazz, dancing and cocktails.'

Mia laughed. 'I'm very … sorry, I'm *dead* grateful for the offers.' She turned to Luke, eyes amused, her smile sweet. 'But Luke's been a good tour guide so far. It seems wrong to sack him just yet.' She turned back to Gary. 'He's already taken me dancing, and as for cocktails, he didn't just buy me one. He concocted the Blue Mia especially for me.'

Phil glanced at him and groaned. 'Mia, please, for all our sakes, stop flattering him. He's already looking obscenely smug.'

'Oh, he was rubbish at the donut racing and his knowledge of art is worse than mine, but cocktails, he's a genius at.' She smiled and gave Luke a brief sideways glance. 'I was thinking, he should offer to make individual cocktails up at the bar. People would really go for that.'

'You think so?' Though he was flattered, Luke couldn't see why someone would choose to drink a ropey cocktail a barman had thrown together instead of a tried and tested classic.

But Phil was looking animated. 'Bloody hell Mia, that's a genius idea. And frankly, with things as they are, anything is worth a try right now.'

Shit no. Luke's stomached dropped. He didn't want the conversation going down that route. He gave his brother a *shut the fuck up* glare.

'We could advertise it as a special service for midweek when business is really slow. Maybe charge a premium for it.' Uncaring or oblivious, Phil carried on talking. 'I mean, it's not going to make up the shortfall, but it could prop things up a bit.'

Luke groaned, briefly slamming his eyes shut and silently counting to ten. He wasn't bothered about the guys hearing Phil's verbal diarrhoea; they knew about the issues with the bar. It was Mia who didn't know. Mia, who was giving him a confused, wide-eyed look that clearly conveyed she felt she was missing an important part of a puzzle.

'I think you've put your rather large feet in it, dear,' Janet said to her husband, giving Luke a sympathetic glance.

Phil winced. 'Sorry mate, didn't realise it was a secret.'

'It's not.' But it wasn't something he wanted to shout about, either. Especially not to the woman he was trying to prove himself to. *Hey Mia, I might have been seeing two women when you met me but I promise I'm not a womaniser. Oh and I might have bought a bar without checking out the accounts properly, even though my brother is a flaming accountant, but I promise I'm not stupid.*

She was still looking at him, huge question marks in her eyes.

'I'll tell you later, okay?' Her answering smile appeared forced, as if she thought he was fobbing her off. As the others started talking about something else, he whispered. 'If you come to the bar tonight we can talk after I've closed up. If you're still interested.'

'Okay.' Her gaze searched his, a hint of … hurt? Disappointment? 'And of course I'm interested. We're friends, remember? If there's anything I can do to help, I want to know.'

Touched, he reached for hand, tightening his fingers around it. 'You're already making a website for me. That's huge, trust me.'

'Good.' Her eyes were fixed on his. 'But if there's anything else you think I can help with, you'll let me know, yes?'

He was tempted to tell her she could sit on his lap and kiss him again, like she had the Saturday before. Let him lose himself in her for a while. And maybe his expression said it for him, because her cheeks turned pink. But she didn't look away. He cleared his throat. 'Deal.'

All too soon Tony snared Mia's attention again and Luke settled back in his chair as his friend moved the conversation on to where she'd gone to university, and why

Manchester uni was better than Bath. Mia argued vigorously against his assertion and soon everyone was piling in with their own uni tales. It wasn't a discussion he could join in with, but instead of feeling left out, he found he was happy just to watch and listen. Content with the knowledge that tonight, he'd have her undivided attention again.

Chapter Twenty-One

Mia felt a sense of heavy anticipation as the last of the customers meandered out of the bar.

Just Bill to go, and then she'd be alone with Luke again. Her belly fluttered as she remembered what had happened the last time she'd stayed behind after the bar had closed.

Bill walked past her, picking up stray glasses. 'Waiting on our Luke are you?'

He gave her a teasing smile and Mia laughed. 'I'm hoping he'll wait on me.'

'And so he should, lovely lass like you.'

'Hey, Bill, hands off. You're too old for her,' Luke shouted from where he was rinsing out glasses.

'Maybe she likes older men.'

Luke pointed to Bill's rounded stomach. 'And overweight older men?'

'Some women go for the teddy-bear look.' Bill waggled his brows at her. 'What do you reckon?'

What Mia reckoned, was she'd never felt more attractive, had such a fuss made over her, than she had today. First Luke's friends, now Bill, all sweetly flirting with her. It said a lot about Luke that the people in his close circle were so friendly, so warm and welcoming, to a virtual stranger.

Luke put his arm round Bill's shoulders and tugged him towards the door. 'Come on old man, time to get you home. Pamela will be wondering where you are.'

'Shh, keep your voice down,' Bill said in an exaggerated whisper. 'I think I might have pulled that lovely lass back there with the blue hair.'

As Luke turned and gave her a sweetly exasperated glance, Mia burst out laughing. She'd heard Luke talk about Bill, about how he'd taught him everything he knew about running a bar, and the affection he had for the older man was obvious.

'Make sure you don't do anything I wouldn't do,' Bill crooned as Luke waved him out. 'Leaves you plenty of scope, mind. Or it would have, in my day. The hips are a bit stiff now, and the ticker not as good as it was. Still, a little blue pill and—'

'Goodnight, Bill,' Luke interrupted firmly. 'I messaged Pamela to say you're on your way, so no dawdling.'

Bill touched his hand to his forehead in a salute, then gave Mia a final wave before heading off.

'Crazy old man,' Luke muttered as he locked the door.

'Yeah, but you love him.'

Luke laughed softly, shaking his head. 'Yeah, I suppose I

do. He's been a hell of a lot more of a father to me than my own, that's for certain.'

Mia raised her eyebrows. 'You're not close to your dad?'

He shrugged his powerful shoulders and she tried not to stare as the muscles flexed beneath his tight polo shirt. 'Not particularly close to either of my parents. Phil still keeps in contact but I was always, well, a bit of a disappointment, I guess.' He pulled a stern face, the next words clearly mimicking his father. 'Doyles are professionals. Not barmen.'

'Being a bartender is a profession,' Mia argued, annoyed for him. 'And now you're a business owner.'

'Yes.' The single word was delivered in a heavy tone, and Mia knew they were about to touch on the subject he'd not wanted her to know about. As his eyes found hers, she saw frustration and sadness. 'Do you mind if we have the conversation I think we're about to have, back at my place?'

His place. So far they'd not been to each other's flats. He'd offered to walk her back last week but she'd declined, worried that if he kissed her goodnight outside her door, she'd invite him in.

Now the worry returned, yet the flash of heat across her skin, the flutter in her belly … they were down to something else entirely. She *wanted* to see his private space. Wanted whatever might happen there, despite the fear that the promise she'd made to herself not to dive into another relationship, was looking shaky.

'Mia?' His concerned gaze found hers. 'You do know I'm not planning some grand seduction? That I've not put black silk sheets on the bed? Hell, I've not even changed the sheets, so you're quite safe, because no way does Luke Doyle tempt a woman into his bed if his sheets aren't clean.'

She laughed at his silliness, but the flat green of his eyes told her he was upset. Hurt, no doubt, at what he believed her silence implied. That she didn't trust him. 'Sorry, I didn't mean to go quiet on you.' She rose to her feet. 'I'd like to see your place.' Walking up to him, she gave his arm a nudge. 'See the famous weight room where you post your messages.'

Amusement flickered across his handsome face. 'You mean the room where you ogle me as I work out.'

'I do not.' The lie burst from her with an impressive degree of righteous indignation. She might have convinced him, if her cheeks hadn't been burning.

'Of course you don't,' he replied smoothly, clearly struggling to keep a straight face. 'Just as I don't put on a show, moving closer to the window when I see you at your desk.' As she tried to take in what he was saying – that he liked her eyes on him – he grasped her hand and led her to the door. 'Come on, I need to get out of this place for a few hours.'

And that, she realised with a mixture of shame and embarrassment, was why he wanted to take her back to his. Not because he wanted to jump her, but because he'd been working for eight straight hours and wanted to get home.

The first thing she noticed when she set foot inside his flat was how neat it was. She'd assumed the carefree bartender with the casual strut and lazy smile would have an equally laid-back approach to other areas of his life. Instead the work surfaces in his kitchen were clear, the sink lacking any lunch/breakfast dishes that hadn't yet found their way into the dishwasher, and his sofa was free of the junk that seemed to collect on hers.

'Bet it looks just like yours, huh?' he asked as he flipped on some low lighting.

'Mine without the clutter.' And that's when she noticed the second thing. 'Err, there's a giant rat with long ears jumping onto your sofa.'

Luke followed the direction of her gaze and sighed. 'Pickles, how many times do I have to tell you, no jumping on the sofa unless I'm on it.' With the ease of a man who'd done it thousands of times before, he scooped the furry animal into his big hands and kissed the tip of its nose. 'Pickles, meet Mia. Mia, meet the woman I share my flat with.'

'Wow.' Mia stared, transfixed, into the rabbit's deep brown eyes. 'Dare I ask why you have a rabbit?'

She wasn't sure if it was her imagination but he looked a little uncomfortable. 'Probably a conversation for another day.' Nodding towards the hallway, he asked, 'Do you want to see the weight/message room?'

'Of course.' She mentally slotted Pickles into the increasing list of questions she wanted to ask him but hadn't yet. Along with why he'd gone straight into bartending when his family and friends were clearly academic achievers. And why he seemed to prefer casual relationships based on sex, rather than anything more meaningful, when it was clear he was a lot deeper than he let on.

She smiled when she saw the pile of poster paper and coloured marker pens as he led her into his spare room. Weights and dumb-bells were stacked neatly along the wall, and a giant multi-gym dominated the centre of the room. 'So this is where you put on your show.'

He grinned, flexing his biceps, and though the gesture was funny, the reaction of her body was far more primitive. She'd never been a woman impressed by male strength, by a ripped body, yet now, when she looked at Luke, she couldn't not see how fit he looked. Couldn't not wonder what it would be like to feel those hard muscles over her, under her. Surrounding her.

Desperate to shake off the increasing arousal, she wandered over to the window, staring into her own flat. 'You know I don't just stare at you when I'm working.'

'There are other dudes flexing their muscles at you?'

He said it with such clear disgust, she had to laugh. 'I was referring to the woman who lives in the flat next to you.' She turned to face him. 'Do you know her?'

Now it wasn't her imagination. He definitely looked uncomfortable, like she'd unearthed some guilty secret he didn't want to share. 'Yeah, I know her.'

Clearly another woman he'd slept with. Jealousy burned through her, and Mia hated both the feeling, and what it represented. She could no longer claim she saw Luke as just a friend. 'I think of her as Immaculate Woman,' she rambled on, because talking was better than thinking. 'She's always so put together. Every morning she's at her desk, dressed all prim and tidy, before I've even managed to fall out of bed.'

It hadn't escaped her notice that of the women she knew he'd slept with, all were glamorous, carefully put together. And very different to her.

Luke did not want to talk about his neighbour. Just as he didn't want to talk about why he, a thirty-four-year-old guy, owned a rabbit. They were conversations for a later date, when Mia knew him better and, he hoped, would judge him less harshly.

'That sounds about right.' When she frowned over at him, he clarified. 'I mean about my neighbour. She's very … uptight, I think you'd call it.' He cleared his throat. 'So, the bar.' It came to something when he'd rather talk about his current screw-up, than a past screw-up. 'Are you still interested? Because if you are, I'm going to need a drink and a sit down.'

'Yes, sure.'

'We could talk about something else if you prefer. Something more fun,' he added so she wasn't tempted to go back to the rabbit or the neighbour. 'Or if you don't want to talk, we could watch a film.' He considered her. 'Maybe dust off my PlayStation? I bet you think you're a whizz on the games console, being a computer nerd and all that.'

She raised an eyebrow. 'Is that a challenge?'

He grinned. 'Nah, think of it as more of a subtle enquiry.

Whether I lay down the challenge depends on your answer.'

'I don't think I'm a whizz.' She put her hands on her hips and gave him a long, slow, cocky smile. 'I *know* I am.'

God, he loved that look on her. 'Bring it on then, super-geek.'

She wagged a finger at him. 'Sure, after you've told me what Phil was inferring about the bar.' She frowned. 'Didn't you say you bought the place from Bill?'

'I did.' He was loath to say too much because Bill was, well, *Bill*. 'Come on, let's get a drink and see if Pickles will let us on the sofa.'

A few minutes later they carried their drinks – two whiskies, he didn't do cocktails in his flat – back to the living area. Pickles frustratingly jumped up to sit between them, twitching her nose like she didn't approve of Mia sitting close to him.

Nursing his glass, Luke leant forward, resting his arms on his knees, and started to explain about the rather large gap Phil had found in the accounts.

Mia gasped. 'Bill was fiddling the books?'

'No, God no. We think it was his bookkeeper. Bill's great at running a bar, but like me, he wasn't so great with numbers. And he was too bloody trusting.'

He could feel Mia's gaze on him. 'You haven't told him about the shortfall, have you?'

'No.' He turned to Mia. 'And please keep this to yourself. The guy's worked his arse off for the last God knows how many years. He deserves a good, long retirement.'

'Semi-retirement,' she corrected. 'He still works for you.'

'Yeah, now and again. Says Pamela likes him better when she's not seen him all day.'

Mia smiled. 'Funny.' Then her face sobered, and as she placed a hand on his cheek, his heart bounced against his ribs. 'You're a really good guy, Luke Doyle.'

He wanted to wallow in her kind words, to lap them up like flowers drink in the sun. Yet it wasn't true, was it? He wasn't all good. He only had to ask any of the long list of women in his phone. Good would be the last word they'd use to describe him. Funny, hot, sexy, maybe. But some would probably say he was hard, unfeeling and selfish, too. Shame rolled through him. He'd thought what he was doing was harmless fun, that he wasn't hurting anyone, yet now he saw it all through Mia's eyes and wondered if that had ever really been the case.

Her hand was still on his face though, her expression soft, as if she really liked what she saw. Not just on the outside, but on the inside. Probably that would change the more she got to know him, but for now he was selfish enough to grab what she offered with both hands. 'Thank you.' He paused while he got his emotions back in check. 'It's only fair to warn you that while the jury is still out on whether I'm a good guy, what is undisputed is that I'm a flaming awesome gamer.'

Mia fell back against the sofa, laughing so hard it upset Pickles, who twitched her nose and scampered off.

Good, he thought as he slid closer to Mia, so close he could feel the press of her thigh against his. He didn't want a bucktoothed chaperone.

They argued for a few minutes over which game to play, in the end settling for *Rocket League* as, in Mia's words, it had less guts and gore than *Call of Duty*.

'I'm not sure if I should admit this,' he said as they waited for the game to load. 'But knowing you play *CoD* actually turns me on.'

Her eyes grew like saucers and then she started to cough, more of a splutter really, like the shock had caused her to inhale her own saliva.

'I'm thinking, by your reaction, I shouldn't have admitted it?'

She swallowed a few times. 'God, I don't know what to do with that information.' Then she pointed to the screen. 'Luckily I don't need to do anything right now, because I'm about to kick your arse.'

He didn't have a chance to reply, because the game started and soon he needed all his focus to stop her from annihilating him.

God, the speed of her thumbs over that controller. It was flaming awesome. As she cursed, yelled and generally behaved like every guy gamer he'd ever played with, Luke took a moment just to appreciate her. It was like having a best mate over, but one he also wanted to make out with. Something he could say, with absolute certainty, he'd never wanted to do with Jim, Tony or Gary.

'You're going down, you sucker!'

At Mia's gleeful exclamation, Luke snapped his attention back to the screen, but it was too late. The game was over. 'Damn it, I never lose.'

'Because you only play in the minor leagues.'

He took in her flushed face, the gleam in her eye, the gloating expression. And felt his heart cartwheel. Shit, hearts didn't do that because you *liked* someone. They did it when you were *falling* for them.

He pushed aside the thought, desperate to find firmer footing. 'No way am I minor league. I'm a pro. You just distracted me with all your shouting and swearing.' She started to shake her head dismissively so he added, 'And with your warm thigh pressed against mine.'

That shut her up. Immediately she glanced down, and though he knew he was right – hell, he'd been hyper aware of her all through the game – it was disappointing to see she hadn't realised, until now.

Then again, she also hadn't moved away. Instead her lips parted, and her breathing became faster.

'Name your prize,' he said huskily, staring into blue eyes that looked as turbulent as he felt.

She licked her lips. Consciously or unconsciously? 'What are the choices?'

'I can kiss you for a minute. Kiss you for two minutes. Or kiss you until you tell me to stop.'

The breath from her laugh fluttered across his face. 'That's quite a narrow choice.'

'What can I say? Loser gets to pick the prize for the winner. House rules.'

A shadow crossed her face. 'Do you always give away kisses?'

He swore under his breath. 'It was a joke. I don't invite women here, Mia. I don't game with them either. Only friends.' He reached to touch her lips. 'And you are most definitely the only friend I've ever wanted to kiss.'

A hint of a smile returned to her face. 'Tony and Gary don't do it for you, huh?'

His lips returned the smile, but his eyes, his focus, remained on her. He couldn't explain why the moment felt so significant, why his heart was racing, his stomach a mess of twisted knots. All because of the woman sitting next to him, her mouth only inches from his. 'You're the only one I want, Mia.' Because he knew she wasn't ready yet, didn't trust him enough, he lightened the mood. 'So, which prize is it to be? A, B or C?'

'C.' Her voice came out in a whisper.

Luke felt his lips tingle, his groin harden. 'Excellent choice.'

Chapter Twenty-Two

Mia stared into Luke's eyes and felt her whole body shudder. God, she was drowning in him. Unable to move away, unable to even untangle her gaze from the intense green of his.

Why had she chosen be kissed until she told him to stop? It might sound the most sensible, giving her the control, but if it was anything like the last kiss she couldn't see herself ever asking him to stop.

'Are you ready?'

Good God, he was sexy. The most gorgeous, most attractive man she'd ever met, never mind kissed. All those average guys she'd dated, the likes of Pete and Danny… Elle was right, she'd *settled*.

Yet was Luke, a ridiculously hot, decidedly un-average charmer, any better for her?

'Mia?' A small crease appeared between his dark brows.

'Sorry.' Stuff the doubts, she was only going to kiss him. 'I'm ready.'

His mouth grazed hers, the mere hint of a touch, and her body trembled. 'I never thought Smurfs would be this sexy.'

She huffed out a laugh, feeling a slow sizzle in her stomach. She'd forgotten to add *insanely funny* to his list of attributes. 'I never thought I'd have to wait so long for my prize.'

It was all the push he needed. Immediately his lips found hers, and this time there was no slow build-up. This time his tongue plundered, his mouth almost feverish against hers. It was like he was trying to inhale her, to drink her in, and the evidence of his hunger, his need, gave her a sharp thrill. Before long he was leaning them both back along the sofa, his powerful body stretched out over hers, the long, hard length of him evident as it pressed against her thigh, creating bursts of heat across her skin.

Still his mouth tortured and teased, but now his hand had moved to her breast, cupping it lightly over her dress. 'Is this okay?'

'Yes,' she croaked. It felt more than okay. It felt like he was searing her skin, even through the material. Her nipples were hard peaks, her core a molten heat. But if they went further, surely the route back to friends would be blocked and God, she did not want to lose this man from her life.

His hand left her breast and smoothed down her side. When he raised his eyes to look at her they were no longer green but flecked with orange, burning like flames. 'Kissing you is like a roaring fire on a cold winter's day. A pint of lager on a sunny day.' He bent his head again, planting a trail of kisses along her jaw, then across her cheeks and up to her forehead. He smiled, eyes crinkling at the corners. 'United winning the Champions League.'

Laughter bubbled in her chest, even as her body ached and throbbed with the feel of him. '*Now*, I'm flattered.'

'You should be.' He nibbled lightly at her lips, causing pleasure to zing through her. 'It's the most romantic phrase a Mancunian can utter.'

'I'm always looking for romantic phrases.'

'Ah yes, for your book.' He was half sprawled across her, his arousal *very* evident, yet he really did seem content to talk, to kiss. To just be with her. 'Stick with me and you'll have plenty of inspiration.'

She didn't reply, couldn't because once again he was kissing her. Lighter than before, more playful than hungry, yet equally as potent. Time passed, and Mia began to feel more and more boneless. If she closed her eyes, she could sleep here, Luke's body nestled against her, his lips dancing across her skin…

She jerked upright as she felt something jump onto her stomach. And stared straight into a pair of inquisitive brown eyes.

'Pickles, how many times do I have to tell you not to jump on guests? It's rude.' Luke sighed and eased himself upright, cradling the rabbit against his chest. 'It's only me who likes you.' He lifted one of her floppy ears and whispered into it. 'And big hint, I won't like you much longer if you scare Mia away.'

As if she understood him, Pickles turned to look at her. 'Does her nose always twitch like that, or is she plotting ways to get rid of me so she can have you all to herself?'

Luke chuckled. 'Her nose always twitches, and the fact that she jumped on you means she likes you. When the guys come round, she scarpers.' After dropping Pickles gently back onto the floor, his gaze skimmed Mia's face. 'Shall we continue where we left off, or has rabbit interruptus effectively killed the mood?'

Snuggling back down with him sounded exactly what she wanted, but Mia was acutely aware that if they did, she might end up forgetting why sleeping with him was a bad idea. 'I'd better get back.' She glanced at her watch, and winced. 'It's three in the morning.'

'Umm.' Reaching for her hand, he entwined their fingers. 'You don't need to go back, you know. I have a perfectly good couch you can sleep on. Or a bed you're welcome to, and I can sleep on the couch.' He paused, and the air around them seemed to electrify. 'Or we could share my bed.'

The saliva from her mouth disappeared, and what seemed like a swarm of butterflies began to flap in her stomach. Her flat was in the same complex, it really wasn't far, yet the thought of just crashing here, with him … the butterflies flapped harder.

It was a big step though. Was it really sensible to make it so late at night, with alcohol potentially muddying the waters? She wasn't drunk, but she had knocked back a few beers, a Blue Mia and a whisky. 'I thought the sheets weren't clean.'

He smiled, releasing her hand to trace a finger down her cheek, his gaze soft. 'I can swap them. Or I can walk you back. Or we can do anything in between.'

Mia swallowed. 'If we share a bed…' she trailed off, her usual ability to say what she thought, deserting her.

'I'm not suggesting we have sex.' He flashed her his heart-stopping smile. 'Of course I'm not *not* suggesting it either, just to be clear, but I can see you're not ready for that step.' He ran his hands up and down her arms, his expression so tender she felt her heart fill. 'It's late, we're tired. Crash here, Mia. I can build a wall of cushions between us if it helps.'

Her brain was so tangled with emotion, she wasn't sure what words would come out if she opened her mouth. In the past, she'd moved from kissing to sex easily, the distinction never feeling as important as it did now, the decision never weighing so heavily. *Because this time, you have something to lose.*

Just because she was scared to lose him though, didn't mean she was ready to dismiss the possibility of more with him. So she rose from the sofa and reached for his hand. 'Let's go to bed.'

After shooting through the bathroom, taking time to inhale his aftershave in between peeing and rubbing toothpaste over her teeth with her finger, Mia eased off her leggings and snuck under the duvet. A few minutes later

Luke joined her, slipping in behind and wrapping his arms around her. She felt cocooned in him, the warmth of his bare chest against her back, the citrus tang of his aftershave invading her senses.

'Excuse Moby,' he mumbled against her neck as she felt a tell-tale hardness pressing against her buttocks. 'I've told him there won't be any action, but he doesn't always listen.'

She bit into her lip, trying not to laugh. 'Moby? Oh, I get it, Moby because he was also a Dick.'

'Yeah. And because he was also frigging huge.'

Laughter spluttered out of her, and along with it a feeling of utter contentment. He felt so *good* behind her. And yes, huge, he wasn't wrong. Also hot, hard and the most incredible turn-on. Yet it also felt natural to be lying like this with him. No awkwardness, as there had been with other dates that had ended up in bed. Just warmth, pleasure – God, so much pleasure – and a real feeling of rightness.

With a deep, happy sigh, she drifted off to sleep.

Luke woke feeling almost unbearably aroused, his morning erection pressed firmly into the most delectable buttocks he'd ever been lucky enough to find himself lying next to.

But doing anything about it was strictly off the cards. He should move away, get up and get dressed. It was without doubt the sensible option, yet also the most ridiculous because who knew when or if he'd ever get the chance to cuddle Mia like this again? So instead he stayed where he was, relishing the ache until she started to stir.

'Moby's still not listening,' he whispered. 'But to be fair, he's not used to waking up against such a gorgeous cushion.'

She turned, ruining his fun, though it was probably for the best. There was only so long he could torture himself before he exploded like an adolescent schoolboy.

'Is that another of those romantic lines I should take a note of?'

Sleepy blue eyes blinked up at him and he felt something shift in his chest. Mia first thing in the morning was headed straight to the top of his list of favourite sights. 'It is,' he confirmed. 'And if you want to hang around for breakfast, I can give you a few more.'

She glanced at his bedside clock and groaned. 'It's nine already. I should get going.' Throwing off the duvet, she slipped out of the bed.

'Hey, not so fast. At least let me make you a coffee.' He scrambled out of bed and immediately felt the heat of Mia's gaze on him.

'Wow.'

She stared at his chest, and he wasn't going to lie, he flexed his muscles, just a little, under her admiring look. 'You've seen it all before.'

'Yeah, but not this close.' Her eyes grew impossibly wide, and he knew what she'd seen.

'Want to have a closer look?' He gave his eyebrows a

comic waggle in an attempt to dial down the sexual tension because his dick was throbbing again.

Her gaze hadn't strayed below his waist though. She walked towards him, eyes on the silver nipple piercing he'd had done when he was nineteen and out to prove something. 'Did it hurt?'

'Nah.' She kept staring and he cleared his throat. 'You can touch it, if you like.'

Her lips twitched. 'Are we still talking about the piercing?'

God, he was in trouble here. 'To be clear, I'd love your hands on all of me, but yeah, you can start with the piercing.' Her fingers tentatively touched the ring and he hissed, the ache between his legs intensifying.

'Why did you have it done?'

Ah. Embarrassed, he glanced away. That was one sure-fire way to cool his arousal. Ask him a searching question about his youth. 'I thought the girls would like it.'

'Is that why you work out with weights, too? To attract the opposite sex?'

Ouch. Now he sounded shallow, and maybe he was, but there was other stuff behind that decision. Stuff he didn't want to tell her yet because it would further dent her opinion of him. 'Is it working?' he asked instead, forcing his mouth into a cocky smile.

She didn't see it, because she seemed intent on watching her fingers as they trailed across his pecs and down to his abs. His muscles quivered as her touch left a burning trail of heat that went straight to the part of him that strained beneath his boxers. He was seconds from pleading with her to touch him there, when she snatched her hand away, as if suddenly aware of what she was doing.

That's when her eyes landed on the side of his ribcage. The tattoo was small; most women didn't notice it or if they did, they weren't bothered enough to ask about it. He *wanted* Mia to ask, to show an interest in *him*, not just his body, even though he wasn't ready to give her an answer.

But instead she turned away and picked up the small black handbag she'd left on the floor by the bed. 'Thanks for the offer of coffee but I need to get back to my desk. I have this website I need to make.'

'On a Sunday?'

'This one is in my own time.'

Damn it. Guilt wormed through him as he realised whose website she was talking about. Yet even as he reached for her arm to stop her, to tell her to forget it, he'd bloody hire someone else to make the damn thing, he saw her guard come down, shutting him out. 'Please don't leave yet, not like this.' He searched her face, trying to work out what was going on behind her gorgeous blue eyes. 'What's going on? You seem upset.'

Her eyes avoided his. 'I'm not. I just need to get back to mine.'

Reluctantly he let go of her arm and grabbed his black jeans from where he'd discarded them on the floor, carefully easing the zip over his now fading erection. 'Okay, I'll see you out.'

She rolled her eyes. 'Your flat has the same layout as

mine. I think I can find the front door.'

He gave her a wry smile. 'Yeah, but you've forgotten there's a beast out there. I don't want you to come to any harm.'

The guard dropped, just a little, but whatever she was about to say in reply was halted by the sound of a female voice.

'Luke, are you still in bed?'

His heart plummeted. Shit, what was she doing here?

'It's my neighbour,' he muttered to Mia, yanking a clean T-shirt from the drawer and shoving it over his head. Her arrival was all he bloody needed. Already Mia was thinking God knows what about his tattoo, about his vain need to attract women…

'Immaculate Woman has a key to your flat?'

'Yeah, though she's not supposed to use it,' he added grimly.

'Then why does she have one? Is it just to look after the place when you're away, or…' she trailed off, the unasked question clear in her eyes. *Or is she another of the women you've been sleeping with?*

'It's complicated, Mia.' It was a crap answer, but now wasn't the time to dump his past on her. Not when a big part of that past had just let herself into his flat.

Pulling the bedroom door open, he strode down the hallway to face the unwanted visitor.

Freya stood in the kitchen, and Luke almost smiled when he saw how she was, indeed, living up to Mia's name for her. Even on a Sunday, Freya was carefully made up, her trousers neatly pressed, her top clearly designer. 'What do you want?'

Her dark eyebrows shot up. 'What sort of greeting is that?'

'The sort of greeting you deserve when you use my key to enter my flat without my permission.'

But Freya wasn't listening now. Her focus was behind Luke. 'I see you have a guest.'

The morning had held so much promise, he thought gloomily as he remembered how he'd woken up. Now it was heading downhill faster than a bloody bobsleigh on an icy track. 'Freya, meet Mia who lives in the flats opposite.' He turned and met Mia's wary blue gaze. 'Mia, meet my neighbour.'

Freya quirked a brow at him. 'Neighbour? Is that all I get?'

He was not ready for this conversation. Neither, it seemed, was Mia.

'Nice to meet you.' She gave Freya a stiff smile before turning back to him. 'I guess I'll see you around.'

'Keep an eye on my window.'

He smiled but she didn't return it. Instead her expression remained uncertain, tense, and his worry about what she was thinking intensified.

Maybe he should have told her everything, his whole history, even if it did only serve to reinforce her opinion of him as some sort of Lothario. At least then he'd know she was damning him for what he had done, rather than whatever the heck her mind had made up.

Mia walked out and once the door had closed behind her, Freya spoke. 'Keep an eye on your window?'

'It's nothing to do with you, Freya. Now tell me what was so important, you had to break into my flat?'

'I hardly broke in.' She gave him a cool look. 'I just thought you'd like to know Grace's flight has landed. I'm on my way to pick her up.'

'Great, a phone call would have done, but thanks for letting me know.'

As he saw Freya out, a little of the misery of the morning melted away.

God, how he needed a dose of Grace's irrepressible, sunny nature right now.

Chapter Twenty-Three

As Mia unlocked the door to her flat, Stan came out of his.

'Morning.' His eyes ran up and down her, no doubt taking in her unbrushed hair, her creased shirt. 'Don't normally see you up and about this early on a Sunday.'

'No.' Shit, was she blushing?

Stan's face took on a broad, shit-eating grin. 'Well I never. You're not up and about early, you're coming back late.'

Damn it. 'I stayed over at a friend's.' A guy she'd slept in the same bed with, but who it turns out has a woman's name tattooed on his rib, and a neighbour – a stunningly attractive neighbour – who thought nothing of letting herself into his flat. And if that wasn't enough, he also has a hot-as-hell body and an intensely erotic nipple piercing, all so he can attract women. *Why did she keep forgetting the reasons she'd decided not to get involved with him in the first place?*

'This friend, he wouldn't happen to be male, would he?'

'Maybe.' Mia pushed open the door. 'Well, it's been good chatting, but I've got things I need to do.' She'd not been lying about the website. She needed to crack on with it, especially now she knew how important expanding Luke's business actually was.

'The male friend of yours wouldn't happen to own a bar,' Stan continued, ignoring her. 'And have a first name beginning with L?'

She glanced back at Stan, who looked at her all smug, like he'd unearthed a big, juicy secret. 'Reckon you've got it all worked out, huh?'

'It's not hard, love. The pair of you have been … what was it you said before, dancing around each other like a couple of frisky peafowl?' He chuckled delightedly at his own joke.

'Ha ha. We're mates, nothing more. We were gaming until the early hours so I crashed on his couch.' *Liar, you slept with his hot, hard erection nestled against your bum. And you loved it.*

This time Stan's chuckle turned into a loud guffaw. 'You're trying to tell me Luke Doyle had a woman stay overnight in his flat and *didn't* get her into his bed?'

And bam, just like that, her sexy thoughts vanished, replaced by nastier ones; jealousy of those that had gone before her, shame that she'd fallen so easily for his charms, despite knowing better.

Yet the fact he hadn't pushed, had seemed happy just to hold her, shouldn't be forgotten. He was a player, but he was also a decent guy. It's just he wasn't one she'd ever be able to trust.

Stan looked expectantly at her, so she did what anyone would when backed into a corner. 'Enough about me. How are things with you and Naomi? Have you summoned up the balls to ask her out yet?'

Yeah, that took the wind out of his sails. 'Why would I do that?'

At his flustered expression, affection coiled through her. 'Because you like her, you dolt. And she likes you.'

'Happen we're just friends.' He gave her a sly glance. 'Like you and Mr Doyle.'

She let out a bark of laughter. 'Well played.' Leaning against the doorframe, Mia gave Stan a sad smile. 'What a pair we are, huh? Both too scared, for whatever reason, to grasp something that could potentially be so good.'

'Aye. Could potentially explode in our faces too, mind.'

'There is that.' She eyed him curiously. 'I know why I'm scared, but what's stopping you?'

Stan glanced down his body, then looked back at Mia. 'I'm a grumpy, overweight, boring old git.'

'Says who?'

'Says the last woman I asked out.' He humphed. 'She stuck with me for thirty-odd years, mind. Buggered off when I retired seven years ago.' A cloud crossed his face. 'Turns out she couldn't carry on with her affairs when I was home all the time.'

'Ouch, Stan. I'm sorry.' She smiled sympathetically. 'If it helps, she was only right about the overweight part.'

He eyed her dubiously. 'You reckon I'm not grumpy?'

'Maybe a little. But I also reckon you know exactly how to charm a woman when you want to.' She gave his middle a gentle nudge. 'So why don't we work on that overweight part and see what happens?'

'I'll have to give up the custard donuts.'

The despondency in his tone made her smile. 'I'm sure we can find another reason for you to go to the café. She does a mean skinny latte, and an excellent granola bar.' Horror crossed his face, and Mia fell about laughing. 'God, Stan, you're so easy to wind up. You don't need to give up everything you enjoy. Climb the stairs instead of taking the lift, don't put sugar in your tea, go for a power walk every day.' She narrowed her eyes. 'Save the bacon butties for a weekend treat. That way I won't be tortured by the smell of sizzling bacon every damn day.'

He gave her a sheepish grin. 'I'll think about it. What about you and the Chipmunk?'

She groaned. 'That is not a good nickname.'

'Doesn't answer my question.'

Mia sighed. 'Truthfully? I don't know. I like him.' Understatement of the year. Gorgeous, funny, sexy, *kind* – her heart had melted when he'd told her about Bill. 'But I'm wary, Stan. I've had too many crap relationships to want to start one that, even from the outset, looks destined for failure.'

Stan shuffled on his feet. 'What I said about him

sleeping with all the single women in the block. It's likely stuff and nonsense. Daft people with nothing else better to do, making up gossip.'

'Good try, but I know it's not all nonsense.'

'A bloke can change, given the right incentive.'

'I don't doubt it.' But realistically, was she, a blue-haired, sloppy-clothed computer geek, incentive enough?

For the rest of the day Mia found it hard to concentrate. By six in the evening she was still thinking of Luke. Mostly of why she shouldn't be thinking of him, yet was unable to stop.

Out of habit, she once again stared into his flat.

And that's when she saw Luke and a woman in his weight room. Not Immaculate Woman this time. Someone dressed more casually, in jeans, her hair flowing freely over her shoulders. She couldn't see her face, she was standing too far back, but she could see her point to where Mia knew he kept the sheets of paper. And from her body language, Mia knew she was laughing.

As Mia continued to watch a cold feeling of unease settled in the pit of her stomach. Shameful as it sounded, if she'd owned a pair of binoculars, she'd have used them. Who was this person he seemed so at ease with? Were they laughing because the idea of messaging across the flats was quaint? Cute even? Or were they laughing at how ridiculous it was that this person he knew, this supposed friend, refused to give him her number, so he had to resort to communication by taping sheets of paper into a window?

It had been nearly a week since Luke had seen Mia. He knew she'd left his flat upset and annoyed, and he could hardly blame her. Having spent most of Saturday night coming on to her, having slept with her in his arms, in his bed, he'd then shamefully not told her exactly who the woman was who'd brazenly walked into his flat.

Figuring it was best to give Mia breathing space, he'd not asked her out this week, settling instead for putting up a few messages she wouldn't have to reply to. That way he could convince himself she was still talking to him.

Monday he'd messaged:

On the PS4 2nite

Honing my skills

Tuesday he'd messaged:

Getting better…

Wednesday he'd messaged:

I'm badass now.

Be afraid…

By Thursday the ache in his chest whenever he thought

of her had become so acute, before he'd gone to bed he'd posted:

I miss U.

Now it was Friday night, and he was trudging wearily home. The bar had been steady, which was something, but Friday and weekends always were. It was during the week he desperately needed things to pick up.

His phone rang as he walked into his flat. At this hour, five before midnight, it could only be one person.

'Hang on a sec, Phil. Just let me feed the monster.' Clattering the phone onto the worktop, he made a fuss of Pickles, who'd scampered over to greet him.

'At least someone loves me, huh?' he crooned, then laughed as she ducked out of the way of his hands and sat expectantly next to her feed bowl. 'Cupboard love, really, that's all there is between us?'

He grabbed a handful of food and dumped it into her bowl, giving her ears another stroke because hell, at least she wanted him, even if it was only for dried pellets. Then he picked up the phone again. 'Okay, I'm all yours.'

'Just thought I'd touch base. Find out how my brother and his budding non-romance was going.'

Luke kicked off his shoes and slumped down on the sofa. 'Not a good time to ask that. Pick another topic.'

'Seriously? You expect me to ignore that massively open goal?'

'Expect, no. Hope, yes.'

'Come on, I'm just showing concern for my kid brother. I thought you looked good together. She's far too smart for you, obviously, but aside from that, I totally approve. I like that she's got this edgy vibe, with the blue hair and the sharp humour, but inside she's clearly a softie. I mean, why else would she make you a website for free? And don't think I didn't notice the definitely-not-just-friends chemistry between the pair of you.'

'Yeah, well, things took a nosedive when Freya decided to surprise us by walking bold as brass into the flat on Sunday morning. Being a dumb twat, I chose not to tell Mia who Freya was, instead I gave her some crap about it being complicated—'

'Whoa,' Phil interrupted. 'Can we rewind that last bit. Mia stayed the night?'

Luke sighed, slumping further down the sofa. Why hadn't he just said *the budding non-romance is fine* and moved the sodding conversation along? 'She crashed at mine because it was late. Sex was not involved. End of story.' Though alarmingly, sleeping with his arms around her in the same bed had felt better than most of the sex he'd had. As for having her touch him the next morning, fingers teasing his piercing, feathering across his chest? Hands down better than any sex he'd had. 'Now what did you really phone for?'

'I did actually phone to ask about Mia, because I liked her.'

The sincerity in Phil's voice touched Luke. 'Thanks. I guess it's kind of obvious I like her, too.'

'Janet would call you out for that statement. She told me she'd never seen you more animated, more besotted over a woman. She reckons you're falling for Mia, big time.'

She's not wrong. Luke felt his throat constrict around the words. He couldn't say them out loud because it would make it too real, and he was shit scared he was falling for someone who didn't feel the same way.

'Okay, so you're not going to take the juicy bait I wriggled in front of you.' Phil sighed. 'Bloody shame that, because it's so long since I've seen you twisted in knots over a girl, I'd forgotten how entertaining it is. Still, I'll cover the embarrassing silence with the second reason for my call. Have you had any more thoughts about holding a designer cocktail evening? Mia's idea was spot on. You can design cocktails for people, or help them design one for that special person. It would really give you a USP.' Luke could almost see the cogs of his brother's mind working. 'You know what, if we found somewhere that could package them up, we could extend it nationwide. Cocktails posted 2 U. It's a bloody brilliant idea.' Luke could hear the excitement in Phil's voice. 'People tell you what the person is like, you know their personality, you design a cocktail for them and we package it off.'

'I hate to deflate you, but there are already companies who send cocktails through the post.' Companies who knew what they were doing. Luke wasn't even sure he could run a bar.

'Yeah, but their cocktails aren't specifically designed for the customer.'

'What if they hate what I've put together? What if I can't mix new cocktails that taste halfway decent?'

'Come on, where's your self-belief? Your ambition?'

Luke hung his head. He could almost hear the demons from the past laughing at him. *Such a disappointment, he'll never amount to much. He's not gone to university, he's working in a bar…*

Clearly aware he'd overstepped, Phil let out a long, drawn-out breath. 'Sorry, I got a bit carried away there.'

Luke grunted. 'You think?'

A pause, and Luke knew his brother was choosing his next words carefully. 'What I think is, you're far more capable than you believe.'

Once again Luke felt emotion claw at his throat. 'Thanks for the show of faith, but on current evidence, learning to walk before I try to run seems like a good bet.'

'Does that mean the design-a-cocktail evening is a goer, but Cocktails posted 2 U is on the back burner?'

God, his brother. Where would he be without him? 'It means I've already talked to Sandy, and next Wednesday we're holding our first Cocktails 4 U evening.'

'You're kidding? You already thought of 4 U? I mean, it's not as cool as *posted 2 U*, but it's not bad.'

'Thanks,' Luke replied dryly. 'Can we call this conversation over now, so I can get out of the clothes I've spent the last twelve hours in and take a shower?'

'Okay, cocktail master. I'll catch you another time.'

Luke smirked. 'Sorry, did you say cock*tail* master or…?'

'Definitely time to call the conversation over. 'Night, brother.'

After his shower, Luke padded to the kitchen to grab a drink of water, then made his way to the spare room. As expected, there was no answering *Miss U 2* message in her window. It was time to push for a response. See if she was still talking to him.

Finding the pen, he scrawled out his message and stuck it in the window. Then sent up a silent prayer that when he woke up, he'd have a positive reply.

Chapter Twenty-Four

Every day this week Mia had woken to a message from Luke. The first few had made her smile, the *I miss U* had actually brought tears to her eyes. Each time she'd thought about sending a reply though, she'd remembered how cross she was with him.

Even if she ignored the kissing, and she was trying really hard to do that, she and Luke were supposed to be friends. She'd admitted all her dodgy relationship history to him. Yet it seemed the sharing only went one way and he was hiding a huge chunk of his life from her.

A chunk that included attractive women who had free access to his flat. Women he'd not told her about. *It's complicated.* The fob-off had really hurt. Her relationship with Pete had turned complicated, but she'd told Luke anyway.

Despite her annoyance though, her pulse picked up pace

when she walked into the spare room and noticed a new message:

Come to mine this a.m.

Plz.

On a second sheet he'd written:

Need 2 talk.

She sucked in a breath, ignoring the dip in her stomach. Maybe he was finally going to open up to her.

Picking up a sheet, she scrawled.

10 a.m.?

Figuring he was still asleep – it was only half eight, she'd woken early to put the final touches to his website – she was about to head off to grab a coffee when she saw movement in his window. A moment later, he'd put up his reply:

Thx

She tried, and mostly succeeded, to get her head down for the next hour or so. There were the occasional glimpses at his window to check him out as he did his usual weight routine. An hour early today, it was impossible to resist now she'd seen his body close up. Touched the hard muscles of his chest and seen them quiver in response.

Heat washed through her and Mia had to take a moment to breathe. To squeeze her legs together to stop the ache between her thighs.

Just friends … yeah, she'd totally mucked that up. Why couldn't she have stuck at liking him? Why did she have to go and fancy him, too?

But it didn't matter, because she wasn't going to act on it. She didn't want to always be worrying about the women he'd told her about, and the ones he hadn't. Those in his phone book, and those who sidled up to him in the bar. A magnet for the opposite sex, a man who loved women so much he went to the trouble of looking good to attract them.

That was not a man a smart woman would fall for.

By the time she knocked on Luke's door, Mia had her hormones firmly locked up.

Then he opened it, and the sight of him freshly showered, his skin glowing, his muscles looking huge beneath the tight white T-shirt … those damn hormones burst free.

'Thanks for coming.' He ran a hand through his still-damp hair and gave her a rueful, endearingly uncertain smile. 'I wasn't sure you would.'

'It doesn't mean I'm not pissed at you.'

'I know.'

He stepped aside to let her in, indicating for her to sit on the sofa but she stood her ground, not ready for that sort of chumminess yet. 'I thought we were friends.' She stared up at him, letting him see how hurt she was. 'But friends talk to each other; they don't evade, they don't lie.' They don't sleep in the same bed with their arms wrapped around each other.

God, she had to stop thinking of that night.

Guilt crossed his face. 'I've never lied to you but yes, I should have said something about Freya before now.'

'It's not just Freya though, is it? I saw another woman in your flat.' Damn, why had she admitted that? 'Not that you can't have women visit you, I mean you're a free agent, it's just…' she trailed off, aware she couldn't say the next words out loud. *I'm massively, stupidly, painfully jealous.*

His eyes narrowed. 'You've been *spying* on me?'

'No.' She'd just accused him of lying and here she was, being a total hypocrite. 'I didn't buy binoculars, though the thought did cross my mind,' she admitted. 'But I do look over at your window, you know I do. And that evening I saw you laughing with a woman who was pointing at where you keep the paper and pens.' Her voice started to shake and Mia had to pause to regroup. 'I figured you were taking the piss out of me.' Finally she met his eyes. 'You know, the weird girl who lives opposite and won't give out her phone number.'

'No, God no.' He looked genuinely horrified. 'Jesus, Mia, how could you think that? You're not weird, you're bloody adorable. I love the way we communicate. It's unbelievably cool.'

A boulder lodged in her throat, making speech impossible.

'Grace thought so too,' he added quietly. 'She wasn't laughing because it was daft, she was laughing because it was, and I quote, *too cute for words*.' He let out a long exhale. 'Grace is my daughter. Freya is her mum.'

'Your *daughter*?' The explanation was so unexpected, Mia struggled to get her head around it. 'I guess at least that explains the tattoo.'

He exhaled sharply. 'Christ, you thought it was the name of an ex, didn't you? Trust me, the only names I'll ever have tattooed on my skin are those of people I want to keep in my life permanently.' Not Freya then? While she was working through that nugget, he nodded over to the sofa. 'Can we please sit down? My legs were feeling wobbly enough after today's workout. They're about to give out now we're talking about personal stuff.'

'Personal stuff? I've known you for three months and you've never mentioned you had a *daughter*. Nor that you were living next to your ex.' She let out a harsh laugh as she walked towards the sofa, her own legs needing some support now, too. 'God, I've not known you at all, have I?'

She watched him sit down next to her and briefly close his eyes, as if in pain. When he opened them again, she could see the regret. 'I'm sorry. I know I should have told you when we were talking about our past, but…' He let out a humourless laugh. 'It sounds stupid now, but I didn't want you thinking badly of me, not until you got to know me more.'

'You thought I'd not want to carry on our friendship because you had a child?' She gaped at him in disbelief.

'No, not because of that.' He hung his head. 'Shit, Mia, I'm saying all this wrong.' Drawing in a deep, shuddering breath, he turned to look at her. 'I'll tell you everything you want to know, but can we please start this conversation again, from the beginning?'

He was a man of effortless charm, yet he clearly wasn't finding this easy. In fact he looked like he was struggling to tell her something important, something he wasn't sure how to articulate. 'It's your story, so tell it however you want.' Relief flashed across his handsome face and she instantly regretted how hard she'd been on him. 'Just know that I'm sorry for being a bitch earlier. I was upset because I felt you'd kept stuff from me, but that's on me.' She was acutely aware she was the one holding him at arm's length. 'I've no right to your full life history.'

Luke stared at Mia incredulously. Had she really no clue how he felt? 'The woman I spent last Saturday night kissing has every right to know about my past.'

Her cheeks flushed and she gave him a small smile. 'Fair point.'

He shifted so he was facing her. 'I met Freya at school. I guess you could say she was my childhood sweetheart, though at the time it felt like a lot more than that. Sure, I was only sixteen, but it felt like IT.' How naïve he'd been, or as his parents had often pointed out, how stupid. He'd been the same age as Grace was now, yet his daughter was so much more together than he'd ever been. 'It got serious between us very quickly, too quickly.' Embarrassed, he glanced down at his hands.

'Was she immaculately turned out even then?'

He laughed softly. 'No, that came once she started work. Back then she was a natural beauty, no need for make-up.' He searched Mia's eyes. 'Similar to someone else I know.'

She waved a hand in dismissal. 'I don't wear make-up because I can't be bothered with it, not because I don't need it.'

He allowed himself the luxury of studying her face. 'Trust me, you don't need it.'

Clearly embarrassed, she rolled her eyes. 'Maybe not now, because you're making me blush, but you should see me first thing in the morning.'

She must have realised her mistake because she turned a deeper shade of pink, making him laugh. 'God Mia, you're so ballsy, so confident, yet you blush at a compliment on your looks. And at the reminder that I *have* seen you when you've just woken up.' He lowered his voice. 'You were beautiful. Hair a bit wild, sure, eyes all soft and sleepy. Lips so naturally pink it took some serious self-control on my part not to kiss them.'

He watched as she bit into those very lips. 'But you didn't.'

Christ, he could feel himself getting hard. 'Because I wouldn't have been able to stop at kissing.'

Her breathing quickened and her eyes darted away from his. 'We're getting off track here. You were telling me about Freya.'

The mention of his ex-wife was sufficient to quell the throb between his legs. 'Yeah, so I was.' Now it was his turn to avoid her eyes. 'She didn't want to go on the pill, because her parents were dead strict and she was scared they'd find out. So we used condoms. Most of the time.' Shameful, furtive encounters in quiet parks, bathrooms at parties, the back of his car once he'd scraped the money to buy one. Old enough to have sex, but not old enough to do it properly, with the right care, in the right surroundings. 'We took stupid risks, and unsurprisingly she got pregnant.'

'How old were you?'

'Eighteen.' He grimaced. 'I guess you could say we were lucky it didn't happen earlier. Freya managed to take her A Levels and get into a local university before Grace was born.' Once again he found himself looking down at his hands, rather than at Mia. Scared to see her reaction. 'I wanted to get married, but Freya refused. She wanted to focus on university, on becoming the lawyer she'd always dreamt of being.'

'So that's what she does at her desk,' Mia mused.

'Yeah. Recently she's got into the habit of doing her emails from home then heading into the office around ten to avoid the traffic.'

'Can't say I'm surprised. She sure fits the image of the sharp lawyer. What about you?' Mia's softly worded question had him jerking his head up to meet her gaze. 'What did you dream of doing?'

He shrugged. 'I wasn't as bright as her. I might have scraped into uni, but one of us needed to earn money so it made sense for that to be me.'

'Did you go straight into bar work?'

She was asking questions, not judging, not getting up and leaving. Luke started to relax. 'Yeah. That way I could take care of Grace during the day while Freya was studying.' They'd fallen into a routine that seemed to work, most of the time.

'Did you live together?'

He let out a sharp laugh. 'No way. Once it became clear she didn't see us having a future together, our relationship was doomed. She lived with her parents until she started work. All she wanted from me was my babysitting skills.' Even now, the pain was still there, hidden deep. To be turned down, rejected. It had fucking hurt.

Mia reached out to touch his hand. 'I'm sure that's not true. You were both so young, dealing with a huge change to your lives in the best way you could.'

True, except he'd wanted the whole deal. Living together, marriage. Being a family. Freya had wanted a career. He pushed the thoughts away and clung to Mia's proffered hand, and the hope it seemed to imply. 'She was probably right,' he admitted. 'We'd never have been a good fit in the long run.' *Yet you're falling for another woman who's far too smart for you.*

Fifteen years on and he still hadn't learnt his lesson.

Mia let go of his hand and rose to her feet. As if she suddenly realised he was no longer the same guy she'd spent last Saturday night with. Now he was a dad.

'I still don't understand why you didn't tell me.' She walked towards the kitchen island and leant against it. 'Being a dad must be such a huge part of you.'

'Grace is the best part of me, by far.' He paused while he swallowed down the ball of emotion. 'I'm as proud as fuck of her, of who she's turned out to be, but am I proud I was stupid enough to have sex without protection? Am I proud that instead of a stable home, for a large part of her life she had to put up with parents who were still kids themselves?' He shook his head as shame rolled through him. 'I didn't tell you because I knew it would reinforce what you already think of me, when what I'm trying to do is change that perception.'

'I don't think any less of you because you have a daughter,' she answered, a touch of exasperation in her tone. 'God, if anything I admire how you put your own dreams on hold to be what she and Freya needed.'

He gave her a tight smile. 'I want to take that, but it isn't the real issue here, is it? You don't want to go out with a guy who's treated women casually in the past. A guy you can't trust.' Deciding it was better for both of them if she didn't have a chance to reply, he added, 'I'd like you to meet Grace, if you're up for it. She already thinks you're super cool.'

Two blue eyes zeroed in on his, her surprise clear. 'What have you told her about me?'

'That you're a computer whizz who's writing a book. That you're smart and funny, brave and down to earth. And that you're an important part of my life.'

'Not that we've ... you know ... kissed?'

He tried to smile but his emotions were too close to the surface. 'No. I didn't see the point in telling her something that might never happen again.'

To his intense disappointment, Mia avoided his eyes. 'Why have I not seen Grace around before now?' She glanced around the room. 'And why doesn't she have any of her things here?'

She's asking because she's still interested, he tried to tell himself, yet the way she'd neatly ignored his comment about her being important, about them kissing again, made it feel unlikely. 'Grace finished her GCSEs a few months ago and since then she's been Interrailing round Europe with her mates. She only got back last Saturday, which was what Freya came round to tell me. As for the second question, Freya didn't like the idea of Grace having two homes, said it would risk her not feeling she belonged in either, so the deal was, we bought flats next to each other. That way she had one base but both parents.' The feeling of loss was something he still carried with him.

'From the expression on your face, that decision must have hurt.'

'Shit, am I that transparent?' He rubbed at the back of his neck. 'It's great that Grace is only next door, but yes, I wanted her to have a bed here. For her to feel this was also her home.'

Mia's eyes filled with sympathy. 'I'm sure she does. After all, you're here. And I presume Pickles is hers, too, and not that you've got a thing for small furry animals.'

He let out a huff of laughter. 'Yeah, I should have got a gerbil. Less poo, less gnawed wires. Shorter lifespan. Grace was supposed to feed her and clean her cage out but the shine soon wore off.' The memory prompted another thought. 'By the way, Freya doesn't have a key to my place, Grace does. Freya must have gone into Grace's room to get it. God knows why. She hasn't done it before.'

Mia frowned. 'You said you've not invited a woman here before?'

'I haven't.'

'Then maybe she heard me and came round to suss me out.'

The idea made him laugh. 'If she did, it was only because she's chronically nosey. Trust me, our relationship was pretty much over as soon as Grace was born.'

When Freya had texted him to say he had a daughter – she'd not wanted him there at the birth – he'd rushed to the hospital, a small diamond ring burning a hole in his pocket; the sum total of all his savings. Dumb as shit, he'd gone down on one knee and proposed. Freya had taken one look and shaken her head. *'Grow up, Luke. I don't need a crappy ring. Get your money back and spend it on something useful, like nappies and baby grows.'*

She'd had a point, but he'd never felt more stupid, more hurt, more unwanted than he had in that moment.

'Hello missy. I wondered where you were.' Mia's voice

cut through his dismal thoughts and he looked over to see Pickles sniffing her Converse trainers.

'See, I told you she likes you. Sniffing feet is like a hug in bunny language.'

Mia's laugh – the first one he'd heard today – bounced around the room. 'You're so full of shit, Luke Doyle.'

His head filled with the things he wanted to say. Where does this leave us? Are we still friends, at least? Can we still go on non-dates? Will you let me introduce you to Grace?

Before he could say any of them, Mia crouched in front of him and kissed his cheek. 'Thanks for telling me about your daughter. I'd love to meet her.'

Reeling from the unexpected gesture, it was a moment before he could speak, and even then the words came out hoarse. 'That's great. Really, really great.'

'I'll see you on Wednesday for your inaugural Cocktails 4 U evening. Such a great idea, I wonder who thought of it?' Smiling, she walked to the door but as she opened it, she glanced back at him. 'Oh and Luke, you're an important part of my life, too.'

She left before he could reply.

Immediately Pickles jumped up into his lap and as he fondled her ears, a grin split his face. 'You know what, there's a chance you might have to get used to sharing me. If I don't balls things up.'

Chapter Twenty-Five

Mia finished the website for the bar on Tuesday, much to Sandy's delight.

When she emailed her the link, Sandy immediately fired back a reply with the heading OMG IT'S AWESOME. In the content of the email were rows and rows of happy emojis.

Wednesday, Mia woke to a message in Luke's window.

U R my

Fav Nerd

TYVM

Considering the tentative stage their relationship was in – friends teetering on the verge of something – the message had held just the right amount of touching humour to cause Mia's chest to ache.

The man was a dad. As she waited outside Stan's door later that evening, Mia mulled over the concept again. It explained some things she'd wondered about. Why he'd gone into bartending and not into further education. Why he had a rabbit. Yet there was still a major part of him that confused her. How did an eighteen-year-old who'd been prepared to settle down and marry, turn into an adult who treated women, and sex, so casually?

She couldn't square the two sides of him.

'Earth calling Mia.'

Stan's voice broke through her muddled thoughts. 'Sorry, I was miles away.'

'I doubt it,' he replied dryly. 'I'm guessing you were downstairs in that bar we're supposed to be heading to. That's if you stop mooning about the owner for long enough to check you've got your purse, or whatever it is you need to buy me a cocktail.'

'I thought you were buying me one tonight?'

'You invited me.' He gave her a cheeky smile as he pulled his door shut. 'I'm getting used to the idea of you buying me drinks.'

'How come you never invite me out?'

Now his smile was more of a smirk. 'I don't need an excuse to see the bar owner.'

'It's the first of Luke's design-a-cocktail evenings,' she explained patiently as they headed to the stairs. 'We're going to show our support.'

'Aye, whatever you tell yourself is alright with me. As long as I get a free drink out of it.'

Laughing, she looped her arm through his. 'We won't be the only locals there.' She paused to make sure she had his attention. 'Naomi's going.'

He came to an abrupt halt. 'Bloody hell woman, why didn't you say?' His eyes travelled down his straining shirt. 'Do I look alright? Did I comb my hair?'

She'd never seen him so unbalanced. It was beyond sweet. 'You look just fine, Stan. I'd have said if you didn't.'

'Right, good.' He gathered himself and started to walk again. 'So what's the score with you and the Chipmunk? Slept with him yet?'

Mia spluttered with laughter. 'Are you sure you want to get so personal? You know you'll have to answer the same questions if we do.'

He hesitated. 'Fine. Are you still doing the mating dance, or have you got stuck in?'

'That is not an improvement, and just so you know, I can't wait to get my own back and interrogate you. But okay, if we're doing this level of sharing, Luke and I have kissed. And he's told me he's a dad.'

'Is he now?' Stan's bushy eyebrows shot up. 'By heck, who'd have thought. Not surprising though, if you think how much … you know … diddling about he's been doing.'

She smiled at the phrase, but the words struck a sad note, reminding her why Luke had been so hesitant to tell her about Grace. There was still the big issue of whether she could ever really trust him enough to be more than friends. She didn't think he'd cheat on her – his loyalty to Bill indicated he wasn't the type. It was more whether she could trust his feelings. He said she was important to him, but how long before he got bored?

'Sorry,' Stan said gruffly, giving her an apologetic look. 'Ignore the mutterings of a jealous old man. If you like him, go for it, or before you know it you'll get to my age and find you're as grumpy as me.'

'I told you, you're not grumpy, you've got a dry sense of humour.' She gave his side a nudge. 'Naomi likes that in a man.'

He huffed. 'You're changing the subject.'

'Only because I know you're right, and it scares the shit out me.' More suitable guys, at least on paper, had let her down, so she knew nothing was certain in life. Did she want to risk her heart for the chance of something potentially great? Or was she better keeping things as they were with Luke and throwing herself into a new independent life up here?

'The thought of asking Naomi out scares me shitless, too.' Stan gave her a weak smile. 'But if I can do it, having been skewered after thirty years of marriage, then a youngster like you can ruddy well do it, too.'

The bar was pleasantly, reassuring, humming when they arrived, but Naomi's big warm laugh reached their ears before they caught sight of her.

'Hell's bells.'

Stan's muted curse, along with his wide-eyed stare, made Mia smile. 'She looks amazing, doesn't she?'

In the café, Naomi always wore an apron over conservative, working clothes. On a night out, she clearly went for it. She was sat on a bar stool, talking with Luke, her black hair slicked back, huge gold ear-rings bouncing as she laughed. The vivid, multicoloured top she wore didn't just draw the eye, it kind of reached out and grabbed it, demanding attention. The whole look was exotic, sexy. And, unsurprisingly, a bit too much for Stan.

'That woman doesn't want the likes of me,' he muttered. 'She wants some strapping, larger-than-life character who can play jazz while doing the samba.'

Mia could understand where he was coming from. 'Funny, I look at Luke and think that guy doesn't want the likes of me. He wants some tall, leggy model who takes care over her appearance and looks dynamite in a tight dress.' She glanced down at her jeans and favourite T-shirt.

Stan grunted. 'Shall we scarper?'

At that moment the people they'd been talking about both turned to look at them.

'The smile Naomi's giving you?' Mia nudged Stan. 'It says she likes you just as you are.'

And the smile Luke was giving her? It said he'd been watching the door, waiting for her to arrive. And now she had, he wasn't just delighted, he was relieved.

'No scarpering then?'

Mia drew in a breath, her eyes on Luke. 'No scarpering, Stan. We man up and go for what we want.'

'Easy for you to say.' When she raised an eyebrow, he waved at her dismissively. 'You know what I mean. Messages in the window, making you cocktails, taking you on dates that you pretend aren't dates. The Chipmunk's been all over you for months. He's a sure thing.'

'Naomi gets custard donuts in especially for you. She sends messages to you via me.' Mia smiled over at the café owner, only to find she was still looking at Stan. 'But if you don't think she's worth sticking your head over the parapet for…'

In a flash Stan left her side and lumbered up to Naomi.

And that's when she noticed Luke wasn't behind the bar anymore. He was standing to the right of her. 'Hi.'

'Hey.' His eyes skimmed her face and when they found hers, he smiled straight into them. 'You've no idea how good it is to see you.'

'You saw me on Saturday.'

He nodded. 'And you still turned up tonight, so I'm taking that as a good sign.' He glanced over to Stan. 'Even though you came with your bodyguard.'

Mia grinned. 'I'm doing a bit of matchmaking.'

'Ah.' They both watched Stan awkwardly hitch up his trousers – she was sure he'd already lost a few pounds – and then point towards the last remaining booth.

'Do you reckon he has a shot with Naomi?'

Luke's gaze slid back to hers. 'I'm more interested in whether I have a shot. With you,' he added. 'In case there's any confusion.'

Luke waited, heart in his mouth, for Mia's reply. Whatever it might have been, she was saved from having to give it because Mateo started gesticulating frantically at him.

'Looks like I'm going to have to wait for the answer.' *It's a Wednesday and the bar is rocking, which is bloody fantastic … that should be your focus. Not Mia.* It was frightening to realise he wanted her even more than he wanted his business to be a success. 'Please tell me you'll stay till closing?'

'I will.' Her lips curved in the hint of a smile. 'I'll use the time to think on my reply.'

The fact she had to think at all didn't bode well, and yet… 'A straight no you wouldn't have to think about, right?'

Laughing, she pushed him towards the bar. 'Go and make cocktails.'

There was something about the glint in her eye, the easy laugh, that sent hope shooting through him. Hope was dangerous, but it was also better than any mood-enhancing drug.

He almost danced back to the bar.

Throughout the evening he caught glimpses of Mia, sometimes chatting with Naomi and Stan, sometimes with Chloe and Tanya who'd turned up despite the fact he'd had awkward conversations with both ladies over the last two months. He also noticed Mia laughing with Gary and Tony, which he tried to be pleased about, because his mates should get along with his girlfriend. Except Mia wasn't one in the usual sense of the word so the standard mate code, the one that prevented mates making a play for your girlfriend, didn't apply.

'Boss, move your arse. I've two more orders for one of your "special",' Mateo mimed quotation marks, 'cocktails.' Then he added under his breath, 'Though God knows what's so special about them.'

'They're *special*, because I make them.' He gave Mateo a cocky grin he didn't altogether feel. What was he doing, mixing new cocktails like he was some sort of expert? *Mia thinks you're a genius at it.* Okay, she might be a whizz at computers, not drinks, but she was smart.

He glanced over at the door, where people were still coming in. And then at the bar, where punters lined up to be served. Many of them had already had a cocktail and were now waiting to order a second.

Maybe she'd been right, and he was a bit of a genius at something, after all.

He was mixing a cocktail for a newly engaged couple – Love Struck, not one of his own, but it seemed to fit the bill – when Mia came up to the bar. Her streaky blue hair stood out among the more boring shades of the other customers. Her T-shirt, showing the evolution of a computer geek from ape to man hunched over a computer, was a far cry from anything the other women were wearing. 'How's the matchmaking?'

She took a peek over her shoulder. 'See for yourself.'

He followed the direction of her gaze to where Naomi and Stan sat. Naomi was throwing her head back in laughter while Stan looked on, his expression one of besotted wonder. 'Bloody hell, I didn't realise old Stan had it in him.'

'He's a real gem, beneath the bluster.'

'Do I need to put him on my hit list, along with Gary, Tony and Mateo?'

'Your *hit* list?'

'Yeah, people who pose a threat. People I might feel the need to hit if they get too close to you.' When her expression turned from confusion to dismay, he swore under his breath. 'Jeeze Mia, I'm joking. For the record, I've never hit anyone in my life. But if I'd said I keep a mental list of people I need to keep a wary eye on in case they start coming on to you, because I'm a jealous bastard, it would have lacked the same punch.' He gave her a crooked smile. 'Hit list, punch, that was pretty funny.'

'God, this is ridiculous.' She sounded exasperated. 'You don't have to keep an eye on anyone.'

He knew the couple were still waiting for their cocktail, that others were waiting to be served. Yet at that moment Mia was the only person who existed for him. Bending towards her, he gently touched her cheek. 'You might not see how bloody amazing you are, but I do. And so do lots of other buggers out there, so it's my mission to get you to see only me.' Reluctantly he took a step back. 'And about that answer I'm still waiting on. My advice is not to think too hard about it.' He knew if she did, he was screwed.

The bar, buzzing an hour ago, was quiet as Luke closed the safe and turned off the office light. Everyone had gone. Except for Mia.

He walked out to find her leaning against the bar, her face illuminated by the green light from the sign. Part Smurf, part Leprechaun, he thought with a smile. *His?*

He faltered on the word. How had he become this man, the one who could only see one woman?

As he made his way back towards the bar, her gaze swung round to meet his.

'So, have you got a reply for me yet?'

'I have.' Her smile was secretive, and again he felt the stirring of hope. Mia wasn't a tease, she was straightforward, so if she was going to give him an answer she knew he wouldn't want, he was pretty certain she'd just come out with it.

Pretty certain, but not absolutely certain.

'And?' He could feel his pulse hammering.

'I've decided to take Stan's advice.'

'Sorry?' His step faltered. 'You're going to take dating advice from an overweight sixty-plus-year-old who hasn't been out with anyone since he was divorced?'

'How do you know he hasn't?'

'I'm a bartender, I listen when people tell me stuff.' The evening felt as if it was unravelling, yet Mia was still looking at him, and still smiling that little smile.

'Then you should listen now, because I'm only going to say this once.' She slipped off the barstool and came to stand in front of him. As he inhaled her, felt her warm, sexy body rest against his, all his nerve endings began to fire. And that was before she leant forward, her lips brushing against his ear as she whispered, 'Take me home with you.'

Immediately all his blood rushed south, between his legs. 'Fuck, yes.' He reached for her, and in his haste to get that smiling mouth on his, he almost knocked her over. 'Shit, sorry, I just…' He groaned when her legs wrapped around his hips as he lifted her up. 'God, I need to kiss you.'

At last his lips found hers and he let out a deep, guttural sound as he began to plunder the wet heat of her mouth, their tongues dancing. Around them there was nothing but dark and silence, yet inside him he felt like a volcano about to erupt. As he edged her onto the bar, as he pressed his aching groin closer to the core of her, he knew kissing was not going to be enough. 'Let's get out of here.'

Later he wouldn't remember if he'd checked the lights were off in the kitchen, or if he'd set the alarm. All he would remember was the joy, the adrenalin rush as he grabbed Mia's hand and ran, literally bloody ran, the short distance to his flat.

Chapter Twenty-Six

She was being rash. Taking all that sensible caution she'd displayed ever since she'd met Luke, and throwing it all into the wind.

Yet she'd never felt so good, so happy, so alive as she did right now, laughing with him as they tumbled into his flat.

They were going to have sex. His track record with women, her inability to pick the right men … she'd shove all those nasty, niggling doubts aside. Tonight was about pleasure.

His hand still clasping hers, Luke shut the door behind them and pulled her snug against him. 'This advice of Stan's.' He kissed her lightly on the mouth, then set about leaving a trail of kisses along her jaw and down her throat, causing her to moan. How had she reached thirty and not realised her throat was an erogenous zone? 'What was it exactly?'

'Ummm.' He wanted her to talk, to think, when he was

kissing her there? As he reached the sensitive spot beneath her ear, she closed her eyes and let desire burn through her. But then his lips left hers and she blinked them back open. 'Why did you stop?'

A sexy grin slid across his face. 'Fuck, you're gorgeous.'

'Then keep kissing me. Here.' She pointed to her neck, then slid her fingers up, along her chin, to her mouth. 'Or here, or anywhere. Just flipping kiss me.'

His deep chuckle sent prickles across her skin. 'I will, after you answer my question.' Another feather-light kiss, this time on her nose. 'What was Stan's advice?'

'Does it matter?' She yearned for him … and yes, that was the first time she'd ever used the word. Never had she felt such a deep ache, a searing desire to rip off a man's clothes and wrap herself around him, over him, under him. Have him push inside her.

Luke lifted her into his arms, just as he had in the bar, as if she was weightless. The strength of the man, the raw power. It was beyond sexy.

Yet as he sat them down on the sofa, her in his lap, buttocks pressed against his powerful thighs, she looked into his eyes and knew it wasn't his body she was falling for. That was just an added bonus. It was the man inside she could no longer say no to.

'I want to make sure we're both on the same page,' he said quietly as his arms tightened around her. 'You know what I want. You and me, to date properly, not just as friends. I need to know that's what you want, too. We don't have to have sex, not if you're not ready, but I want to be able to kiss you.' His gaze found hers, so full of sensual heat she felt the throb of it between her legs. 'I want to touch you in places friends can't touch.'

'Yes,' she breathed, squeezing her thighs against the ache. 'I want all of that. Plus sex.'

He laughed, the husky sound a rumble in his chest. 'Is that what Stan told you to do, have sex?'

'He said if I like you, I should go for it, or before I knew it I'd find I was grumpy and old like he was.'

Luke gave her a comical wide-eyed look. 'Oh shit, are you going to turn into Stan?'

Laughing, she threw her arms around his neck and gave him a brief, hard kiss. 'Only if you don't have sex with me.'

'There's zero chance of that happening.' She felt his thighs tense, ready to lift them both up, but then he groaned as a furry ball jumped onto her lap. 'Sod off, Pickles.' Mia giggled and gave the rabbit's ears a long, luxurious stroke which caused Luke to groan louder. 'Christ, it's killing me watching you do that.'

'Yeah?' Teasing him, teasing them both, she did it again, and arousal flooded through her as Luke hardened beneath her.

Swearing, he lifted them both up and carefully slid her down his body to the floor. 'Wait here, don't move, don't go anywhere. Let me feed the monster.' He gave her a look full of molten promise. 'Then I'll take care of you.'

She watched as he grabbed a handful of rabbit food and dropped it into Pickles' bowl, then went to fill up her water bottle. When he crouched and gave the rabbit a final scratch between her ears, Mia's heart melted that little bit more. Maybe he'd been careless with women over the years, yet all she could really judge him on was what she'd seen with her own eyes. And a man on the promise of hot sex who still made sure to give his rabbit fresh water and a tender stroke, was decent to the core.

'Goodnight Pickles.' Luke stood to his full height, eyes still on the rabbit. 'I don't want any scratching at the door, any squeaking. Behave yourself tonight and you get the biggest carrot I can find tomorrow.'

'What about me?' Mia asked. 'If I behave, do I get a big carrot?'

'Sure.' He smirked. 'Or I can find you something else big to enjoy.'

She let out a strangled laugh. 'Oh God, I hope the sex is better than the innuendo.'

'The sex,' he said softly, eyes blazing, broad chest rippling beneath his shirt as he stalked towards her, 'will be better than anything you've ever experienced.' With that, he swept her into his arms. 'It's time we headed for the bedroom.'

He kicked the door closed behind them and laid her carefully on the bed, his eyes skimming up and down her body. 'I need to see you,' he said hoarsely. 'Without clothes,' he added with a small smile. 'In case that wasn't completely clear.'

She looked at him towering over her and felt the first twinge of nerves. She'd met some of the women he'd slept with and she'd noticed a type; long legs, toned body. 'You first.' Without a second of hesitation, and with none of the flashy moves she'd expected from him, he whisked off his polo shirt and proceeded to unbuckle his belt. 'Wait, slow down.'

He peered up at her in confusion. 'You want me to stop?'

'No, God no. Just…' She smiled. 'I'm kind of weird when it comes to unwrapping presents. I don't like to rip off the paper. I like to take it off slowly, savour it.' Unconsciously she licked her lips. 'Let me enjoy savouring you.'

He groaned. 'God, Mia, if you keep looking at me like that, I won't be able to do slow.'

Her eyes ran hungrily, greedily, over his naked chest; the sexy V dipping into the waist of his jeans, the ridges of his six-pack, the taut muscles of his pecs. When she came across his nipple piercing, she paused, remembering why he said he'd got it done.

But *why* didn't matter. Tonight, she was the one doing the looking, the touching. Swallowing down the jitters, she scrambled onto her knees and beckoned him forward. 'Come here. Let me unwrap you.'

He stepped towards her and when she reached for his belt, his powerful body trembled.

Her heart lurched, and past histories paled into insignificance. This, what they were about to do, felt bigger, more momentous, than anything she'd experienced to date.

Luke gritted his teeth against the flare of need coursing through him. For weeks, months, ever since the first day she'd come into his bar, he'd wanted this.

Yet the moment her gaze had fallen on his piercing, he'd known something wasn't right. He'd tried to ignore it, as she was clearly doing, but it was no good. How could he make love to her, when she still had doubts about him?

'Mia, stop.' His voice sounded strangled, a clear reflection of the effort the words cost him.

Her beautiful blue eyes gazed up at him in confusion. 'You don't want this?'

'I want this more than I want my next breath.' He placed a hand on either side of her face and searched for the right words. 'But I also want *you* to want it, wholeheartedly. Unreservedly.'

'I do.'

'Unreservedly, Mia,' he repeated quietly. 'Without doubts, without fear that you're doing the wrong thing.' He brushed a thumb across her cheek, fighting to keep his words even when calm was the last thing he felt. 'A moment ago, you saw my piercing and hesitated.'

Her eyes avoided his. 'I remembered why you'd had it done.'

'Because I thought the girls would like it?' He exhaled sharply. 'Shit, Mia, you're thinking about me with other women?'

She ducked her head, moving so she was out of his reach. 'I did, briefly.' Her eyes, when she finally met his gaze, brimmed with frustration. 'Why are you doing this? Ruining the mood just when I'd psyched myself up?'

He swore under his breath. 'You shouldn't have to psyche yourself up to make love to me.'

'I didn't mean it like that.' She shifted so her back was against the headboard, knees hugged to her, and his heart ached. She looked hurt, upset.

'Christ, I'm sorry.' He let out a humourless laugh. 'I'm supposed to be the great Don Juan, yeah? But here I am, making a total and utter balls-up of this.' Slipping his shirt back on, he climbed onto the bed next to her, wrapping his arms around her. She felt stiff, far removed from the woman he'd carried to the bed a few minutes ago.

'It's the first time a guy has said no when I was undoing his belt.'

Beneath the bitter words, he heard her vulnerability, and shame rolled through him. He'd not just hurt her, he'd made her doubt herself. 'I've never wanted a woman as much as I want you.' He tucked a hand under her chin, turning her face so her eyes met his. 'But it's more than that now. I'm falling for you, Mia. It scares the living daylights out of me, yet ever since you walked into my damn bar with green streaks in your hair to match my sign, and backchat that was more than a match for me, you caught my attention. Now you're reeling me in.'

She snorted. 'I'm a fisherman now?'

'Yeah, and I'm well and truly hooked.' He pressed a kiss on the top of her head, feeling a little calmer when he felt her relax against him. 'But much as I might want to, I can't delete my past.'

'I know.' She turned to look up at him. 'I wouldn't be here if I thought it was going to be an issue for me.'

He could leave it there. He'd asked the question, received the answer he wanted. Yet if he did, wouldn't he be doing the very thing he was ashamed he might have done with other women over the years; selfishly seeing what he wanted to see? Had the women he'd slept with so readily really all been happy with casual? He recalled the conversation with Tanya when he'd ended things and knew he was deluding himself if he thought his actions had never hurt anyone. 'A few minutes ago it was an issue though, wasn't it?'

'We've both got a past, both slept with other people.' She bit into her bottom lip as she seemed to consider her next words. 'I just can't understand why the guy I think you are, the one who proposed to his pregnant girlfriend, could turn into a man who only wanted women for sex.'

The words stung, but then the truth often hurt. 'I was eighteen when I asked Freya to marry me.' He paused, feeling those long-forgotten emotions bubble to the surface again. 'Do you know what it's like not to be what the person you love, needs? Freya wanted me to change nappies and for occasional sex but not to be by her side. She didn't want my love, not even my emotional support.' His voice caught and he had to pause and take a breath before he could continue. 'I was just the dad and the goodtime guy, so that's what I became.'

'How long were you together after Grace was born?'

'It quickly petered out.' He gave her a sad smile. 'Turns out being rejected is hard to overlook. By the time Grace turned one, we had different lives, me working evenings at a bar, Freya a dedicated student. We only really talked when we handed our daughter over. I hated that, hated never being able to tuck Grace into bed. I missed her so fiercely, I had the tattoo done. My way of keeping her with me.'

Her eyes searched his. 'And the piercing? Did you have that done at the same time?'

'Yeah. The guy in the shop persuaded me it would make me some kind of bad-ass, irresistible to women.' He laughed harshly. 'It sounds so immature, so stupid now, but I wanted to prove to Freya that other women wanted me, even if she didn't. After a while the flirting, the going back with a woman at the end of a shift, it became a way of life.' He stared into Mia's eyes, hoping she could see beyond the surface of him. 'It isn't who I am, only who I became. And I don't want to be that person anymore.' Mia's expression softened and she did something unexpected. She kissed him. 'Not complaining, not one little bit, but what was that for? Just, you know, so I can maybe get another one.'

Her eyes smiled back at him. 'It was for the eighteen-year-old boy who had his heart broken, but still manned up and brought up his child with the woman who turned him down.'

Shit, he could feel the back of his eyes prick. 'Thank you.'

'Tell me about that time.' She turned so she was facing

him, and his heart gave a bump of delight when she entwined her legs with his, keeping the body contact. 'You said you worked in a bar while Freya was at uni, and that Freya lived with her parents. Did you live with yours?'

'Yeah, that would have been useful, but they chucked me out.'

She stared at him, clearly shocked. 'Why?'

'I got a girl pregnant. I was irresponsible.' He shrugged, trying to ignore the pain that twisted through him whenever he remembered that time. 'They never approved of me much anyway. Phil was the one who worked hard at school, didn't get into trouble. I was the one they always thought wouldn't amount to much, and I proved them right.'

'Bollocks.' He couldn't resist a smile at the disgust in her voice. 'You own a bar, Luke. You raised a daughter.'

Now wasn't the time to remind her the bar was slipping out of his hands. 'Grace is so smart, she practically raised herself.' He smiled as he remembered back to when she was small. 'I rented a room in this bloke's flat, and he was into weights, so that's how I got into them. I remember I used to strap her in this bouncer chair when she was a baby and she'd watch me, wriggling away like she was trying to copy. As she got bigger I bought her some pretend dumb-bells and she'd do the lifts along with me. God, she was adorable. Still is, though she's more likely to give me backchat now and tell me I'm being dumb. Back then, she looked at me like I was some sort of hero.'

'You're the dad who looked after her. The one who took

her to the park, who entertained her, made her laugh, who worked at night to make sure she had whatever she needed.' Mia smiled into his eyes. 'You are kind of a hero.'

He wasn't. He'd done so many things wrong, especially in those early days when he didn't have a clue how to take care of a kid. Still, in that moment, Mia's words spinning through his head, he felt better about himself than he could ever remember feeling. 'So where does this leave us?' he asked quietly. Then held his breath.

If she wanted to go back to her place, to cool things for a while, he could work with that. If she'd changed her mind and wanted out, though… The loss of Freya had been brutal, but she'd been a teenage sweetheart, his first love. Could he bounce back if he lost Mia? Because he was terrified the guy who'd spent a large part of his adult life going from woman to woman, had finally found one he never wanted to leave.

Chapter Twenty-Seven

Mia's mind was in a whirl. All her life she'd been getting men wrong. It was entirely possible she'd got Luke wrong, too. The tattoo, the piercing, the reason he'd got into doing weights. All things she'd thought were part of his playboy image, actually had deeper meanings. The tattoo to keep his daughter close, the piercing to help his self-esteem, the weights because it had been a way of keeping fit while looking after Grace. The women because he'd been hurting, and that was the way he'd tried to cope.

'Mia?'

His voice brought her back to his question. *So where does this leave us?*

The expression on his face – the longing he wasn't afraid to show her, overlaid with anxiety he was trying to mask – helped make her answer easy.

'I can't promise I won't sometimes worry when I see you

chatting to a women at the bar, or when Chloe or another of your exes wraps an arm around you.'

He huffed out a breath. 'I was never with Chloe.'

'Would you have been though, if I hadn't turned up?'

He gave her a mild look. 'Aside from the fact that I didn't fancy her, Chloe only ever wanted me as a tool to help her forget her ex. Women go off with the barman at the end of the night because he listens and makes them feel good. Not necessarily because they like *him*.'

Her heart crumpled. Beneath the cocky smile, the blarney, this gorgeous, strapping hunk of a man really had very little sense of self-worth. 'I'm here because you listen, even when it's not what you want to hear. Because you make me feel better than good. You make me feel like I'm attractive, special.' She reached for his hand and held it in hers. 'And because I like you. A lot.'

Like a burst of sunshine, a smile shot across his face. 'A lot, huh?'

'A lot,' she confirmed, her heart starting to beat faster now. She was taking a risk, trusting he was the man she thought she was discovering and not the one she'd believed him to be when they first met.

'Enough to continue where we left off? Not that I'll mind if we don't,' he added hastily, then shook his head. 'That's not true, I don't know why I said that. I desperately want you to stay but I'm trying to be a good guy here, trying not to rush you.' He laughed softly. 'And I'm also freaking out right now because this has never meant so much, never felt so important.'

Her heart swelled, feeling too big for her chest. 'It feels important to me, too.'

He reached to cup her face, eyes glittering. 'Maybe we could freak out together?'

'I'm not freaking.' Feeling oddly powerful now she knew he was nervous, she rested back against the headboard. 'In fact I'm going to sit here and enjoy watching you strip for me.' At her words, she started to laugh. 'Oh God, now I'm remembering what Stan calls you.'

Luke winced as he slid off the bed. 'Do I want to know?'

'Probably not.' But the temptation was too much. 'Chipmunk.' His eyes snapped to hers, his expression so horrified it cracked Mia up. 'It's a long story, one we'll save for when I'm not looking forward to seeing you take your clothes off.'

'Okay.' He seemed to mentally shake himself before lifting at the hem of his T-shirt. 'Do you need some moves with this strip show?'

The brief flash of tan skin and rock-hard abs drained the saliva from her mouth. 'No moves needed. Just…' She swallowed.

His smile was teasing. 'Slow?'

She nodded, eyes fixed on him as he removed his shirt again. This time she was able to savour the slide of muscle over muscle, the smooth expanse of golden skin, the dusting of dark hair that trailed from his belly button into the waistband of his jeans.

But rather than undo his jeans button, Luke reached for his piercing.

'What are you doing?'

'Removing it.' His eyes, dark green now, hot and intense, stared back at her. 'I don't need it anymore.'

Oh God. Her stomach swooped, yet as much as she appreciated the sentiment, it felt wrong. 'No, stop.' She crawled over to him, placing a hand over his. 'This is part of you, part of the journey you've taken. I don't want to erase your past.' Her fingers toyed with the simple silver ring and when he cursed under his breath, she smiled up at him. 'Plus it's freaking sexy.'

'Christ, Mia, it is when you touch it.' His big body shuddered again, and she felt dizzy with power. Bending her head she pressed a kiss his chest, her mouth running over the hot skin of his pecs, across the ridges of muscle.

'Mia.' Her name was a strangled moan. 'You don't know what you're doing to me.'

She placed a hand on the hard bulge in his jeans and squeezed gently. 'I've got an idea.'

He swore again, then grabbed at her wrist, moving her off him. 'Right, that's it, I'm too close to embarrassing myself. It's your turn to take some clothes off.' His eyes trailed up her body until they met hers. 'And my turn to tease the hell out of you.'

'Okay. I'm on board with the teasing.' Her new-found confidence wasn't quite as solid as she'd hoped it was though, and alongside desire, she felt a skitter of the nerves from earlier.

'Stop it.' His voice was gruff, his expression frustrated yet his eyes soft as he cupped her face. 'I want *you*, Mia.

Your short yet perfect legs captivated me when you wore that yellow dress. Your breasts have been the stuff of my fantasies ever since I was crushed against them at the Chill Factore. As for the rest of you, I've danced with you, felt the length of you against me, even moulded my hands across that pert bum before dragging them back to your waist and reminding myself we were only friends.' He smiled. 'I *know* your body already. Taking off your clothes, seeing you naked, is just the cherry on the top of the most delicious cake I've ever wrapped my big mitts around.'

Slipping her arms around his neck, she rested her head against his chest. 'How do you always know the right thing to say?'

His hands shifted, sliding down her back, drawing her tight against him. 'I don't. I'm sure I'll do more than my fair share of pissing you off.' His eyes searched hers. 'But I see you, Mia. I get you.'

Inside her chest, her heart shifted and Mia knew what had gone before had been nothing. Affairs she'd had with guys she'd liked, been attracted to, enjoyed for a while before they'd hurt her, bruised her ego, crushed her confidence. This, with Luke, felt huge. Life changing. Yet on the flip side, it also meant Luke didn't just have the potential to hurt her. He could crush her.

Did she trust him to be careful? To be the person he claimed he wanted to be, and not the one he'd spent all his adult life being?

His eyes pressed hers, and she saw how deeply he felt

this moment, how much he meant what he said. So she took a deep breath, and a huge leap of faith, and pressed her lips against his.

Luke had been on permanent arousal for what felt like the entire evening, ever since Mia had come into the bar.

Now he had her back in his arms for a second time, and he wasn't going to let anything stop them. Not the doubts he felt she still had, nor the single doubt he still had – that she would ever really trust him. The only way he could earn her trust was over time, and he planned on having lots of time with Mia.

Maybe even a lifetime of it.

The thought made his insides clench. He'd thought of a forever once before, and been rejected. Was he seriously thinking he could go through all that again?

But then Mia's lips found his, and his mind short-circuited. All he could focus on was the sweet taste of her, the scent of her, fresh as spring blossom.

Unerringly his hands worked their way under her top, lifting it over her head to reveal her simple white sports bra. He smiled, enjoying the cleavage it created, yet also the fact that this was Mia, true to herself, not trying to pretend to be anything other than who she was; sporty and unfancy.

'Bet you've not seen many sports bras.'

For a split second he worried they were going

backwards again, her thinking of his past, yet when he looked at her face, he saw only dry amusement. 'I like it.' He slid his fingers beneath the elastic, and at the feel of her full breast he hardened even further behind his fly. If he didn't get his jeans off soon, he was going to burst through the damn things. 'I think I'm going to like what's beneath it even more.' With that he eased the bra over her beautiful full breasts, lust raging through him as his eyes feasted on her now naked chest. 'Bloody hell, I've died and gone to heaven.'

She laughed, which caused her breasts to jiggle, and his jeans to feel even more cramped. Yet as much as he wanted to get shot of them, to peel off hers and get them both naked, he wanted to worship her breasts even more. So he ignored the ache and took one of her proud pink nipples into his mouth.

'God, Luke.' Her hands clasped his head as he licked and sucked, his fingers busy on her other breast where his mouth couldn't reach. In the end it was she who pulled back, chest rosy red, breath coming out in pants. 'You're driving me crazy. Get your clothes off.'

Chuckling, he tucked his hands under the waist of her jeans and peeled them over her legs. 'Not until I've got yours off first.' The humour died the moment he slid off her underwear, leaving her flushed and naked before him, all rounded curves and soft lines.

Beautiful. Yet when he sought her gaze, he saw her vulnerability. And when she spoke, he heard it as her voice caught. 'You now.'

'You're perfect, Mia.' He ran his hands over her breasts, across the gentle curve of her stomach. 'Absolutely bloody perfect.'

'That's bollocks and you know it.' But when her eyes dipped to his crotch, the corners of her mouth curved upwards. 'Though it's clear you like me.'

'I more than *like* you.' Deciding he was done with the teasing, he reached for his jeans button and flicked it undone, carefully sliding the zipper over his swollen dick before yanking the jeans off his legs.

'What happened to the strip show?'

'Shelved for a day when we haven't had what feels like a million hours of foreplay.' He grabbed a condom from the bedside table and slid it on before climbing onto the bed next to her, running his hands across her breasts and over her stomach before sliding a finger inside her heat.

Her hips arched off the bed. 'Yes, God yes.'

Easing over her, mindful of his size yet unbearably turned on by the feel of her beneath him, he gazed into her eyes. 'If I don't get inside you in the next few minutes, I think I'm going to explode.'

Her smile was half sensuous, half mischievous. 'If you don't get inside me in the next few seconds, I'm going to flip you onto your back and climb on top of you.'

'Fuck, that's sexy.' Unconsciously his hips thrust against her thigh, the image burning through him. 'You reckon you could do that?'

Before he knew what was happening, he was on his

back, Mia straddling him, her breasts bouncing, eyes laughing at him. 'I'm a black belt in judo.'

'How did I not know that?' She smiled back, holding his stare, and the longer they gazed at each other, the more his nerve endings began to prickle and burn as heat replaced the laughter. 'Hell Mia, just when I think you can't get any sexier, you blow me out of the water.'

Reaching for her face, he brought it down to his and kissed her again and again until he couldn't bear it any longer. Then he positioned himself so she could slide down onto him.

There was a gasp as she seated herself fully – his, hers, he didn't know. All sense of where he ended and she started fled as she began to move over him, finding a rhythm so they moved together as one, his hips punching up as she pushed down. Her eyes never left his, and he felt their connection, the pulse of something that went beyond sex, way beyond anything he'd ever experienced. In that moment she owned him, totally, completely.

Her rhythm picked up and he held onto her hips as he continued to thrust up into her, feeling a throb of satisfaction when her eyes glazed and she groaned out her pleasure. 'More.'

He did it again, and again, and watched in awe as she threw back her head and cried out his name as she fell over the edge.

When her gaze fell back on his she gave him a slow, languorous smile. 'Wow.'

He throbbed, aching for release, yet there was

something about the way she looked at him, the flushed skin, the sensuous expression, the glory of her lush breasts that made him want to hold the moment. 'Wow indeed.' He needed to move, yet for the first time he could remember, the rush to the finish line seemed so much less important than this; the quiet words, the intense intimacy of their connection. 'Being inside you…' His words were thick with both arousal and emotion. 'It's incredible. I don't want it to end.'

She shifted on him, and as he groaned at the sensation she darted him a wicked grin. 'Are you sure?'

His control snapped. Cursing, he gave in to the lust, rolling them over before pushing back inside her. As he felt her heat wrap around him again, pleasure burst over him, snatching the breath from his lungs. This was more, so much more than he'd ever thought possible. A few thrusts later and he let himself go, collapsing on top of her as wave after wave of the most exquisite pleasure rushed through him.

With the last vestiges of his energy he flopped back onto the bed and wrapped her up in his arms. 'Stay the night,' he whispered. 'Please.'

She laughed softly, her breath tickling his chest. 'Umm, I think I'll have to. Not sure I'll be able to move for a while.'

He knew the feeling. She'd drained him of all his energy. And yet, the way her fingers trailed over his abs, the silky feel of her hair across his skin. Those breasts crushed against his side … he bent to kiss her, a strong feeling of contentment brushing happily against the stirrings of arousal. 'Perhaps after a short power-nap we could try again? See if it was just a fluke?'

More light laughter, followed by a yawn. 'Deal.'

Within seconds, she was asleep. Smiling to himself, he kissed the top of her head, and closed his eyes.

Chapter Twenty-Eight

Mia woke to the feeling of a being wrapped in a heavy blanket. A hot and heavy blanket with muscular legs that were entwined with hers. And a hand that was cupping her left breast.

Last night came crashing back to her. The first time, and the second time.

Sex with Luke – it was right there at the top of her all-time favourite things to do. But now she'd discovered it, she was going to want to keep doing it. How did that sit with her need to prove she could be happy on her own? That she was a strong woman who didn't need family round the corner, or a man in her life. Especially one who might hurt her further down the line.

'Mia?' She felt a light kiss on the nape of her neck. 'Is everything okay? You've gone all stiff on me.'

It was an amazing night. You are not going to freak out. She drew in a breath and let the words calm her. 'Isn't that supposed to be my line?' For emphasis she pushed back against the very obvious erection pressing against her bum.

He chuckled, and mixed with the deep timbre of arousal, the sound actually gave her goosebumps. 'What can I say? Moby enjoys waking up like this.' He gave her nape another kiss. '*I* enjoy waking up like this.'

Pleasure hummed through her and she shoved at the dark thoughts that wanted to ruin this. Maybe she'd freak, but later. Now she was going to revel in waking up with a bloody gorgeous man, who was also a friend. 'Well, hello Moby.' Slipping out of Luke's hold, she turned and reached to caress the hard heat of him, staring into the face she was fast becoming addicted to. Forest green eyes surrounded by laughter lines, a square jaw, straight nose, dimples that flashed when he grinned.

He groaned, pushing into her hold. 'Please tell me you don't have to rush off.'

She bit down on her lip, loving the heavy feel of him in her hand, the hopefulness of his expression. 'It depends what you're going to offer.'

Eyes darkening, he trailed a finger over the curve of her breast. 'Pretty much anything you want.'

'Umm, so coffee?' She squeezed him, smiling as he grunted, his hips beginning to thrust.

'If that's what you want.'

'Eggs?' She gasped as his fingers trailed over her stomach, then dipped lower. Okay, so now he was playing at her own game.

'Fried? Scrambled?' His grin turned wicked as he found her core.

Using her other hand, she cupped him. 'Maybe poached. On a muffin oozing with butter.'

He hissed as she fondled him. 'You can have eggs flaming Benedict, as long as you promise to keep doing that.'

She laughed, then it was her turn to groan as he dipped his head and began to tease her nipples with his tongue. She lost the power of speech altogether as he reached for a condom before sliding slowly, exquisitely, breathtakingly into her.

Again his eyes held hers, just as they had last night, and again she felt a tug deep within her chest as his body flowed into hers.

This wasn't sex. It was so much more, and she was terrified she might be the only one thinking that.

'Mia.' He clasped his hands to her face even as he thrust deep inside her. 'Come back to me.'

'Sorry.' She felt the emotion brewing, tears pricking her eyelids. Crap, she couldn't cry. Not during sex, for God's sake.

As if he could read her mind, his eyes filled with understanding. Understanding and something more, something that looked like it was hurting him. 'I feel it, too,' he said roughly, continuing his slow glide in and out of her. 'Whatever it is you're feeling, you're not alone.'

Then he kissed her. It wasn't the searing passion of last night; this was tender, gentle. A caress of lips, a soft touch of tongues. As if he was trying to say with actions what neither of them could put into words because it felt too raw, too new.

She didn't get her eggs Benedict – he offered but she needed to get back to her desk. Instead she swigged at the coffee he'd made her while throwing last night's clothes back on and generally trying not to look like she'd spent the night having wild sex. And the morning… Her heart squeezed and she took another swallow of coffee. This morning had felt an awful lot like making love.

In fact it had felt more like making love than all the times she'd believed she'd been doing exactly that, with men who'd turned out to be bitter disappointments.

'That's one of the ladies in my life sorted.' Luke stood in the bedroom doorway, Pickles resting snug against his chest, the rabbit's blissful expression surely that of every woman who'd ever had the fortune to be cuddled up against him. 'How's the one without floppy ears and a twitchy nose doing?'

One of the ladies … it's a joke, get over yourself. If she really wanted to give this a go with Luke, she'd have to. She gave him a bright smile. 'Dressed and ready. Thanks for the coffee. I'll see you soon?'

'I hope so.' He looked like he wanted to say something more, but then clearly thought better of it. They walked together to his door, where he planted a soft kiss on her lips,

Pickles making Mia laugh as her whiskers tickled her chin. 'I'm working most of the weekend.' Another feather-light kiss. 'Any chance I can persuade you to sit on a bar stool and let me stare at you all evening?'

Her parents were coming down. Her sister. This was the time to tell him. Yet Mia hesitated. Was she ready for him to meet them? Her sister, okay, but parents seemed like a huge step, for both of them. Her, because she'd introduced too many guys to her mum and dad who'd later turned out to be duffers. Yes, her parents loved her. No, they didn't judge. It didn't stop Mia feeling like a failure, though. Elle had found the jackpot with boyfriend number one, and while Mia was still trying to find a man who wouldn't turn out to be an utter prick, her sister had provided their parents with two gorgeous grandchildren.

The next man Mia introduced to them, she wanted it to be The One.

Besides, Luke hadn't been in a relationship since he was eighteen, so he'd surely freak out at the thought of meeting her family. 'I'm not sure what I'm doing yet.' It sounded weak, like she was fobbing him off. The flash of hurt that crossed his face told her that's how he saw it, too, so she reached up to kiss him. 'I'll drop in if I get the chance.'

As she walked down the corridor, still arguing with herself over whether she should have mentioned her parents' visit, she heard a click, and the door of the neighbouring flat opened.

Immaculate Woman stepped out, living up to her name in a smart deep green suit teamed with high heels, her long brown hair neatly coiled into a bun. Mia, blue-striped sex hair, wearing yesterday's jeans and T-shirt, tried not to feel inferior.

'Well hello.' Freya gave her a cool smile.

Mia couldn't deny the woman was extremely attractive with almond-shaped hazel eyes and killer cheekbones. That smile though? Yeah, Mia reckoned she could also be a hard-nosed bitch if she didn't like you. 'Morning.'

The other woman's gaze skimmed over Mia's geek T-shirt before resting back on Mia's face. 'It's Mia, isn't it? I guess if you're coming out of Luke's flat at nine in the morning, you must be his latest.'

Okay, she'd been right. Freya was a bitch. 'And you must be Grace's mum.'

Freya lifted a dark brow. 'He's told you about us then?'

'Why wouldn't he? He's very proud of his daughter.' Mia smirked to herself. Apparently she could do bitch too, given the right incentive.

Freya gave her a cool look. 'Most of his relationships don't last long enough to discuss more than whose bed to use and how many condoms are needed.'

Ouch, there was bitch, and mega bitch. 'Well, it's been … interesting talking to you.' Mia faked a smile. 'I must dash, I've got to replenish my condom stocks.'

Head held high, she walked towards the stairs. Then scampered down them as fast as her trainers could take her. It didn't seem to matter how many times she told herself not to take any notice of the bitch's words, she felt rattled.

Enough that when she came to Naomi's café, she pushed open the door and went inside.

Naomi greeted her with her usual wide smile, though it slipped when she saw Mia's expression. 'Hey girl, what's got into you?'

'Freya,' she blurted without thinking.

Understanding dawned on Naomi's face. 'You mean the Freya who's mum to Grace.'

Mia shook herself. 'Sorry, I shouldn't have said anything. Truth is, she didn't say anything new. I just wasn't prepared for her.' She gave Naomi a considering look. 'And how come you know who Freya is?'

Naomi chuckled. 'Damn girl, I'm the café owner, the daytime equivalent of the bartender. I see everyone, talk to everyone and they talk to me.'

Mia screwed up her face. 'Freya's a customer?'

'Occasionally she comes inside.' Again Naomi laughed. 'Usually she toddles right on by on those killer heels.' Naomi gave her a sympathetic look. 'From what I hear, the woman is obsessed with her career and has no time for anyone else, male or female. I wouldn't take any notice of her.'

'I won't. Next time I'll be on my guard.' After checking nobody was behind her, Mia leaned in and whispered, 'How did it go with Stan? Did you have a good night?'

'You mean after you'd ditched us to go and sit at the bar and flirt with the owner?'

'I'm not having that. You were itching for me to get lost.'

Naomi's dark eyes twinkled. 'Let's just say Stan's dry

humour appeals, and he's a real gentleman. Walked me back to my place after we left.'

'*And?*'

Naomi hooted with laughter. 'Our generation doesn't rush things, not like you young things. We take our time, savour the journey, rather than being focused on reaching the destination.' She gave Mia an appraising look. 'Seems to me you reached your destination, judging by the way you're wearing the same clothes I saw you in last night. Question is, do you get off now, or do you stay on board and see where it takes you next?'

Mia opened her mouth, closed it, then opened it again. 'Café owner and philosopher, huh?'

Naomi winked. 'More like nosey old woman.'

Mia laughed. 'You're not old.'

Again Naomi's rich laughter filled the café. 'Neatly done. I'll not expect an answer to that question, but maybe you can answer this instead. Did *you* have a good time last night?'

Mia willed herself not to blush. 'I did indeed, thank you.' Dear God. Next she'd be saying, *I bid you good day*. She caught the glint in Naomi's eye and burst out laughing. 'Crap, Naomi, I don't know what to say. It's all a bit … new. We've been mates for a while, but now we've crossed a line and I'm still trying to work out how I feel, you know?'

'I do know.' Mia had the feeling Naomi was in a similar place with Stan. 'My advice, don't think too hard, it ties a person up in knots.' She patted her chest. 'The heart is usually the best guide.'

'Not in my experience.' Yet for the first time, Mia questioned whether she'd ever actually been in love. For all the pain the likes of Pete et al. had caused her, she'd never experienced with them what she'd felt last night. Or this morning. A sensation of being out of control, like jumping from a plane and falling through the sky; exhilarating, yet terrifying. Desperately hoping for a working parachute to slow the fall, and a soft landing.

'You're thinking again.' Naomi gave her a sympathetic smile. 'I recommend one of my lattes, a calorie-laden Danish, and something to distract you.'

Mia took her advice. Back at her flat she sipped on her coffee, attacked the Danish and phoned Elle with the latest update.

'Bloody hell, you had *sex*?' There was a pause, and Mia had to stifle a giggle when she heard Dave in the background yelling at Elle. 'Oops, apparently Caitlin's just asked what sex is and who's had it.'

'Jeeze, thanks sis. Way to make me the slutty aunt.'

'Yeah, well forgive me for the screech. Last I heard, you slept in Luke's bed but only cuddled, which I still can't believe if he's as hot as you say he is.'

Mia sighed. 'He is.'

'Right, but if I remember correctly, you gave His Hotness the cold-shoulder for a while because some bitch let herself into his flat the following morning. Then you found out bitch-face was his first love and they have a daughter together, which you were pissed he hadn't told you about. Though you did say you were going to forgive him because he said some stuff about you being important to him and looking nice first thing in the morning. Have I got that right so far?'

Mia rubbed a hand across her forehead, feeling a headache coming on. 'Sort of, but you've missed out some key bits that I'm too knackered to go through right now.'

Elle's voice softened. 'Key bits like the fact you're falling for this man who got a girl pregnant at eighteen and has played fast and loose ever since?'

Mia's voice cracked. 'Yeah, bits exactly like that.'

'So clearly you did forgive him.' Elle paused. 'Am I allowed to ask how the sex was, you know, purely from a sisterly concern point of view and in no way related to the fact that I can't remember why we bothered with it, considering the potential sleep-shattering, life-upending consequences.'

'Which you wouldn't change for a moment.' Mia grabbed at the coffee mug and took a big swallow. 'Best sex ever.' Before Elle could ask any more questions, Mia changed the subject. 'So, what's the plan this weekend?'

'You mean aside from me pinning you down and getting all the sex details?' Elle began to rattle off the arrangements: their parents would stay in the Travelodge; she, Dave and the kids would take over Mia's spare room and 'probably the entire flat'. Unconsciously Mia's eyes drifted to the flat opposite. Luke was stood in the window, ready to begin his workout. He waved, and as she waved back a lump settled in her throat.

He'd introduced her to his friends, to Phil. He wanted

her to meet Grace, and here she was, hiding the fact that her family were coming up this weekend.

He was trying to change, to let her in so they could have a real relationship.

She, on the other hand, was putting her head in the sand and refusing to acknowledge that her heart was opening to him, whether she wanted it to or not. The more she tried to pretend otherwise, to stop him getting too close, the deeper she dug into that sand. And the more she'd end up hurting both of them.

Chapter Twenty-Nine

The last few days the bar had been busier than usual. Luke wasn't sure whether it was down to Sandy's social media promos, Mia's new website, the Cocktails 4 U night or a total bloody fluke. Either way, when Phil had taken Luke through the accounts this morning, he'd reckoned there'd been enough of an uplift in customers through the door this week, to give him hope the bar might just make it.

Luke wasn't sure he could say the same about his tentative relationship with Mia. Wednesday had been a turning point, the beginning of a new phase where they still were friends, still went on dates, still enjoyed the hell out of each other's company. But also had frequent, frigging awesome sex.

Or so he'd thought.

'Comes to something when the accountant has to get his own bloody coffee.' Phil wandered back into the spare room, clutching at the mug he'd had to go to such extreme lengths to acquire.

'I made the first. If you're greedy enough to want a second, that's on you.'

Phil plonked himself down on the chair in front of the computer. The one with the spreadsheets they'd just been peering over. 'It's not greed. It's my way of ensuring you don't kick me out of the door before you've given me the rundown on you and Mia. Are you still not going on dates and not having sex?'

Bugger it. Luke rubbed at the back of his neck, trying to knead out the tension. 'I'm not in the mood for a cross-examination of my sex life right now.' Aware he was being stared at, Luke turned to face him. 'What? A guy's allowed a bit of privacy, even from his brother.'

'First, this brother has just spent his Saturday morning supplying free accountancy advice, so the least you can do is provide salacious details in return. Second.' A gleam entered Phil's eyes. 'You've just admitted you're having sex.'

Luke groaned. 'You should have been a frigging lawyer, not an accountant. But okay, we did have sex.' He rubbed at his eyes with the base of his palm, wondering whether to admit what he was feeling. 'I'm just not sure if it's going to happen again.'

Phil's eyes boggled. 'It was that shite?'

'No, you dumb-arse. It was the most awesome bloody sex I've ever had. And before you say anything, I was under the impression she thought the same. Except now I'm not sure because she didn't turn up to the bar last night.' And he should know because his head had popped up like a meerkat's – Mateo's description – every time someone had come through the door. A lot of head popping, leading to a shit-tonne of disappointment.

'Did she say she would?'

'She said she'd *drop in if she got the chance.*' It had made him feel like a chore she'd have to cross off.

'So? Clearly the lady has better things to do than sit in a crowded bar just so she can snag a few seconds of your precious time in between customers.'

Luke let the words sink in. Not for the first time, his brother had a valid point. 'You're saying I'm reading too much into it?'

'I'm saying, you're acting like a thirteen-year-old kid who thinks his girlfriend doesn't like him anymore just because she didn't sit next to him in class.' Phil pushed his chair back, clearly making himself more comfortable. 'You know you could always phone her. Ask her if she's planning on coming tonight.'

Yeah, maybe he could, if he'd not bottled it on Thursday morning. Then again, maybe she'd have said no. 'If you'd listened to a word I've been telling you over the last few months, you'd know I don't have her number. Hence the messages in the window.' He gave Phil a hard glare. 'The ones you told me were creepy.'

'Ah.' Phil looked at him pensively. 'I kind of assumed after all this time, you'd have it by now.'

He knew Phil didn't mean it to sound mean, but it

pricked nonetheless. 'She was burnt by her last boyfriend so she's only given her new number out to key friends and family.' *People she could trust.* Hence the reason he'd bottled asking. He could bitch and get frustrated all he liked, but considering her track record with men, and his track record with women, he could also understand why she hadn't trusted him with it yet. Didn't stop it hurting like a bugger though.

The way Phil winced, the fact he didn't respond with a smart-arse wise-crack, said it all.

Luke was back at the bar by two, where Bill and Sandy were taking care of the Saturday lunch session. Sandy caught his eye and walked over.

'Hey boss, you didn't tell me Mia's family were up this weekend.' He blinked and knew his poker face had failed him yet again when her expression turned from mildly irritated, to sympathetic. 'Ah, you didn't know, huh?'

'Just because Mia and I are friends it doesn't mean we have to tell each other everything that's going on in our lives,' he retorted far too defensively.

'Is that the same way friends don't need to tell each other things like the fact they have a sixteen-year-old daughter, and an ex living next door to them?'

'She knows that. Now,' he added, uncomfortably aware that when it came to discussing family with Mia, he wasn't totally blameless.

'Good. Has she met Grace yet?'

'No. But she will.'

Sandy narrowed her eyes. 'And now I can see why

you're looking so upset. Mia's becoming really important to you, isn't she? Which is why it hurts that she's not suggested you meet her family when you're ready for her to meet yours.'

He could lie, but what was the point? Sandy knew him too well. 'I'm a bit pissed, yes. I think I get why she's not ready, that she's still wary of me, of us, but yeah, it stings.'

He started to walk into the bar but Sandy put a hand on his arm. 'Hold up, where are you going?'

'To work?'

'Even though I happen to know Mia is with her family in Naomi's right now?' When he grimaced, Sandy shook her head. 'Mia's sister has two kids, dumb-wit. A baby and a really cute three-year-old. The bar isn't exactly a suitable place for them to have lunch, is it?'

'Fine, thanks for letting me know.' He was still smarting from it all. If Mia had told him her family were coming up, he could have met them for lunch, damn it.

Sandy moved to stand in front of him, blocking his path. 'Are you really turning into that guy? The one who gives up?'

'I'm not giving up. I'm respecting Mia's wishes. If she'd wanted me to meet them, she'd have said.' And ouch, there came another punch to his gut. He was the guy women had fun with. Not the one they introduced to their parents and settled down with.

'Maybe it wasn't a question of whether she wanted you to meet them, but whether she thought it was too soon.' Sandy stared at him, a glint of challenge in her expression.

'Why don't you go and prove her wrong? Prove that you can meet up with your *friend's* family without it having to be all weird.'

He wanted to sulk a bit more, to ignore Sandy and her unwanted advice, but it was damn hard to when she was looking at him all cocky and know-it-all. 'You know I could never resist a dare,' he muttered, dragging a hand through his hair. Shit, could he really do this? Walk casually into Naomi's and meet Mia's family, as if it wasn't a big deal, when meeting the important people in her life was huge?

Sandy grinned triumphantly. 'Okay then. I officially dare you to walk into Naomi's and meet Mia's family.'

Luke swore. Then turned round and headed towards the café.

Yet again, Mia watched her sister's eyes drift towards the door of the café.

'Stop it,' she hissed under her breath, not wanting to attract the attention of her parents, who were happily playing a game of hide the teaspoon with Caitlin while Dave paced up and down outside, trying to get a grumpy Jacob to sleep.

Elle frowned at her. 'Stop what?'

'Looking at the door, waiting for Luke to come in. I told you, he won't.'

'But Sandy, that was her name, yes, the woman who came in to borrow some napkins from Naomi for the bar?'

Mia sighed. 'Yes, that was Sandy.' Mia had wanted to hide under the table when Sandy had strolled in. She hadn't, because her cowardice apparently only ran as far as not telling Luke her family were visiting. Now he'd know, because no way was Sandy not going to blab. And now he'd be hurt/upset/offended/confused/annoyed that she'd not told him herself.

God, she felt terrible. And pathetic. And don't forget downright mean.

'Sandy said Luke was due at work,' Elle glanced down at her watch, 'five minutes ago.'

'So?'

'So, he'll now know you're here. Why wouldn't he pop in and say hello?'

'Because I didn't tell him you were coming, okay?'

'Oh.' Elle paused, which Mia was grateful for, because it meant whatever came next wouldn't be the unfiltered *why the bloody hell not?* she'd have received if they were by themselves. 'I'm sure you had your reasons.'

'I did.'

Elle raised an eyebrow. 'Just out of interest, how are you feeling about these reasons now?'

'Pretty shitty, if you must know.'

Elle smirked. 'Thought so.' Again she paused, only this time she nodded towards the door, and the huge window next to it. 'And if you take a look outside now?'

'Shit.'

Both her parents turned to face her.

'Mia Jessica Abbott,' her mum scolded. 'Young ears are listening.'

Ignoring her mum's disapproving look, and Elle's attempt to muffle her laughter, Mia stared out of the window at Luke, who was chatting to Dave. And, oh my God, now he was holding Jacob in those big muscular arms, easing him so he was face down across his forearm, his hand supporting Jacob's belly. Swaying him gently.

'That is seriously hot.' Elle pretended to fan herself. 'I mean, I love Dave with all my heart, but he does not look as sexy holding Jacob as that guy outside does.' She gave Mia a sideways glance. 'I presume that's Luke?'

Mia cleared her throat so she could speak. 'Yes.'

The conversation caught her mum's attention. 'Is that the friend you made, Mia? The one you told us about who's been showing you the city?'

'He's been showing her more than that,' Elle murmured.

Mia glared at her but it was too late. She now had the full focus of both her parents.

'He's your boyfriend?' Her mum looked hurt. 'Why didn't you tell me? You kept saying he was just a friend.'

'He *was* just a friend.' Mia couldn't take her eyes off Luke. The way he was holding baby Jacob so naturally. *Of course he is, he's been in Dave's shoes.* On one level she knew that, yet seeing it with her own eyes was huge. No longer was she looking at a sexy charmer, a player. She was looking at a dad. A guy who'd been there for his daughter through sleepless nights, changing her nappy, calming her like he was doing to Jacob. No doubt he'd had to handle toddler tantrums, the nerves of starting school.

Just then he turned to look into the café, and their gazes collided. Mia couldn't describe the jolt she felt, how much it turned her inside out.

'Mia?'

Her mum's voice broke through her trance. Shaking herself, Mia turned to her parents. 'Sorry.' She swallowed. 'Would you like to meet Luke?'

'If he's important to you, of course we would.'

Mia swallowed again, trying to ease the tightening in her throat. 'He is important to me.' With that she stood and, heart in her mouth, walked towards the door.

When she stepped outside, both Dave and Luke turned to look at her.

'Hey Mia.' Dave smiled. 'I've been chatting to Luke. He says he knows you.'

She raised her eyes to Luke's. 'He does.'

'I told him I own the bar round the corner,' Luke supplied, his gaze not leaving hers.

A ball of emotion rushed into her throat as she realised what Luke was doing. Pretending they were casual acquaintances.

Clearly oblivious to the undercurrent between them, Dave carried on talking. 'I don't know what owning a bar is like, but if you ever fancy a change of jobs you're a bloody marvel at calming tetchy babies.'

Luke smiled, and it was only because Mia knew him so

well that she could tell it was strained. 'I've had one of my own. Tried every trick in the book.' He glanced down to where Jacob was now fast asleep, nestled in his arms. 'Grace would only settle when I held her like this and rubbed her tummy.'

'Ah, how old is your daughter now?'

'She's sixteen.' Mia could see Dave's dawning shock as he worked the ages out in his head. 'I was a young dad,' Luke supplied with a wry smile. 'Though thanks for the look of surprise. It's a killer when people don't bat an eyelid and assume I'm forty-odd.'

Mia could see Dave ready to ask another question so she cleared her throat. 'Luke, have you got time to come inside?' She made sure to catch his eye. 'I'd love you to meet my sister Elle and my parents.'

Those bright green orbs widened, but still he didn't smile. 'Are you sure?'

She held his gaze steady with her own. 'I'm sure.'

His face lit up, the joy so visible it made her curse that she'd made him doubt how important he was to her.

As Dave went to open the door, Luke shot her a dimpled grin. 'What are we waiting for? I've always wanted to meet Papa Smurf.'

Mia burst out laughing and as she threaded her arm through his, happiness flowed through her. She hadn't broken what they had. That fact that he'd come to confront her when he knew her family were here, rather than sulking, showed that he was open and straightforward. More than that though, it proved they'd built something over the last few months that could withstand lapses in judgement on either side.

For the first time, Mia started to believe the nerd and the cool kid might actually have a shot at making this thing work.

Chapter Thirty

Sat on a picnic blanket, his arms around Mia, Luke watched in contentment as little Caitlin chased Grace round the duck pond. On the other side of the blanket sat Elle and Dave, a gurgling Jacob flat on his back between them, arms and legs waggling in the air. Behind them, sitting on two deckchairs Luke had managed to find in the depths of his junk cupboard, Mia's parents were shouting encouragement to Caitlin. Luke had found her dad quiet but with a ready twinkle in his eye. Her mum, on the other hand, was a riot. It wasn't hard to see where the daughters got their forthright sense of humour from.

Yesterday he couldn't have imagined this scene. When Sandy had practically shoved him over to the café to meet Mia's family, he'd not had a clue what he was going to say. Or how she'd react.

Yet somehow it had all worked out. A fact Sandy had gloated over when he'd returned to the café and admitted he'd not only met Mia's family, he was joining them for a picnic lunch the following day.

Oh and Mia had suggested he invite Grace, too, because his daughter might find it easier to meet her in a group when there was also a baby and a three-year-old to create distractions.

'Grace is really good with her.' From her position on the other side of the picnic blanket, Elle smiled over at him.

'She doesn't get to see tots too often. She's enjoying playing with the squirt.'

Mia dug her elbow into his ribs. 'You can't call my niece that.'

'She likes it.'

Elle laughed. 'Yes, thanks for that. She spent the rest of yesterday going round saying *I'm a squirt* in a proud voice to everyone she met.'

Luke chuckled. 'Grace was the same when she was that age. I used to call her a pickle and when people would say, "Grace, please come here," or whatever, she'd turn around and say, "I'm not Grace, I'm a pickle."'

The woman in his arms started to shake with laughter and he hugged her closer, resting his chin on Mia's head, breathing her in. Enjoying her. 'Is that why the rabbit's called Pickles?'

'Whoa.' Elle put up a hand. 'What rabbit?'

'Pickles is a dwarf lop,' he explained. 'For her tenth birthday, Grace insisted she wanted a rabbit. Her mum wasn't keen on the idea, thought rabbits should be outside, so I was the sucker who bought Grace one. She was the crazy person who called it Pickles.'

Elle cleared her throat. 'Is this the part where I pretend I don't know that Grace and her mum, who's called Freya, live next door to you and instead ask if they live in a flat, too?'

Mia groaned. 'Excuse my sister, she's so embarrassing. But okay, as she's so subtly pointed out, I will admit I tell her pretty much everything.'

Luke thought of his own relationship with Phil. 'I'm the same with my brother. That's what siblings are for.'

'Don't forget parents like to hear everything, too,' Mia's mum piped up, her attention temporarily diverted from her granddaughter. 'I hope you're better at keeping yours informed than Mia's been recently.'

Luke's stomach dropped as he searched for how to reply but thankfully Mia spoke into the silence. 'That's not fair. I know everything I say to Elle gets back to you, so there's no point repeating myself.'

'Umm, but now and again we like to hear what's happening first hand. Especially if it's important.' Mia's mum looked over at him. 'Do your parents have to hear about your relationships from your brother?'

Damn, seemed he wasn't going to escape this after all. 'I'm afraid they do.' He knew from the shocked expression on Mia's mum's face, the way Elle stilled, that he couldn't leave it there. Still, this wasn't an area of his life he wanted to discuss with the very people he wanted to impress. 'We had a falling out a while ago. Phil's still part of their lives but I'm…' Not wanted, not liked. 'I'm no longer in touch with them.'

'Is this the part where I pretend I'm not interested and change the subject?' Mia's mum smiled gently at him as she repeated Elle's words from earlier. 'I hate to disappoint you but I'm nosey, so that's not going to happen.'

He let out a choked sound, part laugh, part shock. 'Noted.'

'So what was the falling out about?'

Mia shifted so she was no longer sitting between his legs but facing him. 'Mum's nosey but you don't have to reply. You can pretend your phone's vibrating with an important call, or you need to take a pee, or—'

'Or I can just answer the question,' he cut in, smiling to let her know he appreciated her having his back. 'I had Grace when I was eighteen. My parents are pretty rigid in their views and couldn't deal with their son being a dad when he'd only just left school, and them having a granddaughter born out of wedlock.' He'd wanted to make things right, wanted to man up to his responsibility. His parents hadn't been able to see past his initial mistake.

'So they, what, disowned you?' Elle looked appalled.

'Pretty much.' He glanced over at Grace, who'd picked up the squirt and was now tickling her, leading to squeals of giggles from Caitlin. 'They never got to see Grace growing up. Never got to see the amazing person my careless, irresponsible, shameful actions – their words –resulted in.' He swallowed down the bitterness. 'Their loss.'

'Did Freya's parents help out?' Elle gave him a sheepish

smile. 'I'm my mother's daughter when it comes to the nosey part.'

'Freya lived with them in the beginning so yes, in a way, but they didn't look after Grace, if that's what you mean.' He looked Elle straight in the eye, determined that at least one part of this story would leave the right impression. 'I didn't want them to. Grace was my daughter, I wanted to bring her up as much as I could.'

'Then she's a credit to you.' Mia's mum had a warm smile, just like her daughter, and right now Luke was humbled to find it directed at him.

'She's a credit to herself, mainly.' Luke shrugged. 'I'd like to take some of it, so would her mum, but truth is she's making her own way in life.'

Mia, who'd been silent until now, reached for his hand. 'You gave her a stable childhood. Her parents weren't together in the traditional sense but she saw them as often, if not more, than most kids see theirs. Heck, you even bought flats next to each other so she can pop round whenever she wants. You were there for her, Luke. *That's* to your credit. And it's a shame your parents can't see you now to realise it.'

Luke wasn't sure, even if he knew what to say to that, that he'd actually be able say it.

Thankfully Grace chose that moment to bring the still giggling Caitlin over to them.

'She's worn me out.' Grace dropped onto the blanket next to him and threw her arms around his shoulders in a gesture that always made his heart squeeze, no matter how often she'd done it over the years. Her face was flushed and her green eyes – yeah, he was going to take credit for those at least – danced.

'Youngsters today, right bunch of snowflakes.'

She shoved at him. 'Thanks Dad. Why don't you try and keep up with her then?'

Maybe it was what he needed. A break so he could get his emotions back into line. Jumping to his feet, he looked down at the cute little tot with blonde curly hair and a cheeky smile. 'So Squirt, want to go and talk to the ducks?'

'Quack. Ducks go quack.'

He reached for her hand and hauled her up onto his shoulders as he used to do with Grace, much to her delight. 'Sure they do. They also go hoot and squeak and hiss if you listen carefully enough.'

'Hoot, hoot.' She grabbed at his head, giggling.

Luke glanced over to Mia's parents and smiled. 'How about we ask Grandma and Grandpa if they want to come too? They can help us listen.'

He wasn't sure what Caitlin's reaction was, but Mia's parents immediately got to their feet, so he guessed it was a good move asking them.

As Luke strolled off with a large part of Mia's family, he marvelled at how relaxed the morning had been. Sitting in the sun with his arms around Mia, talking to her family, watching Grace enjoy herself. It had felt far easier than he'd expected.

Having spent the whole of his life not measuring up to what people expected of him – his parents, Freya … himself

– yeah, having that in his head, he'd been shit scared of meeting Mia's family. Not that he'd have ever admitted as much to Sandy. Now, though he didn't know what they thought of what he did for a living or whether he was good enough to date their precious daughter, they were at least happy to walk by his side. And considering the conversation they'd just had, that was a pretty amazing result.

Not quite as amazing as the way Mia had come to his defence, though. For the first time in his life someone had told him he'd done something good, something to be proud of. Tears burned his eyelids and he had to force himself to focus back on Caitlin's chatter before Mia's parents were subjected to the embarrassing sight of their daughter's boyfriend crying.

As soon as Luke and their parents were out of earshot, Elle turned to Mia. 'Holy crap, that man is amazing with my kids. Please let me take him home with me.' Dave cleared his throat and Elle giggled. 'Just to keep the small people entertained, you muppet.' Once again her sister's gaze sought Mia's. 'Guess he's not just a hot guy with a great body, huh?'

Mia glared at her, desperate for her to shut up because Grace was still with them. Luke's *daughter*.

'What?' Elle gave her a quizzical look. 'You're the one who told me you used to ogle him while he worked out.'

While Mia turned a shade of tomato red, Grace burst out laughing. 'Seriously? You can see Dad do his weights from your place?'

Once again Mia levelled a death glare at Elle before turning to Grace. 'Excuse me later when I accidentally shove my sister into the pond.' She rubbed at her face. 'God, I can't believe we're having this conversation but yes, I may have noticed your dad when he did his workout every morning.'

'At ten o'clock,' Elle supplied unhelpfully.

Grace's wide-eyed stare swivelled from Mia to Elle and back to Mia. 'Is that how you started messaging each other?'

'Well, we met at the bar first but yes, I guess he knew when he put a message up in his window I'd be able to see it.'

'That's so sick,' she exclaimed. 'Way cooler than using a phone.'

'It was your dad who started it but yes, it's been fun, if a bit weird considering I'm a tech person and writing notes on paper to stick into a window is about as untech as it gets. It's also been challenging having to work out what he's trying to say from his cryptic symbols.'

Grace laughed and Mia immediately saw the resemblance to Luke. Not just the sparkling green eyes or the dimpled smile but the same easy way he had. As if nothing else existed but now, and enjoying it to the full. 'He told me about them. Sometimes he'd text me asking where to take you and what symbols to use in the message.' She gave Mia a sly look. 'He was trying to be dead clever so he'd impress you. The first one, the donut with the frost symbol, that was the best. I wouldn't have got it.'

'I nearly didn't. I had to google it.' She paused. 'Thank you for joining us today. I hope it hasn't been too weird. Aside from Elle and her big mouth, of course.'

Elle humphed. 'Hey, it's only fair Grace knows you think her dad's hot.'

Grace sniggered. 'Yeah, like that's such a big deal. Loads of women think he's hot. Sometimes when he lets me help out at the bar I have to look away 'cos it's just too embarrassing, watching them trying to get his attention.' She glanced at Mia. 'You're different though.'

'Yeah? Not the first time I've been told that.' She tugged at her blue-highlighted hair. 'Your dad called me a Smurf when I had this dyed.'

Grace groaned and put her head in her hands. 'He thinks he's funny but some of his jokes are like, so bad.'

Mia smiled, enjoying not just the interaction with Luke's daughter, but the glimpse of the other side of him. The embarrassing dad. It made him feel normal, a man she could see herself having a real relationship with. The hot bartender who had women fawning over him was too much of a stretch from who she was, but the man Grace was talking about. The one who told bad jokes and had such a grounded, loving relationship with his daughter. He was someone she could relate to.

'Mum used to find him funny,' Grace added, and immediately Mia felt a tightening across her chest at the mention of Freya. 'But then she got too stressed with her job and started getting annoyed instead. She'd be like, *not everything's a joke*. I mean it's true, but he was only trying to cheer her up, you know?'

Mia wasn't sure how to respond. Freya was Grace's mum, but equally to Mia she'd been less than friendly. And damn it, there was the bite of jealousy too, the knowledge that Freya was the one woman Luke had really cared about. The woman he'd loved enough to ask to marry him. 'I'm sure she realised that later.'

'Maybe. I guess I always thought Mum and Dad would end up together at some point. She's never really dated anyone else and I know Dad's had girlfriends but none that he's ever introduced me to.' She slid Mia a sidelong glance. 'Until now.'

Mia's heart thumped, her brain frazzled by the two seemingly opposing statements. If Grace believed they might get back together, were Luke and Freya closer than she'd thought? But did that matter, because of all the women Luke had dated, *she* was the only one he'd wanted to meet his daughter.

Thankfully she didn't need a reply because Luke and his entourage were heading back. Caitlin had her hands in his hair, tugging, spewing out words that didn't all make sense. Luke was replying though, clearly uncaring of the way his hair was being pulled, and her parents were laughing.

'Did you find some ducks?' Dave asked, reaching up to lift Caitlin off Luke's shoulders. Quite a task considering Luke was a fair bit taller than Dave. And Caitlin clearly wasn't ready to come down yet.

'What do you reckon, Squirt?' Luke tucked her under the chin, the motion enough to grab her attention and stop the tantrum that had been about to blow. 'How many ducks did you see?'

She held out her fingers. 'One, two, three, four…' She pulled out her other hand and grinned. 'Ten ducks.'

He chuckled. 'Exactly. More ducks than an England score sheet.' He lifted his eyes to Mia's, laughter creasing them at the edges. 'That's a cricket joke, in case you missed it.'

God, this man with his sexy, twinkling eyes. Was he really hers, or was he only on loan? 'That's a sexist remark, in case you missed it.'

'Didn't mean it to be.' He gazed at her, his expression both amused and, she thought with another heart bump, *adoring*. 'It's just, you once told me City were better than United, so I wasn't sure whether you understood sport enough to get the joke.'

Everyone laughed and the connection between her and Luke was broken, yet as they cleared up Mia felt a bubble of happiness. It had only been three months, yet she felt settled up here. As if she'd never lived anywhere else. The only small dent to that happiness was the worry that Luke was the cause of it. When he decided he'd had enough of dating the nerdy Smurfette, where did it leave her?

Chapter Thirty-One

Luke watched the man enter the bar, his gaze skimming over the faces of the customers, clearly looking for someone.

There was something about him – was it was the way his eyes constantly shifted? The fancy leather jacket that looked too designer, too pretentious in a Manchester bar, even on a Saturday night? Luke couldn't put his finger on what it was, but he felt a prick of unease.

Hell, maybe he was being paranoid. His life was going so bloody perfectly right now, perhaps too perfectly. His mind was making things up to disrupt it.

He exhaled, turning away from the fair-haired stranger. Nope, he wasn't going to let anything get in the way of how he was feeling right now. He had a bar that was starting to pick up, a daughter who was settled in college and starting her A Levels. And a girlfriend he'd seen four times already this week, but who'd still promised to drop by later.

A girlfriend he couldn't ever imagine not being with.

Next to him, Mateo groaned. 'For God's sake lose the dopey expression. It's making me ill.'

Luke grinned. 'Jealousy isn't pretty.'

'Neither is bragging,' Mateo grumbled. 'Still don't know why she chose you over me. I thought she was smarter than that.'

'She's far too smart for either of us.' Luke let the words drift round his mind but where he'd usually feel a bite of inferiority, now it was more of a nibble. Mia saw things in him others didn't. She admired how he'd brought up Grace, and how he ran the bar. Hell, she even thought he was a genius at making cocktails.

'Excuse me.'

He was shaken out of his happy buzz by a posh-sounding voice in a southern accent. When he turned he found himself face to face with the guy in the posh leather jacket.

'What can I get you?'

The man shook his head. 'Thanks, but I'm not here for a drink. I'm looking for someone. Female, blonde and blue eyes, about five foot three. Might have coloured streaks in her hair.'

His pulse kicked but Luke worked hard to keep his expression bland. 'We get a lot of women through this door, many of them short with blonde hair. Have you got a name for her?'

'Mia Abbott.'

Okay then. 'Is she a friend of yours?'

'You could say that. We used to date, but then we lost touch when she moved up here.'

Luke reached for another glass to dry so he had something to do with his hands. 'You can't just give her a call?' And yes, he was aware of the irony of that statement, given he was pretty sure the lowlife was Mia's ex, Pete.

'I lost her number.'

At least you had it once. Luke shrugged off the bitterness and instead directed his anger at the man in front of him. He was the reason Mia was now scared to trust people – trust *him* – with her new number. 'But you know where she lives?'

The man looked uncomfortable. 'I used to know, obviously. I mean, I used to almost live there, but I don't have her new address, no. I only know she must come to this bar because she liked it on Facebook.'

Shit. Looks like Sandy's social media campaign had had an unintended consequence. And if this guy was as tenacious as Mia had implied, he was going to keep coming back until he saw her here.

Not going to happen.

'What's your name?'

'Pete. Pete Michaels.'

Luke nodded, wiping a non-existent mark on the glass while he fought the desire to reach across the bar and grab the guy by the lapels of his fancy jacket. 'Well then Pete, you're right, Mia does come to this bar.' He stared straight into Pete's light-coloured eyes. 'She's my girlfriend.'

Pete blinked, rocking back on his heels. 'Oh, right.' Luke watched as he visibly swallowed. 'Congratulations.'

Luke inclined his head but kept quiet.

'I don't suppose you could tell me where she lives now though? Just so I can say hi.' He lifted his shoulders. 'You know, for old time's sake?'

And how galling, how humiliating, that this prick hadn't just once been Mia's ex, he'd slept with her in her house, in her bed, called her on her phone. Whereas Luke hadn't been able to do any of that, despite how close he'd felt to her since meeting her family. 'You think Mia would want to see you land on her doorstep?'

Ha, that got the bastard flinching. 'I don't know.'

'Well I do.' Signalling to Mateo that he was going to be a minute, Luke brusquely told Pete to follow him. When they entered the office, he shut the door and stood nose to nose with him. 'Mia came up here to escape you, you snivelling bastard, so you'd be about as welcome on her doormat as a dog turd.'

Pete stepped backwards. 'Whoa, no need to be aggressive. I only wanted to say hello to her.'

Luke took another step forward, needing to impress on Pete his superior height, his bulk. The uselessness of a slick leather jacket when it came to a show of brawn. 'If she'd wanted to hear from you, she'd not have changed her phone number.' He lowered his voice, letting his anger show. Anger at the git for upsetting Mia, hurting her so much she was now wary of letting Luke in. 'Think you're a big man, do you, harassing a woman?'

'I didn't harass her.' Luke noticed Pete was no longer able to look him in the eye.

'Maybe in your mind you didn't, but let me make it plain. Try to see her again, try to contact her, and you'll know exactly how it feels to be hounded, to be fearful. To be scared of what the other person might do to you.' He felt a dart of satisfaction when he saw the fear enter Pete's eyes. 'Are we clear?'

Pete opened his mouth to speak, but no sound came. Then he coughed and tried again. 'We're clear.'

As Luke watched Mia's ex walk out of the bar a few moments later, he wondered what Mia had ever seen in the guy. Then he realised he should be wondering what she saw in him, because Pete, with his trappings of wealth, his cultured accent, his air of entitlement, was one hell of a long way from a guy who spent his days working in a bar.

Mia rolled her shoulders and looked at her watch. Nine o'clock – time to hit the bar. She'd promised Luke she'd head over there once she'd written her target 3,000 words for the day. She could have done more, but she'd woken in his bed this morning and not wanted to leave. It was only when he'd headed to work that she'd finally made it back to her flat. Heat flashed through her as she remembered how they'd spent the time. Yep, totally worth it.

As she closed the door to the flat, her phone pinged with a message from her sister.

Advance warning, Mum is muttering about inviting you and Luke down for her birthday. E xx

Mia sighed. It was great that her mum was taken with Luke – *such a handsome lad, so sweet with Caitlin and so easy to talk to, not like that last one.* Still, Mia was worried she seemed to be racing forward at a million miles an hour while Mia, many times burned, was desperate to take things slow. Feeling a little panicked, she fired off a quick reply to Elle:

Remind Mum of my track record for picking men. That should make her pause. M x

It was only as she pressed send that Mia realised she hadn't picked Luke. In fact she'd tried her hardest *not* to. So maybe this time it really would be okay. Maybe this time she could let her heart do what it so badly longed to do, and open up to him fully.

She heard the hum from the bar as she rounded the corner. It was a mild September evening and many people were sitting outside. Mia strolled past them, waving to a few of the regulars she'd got to know over the last few months of coming here.

Speaking of regulars, Tanya was standing at the bar. She'd not spoken to her since she and Luke had started sleeping together. Crap, what did you say to your boyfriend's most recent ex? Or maybe you didn't say anything. Maybe you just turned around and hot-footed it out…

Mia squared her shoulders and eased into the space next to Tanya. 'Hi.'

Tanya turned and smiled. 'Hi yourself. We didn't realise you were here.'

'I've only just arrived.'

'Oh, right. Are you going to come and join us?' Tanya paused and glanced at the other end of the bar where Luke was busy shaking cocktails. 'Or maybe you're here for another reason.'

Shit, she really wasn't good in these situations. 'I'd love to come and join you guys.' She hesitated. 'After I've said hi to Luke.'

Tanya's eyes searched hers. 'So you and Luke really are a thing now? We watched you both at the Cocktails 4 U bash. It was obvious you couldn't keep your eyes off each other.'

'At the time we were only friends,' Mia stated quietly. 'That was the night things changed.'

Tanya nodded, eyes on the empty glasses in front of her. 'When we broke up, Luke told me he didn't want to see me anymore because his head was full of another woman. I thought it was Chloe.' She turned to look at Mia. 'Turns out it was you.'

God, this was hard. She liked Tanya, the others too. Different to her, but they'd taken her under their wing anyway. 'I didn't think it was me. Not then. But the more we saw each other as friends, the closer we got.'

Tanya smiled. 'And you finally realised how hot he was, huh?'

Relieved at the easing of tension, Mia laughed. 'I always knew he was hot, but that's not the type I usually go for. Or the type that goes for me.'

Tanya sighed. 'Well maybe you did it right, being mates first. I mean looks are great, and so is sex, but there has to be more if it's really going to work.' Her eyes drifted over to Luke. 'I wanted it to work with him, but I always knew it wasn't what he wanted.'

Her heart ached for the gorgeous woman who looked uncharacteristically lost right now. 'You deserve more from a guy than just sex, Tanya.'

She gave Mia a wry smile. 'That's what he said, too.' Her arm nudged Mia's. 'He's a good guy, but you're cool, too. I hope it works out for you both.'

A lump rose in Mia's throat and she squeezed Tanya's hand. 'Thank you.'

The moment was broken by a well-spoken voice behind them. 'Fancy seeing you two here.' Mia turned sharply to find Freya. *Perfectly put together* Freya; hair down in glossy waves, make-up discreet, black flared trousers that showed off her slim figure and looked effortlessly classy.

Tanya was the first to speak. 'Hi Freya. It's been a long time since we've seen you here.'

'I've been busy with one thing and another. Just had a hankering for my favourite cocktail tonight.' She lifted her slender shoulders in a small shrug. 'Only Luke seems to make it just how I like it.'

Mia didn't want to get into a sparring game with the woman, but it was hard to forget what a bitch she'd been the last time she'd seen her. 'He is a genius at cocktails,' she remarked mildly.

Freya smiled, though it didn't reach her eyes. 'It seems he's also a genius at keeping women interested. Look at us, his first, his latest and the one before her. All hoping for some attention from him.'

The atmosphere became charged and while Mia quietly fumed – *his latest*, gee, thanks – it was Tanya who made the first riposte. 'You must be talking about yourself, Freya. I'm only here to order some drinks.'

At that moment Luke glanced over at her. His huge smile, the sexy wink, were exactly what she needed. 'And the advantage of being his *latest*,' Mia added, 'is I'm not hoping for attention.' She made sure to catch Freya's eyes. 'I know I'm going to get it.'

Murmuring to Tanya that she'd go and find Chloe and the gang, Mia walked away, her mouth curving in a tacky, but hugely satisfying smirk.

By eleven o'clock the bar was quiet enough for Luke to come and find Mia. Taking her hand, he gently pulled her away from the girls. 'Come with me. I've got something I need to talk to you about.'

'Oh?' she grinned. 'Is that a euphemism for something, because if it is, I'm totally up for it.'

He cocked an eyebrow, the green in his eyes darkening. 'Oh yeah?' He tugged her into his office.

As soon as he'd closed the door, he pushed her against it and lowered his head. 'God, you're sexy.' His eyes fell to her lips. 'I so want to kiss the hell out of you right now.' He heaved out a sigh. 'But it's going to have to wait, because I need to get back out to Mateo.'

When she looked up at him, she saw a smidgen of tension on his face. 'What's wrong?'

He reached for her hand. 'Pete came into the bar earlier.'

Mia tensed, a chill running through her. 'Pete, as in my ex?'

'Yes. He was looking for you.'

Unbalanced, Mia wrenched her hand from his grasp. 'How the hell did he find me here?'

'Apparently you liked one of the posts about the bar. He put two and two together and came here.'

'Shit, I forgot to unfriend him.' She started to pace the small room. 'How stupid am I? I went to the trouble of getting a new number and I didn't think to bloody remove him from my Facebook friends.'

'Hey, it's okay. I don't think he'll trouble you again.'

Though his smile was clearly meant to reassure, there was something in Luke's dark expression that sent a shiver across her skin. 'What did you do?'

'I warned him off.'

'Jesus.' She couldn't believe this was happening. Not just that Pete had followed her up here, but that Luke had met him and seen with his own eyes how appalling her judgement had been. Worse even than that though, was that he'd felt the need to scare Pete off. It was mortifying. 'That wasn't for you to do. He's my issue.'

'Not if he's a threat to *my* girlfriend.'

Anger fizzed now, alongside the embarrassment. 'You should have asked him to wait. You knew I was coming to the bar.'

Luke's jaw tightened, his expression hardening. 'Sure, I could have done that. Even better, I could have phoned you to warn you he was here. Dashed up to your flat to tell you in person. But I couldn't do either of those things, could I?'

Slowly her anger cooled, replaced by shame. What sort of girlfriend was she if she couldn't trust the man she was sleeping with enough to give him her ruddy phone number? Her address?

The strained silence was broken by a knock on the door and Mateo's voice came through the woodwork. 'Need you out here, boss.'

Luke exhaled sharply and walked towards the door. Gripping the handle, he turned and gave her a sad smile. 'Sorry, but I can't apologise for what I said to Pete. He needed to be told, so he wouldn't come and pester you again.'

Maybe he was right, but she'd moved here to prove she could manage by herself without her family. Without a boyfriend. Now she'd not only found herself with one, she was terrified she was becoming dependent on him. 'I think it's best if I go home.' Pete being here, the altercation with Freya at the bar… Mia needed to go back and regroup.

Hurt flashed across Luke's face. 'If that's what you want.'

'It isn't, but it's what I think I should do.' With a heavy heart, she pointed to her head. 'I've got stuff going on in here that I need to work through.'

The ache in her chest intensified as he gave her a final searching look before walking out and closing the door behind him. Left by herself, she cursed Pete for turning up and buggering up the Saturday night she'd been looking forward to all day.

It was only later, when she was back at her flat, that the truth dawned on her. It wasn't Pete who'd ruined the evening. It was *her*, for letting him.

Chapter Thirty-Two

Luke woke the following morning to an empty space beside him, and a gnawing emptiness in his chest. Alone in his bed, he went over and over the conversation with Mia in his office from last night, trying to see it from her side.

Had it felt like he was interfering in her life? She'd told him many times how much she needed to prove she could manage by herself. It had been part of why she'd been so determined not to start a relationship with him. So yeah, maybe he'd been heavy handed. With guys like Pete though, sometimes only a threat would work. Could he have done it more subtly though, and in a way that left Mia in control?

If he'd told Pete to come back to the bar later, talk to her when the bar was shut, he could still have protected her, still have made sure Pete knew he had her back, but done it by staying in the background.

Damn it, he'd cocked up.

Pushing the duvet off, he strode into the spare room and headed to the sheets of paper. He'd message her, apologise for being an overbearing prick. But when he glanced at her window, he saw she'd beaten him to it.

Can we talk

Plz

His heart sank. How many times in life did the words *we need to talk* lead to anything good? Grabbing his marker pen, he scrawled:

Here?

Now?

A few seconds later, his heart flip flipped:

U 2 me?

A moment later a second message:

Flat 214

He inhaled sharply, his mind a jumble. Could this really be bad news if she was finally telling him where she lived? Or had she been forced to do that because she'd lost her key/had to stay in for a delivery/any other crappy reason he could drive himself mad thinking about? Quickly he messaged back:

OK

5 mins

He spent two of those minutes in the shower, one shoving on a pair of jeans and a T-shirt, and then legged it out of the flat, just remembering to pick up his phone and keys before he slammed the door behind him.

A minute and a bit later, he knocked on the door of flat 214.

The woman who opened it, the one who made his heart leap whenever he looked at her, threw her arms around his neck. It took him so much by surprise, he stumbled backwards.

'Whoa.'

'God, I was such a cow yesterday.' Not giving him a chance to talk, she dragged him inside and began to plant kisses all over his face. The gesture was more exuberant than sexy but God, it did more to lift his heart, and his libido, than any artful seduction. 'Sorry,' she repeated, with another flurry of kisses. 'Sorry.'

Groaning, he lifted her so she was able to put her legs around his waist. 'No, it's me who needs to apologise. I should have let you handle your ex, your way.'

She buried her face in his neck. 'Maybe, or maybe if I

had it wouldn't have worked and he'd still be here, waiting for me.' She eased back and the eyes that found his brimmed with apology. 'Mum phoned this morning to say Pete had just come to see her. He asked her to tell me he's sorry, he realises he went too far but he's got the message and won't try and contact me again.'

Relief settled over him and he hugged her tighter. 'Good.'

'Yes.' She rested her forehead against his. 'I wanted to handle it myself, but I also appreciate how you stepped in, which I know sounds backwards.' Her sigh fluttered against his face. 'Truth is, much as I want to be independent, I also love having someone in my corner, so thank you for being that someone.'

'Anytime,' he told her gruffly, his heart full. 'I'll always be there for you, in that corner, fighting for you.' He wanted to add, *because that's what people in love do*, but he was terrified it was too soon for either of them to hear it. A man who'd played fast and loose all his adult life wasn't someone who should rush into saying the words. And a woman who'd only just trusted him with her address wasn't someone he should rush.

His lips found hers and he took over the kissing, teasing her, enjoying her. It wasn't long before arousal pulsed through him and as his knees began to weaken he walked them towards the wall, pushing her back against it and shifting so her core was aligned with his. Relishing the heat of her, he deepened the kiss. Just as it threatened to get out of hand, she leant back, her breathing as uneven as his own. 'Have you got your phone?'

'My phone?' He laughed softly. 'I must be losing my touch if you're thinking of making a phone call while we're making out.'

'Not a phone call.'

Intrigued, he allowed her to slide down his body until her feet hit the floor. Then he snagged his phone from his back pocket, opened it up and gave it to her. 'Do you want to see my text messages? Is that what this is?' He tried not to feel too insulted and instead remembered the reason why she'd been wary about him. 'Because you can, I don't mind. I've got nothing to hide.'

Mia stilled, a look of horror crossing her face. 'Oh God, you think I'm checking up on you?' Before he could reply, she was talking again. 'Of course you do, because why wouldn't you when the woman you're sleeping with hasn't even had the decency to give you her phone number?'

With that, she tapped something into his phone. When she handed it back to him, he saw that she'd added *Mia (girl opposite)* and her phone number. Feeling choked, he just about managed to squeeze out a thank you before pushing it back in his pocket.

Her expression was solemn. 'I should have done it sooner and I'm sorry I didn't. I let my experience with Pete totally cloud my judgement, which wasn't fair on you. You're so far removed from him,' she shook her head, 'I can't even tell you how much.'

'I don't wear posh designer jackets, that's for certain.'

She looked at him aghast. 'God, don't even think about comparing yourself unfavourably to that bastard. I'm embarrassed I ever went out with him.' She gave a little shudder. 'My family have never gushed about a guy I've introduced them to like they did about you. Mum thinks you're handsome and charming; Dad says you're solid, which – trust me – is real praise; and Elle would have your babies tomorrow if she wasn't already married.'

He smiled, reaching a hand to touch her cheek. 'That's great to hear, but it's what *you* think that counts. Because I'm telling you right now, I've never felt for anyone what I feel for you.' He'd just told himself he wasn't ready, *they* weren't ready, but he couldn't contain what he felt inside any longer. It was too big, too important to keep quiet. 'Mia, I'm no longer falling for you. I've *fallen*. Arse over tit, head over heels, however you want to phrase it. For years I was cut up about Freya but now I realise that was young love. This, what I feel for you, it feels like true love.'

Breathe, Mia, breathe.

But it was hard to when your chest felt so tight. And your eyes burnt with unshed tears.

'Mia?'

He looked so concerned, she forced her mouth to smile. 'Sorry, I'm trying to wrap my head around what you've just said.'

'Is it okay that I've said it? Because I'm not expecting

you to say anything back. I'm aware this is too soon for you, and I was going to keep quiet for a bit, but you need to know I'm not going to get bored of you. I'm not going to start looking for someone else.' He clasped the side of her face, his eyes devastating in their intensity. 'Why would I, when I've found *you*? Best friend, sexy siren, cute nerd, funny Smurf, all rolled into one?'

Half laughing, half crying, she wrapped her arms around his waist. 'I wasn't expecting this when I moved up here. I thought I'd have time to get settled, to learn to live by myself, to find friends, before I started dating again.' She peered up at his gorgeous face. 'And if I'm honest, you're not the type of guy I expected to fall for.'

She heard his intake of breath. 'Fall for?'

'That's what I said.'

She felt the tension leave his body. 'You've got no idea how fucking good that sounds.'

She laughed against his chest. 'Yes I have.'

For a moment they stood in silence, content, arms around each other.

'This type,' he said finally as he eased her away, taking hold of her hands. 'Are you talking the cool-guy/nerd-girl shite again, or me the player?'

'Both.' She glanced down at their entwined hands, noticing for the first time how long his fingers were. How masculine and deeply sexy, like everything else about him. 'I was wary of the player side of you but I know that's not you now. What is still you, is a vastly good-looking guy with a ready smile that has, in the past, attracted some seriously gorgeous, immaculately put-together women.' She glanced down at her leggings and oversized shirt. 'That isn't me.'

He laughed, a low chuckle that made her insides melt. 'I don't give a rat's arse what you wear, as long as I can strip you out of it.' His expression turned serious as he gazed into her eyes. 'I told you before, I went with women who were confident and knew what they wanted, not because I saw a future with them, but because I didn't. They were only in it for the short term, like me. Then I met you, and you were so different. You made me think, made me question. Made me want to spend time with you outside the bedroom.' He gave her a dirty, sexy smile. 'Inside, too, but you kept me at arm's length so I had to quash all my usual instincts.'

She nudged him. 'You didn't quash them that well. You were pretty hard to resist.'

'When I want something, I can be pretty relentless, so fair warning.' He dropped a kiss on her mouth. 'Are we really doing this then, Mia Abbott? Going steady? Not just sightseeing non-dates, messages in the window and you coming to the bar, but real dates, spending time in each other's flats. Phoning when we can't see each other?'

It sounded so good, so exactly what she wanted, now she'd stopped letting the past interfere with her future. 'Yes, to all of it. By my reckoning there are still ninety-two places in Manchester you've still to show me, and I definitely want to phone you but also I don't want to lose the messages in the window, because it's us.' She gave him a cheeky smile.

'Oh and I can't wait to see what Luke Doyle does on a real date, because his non-dates have been pretty spectacular.'

'Err, a real date will be pretty much like the non-date.' He waggled his eyebrows. 'The difference is, you don't get to leave me at the end of it.'

'Deal.' She held out her hand to shake on it, but he shook his head.

'Oh no, we don't seal a deal by shaking hands.' For the first time his eyes skimmed beyond the tiny hallway they were in and down the corridor. 'How about you show me where you work, so I can picture you when I look over at your window?' He drew a hand around her waist, pulling her tight against him before bending to whisper in her ear. 'And then we can seal the deal in your bedroom, so when I'm not with you I can picture you there, naked.'

Just as he went to grasp her hand though, his phone rang. He sighed, pulling it out of his back pocket, before giving her an apologetic look. 'It's Freya, mind if I answer? I'll get rid of her quickly.'

'Of course.' Mia reminded herself Freya was Grace's mum, so of course he had to talk to her. Even though a second before, he'd been focused on them getting naked.

Because she didn't want to overhear – okay, bollocks to that, she wanted to listen to every word, but that wasn't polite, reasonable or trusting, and Mia tried to be all those things. So she walked through into the kitchen where she could only hear the deep hum of his voice. And the occasional lilt of laughter, which caused her gut to twist.

He's just told you he loves you, for God's sake. She reminded herself of the incredible things he'd just said. Things she'd like to bet he'd never told any of the other women he'd been with. *Except Freya.*

'Sorry about that.' Luke strolled into the kitchen and wrapped his arms around her. 'Now where were we?'

Mia wanted to go back to the time before the phone call, but her mind wouldn't let her. 'What did she want?'

'Oh, just some gripe about a light switch that's not working. I'll take a look later.' He peered down at Mia, understanding dawning across his face. 'Freya is Grace's mum, her flat is Grace's flat, too. The occasional stuff I do for her, I do because of that, and only because of that. Okay?'

Mia closed her eyes and relaxed into him. Starting a new relationship when her last few attempts had gone so horribly wrong was hard. Yet comparing him with the likes of Pete, of Danny and Andy, was terribly unfair. As Elle had said, she'd settled for guys who were average, believing that was her, too. Yet now she had the chance of a man who was extraordinary. And she wasn't going to allow her irrational fears to muck it up.

Chapter Thirty-Three

The next month passed in a blur. Luke both cursed and loved the fact that the bar was busier than ever. The Cocktails 4 U evenings had been a hit, getting them a write-up in the local paper and, unbelievably, squeezing The Bar Beneath into the top-ten list of best places to get a cocktail in Manchester.

It meant his chances of keeping the bar had gone from low to high, and that he was actually proving to the staff, to Phil, to himself that he could run a business.

It also meant he spent long hours away from Mia.

On the plus side, Mia never once complained and if part of him would have liked her to gripe, just a bit, that she missed him, mostly he was thankful for her understanding. Of course, Mia being Mia, she wasn't sitting in her flat waiting for him to turn up. She was writing.

He was changing the vodka optic early evening on a slow Sunday when his phone beeped with a message he knew was from Mia because he'd given her a special sound. The Smurf theme tune. Finishing the job at double speed, he grabbed at his phone.

Just written The End. Need to celebrate!

'What's brought that smile to your face?' Sandy raised a hand. 'Actually no, don't tell me. You remember when I said I could guess it was your latest booty call messaging you, from the leering expression you made?'

The memory sent an uncomfortable shiver down him. 'I'm not that guy anymore.'

'God, don't I know it. Now when you look at your phone you mostly have this half-soppy, half-downright smug grin on your face and I don't have to guess who the message is from. I know it's Mia.'

'She's finished her book.'

'Wow, that's amazing. We should help her celebrate.'

He eyed up Sandy, his mind spinning with an idea. 'Can you get your hands on any balloons? Maybe pink but it doesn't really matter. Oh and a congratulations banner?'

'Probably. What are you thinking?'

'I'm thinking I'd like to show Mia how many friends she's made up here, and how proud we are of her.'

Sandy's expression softened. 'God, you really are gaga over her, aren't you?'

He nodded happily. 'Yep, I really am.'

Sandy reached up to kiss his cheek. 'I'm so bloody pleased. She's exactly right for you. Gorgeous but not showy, crazy smart yet not highbrow, punchy without being aggressive. Plus she isn't going to sit at the end of the bar and mope, waiting for you to finish work and resenting the time you spend at it. She'll do her own thing and find you later.' She grinned. 'Of course it does mean you're destined to eat curry on your lap in front of *Britain's Got Talent*.'

'No way, not me and Mia.' He smirked. 'I'll take the curry, but we'll be gaming, not watching TV. And after that's got her all hot and worked up, we'll go to bed, where I'll get her hot and worked up—'

Sandy pushed her fingers in her ears. 'No, no. I do not want to hear about your sex life.' She nodded to his phone. 'You focus on your end of things, I'll sort out the trappings.'

Was he crazy to be doing this? Mia wasn't an extrovert, like him. She might not want the attention. There was also the fact she might think it was too much – she'd finished the manuscript, not found anyone who wanted to publish it.

He shrugged the doubts away. She'd said she wanted to celebrate, he was going to help her.

Before he could call the first person on his list, his own phone rang.

'Hey, Pickle.'

Grace let out a heavy sigh on the other end of the phone. 'I thought we agreed you'd stop calling me that when I turned sixteen.'

'You asked me to stop, I said I'd try, but a sixteen-year habit is hard to break, so suck it up, kiddo. Now, what did you want?'

'I've got maths homework to be in by tomorrow and I can't fucking do it.'

'Hey, what's with the language. Does your mum let you say the f-word?'

Another sigh. 'You're not Mum though, are you?'

He'd always been the soft touch. Freya had treated motherhood much as she had her career – committed, dedicated, organised, with a spine of steel. For him, it had been his sole focus, the reason he got up in the morning. Bar work had paid the bills, but being a dad had fulfilled him. Still did, even though Grace needed him less and less now. Which brought him back to the phone call. 'Fine, you can swear to me, but not to any other adult. Now about this maths, I hate to say it but your mum is the bright one. The only numbers I'm good with are working out the change from a tenner, and even with that I'm rusty, as most people pay by card now.'

'Duh, I know you can't help.' He knew the slight was unintended. He might not have followed the academic path but in his daughter's eyes, he still walked on water. Some of the time. 'Do you think Mia will be able to? She's into computers, and my friends who do computing say a lot of it is maths so I figured she might be good at it.'

A warm, fuzzy glow settled in his chest. He loved how Grace and Mia had bonded over the last few weeks. 'I'll ask her.'

He had half a mind to ping Grace Mia's number so they could talk direct, but though Pete had not resurfaced in real life, Luke knew the bastard still lurked in Mia's subconscious, preventing her from fully moving forward.

It had to be the reason she'd yet to tell him she loved him, even though he'd said the words several times to her since that first time in her flat.

Or maybe she doesn't feel as strongly as you do, dumb arse.

He guessed that was the other explanation.

Shoving the unhelpful thoughts aside, he made the phone calls on his list, finally ending with one to Mia.

'Finished the book huh? How many words?'

'Just under 92,000.'

He smiled at the obvious pride in her voice. 'That's one hell of a big number. Definitely needs celebrating. How about you come over to the bar in a couple of hours and I'll make you a special cocktail?'

'Sounds good.' She paused. 'No Smurfs though, because I'm going to dye my hair a new colour for the occasion.'

'Oh yeah?' He liked the blue. Then again, he reckoned he'd like her in any colour. 'Do I get to hear what colour?'

'Nope, it's a surprise.'

'Okay, I'll look forward to it. In the meantime, if you've got a spare moment, Grace is stuck with her maths homework and wonders if you're any good at the subject.'

There was a slight pause. 'Really? She asked you if I could help her?'

'Well yeah, but no worries if you can't. She thought people who were good at computers were also good at maths, but I'm a master at computer games and I can't even spell trigonometry, so—'

'God, I'd love to help her if I can. I did maths A Level so I might remember some of it. Did you give her my phone number?'

'No. I wasn't sure if you wanted that.'

He heard her sigh. 'I really was a head case about not giving out my number, wasn't I? But I'm done with all that crap so yes, please, give her my number and I'll see what I can do.'

So it's not all the crap with Pete that's holding her back. Nope, he wasn't going to second guess how she felt. She'd tell him when she was ready.

Mia glanced at her watch. Good, another ten minutes before she'd promised Luke she'd be at the bar.

'We've just got time to finish this last question.'

Grace, who was sat next to her at the kitchen table in Freya's flat, groaned. 'This is like torture.'

Mia had to work hard not to laugh. 'You said you wanted help.'

'Yeah, but I didn't think you'd make me do all the questions,' Grace mumbled. 'Miss would have been happy with the first five.'

'But by doing all ten you now really understand how to do them.'

Just then the front door opened and Freya walked in. She did a double-take when she saw Mia and wow, that was not an I'm-pleased-to-see-you expression.

'Hey Mum, Mia's helping me with my maths.'

'And Grace is really happy about it,' Mia added, hoping to lighten the tension she felt pinging round the room.

Grace didn't seem to be aware of it, because she sniggered. 'Yeah, right. I'll be happy when we're done.'

'And how long will that be?' Freya asked, and bloody hell, the woman had clearly come back from the supermarket yet she was dressed in the cleanest, bluest jeans Mia had ever seen, and what looked to be a fancy cashmere jumper.

'Mia said I have to do one more question.'

Mia slid a little down her chair. Way to make her out to be the bad guy in front of the woman who clearly, if she didn't hate her, definitely didn't like her. Because she was dating Luke? Because she was helping Grace? Or because she didn't like scruffy women with funny-coloured hair?

Thankfully Grace had got the hang of the problems and five minutes later Mia stood to go. 'You've got my number now, so call me any time you're stuck, okay?'

Grace shocked her by giving her a hug. 'Thanks, Mia, you're ace.'

And yep, Mia didn't miss the way Freya's expression hardened when she turned to say goodbye to her. 'I'm sure Grace appreciates your help.'

Message between the lines: *I don't appreciate you being in my space.*

Thankful to be out of Freya's death stare, Mia scampered down the stairs. If things between Freya and Luke were really as over as Luke claimed, why was Freya being such a bitch to her?

The thoughts percolated in her head all the way to the bar, but when she opened the door, Freya's unpleasantness was pushed to the furthest corner of her mind.

Applause echoed around the room. Pink balloons were everywhere. Across the bar hung a banner saying CONGRATULATIONS, and scrawled on a few pieces of paper after that, in what looked like Luke's handwriting, were the words AUTHOR-IN-THE-MAKING.

People, faces she knew, smiled broadly at her.

Naomi, Stan – Mia felt a pulse of satisfaction as she saw how close they stood next to each other. Beside them were Phil and Janet, Sandy and Jim, behind them Gary, Tony and Bill.

And oh God, the girls were there too. Chloe, her face beaming, and alongside her Donna and *Tanya,* who had reason enough to hate her. A lump rose in Mia's throat. All these people had come here for her.

Her eyes slid over to the bar, where Mateo winked in that flirty way he'd always had with her. Finally, next to Mateo, was the man who made her heart leap when their eyes connected. Luke's smile, the one she'd first fallen for, was in full force, crinkling his eyes at the corners, dimples flashing. In his hand he held a lurid pink cocktail, complete with pink feather stirrer.

When their eyes met, laughter bubbled inside her, along with a tonne of emotion that made her chest feel tight and her throat almost impossible to speak out of.

'Snap,' she managed, tugging at her newly dyed hair which she'd streaked with pink, in celebration of finishing the rom-com.

Or maybe it had been in celebration of romance, because this surely was one hell of a romance playing out right in front of her eyes. And incredibly, she was at the heart of it. She was the heroine.

Shaking her head, she looked at her friends. Her *friends*. And felt choked all over again. 'I can't believe he forced you out on a Sunday evening just to celebrate me finishing my book.'

'Forced us?' Stan rasped. 'Nobody forced us, love.' He glanced over at Luke. 'He did promise us a free drink, mind.'

Everyone laughed, and then, thank God, started talking because as much as Mia loved the show of support, she hated being the centre of attention.

Naomi was first to come up to her, squeezing her arm. 'You're a dark horse. I didn't have our local computer whizz down as a romance writer.'

'Whoa, you can't call me a writer. I'm still a long way from getting anything published.'

'Luke said you'd finished writing a book.' Stan joined them, looking smarter than she'd seen him with a neatly trimmed beard and new haircut. 'That makes you a writer. Not sure about the romance, mind. If it'd been a thriller I might have read it.'

Mia spluttered with laughter. 'For that, I'm going to

make you read it anyway.' She gave Naomi a sidelong glance. 'Who knows, you might learn something.'

The others came over and Mia lost count of the number of times she had to tell people not to get carried away. Only a few writers ever get their work published. It was what she said to Luke, too, when she finally managed to talk to him.

'But writing a book, writing ninety thousand words, is one hell of an achievement. You should be proud, shout about it.'

He was so happy for her, Mia almost couldn't look at him because she felt too much. 'Well thanks to you I am shouting about it.'

Some of the light in his eyes dimmed. 'Was this the wrong thing to do?'

Her heart burst open. 'This was the most amazing thing to do.' Reaching across the bar, Mia gave him a fierce kiss. 'I can't believe you persuaded everyone to come, though. How many cocktails have you had to give away?'

'You really think I needed to bribe anyone? That these people weren't so utterly thrilled for you, they couldn't wait to congratulate you?'

Her heart bounced. 'Really?'

'Really.' His eyes looked deep into hers. 'You've made friends here, Mia. Friends who care about you.'

She glanced back over her shoulder at the people who'd come out to support her and felt a burst of pride. She'd been so worried about starting a relationship with Luke, about being dependent on him for her happiness, yet without realising it she'd made other friends, too. Friends who'd still be there for her even if she and Luke didn't make it.

'It seems I've also found a boyfriend astute enough to plan this celebration to show me exactly that.'

He let out a bark of laughter. 'Okay, I like *astute*, so I'll admit I hoped you'd see this as more than a celebration of your writing. It's a celebration of what you've achieved in four months of living in Manchester.'

'Friends, a finished book.' She placed a hand on his cheek. 'And an awesome boyfriend.'

He waggled his eyebrows. 'An awesome boyfriend who can make you romantic pink cocktails to match your hair.'

'What do you think of the pink?'

His eyes skated slowly over her hair and then across her face, the green getting more intense when they finally rested on her mouth. 'I think you're the sexiest flamingo I've ever seen.' As she struggled between laughter and wanting to pour her cocktail over him, he grinned. 'Nah, only kidding, you've got far better legs than their spindly efforts. You're more ... Snagglepuss? No, wait, I've got it. Pink Panther, except he was a boy, and tall, and had big eyes like you, but they were yellow, not blue.'

God, he wasn't just sexy and hot, he was adorable. 'Is that it then, you're stumped for a new nickname for me?'

He shook his head, a slow grin forming across his face. 'I've got it. That Cartland woman who wrote all the romance novels and always wore pink.' Taking her hand, he kissed her knuckles, then slowly slid his gaze up to hers. 'I think you're the sexiest Babs I've ever met.'

As always, he cracked her up, but as the laughter died, her feelings for him grew, leaving no room in her chest. She loved him, she knew that now, but it wasn't the time to tell him. Instead she clasped his hand and brought it to her lips. 'And I think you're the sexiest, most thoughtful boyfriend I could ever have wished for.'

Chapter Thirty-Four

Luke walked into his spare room to do his usual weights on Tuesday morning, and smiled when he saw a message in Mia's window. The woman loved communicating this way and he had to admit, walking in to find a message in her window gave him a bigger kick than reading one on his phone.

Coffee?

Naomi's

11 a.m.

Bending to grab a pen, he scribbled back:

Missing me?

They'd spent Saturday night through to Monday morning together when he hadn't been working. It wasn't nearly long enough. Increasingly he, the man who'd bounced from woman to woman in casual, no-strings relationships, was getting frustrated at not seeing Mia enough outside work. He knew she had her judo classes now, and that in between her day job she was busy editing her book before sending it out to publishers. Still, he wanted more of her time. Wanted more of her.

Movement in the window opposite signalled she was putting up a reply:

Maybe

Another flicker of movement, and another message:

Or I just

Need U 2

Buy me

Coffee

He laughed, though he had to admit one of the down sides of dating a woman with a sharp mind was he didn't always know when she was joking.

After posting a thumbs-up picture, he began his work-out.

Fifty minutes later he'd just got out of the shower when he heard a knock on the door. And Freya walked in. 'Only me.'

He swore as he grabbed at a towel. 'I thought we agreed, no using the key unless it's an emergency.'

'It is.' She appeared in the doorway to his bedroom, her slender figure squeezed into a slim-line skirt and bright red blouse. A mile away from Mia's casual approach to dressing. Her eyes flickered to the towel he was clutching round his waist. 'No need to be shy on my account. I've seen it all before, remember?'

'It's been a while,' he muttered, feeling uncomfortable.

'Sure.' Her eyes ran over his chest. 'Though not as long as Mia thinks, I suspect.'

Anger spiked. 'Keep Mia out of this. And speaking of keeping out, get out of my bedroom, out of my flat.'

'Hey, no need to be tetchy. I came to ask if you'd come and sort the kitchen sink. It's leaking all over the floor.'

'Fine. I'll be over later.'

Freya cleared her throat. 'Did you hear the part about it causing great puddles of water—'

'Fine,' he interrupted sharply. 'Let me put some clothes on.'

She smiled. 'Again, no need to worry on my account. I'll leave the door open.'

'Freya,' he warned, but she wasn't listening. He swore she swayed her hips as she walked back along the corridor.

He glanced at his watch and grimaced. Damn it, five past eleven. Mia would be at Naomi's by now. Reaching for his phone he called her number, swearing when it went into voicemail.

After yanking on his jeans, he pulled a long-sleeved T-shirt over his head and grabbed his tool box.

'I'll be back in a jiffy,' he told Freya, dumping the tool box on the floor next to the dodgy sink.

'What? Wait, where are you going?'

'I'm supposed to be meeting Mia at Naomi's for coffee. I can't catch her on the phone so I've got to pop down and see her.'

Freya placed a hand on his arm. 'Why don't I go and let her know you'll be late, while you fix the sink? That way you'll still get your coffee.'

It felt wrong, his ex sending apologies to his girlfriend on his behalf, but it would save time. 'Okay. Tell her I'll be fifteen mins, max.'

As Freya strode off, he reluctantly wedged himself underneath the sink. If the waste pipe needed more than a quick tighten he was going to call a bloody plumber.

He'd just found the problem, hallelujah, when he heard Freya come back.

'You find Mia okay?'

'Of course.' From his vantage point beneath the sink, he saw Freya's patent black stilettoes come into view. 'With her odd-coloured hair, she's hard to miss.' There was a beat of silence and when she spoke again, it was so quiet he almost didn't hear. 'This one seems important to you.'

'She is.' He held his hand out. 'Pass me the wrench, the large one.'

Freya placed it into his waiting palm. 'How important?'

'That's my business.' He focused on tightening the joint that had become loose and then scooted out from under the sink. 'That should do the trick.'

Jamming the torch and wrench back into the tool box, he strode towards the door. As he opened it, he glanced behind him. Freya no longer looked like the in-charge career-driven Freya he'd come to know, but the scared, pregnant eighteen-year-old he'd once loved. It caused him to pause. 'What's wrong?'

'Nothing. Not really.' She tried to smile, but it looked off. 'I guess I never thought this day would come.'

'What day?'

'The day you fell in love with another woman.' She smiled sadly at him. 'You loved me once.'

'I did.' He stared back at her, unsure where she was going with all this. 'But then you broke my heart.' Anxious to find Mia, he went to open the door. 'I'll catch you later.'

After dumping his tool box back at the flat, he legged it down the stairs.

The door to the café opened and Mia looked up. Then sighed when she saw the mum and her toddler walk in. She went back to staring at her coffee. The talk with Freya had left her unsettled. It wasn't so much that Luke was apparently fixing his ex's leaking sink, but that he'd insisted on doing it now, when he was supposed to be meeting her.

Couldn't it have waited half an hour? And why hadn't he come down and told her himself?

Mia huffed out a breath and swigged down the last of her coffee.

'You want another?' Naomi had left her position behind the counter to slide into the seat opposite.

'I'm meant to be meeting Luke here, but apparently mending Freya's sink has trumped me. Or so she was delighted to tell me.'

Naomi let out one of her hearty chuckles. 'Sounds like you two had another run-in.'

'No, not exactly.' Mia fiddled with the teaspoon. 'But the woman definitely doesn't like me.'

'Ah.'

Mia glanced back at Naomi. 'That sounds like you know something I don't.'

'I don't know, but I'm guessing she feels her nose has been pushed out of joint. Luke's always been hers, so to speak.'

'Hers? She turned him down years ago.'

'Well yes, but it doesn't mean she isn't a bit peeved that someone else has come along and taken her place. I mean, he's had his fun with other women, but none of them have been serious. None have threatened Freya's hold over him.'

Mia felt her heart jump. 'You think she still has a hold over him?'

Naomi patted her hand. 'I think Freya believes that, yes. But anyone who's seen you and Luke together can tell who has the hold over him now.'

The door jangled and when Mia turned round, she saw Luke stride in. He looked harassed, his chest heaving as if he'd just run here.

His eyes met hers and he visibly sagged. 'Thank God you're still here.' Walking over to them, he smiled at Naomi. 'Excuse me while I kiss the living daylights out of my girlfriend and then grovel at her feet.'

Naomi boomed out a laugh and eased off the chair. 'I'd grovel first if I were you.'

'Damn it, yes, great idea.'

Much to Mia's embarrassment, as Naomi walked away, Luke knelt on the floor and looked at her solemnly. 'I'm really bloody sorry for being late.'

Mia tried to remember she was annoyed. 'I guess you're forgiven. Please rise.'

The twinkle returned to his eyes. 'Does that mean I can proceed to step two?'

She smiled in anticipation. 'You may.'

It was a few seconds before she felt the touch of his lips against hers. Another few before she realised this wasn't a quick peck, but a meltingly tender exploration of her mouth with his. 'I've missed you, Babs.'

'So much so that you prioritised Freya?' Oops, seems the kiss hadn't dispelled all her irritation.

Luke heaved out a sigh. 'What was I supposed to do? Tell her to call a plumber and walk away, leaving her with a pool of water on the floor?'

You're better than this. Mia forced down the nasty spikes

of jealousy. 'Sorry. Of course you had to help her. It's just, I was looking forward to having coffee with you.'

His eyes turned a soft green. 'Me too. It's felt like an eternity since I last saw you.'

'It's been twenty-four hours.'

'Exactly. Far too bloody long.' He picked up her hand, holding it in his. 'Sorry I wasn't here at eleven. And sorry I had to send a message via Freya. I did try to phone – you know, that novel way humans have of communicating – but you didn't pick up.'

'Ah, I left it in the flat. Didn't think I needed it.' She glanced down at their hands, allowing the warmth from his to melt the places jealousy had left cold. 'Did you fix the leak?'

'Yep, it was just a joint that needed tightening.'

'Maybe you should teach her how to do it herself, in case you're ever not there.'

He gave Mia a half-smile. 'I have done, but her head's too full of long lawyer sentences. Not sure she can grasp the practical.'

The conversation with Naomi flooded back to her. Was this Freya trying to keep her claws on Luke? And was he too naïve, too trusting, or too enthralled with her still, to see it?

His hands tightened around hers. 'I'm off tomorrow. Any chance we can use the day to cross off another Manchester hot spot?' He saw her hesitation and sighed. 'You have to work, I know. Don't worry. Maybe I can cook you dinner?'

She jiggled the dates around in her head. 'Or maybe I can shift tomorrow afternoon's work into Saturday afternoon… Wait, where are you going to take me?'

He raised his eyebrows. 'Wow, when we weren't dating, you were happy to come out with me based on a dodgy clue in the window. Now you'll only see me if the venue is up to scratch?'

Amused, she shrugged. 'I'm just making sure your standards aren't slipping.'

He huffed out a laugh. 'Okay then, game on. But I'm not telling you where we're going. You'll have to watch my window for a clue.'

It was after eleven that night when Luke posted his message. Mia knew because, sad cow that she was, she'd waited up to see it on the pretence of finishing the edits on her book. As she watched the sheet of paper going up, the familiar buzz shot through her, the one she'd experienced right from the start, when she'd been telling herself they were just friends. While actually she'd been falling in love.

When the sheet was in place, she did a double-take at the drawing of a bird in flight and the words:

U + Me xx

Okay, so she had no clue what she was doing. Going to an aviary? Feeding the ducks? Was it a love-bird symbol? Were they going to spend the day in bed?

A second later her phone pinged with a message:

Meet at mine at 1 p.m. And be prepared to stay the night L xx

Another message quickly followed:

Err, I should say staying over isn't compulsory.

A final message:

But your tour guide would be ecstatic if you did. Sweet dreams L xx

She still didn't know what the day had in store. But she did know that whatever they did, she'd love it, because she'd be doing it with him.

Chapter Thirty-Five

Luke peered at the bedside clock and winced. How annoyed would Mia be if he ignored the time and snuggled back into bed with her?

Wrapping his arms around the warm body next to him, he couldn't believe that only six months ago, if he found himself waking up next to a woman, he'd eased out of her bed as quietly as possible. Now all he wanted to do was keep Mia in his bed, in his flat, in his life. Permanently.

She stirred, and he kissed her nose. 'I don't want you to go, but it's eight o'clock.'

She groaned, turning in his arms. 'Why am I so knackered?'

'Because you can't keep up with me? Because I wore you out yesterday with all that vigorous—'

'Sky diving,' she interrupted, giving him a dig in the ribs. 'It was all that floating over a wind tunnel that wore me out. I didn't even know indoor skydiving was a thing.'

She laughed softly into his chest. 'God, to think, I believed you were taking me to feed the ducks.'

'Well now you know. My standards don't slip.' He nudged her so she looked up at him. 'They get higher and higher.'

She smiled, blue eyes still cloudy with sleep. 'Is that a promise?'

'Yes.' They were teasing, joking around, yet he felt the certainty of his promise all the way through to his bones. He wouldn't take her for granted, he wouldn't become complacent. He'd try to do his best by her. Always.

Yawning, she sat up and pulled off the duvet. 'Much as I'd love to stay here and discuss your increasingly high standards, I have to get going. I'm half a day behind now.' She gave him a sly smile beneath her lashes. 'But it was totally worth it.'

'I'll make us a coffee.' He halted. 'Damn, I can't remember if I've got any milk.' She was busy slipping on her bra, and for a moment he watched the beautiful breasts he'd enjoyed last night being tucked neatly away.

'No worries. I can wait till I get back to mine.'

'No.' Desire made his voice hoarse. 'I just promised you my standards weren't going to slip. Let me message Freya.'

As he was still watching her get dressed, Luke saw the way Mia stilled, her movements a little stiffer as she pulled on her jeans. Damn, there was something going on between Mia and Freya. Grace had mentioned her mum being a bit frosty with Mia the last time she'd helped with her homework.

He'd have to talk to Freya because the pair of them needed to get along. Mia was a part of his life now – if he had his way, a permanent part – and Freya was going to have to get used to it.

A message pinged back and he glanced at his screen. 'She's going to bring some milk over.'

'Very good of her.'

It wasn't the words, it was the way Mia didn't meet his eyes. 'Hey.' Finally she looked up at him. 'You know it's you I want, you I can't stop thinking about. You I love.'

He held his breath as he watched her swallow. *Tell me you love me, too.*

He'd never know if she was going to say the words he longed to hear, or if she was going to smile and ignore them again, because Freya banged on the front door.

When he opened it, she handed over the milk carton, but her eyes narrowed as they focused over his shoulder.

'Oh, sorry, I didn't realise you had company.' Instead of leaving, as he expected, she stepped into the flat. 'Hello Mia. How are you?'

'Good, thanks.' Mia's words sounded stilted and her usually warm smile didn't reach her eyes.

Freya's gaze swivelled between him and Mia. 'It's a bit awkward, isn't it, having me living next door?'

'Why would it be?' He nodded at the milk in his hand. 'You've just saved our morning.'

Freya gave him a small smile. 'Still as disorganised as usual, I see. I wonder if everything else about you is the same as it always was.' She glanced back at Mia. 'Does he still have his nipple piercing? I know I got a shock when I first saw it because he hadn't had that when he was eighteen, but then I realised it was actually kind of sexy.'

Luke glared at Freya. 'What are you trying to do here?'

'I'm not trying to *do* anything, but I do think she has a right to know.' Freya stared unapologetically back at him.

'Right to know what?' Mia's voice was quiet but steady.

Freya looked at her. 'That we're not just Grace's parents. That we've been lovers over the years, too.'

Luke watched in horror as Mia's face paled.

'That's enough.' Anger burned through him, along with a whole bucket full of frustration and a worm of guilt. Marching to the door, he flung it open. 'Thanks for the milk. I'll return it when I'm done.' Whatever their difficulties, he'd always admired and respected Freya, but right now he didn't like her one little bit.

When she was gone, he turned back to Mia, and the bottom fell out of his stomach. Anger he could take, surprise, annoyance, he'd deal with it.

But Mia's expression held none of that. Instead she looked gutted, as if the stuffing had been knocked out of her. And he had a feeling it wasn't disappointment in the situation, but in him.

Mia felt blindsided. *We've been lovers over the years, too.* Should she have known?

'Talk to me, Mia.' As if he sensed her fragile emotional

state, he put his hands out in a placatory gesture. 'I know you have questions.'

'Questions?' Anger bubbled. 'You've made me look stupid. Made me feel stupid. All the times we talked about Freya, you always implied it had been over since Grace was born. Why the hell didn't you tell me you were still sleeping with her?'

A muscle in his jaw ticked. 'Slept, past tense. What did you want from me, a detailed list of everyone I've ever had sex with?'

She snorted, the shock, the bitter sense of betrayal leaving her feeling cold, hard. 'I doubt you could produce one. You probably can't remember most of their names.'

'Fuck, Mia.' He exhaled sharply, staring down at the floor for a few seconds before finally lifting his gaze to hers. 'I thought we were done with this.' Pain laced through his voice, was clearly etched on his face. 'You know my history. You know why I kept things casual.'

It didn't change the fact that she felt like she'd been attacked, that everything she thought she knew had suddenly been turned on its head. 'Freya wasn't just a casual hook-up though, was she? She was the woman you loved, the one you wanted to marry.' Damn it, her voice was cracking. Dragging in some air, she forced herself to focus on the facts. The emotion she'd deal with later. 'That's true, isn't it?'

'*Sixteen years* ago.' His eyes pleaded with her. 'Come on Mia, that's a lifetime ago. I've changed, she's changed.'

'Yet you still fancied her enough to sleep with her.'

'Twice, four years ago,' he said tightly.

Okay. That sounded better than Freya's *we've been lovers over the years*. As long as he was telling the truth. 'You still should have said something.'

He hung his head, his big shoulders moving as he clearly struggled to control his emotions. When his eyes found hers, she saw his pain. 'What was I supposed to say? By the way, that long list you have of people I've slept with, you need to add Freya for the two occasions we fell into bed when we were at a low ebb and the worse for drink?'

'No, when I asked about Freya, you were supposed to say you're not over her.' The niggles, the doubts that had surfaced every time she'd spoken to Freya burst onto the surface. 'Because clearly that's the case.'

'Christ, you could not be more wrong.' He stared down at her, his huge body almost vibrating with, what? Frustration, anger? 'I love you, Mia. How many times do I have to tell you before you start to believe me?'

'Apparently a few more yet.' She looked at her watch even though whatever time it said, she knew it was time she left. 'I've got to get back to work.'

'So when are we going to talk about this?'

'I'll let you know.' Right now she needed to escape from his sad expression, the hurt in his eyes, the barely suppressed frustration.

'Right, fine.' He glared stonily back at her. 'But remember I have your number now, I know where you live. I won't let you stay away for long.'

Cold washed through her. 'Is that a threat?'

His face crumpled. 'Shit, sorry, no, of course not. I'd never…' He raked a hand through his hair, his expression bleak. 'I'm not Pete, Mia,' he added quietly. 'I'm not any of those bastards who came before. I love you, I won't let you down.'

'So why do I feel you just have?'

Back in her flat, Mia found it hard to focus on work. There was too much going on in her head, too many questions, too many swirling emotions. She picked up the phone to talk to Elle, but it went to voicemail. She couldn't talk to her parents, not until she had her thoughts straight. They liked Luke, and if there was a chance they could get through this, she didn't want their view of him tainted by her unvarnished thoughts.

But she needed to talk, to get another viewpoint. Someone to tell her she was over-reacting, or that she was entirely justified. Or anything in between.

By 6.30 p.m. she gave up all pretence of work, turned off her computer and walked into the kitchen. Reaching for the kettle, she glanced at the wall dividing her flat and Stan's. Her neighbour with his no-nonsense attitude yet big, soft heart. The first person she'd spoken to when she arrived in Manchester.

Putting the kettle back down, she tucked her keys into her pocket, walked out of the flat and knocked on his door.

He opened it without looking at her. '*Eggheads* is on in five minutes.'

Mia followed him in and closed the door behind her. 'I'm fine, thanks for asking. How are you?'

He paused as he entered the living room. 'I didn't ask.'

'No, but you should have. It's polite.'

'Aye, but I don't have to be polite with you.'

'Err, why not?'

'You're Mia.' He shuffled his feet. 'We're friends, aren't we?'

She hadn't realised how much she'd needed to hear that, how much she'd needed an arm around her, until that moment. 'Yes,' she swallowed down the golf-ball-sized lump in her throat. 'We are.' Tears that had been building all afternoon started to spill down her cheeks.

'Hey, lass, what's wrong?' Clearly alarmed, he peered over at her.

'Nothing, probably.' She drew in a shuddery breath. 'I hope you'll help me figure it out.'

'Come here.'

He held out his arms and Mia collapsed into them. Shorter than her dad and wider, nonetheless he felt like a safe haven.

After a while he cleared his throat. 'So, *Eggheads*. Am I recording it?'

A bubble of laughter whooshed out of her. 'Is that okay?'

'It is if you stop crying.' His smile took the heat out of his words. 'I'm not good with crying women. I don't have the fancy words.'

She used the sleeve of her shirt to wipe the wet from her cheeks. 'No more tears, I promise. And I don't need fancy words. I've come round for a bit of your blunt honesty.' Drawing in a breath, she nodded towards the TV. 'You record *Eggheads*, I'll make the tea. Then I need you to listen and tell me what you think.'

She spilled everything, the snide asides from Freya, the way Luke seemed to drop whatever he was doing to answer her calls, the leaking tap and finally today's bombshell.

He only spoke when she'd finished. 'What's the real issue here? That you're angry he didn't tell you he'd slept with Freya a few years ago? Or you think he still has feelings for her?'

Mia clasped a hand around her knees. 'That's good, distilling it down like that.'

He let out a gruff-sounding laugh. 'What's the answer then?'

'I want to say both, but is that a cop-out?'

'Your feelings are your feelings.' He scratched at his beard. 'But if you want to know what I think, I'd say if the man wanted to get back with his ex, he's had ample opportunity. Instead he started dating you, organised a shindig for you the other night, told you he loves you.' He gave her a half-smile. 'Do I need to go on?'

'You think I'm making a fuss over nothing.' Mia wanted to believe that too, but she'd trusted before, believed in someone before, and had it explode in her face.

'I think this woman is trying to drive a wedge between the pair of you, and you're allowing it.'

She winced. 'Ouch.'

'You asked for my opinion. I've given it. No point complaining you don't like it.'

She gave him a pouty look. 'You're supposed to be on my side.'

'I am, lass. I am.'

She mulled on Stan's words for the rest of the evening.

When she woke the following morning, she posted a note in the window.

Can we talk again?

Yours @ 10 a.m.

Chapter Thirty-Six

It was 9.45 a.m. and Luke was in the kitchen fixing himself his usual wake-himself-up coffee when there was a knock on the door. Opening it, he was surprised to find Freya. Again.

'What do you want?' After her behaviour the previous morning, he didn't feel particularly friendly.

'Grace needs a lift to college and I've got a meeting I need to get to. Will you take her?'

'Of course.' He was about to ask if she needed to go right that minute, when Freya stepped back into her own flat and shouted Grace's name.

'Calm it, I'm coming,' came a clearly exasperated voice.

'Okay, I take it we need to leave now,' he murmured. He might as well have been talking to himself because Freya was busy telling Grace to hurry and Grace was busy telling Freya to stop being such a nag.

When Grace appeared in the doorway she gave him a

pained look. 'Tell Mum to focus on her own life and leave me to sort mine.'

He wanted to agree, to tell Freya to keep out of his life too, but he and Freya had made a vow when Grace was born to never undermine each other in front of their daughter. Just because they weren't together in the traditional sense didn't mean they weren't a unit when it came to parenting. 'Your mum is only trying to make sure you get to your class on time, so cut her some slack.'

'Yeah, but—'

'Have you got everything?' Freya asked sharply.

Grace rolled her eyes. 'Jeeze, yes, take a chill pill.'

Figuring the best way to defuse the situation was to get on their way, Luke shot back to his flat and picked up his keys. 'Come on kiddo, let's get out of your mum's hair.'

'She's been in a dead weird mood recently,' Grace muttered as they climbed into the TVR.

'Maybe she's stressed about work,' he offered.

'Nah, work never stresses her. She loves all that crap.'

He flicked Grace a look. 'I'm tempted to say it might be her time of the month, but I'm scared you'll clock me one.'

'You're right to be scared.' Glancing down at her phone, she sighed. 'I can't even play my music, can I, 'cos your dumb car doesn't have Bluetooth.'

He chuckled, tapping the console. 'Nope, it's better than that. It has a radio.' He flicked it on to the local station.

Fifteen minutes later he pulled up outside the school gate. 'What happened to the bus today?'

Grace shrugged. 'Nothing. I was going to take it, but

Mum said she'd drop me. Then she said she couldn't and she'd get you to do it.'

'Her meeting must have been last minute then.'

'I suppose.' She glanced down at her watch. 'Guess I'd better head to the study room.'

'I thought you had a lecture?'

'Yeah, but not till half eleven.'

'What was all the rush then?'

She frowned at him. 'You're kidding. Mum said I had to go now or you couldn't take me.'

'But it's Friday. She knows Bill covers lunch and I don't go into work until later.'

They shared a look, both clearly trying to work out why the scarily organised woman they knew had forgotten that fact. 'Maybe she just forgot.'

'Maybe.' But he knew the explanation couldn't be as simple as that, because Freya didn't 'just forget' anything. She also didn't have last-minute meetings, because again, that implied something had come up she hadn't anticipated, and that simply didn't happen in her world.

Was she still smarting from the dressing down he'd given her yesterday when he'd returned the milk? Upset both with her and the situation, he'd accused Freya of meddling, which of course she hadn't appreciated. She'd rebuffed him with words along the lines of *Don't blame me, it's your dishonesty that's got you into the mess.*

'Dad?'

Grace's voice brought him back. 'Sorry Pickle, I got lost in my head for a bit.'

'Is everything okay?'

She looked so concerned, he bent to kiss her forehead. 'Of course. Mia and I just had a bit of a falling-out yesterday. Nothing we can't fix.' Even as he said the words, his stomach knotted and he felt a desperate need to cross his fingers in the hope the gesture would somehow help.

'What did you row about?'

Your mum let slip that we'd slept together a couple of times around that really shitty Christmas when your gran fell ill. 'That's kind of personal.'

She nodded, her green eyes, so similar to his own, giving him a steady scrutiny. 'Do you love Mia?'

'Yes.' He reached across, holding Grace's chin in his hand. 'It doesn't mean I love you any less, or that I'll have any less time for you.'

She smiled and the look she gave him was so mature, so much the young lady rather than the kid he needed to protect. 'I know, Dad.' Her breath came out heavy as she sighed. 'It's not me you need to worry about. I think maybe Mum's the one having a hard time over Mia.'

'Your mum? Why?'

'I don't know. Just the way she's been a bit weird around her, and if I mention her name she gets all frosty. It's like she's jealous or something.'

He barked out a laugh. 'If your mum's jealous of anything, it's not me and Mia, it's you and Mia. Might be she's feeling a bit wobbly, what with Mia helping with your maths homework.' He gave a strand of her hair a gentle tug, like he used to do when she was young to get her attention. 'Don't worry. It takes time for people to adjust. We'll work it out and Mia and Freya will find a way to get along.'

He mulled it over on the way back to the flat. How would he feel if Freya brought a guy over who started to do stuff with Grace that he usually did? Yeah, he wouldn't like it, either. He just had to give Freya time to get to know Mia. Once she did, she'd realise Mia only wanted to help.

His stomach tightened. Of course there was the distinct possibility Freya wouldn't get that time. Because Mia would ditch him.

Mia rang the bell on Luke's flat again. Maybe he had the radio on and couldn't hear her. Bugger it, why hadn't she brought her phone with her? That was the trouble with not having many people know her number, she'd got out of the habit of taking it with her wherever she went.

Next to Luke's flat a door opened, and Mia's heart sank as she saw Freya come out.

'He's not in.' Living up to her nickname in a sharp black trouser suit, Freya gave her a small smile. 'I asked him to take Grace to school.'

'Oh, okay.' Maybe he hadn't seen her sign then.

Freya took a few steps towards her. 'Despite what you might think, I like you, Mia. You've been good to Grace, which is important to me. So I think I should warn you that this, Luke putting his family first, will happen a lot.'

Mia wasn't sure she'd ever felt less liked, by anyone. 'Of course Grace will come first.'

Freya gave her one of those small smiles that didn't reach her eyes. 'It's not just Grace though, is it? Luke, me, Grace, we're a unit. That was how we agreed we would raise Grace. Not as two separate parents, but as a family.'

Mia looked Freya straight in the eye. 'Let's not beat about the bush here. Say what you want to say so we can both be clear.'

Another practised smile. 'I appreciate your candour, so I will give you the same courtesy. Luke is loyal, almost to a fault. It's why Bill still works for him, even though a younger guy would be much better for business. But Luke's got a soft spot for him, so…' She sighed, hitching her handbag further onto her shoulder. 'That same loyalty is magnified when it comes to his family. You have to ask yourself whether you can put up with being not the most important person in his life, or even the second, but the third most important.'

She wanted to rattle the woman. To push, to unsettle her, but right now she was too gutted to muster the energy. She'd come here ready to talk things out, to put her and Luke back on a firm footing, but instead she was left feeling further adrift from him. Once again she'd been effectively stood up, and Freya was the reason. 'I take it you're happy with second place?'

'Of course,' Freya returned smoothly. 'I expect to come behind Grace. The question is, are you happy to come behind me?'

Don't let her get to you. She'd been here before. Bitchy girls at school, trying to needle her, get a rise out of her. Mia squared her shoulders. 'Or perhaps the question is, are you worried that you will soon be behind me?'

Before Freya had a chance to come back with another tart remark, Mia turned and shot down the stairs. When she arrived back at her flat she slammed the door shut and slumped onto the floor.

Damn Freya and her bitchiness.

And damn Luke for making her fall in love with him. She didn't want Freya's words to matter, yet the woman had prodded and poked at the place Mia felt most vulnerable. Luke said he loved her, but did he, really and truly? She woke in the morning thinking of him, went to bed dreaming of him. When she wasn't with him, she counted down the hours until she would be. She loved her family, but somehow, without her wanting him to, Luke had become the centre of her world. She only had to think of that moment when she'd finally finished her book. *He* was the first person she'd wanted to tell.

But could she continue in a relationship where he didn't feel as strongly? Where instead of being at the centre, she was simply a nice addition to his life, someone he could slot into the moments when he wasn't working or focused on what Freya had called *his family*.

And now she came to the crux of the matter. Had he really ever got over Freya? Was his first love going to also be his last love?

The sound of her phone burst through the flat and Freya

jumped to her feet and walked into the spare room where the phone was vibrating around on her desk. Her heart thumped when she saw who was phoning.

After sucking in a breath, she pressed answer. 'Hi.'

'Damn it, I've just seen your message.'

'It doesn't matter.'

She heard a rush of breath. 'Are you kidding me? Of course it matters. I want to talk to you, I need to talk. It's just, I had to take—'

'Grace to school. I know, Freya told me.'

There was a pause on the other end of the phone. 'Can I come round now?'

'No.' She rubbed at her eyes with the heel of her hand. 'I've got too much to do.'

She heard his heavy exhale. 'Why does that feel like an excuse?'

'It's not.' But she couldn't lie to him. 'I have got stuff to do, but I'm also not in the right frame of mind to hash things out just now.'

'Hash things out? What things? You're scaring me.'

Her heart ached at the panic in his voice and Mia cursed Freya for putting doubts in her head. 'I don't mean to. It's just…' she trailed off, feeling miserable. She desperately wanted to see him, to feel his arms around her. Maybe then all these worms of worry would disappear. 'I'll see you soon.'

'Soon?' A beat of silence, and when his voice came back it sounded so tight, as if his windpipe was being squeezed. 'Look at me, please.'

Lifting her eyes, she stared over at his window and her heart cartwheeled at the message he'd left.

I ❤ U

'Mia? Can you see it?'

Tears streamed down her face. 'I can see it.'

'Then you'd better believe that I'm not giving you up without one hell of a fight. So take whatever time you need and let me know when you're ready to talk. I'll be waiting for you.'

Thank you, I'm sorry. I love you, too. All words she wanted to say, but her mind was too confused, and her heart too heavy to utter them.

A moment later, he ended the call.

Chapter Thirty-Seven

Mia spent a good portion of Saturday working. What with the afternoon out at the indoor skydiving – God, that seemed a long time ago – and the fact that her head hadn't been in the game ever since, she had a lot to catch up on.

But by six she was done, and her heart just wasn't in it to work on her book.

Stretching, she stared over at Luke's window. The sign he'd left her was still there, and once again she felt that tight feeling in her chest, her heart hurting as she remembered his words from yesterday. The pain in his voice.

What had Stan said? *She's trying to drive a wedge between the pair of you, and you're letting her.*

Freya was a lawyer, good with words, good at persuading a person to her point of view. But it was Luke's words, Luke's perspective that was the only one that mattered.

Her phone buzzed with a call.

'Grace.' Glad of the distraction, Mia stood and wandered into the living room. 'Everything okay?'

'Yes.' She paused. 'Is it okay if I come round?'

On the few occasions Mia had helped Grace with her homework, it had always been on Grace's turf. 'Of course, or I can come to you if you prefer.'

'No.' The word shot out like a bullet. 'It's better if I come to you.'

After giving her the flat number, Mia ended the call with a nudge of unease. It didn't sound like everything was okay, but maybe that was just teenagers, making a drama out of nothing.

Five minutes later, Grace was sat on her sofa and looking on edge.

Mia perched on the coffee table and squeezed Grace's hand. 'Whatever it is that's bothering you, I'm here if you want to talk, but if you don't, that's okay, too. I can put on the telly, we can fire up the PlayStation—'

'I need to tell you something.' She drew back her hand and twisted it in her lap in an agitated gesture. 'I don't want to get Mum in trouble but if I don't say this, it might hurt Dad.'

'Okay.' Sensing Grace needed space, Mia went to sit on the armchair opposite. 'Whatever you have to tell me can stay between us.'

Grace nodded. 'Please.' Then she rubbed her hands down her face and drew in a deep breath. 'Mum can see the messages you post to Dad.'

Mia rocked back in surprise. 'Well, I don't suppose that matters.'

Grace jiggled her legs up and down restlessly. 'But it does. I only found out yesterday 'cos it was so crazy that she asked Dad to take me to school instead of me getting the bus. I went into her office to see if there was anything in her diary about a meeting and there wasn't. That's when I saw the binoculars on her desk.' Grace glanced around the room. 'God, this sounds so bad. Mum isn't really like this. I know she's been dead mean to you but that's not her. She's not as friendly as Dad, but she's not a bitch, you know?'

'I do know.' Mia's mind was stuck on the binoculars. 'She's played a huge part in raising you, she's part of you. She must be an amazing person.' The words were true, so all Mia had to work out was why Freya had been so mean to her.

And really, it was quite obvious.

'You think your mum is still in love with your dad?' she said quietly. 'That's why she doesn't like me?'

Grace shook her head. 'I thought that at first, but then I asked her why she was spying on your room. She denied she was at first, but I said I'd seen the binoculars, I knew she'd seen the message about you meeting Dad, and that must be why she'd got him out of the way.'

Wow. Mia's heart began a slow thump. It would explain the leaking tap, too. Freya had seen Mia's messages and decided to meddle.

'She looked dead scared when I said that.' Grace's voice started to wobble. 'I mean like she was proper horrified that

I'd sussed her out. Then she stared to cry and tell me she was sorry. It wasn't like she loved Dad, she said, not in the way he loved you. It was just she'd got used to him being there for her and now she was scared you'd take him away from us.'

'Oh God Grace, I wouldn't.' Mia leapt to her feet and crouched in front of Grace. 'He loves you so much. Why would I want to take him away from people he loves?'

'That's what I said to her.' Finally, finally, Grace met her gaze. 'I said you were dead lovely and you'd never make Dad choose between us.' She gave Mia a tentative smile. 'I also told her you were smart, like she was, so the pair of you were bound to sort it all out.'

'We will.' It felt like a weight had lifted off Mia's shoulders. 'Did your mum really say she thought your dad loved me?'

Grace rolled her eyes. 'Err, duh, of course. He always told us he wasn't going to settle down so there was no point in us meeting any of his girlfriends. Then you come along and I get Mia this, Mia that. And then he's asking if I'll come to a picnic with you and your family. Like, double whammy.' Grace's smile faded. 'Will you tell Dad about the binoculars, about Mum spying?'

Mia rose to her feet and gave Grace a hug. 'That's not my tale to tell. The only thing I'm going to say to your dad is something I should have told him weeks ago.' Grace looked at her questioningly, and Mia laughed. 'You've got a key to his flat. I'm sure he won't mind you taking a look at the message I'm going to leave him in my window.'

The bar had gone crazy. Luke felt his work life and his love life going in two diametrically opposite directions. The bar was taking off, just as his love life was heading down the toilet.

He slammed the till drawer shut and Phil, coerced into helping once he and Mateo had started to struggle, winced. 'Abusing the bar furniture, or the staff, I might add, isn't going to help.'

'No, but it makes me feel better.' His heart leapt as another customer walked through the door. Then took a nose dive as yet again it wasn't a gorgeous pink blonde he wanted to spend the rest of his life looking at. And touching. And, damn it, *talking* to.

Phil gave him a nudge. 'Will you just bloody relax or you'll scare off the customers.'

He grunted and gave Phil's shirt – black with vibrant pink flamingos – a cursory glance. 'I'm not the scary-looking one here.'

'Hey, this is my going-out shirt.' He smoothed a hand down the front. 'In case you forgot, I wasn't expecting to work tonight. I was expecting to take my wife out to dinner.'

Luke raised a brow. 'And Janet's good with that look?'

Phil screwed up his face. 'Not exactly. She told me to change out of the shirt I'd planned to wear with her because *you don't want to get it ruined.* With such little advance warning,' he added pointedly, 'I couldn't immediately locate my bar shirt so Janet found this. Apparently getting cocktails sloshed down it would be an improvement.'

'She's not wrong. And I might help that along if you don't stop looking at me like that.'

'Like what?'

'Like you feel sorry for me,' Luke grumbled, nodding to a customer and pulling him another pint. 'Everything is going to work out with Mia.'

'I have no doubt.' Phil began to collect the empties off the bar.

'I mean, it has to, because we're so flaming good together.'

The bar now clear, Phil began to wipe it down. 'You are.'

'Jesus.' Luke huffed under his breath. 'Stop being so bloody agreeable.'

Phil finally turned to look at him. 'You want me to say you're not good together? That things won't work out?'

'No, of course not.' God, it wasn't just pulling teeth. It was trying to yank on them while the dude with the teeth had his mouth slammed shut. 'I want you say it like you mean it. And not like you're trying to placate a gnarly animal.'

The corner of Phil's mouth twitched. 'You are pretty gnarly tonight.'

'Yeah well, so would you be if the woman you loved was avoiding you.'

Phil opened his mouth to say something, but an influx of customers arrived at the bar. Luke pasted a smile on his face and acted like the cheery bartender they expected. And not the pathetic lovesick sod he felt inside.

It was only as the last customer left and they began to clear up, that he was able to touch base with Phil again.

'Thanks for helping out.'

'Yeah man, we appreciate it,' Mateo called out from where he was loading the dishwasher.

'No worries, it's great to see the place so busy.'

'The crowds I could have coped with,' Mateo yelled before Luke could get a word in. 'It's your brother's hangdog expression I couldn't handle.'

Phil barked out a laugh. 'I hear you, mate.'

Luke cleared his throat. 'Do I need to remind you guys who pays your wages?' He flicked a finger at Phil's shirt. 'And from the look of your wardrobe, you need the money.'

Phil grinned and rested a hand on each of Luke's shoulders. 'I promise not to wear this shirt again to your bar.' Slowly the grin left his face, and his eyes fixed on Luke's. 'And back to what we were talking about earlier, I also promise to always tell you the truth. You and Mia will make it. You just have to be patient with her. Imagine if she was the one with the ex who lived next door? The one who she'd wanted to marry but had turned her down. How comfortable, how *secure* would you feel?'

'I'd hate it.'

Phil beamed like a proud teacher. 'Exactly.'

'You really believe she thinks I've still got a thing for Freya?'

'Put yourself in her shoes. The first time she stays over, Freya barges into your flat using her own key. She nearly gets stood up the other day because you were fixing Freya's tap. Add to all that the fact that she thought you guys were over years ago and then finds out you slept with each other recently.'

'Four fucking years ago,' he reminded Phil between gritted teeth.

'But that's recently compared to the sixteen years ago Mia thought it had been,' Phil pointed out.

And damn it, Luke hated it when his brother was so calm, so considered. And so flaming right. 'Okay, okay.' He drew in a breath. 'Patient. I can do that.' Unconsciously he drew out his phone to check his messages. A big fat nothing. 'This patience. How many days does it have to last, exactly?'

Phil chuckled and gave him a hard thump on the back. 'You'll work it out.'

Just then his phone began to vibrate and Luke's pulse kicked in. When he saw the message was from Grace, not Mia, he was ashamed that he felt disappointed. But when he clicked it open, his heart almost detonated.

> You need to come home ASAP. Message for you in Mia's window. G xxx

'Shit, what is it? You've gone pale as a sheet.'

His hand trembling, Luke showed Phil the message. 'Do you think it's good news or bad news?'

Phil gave him a push towards the door. 'Only one way to find out.'

Chapter Thirty-Eight

As he unlocked the door to his flat, Luke's heart was pounding so hard he was half afraid it would burst out of his chest and start bouncing round the floor.

In his desperation to get to the spare room, he almost tripped over Pickles.

'Damn it.' The rabbit gave him a wary look and Luke scooped her up. 'Shit, sorry love. I didn't see you there.'

She nudged her nose against his neck. 'Guess I'm forgiven, huh?'

The bigger question was, had Mia forgiven him, too?

'Okay then, let's do this together.' He clutched the lop-eared fur-ball against his chest. 'Sorry for the heart hammering. Turns out I'm more terrified of going into this room than I've ever been in my life.'

Of course, since she was a rabbit, he didn't expect Pickles to give him much in the way of encouragement. Still, she didn't seem to realise how shit scared he was. In fact the way she was nudging him, he had a feeling she was more bothered about getting fed.

'Okay, okay, but you've got to wait. There's more important stuff going on right now.'

Still holding her like a safety blanket, he forced his legs to walk along the corridor and into the spare room.

'Christ, I almost can't bear to look, but I don't suppose you're going to read it for me.'

Striding up to the window, heart in his mouth, he stared at the window opposite. The one that would, perhaps, seal his destiny.

And as his eyes took in the message, his mind became stuck. He had to read the single sheet of paper again and again before it finally sank in.

I ❤ U 2

Knees buckling, he slipped to the floor. 'She loves me,' he mumbled against Pickles' fur. 'She loves me,' he repeated, voice stronger. Then he started to laugh, lifting Pickles up in the air. 'Can you bloody believe it!'

Clearly less than impressed, Pickles wriggled out of his arms and scampered off but Luke took a moment to just sit and look at the sign. His heart felt so full now, brimming not just with love but with hope.

His phone beeped.

Did you see it? G xx

He wondered how she knew, but decided it was a conversation for another day, so he simply messaged back a yes.

A second later he received another message from her:

Aw, true love ❤❤❤

Just as he was clambering to his feet, his phone beeped again. And this time his heart skipped a beat.

Grace tells me you've seen the message. Can I come round? M xx

This was quickly followed by:

I feel the need to kiss the living daylights out of you. M xx

Laughter rolled through him at her use of his phrase, but being emotionally wiped out, he was fresh out of witty replies so he went with a heartfelt one instead:

Yes please. L x

It seemed like hours before she arrived, though probably it was only minutes. He just about had enough time to feed Pickles, stroke her ears and tell her not to disturb him for the next twelve hours.

Then there was a knock on the door and he flung it

open, lifting the gorgeous woman on the other side of it into his arms and carrying her through the flat to his bedroom.

'Err, hello.' Her hands were either side of his face, her mouth raining kisses over it.

'Hello yourself.' He threw her inelegantly onto the bed where she landed with a soft thump and laughed back up at him.

'Are you in cave-man mode?'

'I'm in *I need to bury myself inside you so I can be absolutely certain this isn't a dream*, mode.'

Her expression softened and she reached for his hand. Tugging him down onto the bed before rolling over, she stared down at him. 'I'm sorry it took so long for me to tell you.'

Emotion balled, clogging his throat. 'Don't be.' With his finger he traced the curve of her cheek, the outline of the mouth he never wanted to stop kissing. 'You had to be certain.' His eyes found hers. 'You are, aren't you? Certain, I mean. Because if there are any doubts I want to know.'

Her lips found his, soft, teasing. 'I'm one hundred per cent sure I'm in love with Luke Doyle,' she stated solemnly.

His body relaxed, his heart filling. 'I feel I should state, for the record, that I am also one hundred per cent certain I'm in love with Mia Abbott.' As she sighed and snuggled into him he felt the need to add, 'I do still think we need to make absolutely sure this isn't a dream.'

The breath from her laughter fluttered across his skin. 'I'm inclined to agree with you.'

'*Inclined to?*' He dug his fingers into her side, tickling her. 'What are we, a Charles Dickens novel?'

'Jane Austen, please.' Her hand slid under his T-shirt until she found his piercing and the tweak she gave it travelled all the way to his groin. 'So, are we going to do some basket making?'

He spluttered out a laugh. 'Is that what she called it?'

'No, she wasn't so vulgar.' She reached up until her lips feathered across his ear. 'But I can be.'

And that was it, he was done talking.

Mia woke slowly. When she tried to move, the big arm draped across her tightened and she smiled, happy to stay where she was a while longer.

'Morning.' His voice was gruff with sleep.

She wriggled round. 'Morning yourself.'

His eyes skimmed over her face, as if he still couldn't believe she was there. 'You have anywhere you need to be in the next few hours?'

'Yes.' His face fell and she kissed him. 'Here, you muppet. This is where I need to be for the next few hours.'

'Good.' God, she could lose herself in his eyes. It wasn't just that they were a beautiful colour. They told her so much about what he was thinking; glinting when he was amused, darkening when he was turned on, vivid and intense when he was emotional, like he clearly was now. 'We didn't get a chance to talk last night.'

'No. Somebody threw me onto a bed and ravaged me.'

He grinned. 'We made a lot of baskets.'

'That we did.'

He brushed at her hair. 'But perhaps we should talk now. About Freya.'

Mia swallowed. Following her chat with Grace, she no longer felt that burning jealousy, or the cramping fear that Freya was Luke's real love. Still, she didn't want to betray any confidences. 'What about her?'

'Grace said something in the car the other day, about Freya having a hard time getting used to you and me. It made me wonder if she'd been making life hard for you?'

She didn't want to lie to him, but if she had any hope of getting on with Freya, she couldn't tell him the truth, either. 'Everything is fine,' she reassured. 'The only problem was in my head.'

He nodded, his hand in constant motion, trailing down her face, up and down her arm. As if he couldn't stop touching her. 'But now you know what I felt for Freya was a long time ago, and it was nothing like the all-consuming love I feel for you.'

'Now I know.' He opened his mouth to speak, then stopped himself. 'Say it,' she urged him. 'We have to be able to talk about stuff that's difficult without worrying if the other person is going to get upset.'

'Okay.' His Adam's apple bobbed up and down. 'But I don't want to upset you.'

With a laugh, she pushed at him. 'I can't promise not to

get mad, but I can promise I will always stay and argue. I won't run off.'

His chest heaved as he drew in a deep breath. 'I was going to talk about why I slept with Freya those two times. To explain it wasn't because of any rekindling of feelings. It was Christmas Eve. Her mum was in hospital and I'd just broken my ankle playing five-aside football, so I couldn't drive anywhere. We were both stuck in our flats and feeling miserable. Two nights on the trot, when Grace had gone to bed, Freya got out the tequila. By Boxing Day we'd both had enough of each other and tequila.'

Mia pressed a kiss to his lips, silencing him. 'You convinced me at tequila.'

He laughed softly, and she could hear relief as well as amusement. 'One thing I'm confused about, and I'm not sure if you can help clear it up or not.'

'Oh?'

'Grace texted me last night to tell me there was a message in your window for me.' His lips twitched in a wry smile. 'The run from the bar to here nearly gave me a heart attack.'

She patted his cheek. 'Aw, you poor old thing.'

He snatched at her hand. 'Less of the old.' Then his eyes narrowed on hers. 'What I'm trying to work out is, how she knew there was one.'

Mia was crap at poker, but she tried her best to keep her expression bland. 'She's got a key to your place. Maybe she came in and saw it.'

'Umm, maybe.' His eyes searched hers. 'Why do I get

this feeling that you and my daughter have been talking about stuff other than maths?' But then he smiled. 'You know what, I don't need to know. I love that my two favourite females are building a relationship.'

'Your daughter is amazing.'

Another smile. 'My girlfriend is amazing, too.'

Just then the door to his bedroom creaked open and Pickles jumped onto the bed.

Luke groaned and sat up, lifting her into his arms. 'The deal was, you gave me twelve hours.'

Mia shifted so she could fully enjoy the sight of this sexy man lying in bed, muscled chest on full display, arms around a smug-looking rabbit. 'She clearly heard you call me and Grace your two favourite females.'

'Damn.' He peered down at Pickles. 'Are you jealous?'

'She doesn't need to be. There's room for the three of us.'

His eyes caught hers and the smile he gave her caused a zing from her head to her toes and in all the places in between. 'Not in this bed. She needs to understand the only person I want in my bed from now on, is you.' And just as she started to melt, he waggled his eyebrows. 'Though if you fancy putting on one of those hot bunny costumes from time to time, I won't stop you.'

Epilogue

The following summer

Luke knew he was driving Grace mad but he couldn't seem to stop himself. He was so stupidly, unbelievably, uncontrollably … shitting himself.

'God, Dad, I swear if you ask me one more time if this is going to work, I'll clock you one.'

He grimaced. 'Yeah, that might not be a good idea, what with this being quite a public thing I'm about to do.'

They were stood in the centre of quadrangle, the garden area that was surrounded on all four sides by the flats. Luke looked up towards his flat and wondered whether this really was such a great idea after all. Not the plan itself, that was a no-brainer. It was the execution he was getting angsty about.

His phone buzzed with the call he'd been expecting and Luke jammed the thing to his ear.

'We're heading back.' Freya's voice drifted through to him, along with a bucket-load of car engines and background chat. 'She's just gone to the loo so I've only got a few minutes.'

'What time do you reckon you'll be here?'

'We've been through this.'

'Humour me and go through it again.'

Freya let out a long, frustrated breath. 'Fifteen minutes, if she doesn't want to pop into any more shops.'

'You've been shopping all bloody morning.'

'Because you wanted us out of the way,' Freya reminded him mildly. 'I don't think either of us really wanted to shop together, we hardly have the same tastes.'

'Yeah, yeah, I know.' But he'd been desperate to get Mia out of the way so they could rehearse what he'd planned. Getting Freya to ask Mia if she fancied going shopping had seemed the easiest way. He couldn't say the pair of them were best buddies now, but they were a lot more comfortable with each other, which counted for a lot.

'Thankfully we do have the same tastes in coffee houses, so that's why we're a little later than planned.'

'Half an hour later,' he grumbled, which caused Grace to sigh. 'Okay, doesn't matter, you're on your way. That's good.' His throat began to tighten up. 'It's all good.'

The moment he ended the call, Sandy bound up to him, walkie-talkie in hand. 'Are we set? Is the Eagle about to land?'

Grace giggled, and normal Luke (not the Luke who was currently shitting bricks) would have bust a gut laughing. But this Luke was too tense. 'She'll be here in fifteen.'

'Okay, I'll warn the troops.'

'She's kind of bonkers,' Grace said, watching Sandy as she scurried off into Luke's block. 'I guess that's why you've been mates for so long.' She glanced over his shoulder and her face split into a grin. 'Mia's family have just arrived.'

'Christ.' All his nerve endings started to twitch. 'What the hell was I thinking, inviting them along? If this goes tits up—'

'Which it won't,' Grace interrupted. 'So you can stop the meltdown and put a smile on your face.'

He glanced sideways at his now seventeen-year-old daughter. 'When did you become the grown-up here?'

'Since you fell in luuuuurve.' Flicking him a smile, she started towards Mia's parents, or more precisely towards little Jacob who was tottering between them; Elle, Dave and Caitlin bringing up the rear.

The next ten minutes was a chaotic whirl of greeting people. It wasn't just Mia's family he'd decided, in his wisdom, to mention today to. Phil and Janet were here, and Naomi and Stan, too.

'Don't worry,' Naomi murmured, clearly sensing his jitters. 'She'll love it.'

He was about to express his thanks when Stan decided to add, 'That's one possibility. The other is, she'll run away screaming.' He shook his head. 'You've got to be daft in the head to do it this way.'

Luke was desperate to tell Stan he was talking bollocks, but right now he couldn't fault the man's statement.

'Nonsense. It's romantic.'

Stan did a double-take at Naomi's reply. 'You *like* the idea of public humiliation?'

'Christ.' Luke really didn't need to hear any more from Stan right now.

Naomi winked at him. 'I'll take this mood killer aside and put him straight.' She reached up to kiss him on the cheek. 'You relax and enjoy the moment.'

Enjoy. Yes, that's exactly what he needed to do. And he would. Once it was over.

Mia glanced sideways at Freya as she gripped her arm.

'Are you going to tell me why we're in such a tearing hurry to get back to the flat?'

Freya shook her head. 'We're not. I just told Luke I'd have you back by one o'clock, and it's already quarter past. I don't want to get into trouble.'

Mia laughed. 'Because he's soooo scary.'

Freya's lips twitched. 'There's always a first time.'

If someone had told her last year that she'd be sharing jokes with Freya, spending time with her, just the pair of them, Mia would have asked them what they were smoking. But somehow, against the odds, they'd managed to find a way to get on. Mia knew it had helped that she'd kept Freya's secret and never told Luke how she'd tried to meddle. In one drunken moment Freya had even admitted it had started before the messages, when she'd first heard her voice outside Luke's flat. And deliberately chosen to take Grace's key and walk in on them the following morning.

Freya looked again at her watch. And increased the pace as they threaded their way through the car park. When Mia turned towards the stairs, Freya shook her head. 'I said we'd meet Luke in the quadrangle.'

Odd, but okay. Maybe he was soaking up some sun before his long Saturday shift.

Yet when they stepped into the quadrangle, the oddness went up a few levels. Stan, Naomi? Phil? And oh my God, what were her parents doing here?

That's when Luke walked into view. Luke of the dazzling eyes, the Greek god-like body, and the … whoa. 'Is everything alright?' Her heart began to race as she stared at him. 'You're looking green.'

'Everything…' He coughed, drew in a breath and started again. 'Everything's fine.' Then he swallowed and reached for her hand.

Now her heart was having a proper thump. 'What are my family doing here?'

'Celebrating.' He swallowed again and gave her a weak smile. 'Hopefully.'

Okay, that sounded better. 'Celebrating what?'

He looked towards Sandy, who gave him the thumbs up and spoke into her walkie-talkie. 'It's a go.'

'What's a go?' Confused, Mia glanced around, only to

find nobody was looking at her. They were all focused on the windows in Luke's block.

She angled her head up to see what all the fuss was about and the bottom fell out of her stomach.

There, across Freya and Luke's flats, letters appeared one at a time in each of the windows, quickly spelling out:

WILLUMARRYME?

And in the final window:

PLZ

Her heart slammed against her ribs and when she turned to Luke she found him staring at her, his heart in his eyes. 'Stan told me I was mad doing it this way. That you might run off.' He reached for her hands and grasped them in his. 'You don't need to say yes, but remember you promised me once you wouldn't run. That you'd stay and argue. So if we need to do that for a bit, if you need me to go through the long list of reasons why this is the best idea I've ever had, we can do that.' He heaved in a breath. 'Now would be a good time for you to speak.'

Oh my God, she'd never been so utterly overcome. The proposal, the way he'd done it. The fact he'd asked her parents to witness it. Tears welled in her eyes. 'I don't want to argue.'

'Yeah, that's good, but right now I need an answer…' he trailed off, his eyes widening. 'Wait, does that mean you're saying yes?' His hands tightened around hers. 'Or that you're about to run away?'

Laughing now, happiness flooding through her, she reached up on tiptoe and kissed him. 'You goof, I'm saying yes.'

A loud whoop went up around them and everyone started clapping. Beside her Luke's face was no longer green but flushed and beaming. 'Thank Christ for that.' To her surprise he grabbed the hem of his shirt and lifted it up. 'If you hadn't, I'd have been left with a problem.' Tattooed next to Grace's name, she saw her own, and felt tears spill onto her cheeks as she remembered his words: *The only names I'll ever have tattooed on my skin are those of people I want to keep in my life permanently.*

As she wiped her face, he pointed up to the flats. And now Mia could see how he'd done it. Chloe, Tanya, Donna, Mateo, Bill, Gary, Tony … others she recognised from the bar. They each stood in one of the windows, waving down at her. 'Wow, this has taken some organisation.'

He laughed. 'I want to say it was nothing, but I've been a basket case all morning. Would the gang turn up, did they have the right letter in the right window, would they put it up too soon, not soon enough, not at the right time?' He held her gaze. 'Would you hate me asking you so publicly, being put on the spot like this?'

Just when she thought she couldn't love him more, he showed her the vulnerability that was usually so well disguised. 'I love that you did it this way because this is *us*.'

Wrapping her arms around him, she smiled into his eyes. 'A bit geeky, a bit flashy, a lot crazy but totally wonderful.'

It wasn't long before they were bombarded by family. Her mum had tears in her eyes, her dad couldn't stop smiling. Elle was a wreck. When she glanced over to Luke she saw he was being clapped on the back by his brother and hugged by Grace. He caught her eye over her shoulder and the small smile he gave her fizzed down her spine. *I can't wait to get you alone*, it said.

'My little gumdrop, going to get married!'

Mia turned to her mum, who was wiping her eyes with a tissue. 'I'm waiting for you to tag on a *finally*.'

'Oh hush you, I always knew it would happen.'

'Next she'll be waiting for you to produce little gumbabies,' her dad added dryly, a glint in his eye.

As Elle snorted with laughter, Mia shook her head. 'One step at a time, please. Besides, you've got enough grandchildren to be getting on with for now.'

'I knew he was the one for you, I just knew it, right from that first message he put in the window.' Elle let out a long, dreamy sigh. 'I mean, who thinks to do that?'

'A guy who was besotted right from the start, and fell deeper in love, the more he saw her.' Mia turned to find Luke staring down at her. 'It took a few months, and a forest of paper, but thank God she finally got the message.'

Acknowledgments

My first big thank you is to the fabulous One More Chapter. This is my fourth book with them and from concept to finished book, they have been a joy to write for. Charlotte Ledger, editor extraordinaire, is the most inspiring person to work with. The messages in the window were her brain wave and I absolutely loved the challenge of figuring out how to use the idea to build the relationship between Luke and Mia. Such a romantic concept, but fun, too. At least I hope you'll find it fun when you read it! While the messages in the window were a joy to write about, I'm sure they weren't a joy to actually put into print, so a big thank you too, to Bethan Morgan for patiently (painstakingly?) sorting them out, along with the edits. Finally, I adore my One More Chapter covers and I think *Mr Right Across the Street* is my favourite so far. So thank you Lucy Bennett for yet another gorgeous creation.

I chose Manchester for Mia's new home because I've

spent many happy times there, so my next big thank you is to my dear friend Charlotte England. And please excuse me while I use this opportunity to warn her I'm looking forward to many more visits, including checking out some of the new places I found when researching this book!

While writing is a solo affair, I'm lucky to be part of a writing community that ensures I never feel alone, so thank you also to the amazing bloggers and fellow authors out there who do so much to support each other, and me.

Speaking of support, thanks to the following people who are kind enough to still show an interest in my writing; my in-laws, Anne and Keith, cousins Shelley, Karley, Kath, Kirsty and Hayley, my sis-in-law Jayne, friends Laura, Sonia, Jane, Carol, Tara and Priti. And of course I can't forget my own lovely mum. I suspect she thought I'd stop after a few, but here we are, 15 books later and, at the age of 86, she's still managing to keep up to date.

My husband and sons put up with endless bizarre questions from me when I'm writing a book, whether it's for ideas, for cool names, or in this book odd computing questions for my youngest who's studying computer science. Thank you for putting up with having a romantic fiction writer as a wife/mum.

Finally, I want to thank you, the reader, for buying *Mr Right Across the Street*. If you'll forgive the terrible pun, I sincerely hope it's right up your street!